A Hint of Danger

As he abruptly turned to go I caught at his arm. "Ian . . . I didn't mean to pry. Isn't it possible, though, that you might have misinterpreted my grandfather's attitude?"

He jerked his arm away. It was darker now, and in the half light I couldn't see his face distinctly under the jaunty cocked hat, but there was no mistaking the throb of anger in his voice. "You're the new lady of the manor, and I work for your family, but there's nothing in the terms of my employment that requires me to discuss my personal affairs with you."

My heart felt flayed, and there was no intelligent reason why I should have invited any more punishment, but I heard myself saying, "Ian, must we quarrel? Can't we be friends?"

"Friends? Oh, God." Suddenly he reached out for me, wrapping his arms around me in a bruising embrace while his lips ravaged mine in a kiss that ignited a torrent of unfamiliar fiery desire.

He finally lifted his head, his breathing hard and uneven, his gray eyes no longer cold but alive with dancing flames. "I can give you this, any time you want it, but not friendship, Kirstie MacDonell Cameron."

MORE THRILLING GOTHICS FROM ZEBRA BOOKS

THE MISTRESS OF MOONTIDE MANOR (3100, $3.95)
by Lee Karr

Penniless and alone, Joellen was grateful for the opportunity to live in the infant resort of Atlantic City and work as a "printer's devil" in her uncle's shop. *But her uncle was dead when she arrived!*

Alone once more, she encountered the handsome entreprenuer Taylor Lorillard. Danger was everywhere, and ignoring the warning signs — veiled threats, glances, innuendos — she yearned to visit Moontide Manor and dance in Taylor's arms. But someone was following as she approached the moon-drenched mansion . . .

THE LOST HEIRESS OF HAWKSCLIFFE (2896, $3.95)
by Joyce C. Ware

When Katherine McKenzie received an invitation to catalogue the Fabulous Ramsay oriental rug collection, she was thrilled she was respected as an expert in her chosen field.

It had been seven years since Charles Ramsay's mistress and heiress had mysteriously disappeared — and now it was time to declare her legally dead, and divide the spoils. But Katherine wasn't concerned; she was there to do a job. *Until* she saw a portrait of the infamous Roxlena, and saw on the heiress' finger the very ring that she herself had inherited from her own mysterious past.

THE WHISPERING WINDS OF
BLACKBRIAR BAY (3319, $3.95)
by Lee Karr

Anna McKenzie fulfilled her father's last request by taking her little brother away from the rough gold mining town near City. Now an orphan, Anna travelled to meet her father's sister, whom he mentioned only when he was on his deathbed.

Anna's fears grew as the schooner *Tahoe* reached the remote cove at the foot of the dark, huge house high above the cliffs. The aunt was strange, threatening. And who was the midnight visitor, who was whispering in the dark hallways? Even the attentions of the handsome Lyle Delany couldn't keep her safe. For he too was being watched . . . and stalked.

Available wherever paperbacks are sold, or order direct from the Publisher. Send cover price plus 50¢ per copy for mailing and handling to Zebra Books, Dept. 3516, 475 Park Avenue South, New York, N.Y. 10016. Residents of New York, New Jersey and Pennsylvania must include sales tax. DO NOT SEND CASH.

THE LOST BRIDE OF KILDRUMMOND

LOIS STEWART

ZEBRA BOOKS
KENSINGTON PUBLISHING CORP.

For Don and Marne
my medical researchers

ZEBRA BOOKS

are published by

Kensington Publishing Corp.
475 Park Avenue South
New York, NY 10016

First printing: September, 1991

Printed in the United States of America

Chapter I

There was nothing about that sunny afternoon in April, 1770 to warn me that before nightfall I would lose my father, my home and my very identity.

The music room at the Château Bassincourt faced the gardens. The windows were wide open on this warm and lovely spring day, and as I sat at the harpsichord the fugitive scent of hyacinth and violets and the distant cooing sounds from the dovecote kept distracting my attention from the accompaniment I was playing. A sudden discordant clash caused me to drop my hands from the keyboard, and I turned my head to chide my pupil gently. "Please repeat the passage, *ma petite.* You forgot the accidentals."

Marie Christine de Bonnard put down her cittern on the table next to her chair with such emphasis that the strings twanged in protest. "It's no use, Mademoiselle MacDonell," she exclaimed, her woebegone fourteen-year-old face expressing her frustration. "I'll never learn to play this—this thing. Or the harpsichord, either. I'm like Papa. I have a tin ear. The notes all sound alike to me."

"Nonsense. You're coming along very well," I said encouragingly, but I knew that if my livelihood depended on making a musician out of Marie Christine I would soon be unemployed. She *did* have a tin ear, but fortunately she was an apt pupil in other subjects, such as literature and foreign languages. "We'll try the passage again tomorrow," I continued. "It may come easier then. For now, let's see what you've done with your Italian translation."

Christine was reaching for her volume of Dante when her mother entered the room. The Comtesse de Bassincourt was a sweet-faced woman whose unassuming manners failed to proclaim the fact that her family's title and estates were among the oldest and most noble in France. The Bonnards of Château Bassincourt were *noblesse* of the sword, and they had served their king faithfully over the centuries, but they took no part in the splendid court life at Versailles. They were content to live out their lives in modest comfort on their snug acres in this wooded valley of the Norman *Bocage*. I was very fond of madame. She'd had been endlessly kind to me during this past year since I'd assumed my father's duties as Marie Christine's tutor.

The welcoming smile froze on my face as the comtesse said, "Mademoiselle, I'm so sorry to be the bearer of bad news."

I felt my heart constrict. "My father? Is he . . . ?"

"No, no, *ma chérie,*" she replied quickly. "Monsieur Mac-Donell isn't dead. But your maidservant has sent word that he's fallen ill. It may not be serious—let us hope so—but I think you should go to him. I've ordered Michel to bring the carriage around."

I accepted the offer of the carriage gratefully. The château was only a mile from the village, and I usually made the daily trip from my home and back again on foot. But today I didn't want to lose an instant in reaching my father. His first seizure a year ago—agonizing chest pains that the doctor had called angina pectoris—had left him an invalid, and Doctor Gontier had warned me that a second attack could occur at any time and might well be fatal.

As we rolled down the long driveway of the château and emerged into the rutted road leading to the village, I huddled into a corner of the carriage with my shawl wrapped tightly around me and my eyes squeezed shut while I bombarded the Lord with silent, desperate prayers. I couldn't lose Father. He was the only relative I had in the world, and despite his fecklessness and his checkered past I loved him dearly.

He and I had lived in this tiny village in the remote Norman countryside for fifteen years, since I was four years old. Bassincourt was an unlikely residence for a Scotsman of good family like my father, whose clan, the MacDonells of Aultnaclunie, was a cadet branch of the powerful MacDonells of Glengarry. But Calum MacDonell had been ostracized by his family. I knew only the sketchiest details of his early life, garnered from my mother's scattered, unwary confidences before her death five years ago and occasional unguarded remarks dropped by my father. Wild living seemed to sum it up: mountains of gambling debts, excessive drinking, an unsuitable marriage to the daughter—my mother—of an Edinburgh tavern owner at whose establishment Calum spent most of his time. And something else, darker and more sinister, the reason for his long exile on the Continent.

My mother had only hinted at the story, and Father had never spoken a word about it. So while I couldn't be sure of all the facts, I believed Calum had been caught cheating at cards and had fought a duel with the man who accused him. The man died, and, since he was the son of the Lord Provost of Edinburgh, Father had had to flee the country to avoid social disgrace and possible imprisonment. I was born shortly after my parents left Scotland. For a few years, I'd gathered, Father had attempted to make his living in the gambling halls of Paris and the spa towns of the Rhineland. When those attempts failed, he'd settled down in the obscure hamlet of Bassincourt, where he gave lessons in music and English and Italian to the children of the minor landowners in the area and later to the daughter of the Comte de Bassincourt. When he became too ill to teach after that first attack of angina, the Comtesse de Bassincourt had engaged me as Marie Christine's governess.

As soon as the carriage stopped in front of our tiny house on the outskirts of the village, I pushed open the door and jumped to the ground before the coachman could let down the steps. Dashing through the gate, I sped past the neatly tended flower beds to the door. Before I could put my hand to the latch, the door opened and Emily Robertson threw her arms around me, saying with a catch in her voice, "Ach, Mistress Kirstie, I'm sae glad ye're here."

Almost immediately she drew back, looking faintly sheepish and drawing a handkerchief from the pocket of her capacious apron to blow her nose loudly. She was a dour, long-faced, angular Scotswoman who had been in my parents' employ since before I was born, fiercely devoted to all of us but never one to display her emotions.

I patted her bony shoulder. "How is Father, Emily? The comtesse said you'd sent word he'd been taken ill."

"Then she was trying tae spare yer feelings," replied Emily, reverting to her usual grim stoicism. "The doctor's wi' him noo, but I dinna need a doctor tae tell me Maister Calum's in a verra bad way. He's had anither of those dreadful seizures, Mistress Kirstie."

My heart sank. I'd been hoping that Father had merely had one of his sinking spells, or at worst a recurrence of the sharp, short attacks of pain that left him prostrate but didn't seem to worsen his condition.

"I canna say I'm that surprised," Emily remarked after a moment. "The maister ha' been sae restless these past few days, always asking if a letter ha' come fer him."

"A letter?" I looked at Emily blankly. We never got letters. Who was there to write to us? For all the notice the outside world took of us, we might as well be resting in the village cemetery. Perhaps Father's mind had started to wander. He'd been forgetful so often of late.

I looked up anxiously as Doctor Gontier came down the stairs. He was an old friend by now, having treated my childhood ailments and attended my mother in her last illness.

He came up to me, taking my hands and squeezing them gently. "You're a strong young woman, mademoiselle. I know you'll want to know the truth. Monsieur MacDonell is very near death. His life is hanging by a thread."

"You can't do anything, Doctor?"

He shook his head. "Nothing. We must just try to keep him as comfortable as possible in mind and body. Unhappily, it won't be for long. *Au revoir, ma petite.* I'll look in this evening."

After the doctor had left I walked slowly up the stairs, turning left on the landing into one of the two tiny bedchambers on the second floor of the cottage. Father was lying on his back in the bed, a nightcap covering his head in place of his usual neat wig, his arms lying limply outside the coverlets.

I stood quietly by the bedside looking down at his still face. His eyes were closed, and his skin had a faintly bluish tinge. He'd become very thin during this past year, and the long slender fingers lying on the coverlet looked almost transparent. As if aware of my presence, he aroused, opened his eyes, his lips curving in the smile of pure charm that had always made it so easy to excuse his shortcomings.

"There you are, my love, my darling," he said in a thready voice. He spoke in the Gaelic, which I understood but spoke haltingly. "I'm so sorry to be such a worry to you."

"Oh, Papa, you're no worry to me," I exclaimed with a catch in my throat. I bent down to kiss his thin cheek, and then, drawing up a chair, I sat down, catching his hand in mine. "No worry at all, except that I want you to get well."

He shook his head. It was obvious that even the slightest movement was an effort for him. "You know better than that, my Kirstie," he whispered with the ghost of a chuckle. "You've hidden the claret bottle for the last time, and you'll never wait anxiously again for me to come back from a gambling binge in Caen."

The smile faded from his lips, and his dark eyes stared up at me with a look of such unutterable sadness that I could scarcely bear to meet his gaze. "I don't mind going, you know," he murmured. "I've been between the living and the dead all this past year, no use to you or to me, either. My only regret is that I'm leaving you alone and penniless in a foreign country. Kirstie, I've been such a bad father." His voice trailed away and his eyes closed again. He began muttering to himself. "Why haven't they written? Have they changed their minds? I've got to hang on . . . hang on . . . "

A cold vise clamped around my heart. I'd heard that dying people often became irrational, disoriented, in the last hours before death. Father wasn't making sense. Who were "they"?

The door opened quietly behind me. "Mistress Kirstie," came Emily's excited whisper in my ear. "There's a strange gentleman below tae see the Maister. A Scottish gentleman."

"Father can't see any strangers now," I whispered back angrily without thinking, and then paused, struck by the sheer unlikelihood, no, the impossibility, of what Emily was saying. A Scottish gentleman? Emily might as well have said a Turk or a Red Indian. We hadn't had a visitor from outside the immediate vicinity in all the years we'd been living in Bassincourt. I hesitated, looking at Father, who seemed to have drifted off into an uneasy slumber again, and rose from my chair. "Stay with Father, Emily. I'll talk to this gentleman, whoever he is."

Downstairs, I gaped at the tall man with the powerful shoulders who faced me across the small, cramped parlor. He was certainly Scottish. He was wearing a kilt. Not that I had ever seen one before, but it was unmistakable, a length of plaid material in a dark green tartan, worn around the waist like a skirt, with the end of the plaid pinned behind the left shoulder and trailing down beside the arm. With it he wore a bright red coat and a loosely draped fur cap with a hackle.

However, it wasn't the man's clothing that transfixed my attention. It was his eyes, cold and penetrating and glacially gray as a sunless winter morning. They dominated the austerely handsome, strong-boned face beneath the powdered wig and the fur cap. No, it wasn't a wig. It was his own thick, springing hair, powdered and curled and tied in a queue at the back of his head.

He returned my stare in silence, his cool, unfriendly gray gaze boring into my face and figure until I began to feel inexpressibly dowdy and provincial in my simple gown of dark Indian cotton, worn without even modest pocket hoops and adorned only with a plain muslin fichu.

At last he spoke. "Would you be Mistress Kirstie MacDonell?" he asked curtly. I could hear the soft Scottish burr that by now, after all these years of lonely exile, was only an echo in my father's voice.

"Yes, I'm Kirstie MacDonell," I said firmly, lifting my chin. The sound of his voice had disrupted the confused, almost trancelike state into which I'd fallen beneath that mesmerizing, arrogant stare. I reminded myself that I was the mistress of this house, and he was a stranger here on my sufferance. "May I ask who you are and why you are here, sir?"

"My name is Ian Cameron. Major Cameron, to be precise, of His Majesty's Forty-second Regiment of Foot. The Black Watch," he replied. He paused, giving me another long, measuring look. "You seem unfamiliar with my name," he said abruptly.

"That's quite correct, sir. Is there any reason why I should know you?"

A frankly skeptical note crept into his voice. "I would certainly have thought so. Your father *is* Calum MacDonell of Aultnaclunie?"

"He is. Or was. He hasn't lived in Scotland for many years."

"Then he's the man I've come to see. Pray inform him that I've arrived."

Nettled by his air of calm, indifferent certainty, I said sharply, "That will be impossible, Major Cameron. My father can't possibly receive you. He's very ill." My voice

11

broke, and I turned my face away, trying for composure. After a moment I looked back at him. "He's more than ill. My father is dying."

"I'm sorry to hear that." The tone was perfunctory, without the slightest shade of feeling. "Nevertheless, I must ask you to tell Mr. MacDonell that I'm here."

"I can't do that." I eyed him coldly. "You may state the reason for your visit to me, and then, if I consider it important, I'll mention it to Father."

I had reached him at last. There was a spark of anger behind those chilly gray eyes as he said, "Think again, Mistress MacDonell. I'm here at your father's invitation." Reaching into the fur pouch hanging from his belt—I later learned it was called a sporran—he took out a letter and handed it to me. Puzzled and faintly alarmed, I looked at the superscription. It was in my father's familiar handwriting.

As I was about to open the letter, Major Cameron put out his hand and removed it from my grasp, saying coolly, "You'll pardon me, but my business is not with you, but with Mr. Calum MacDonell."

As he took the letter his hand brushed my fingers, and my heart gave a sharp erratic thump and seemed to cease beating for several seconds. I took a deep breath and moved a quick step backward, trying to block from my mind a sudden jolting image of myself cradled against this stranger's broad, powerful chest. My pulse was racing, and I felt light-headed. Never before in my sheltered life had I been so intensely, achingly aware of a man's physical presence.

Major Cameron's incisive voice said, "I fear I must insist that you notify Mr. MacDonell of my arrival."

"Very well, I'll tell him, but I don't promise anything," I said hastily, and turned to mount the stairs, glad to escape from that searching hostile gaze. How much of my absurd emotional confusion had he noticed?

Father was awake again when I entered his bedchamber, where Emily Robertson sat watchfully by his bedside, and he seemed to be fully conscious. "A Scottish gentleman is here to see me?" he repeated. His exhausted eyes brightened, and a faint color warmed his cheeks. "Emily, ask the gentleman to come up."

"Papa, are you sure you feel strong enough to see this man?"

He made a feeble movement with his hand. "I must see him, Kirstie. Be a good child, now, and look on the shelf of the wardrobe, under my shirts, for a packet wrapped in oiled silk."

I was standing beside Father's bed, gazing with mystified eyes at the slim packet I'd taken from the wardrobe, when Major Cameron entered the bedchamber, instantly dwarfing the dimensions of the little room with the vitality of his presence. He made a formal bow to Father. "Good day to you, sir. I regret to find you ill. I'm here in answer to the letter you sent to Lord Carrickmore."

"Kirstie, will you put another pillow beneath my head, please? Thank you, now I can see our guest better." Father's voice sounded stronger. He looked curiously at the major, his eyes lingering on the uniform. "Naturally, I didn't expect to see his lordship himself, but—would you be his nephew, Murdoch Graham? Who I would have thought was somewhat older than you appear to be. . . . "

Ian Cameron's face altered, becoming completely expressionless. "No, I'm not Murdoch Graham. Nobody quite that important," he said drily. "I'm a clansman. My father was Cameron of Inverloch."

"Ah." Father nodded thoughtfully. "I remember. Inverloch, the chieftain of the senior sept of Clan Cameron. He went out with the prince in the Forty-five."

"And was hanged for high treason and had his estates forfeited," said the major with a bitter finality. "Can we get on with this, Mr. MacDonell? According to your letter, you have important documents for the Earl of Carrickmore. His lordship has authorized me to examine them."

13

"And after that?"

"After that, if the documents seem genuine, we'll talk about your claims."

"Fair enough. Kirstie, please give that packet to the major. And Emily, will you find a chair for our guest?"

Sitting down in the chair that Emily drew up for him at the end of the bed, Ian Cameron extended his hand to me. "If I may?"

Numbly I handed over the packet. Then, emerging from a state of tongue-tied perplexity, I turned to Father, exclaiming, "Papa, I don't understand. What documents? And what's this talk of 'claims?' Claims to what?"

"Wait, love, until the major finishes his examination of the documents," said my father gently. He tried to smile, but it was a travesty of a smile, clouded by weakness and pain and some other emotion I couldn't place. It couldn't be fear. What could my father have to fear from the Black Watch major and that thin packet of "documents"?

So we waited, Father and I—and Emily, too, standing silently by the door—while Ian Cameron carefully studied the papers that he withdrew from their oiled silk wrappings. From where I stood, several feet away from him, I couldn't see the papers clearly, but there appeared to be one official-looking document and several letters. At one point the major opened his sporran and removed some letters of his own, placing them beside the ones Father had given him, and obviously comparing the styles of handwriting. At the end of ten minutes Ian Cameron lifted his head, saying to Father, "You spoke of some jewelry?"

"Yes. Kirstie, if you'll look in the wardrobe again, in the same place, you'll find another parcel, wrapped in one of your mother's old shawls. Give it to the major."

More puzzled than ever, and imbued now with a vague sense of apprehension, I found the parcel and gave it to Ian Cameron. Emily was a demon housekeeper, I reflected. She hadn't mentioned finding the packet of papers or this parcel

14

in Father's wardrobe when she'd turned out the contents of his bedchamber several weeks previously. Had Papa concealed the objects temporarily, under his pillows, perhaps, until her housecleaning frenzy had abated? Then I glanced across the room at the old servant, as she stood watching the major intently, and I knew, without knowing how I knew, that the objects Father had placed in his wardrobe came as no surprise to her.

I kept my eyes fixed on Ian Cameron as he unrolled the shawl and uncovered a small silver box, from which he removed a gold brooch. Opening the brooch, he studied the tiny portraits inside, almost as though he was memorizing the painted features. Then, laying aside the brooch, he picked up and examined a bracelet set with cameos and several hair ornaments in the shape of jeweled butterflies.

Slowly, deliberately, the major replaced the jewelry in the silver box and stood up, holding the papers in one hand and the box in the other.

"Well?" said Father, his fingers intertwined so tightly that his knuckles showed white.

"In my opinion these documents and the jewelry are authentic," said Ian Cameron curtly. "You've made your case, sir. I have Lord Carrickmore's authorization to proceed."

Expelling his breath in a long, tired sigh, Father relaxed against his pillows. "Pray indulge me, Major. Before we have any further discussion, I'd like to speak privately with my daughter."

Ian Cameron bowed, and Emily silently opened the bedchamber door for him. At a slight movement of my father's hand, she, too, left the room, closing the door behind her.

"Papa, what does all this mean?" I burst out as soon as we were alone. "Where did those papers and that jewelry come from? What have they to do with us? And who is this Lord Carrickmore?"

"All in good time, child. Draw up your chair beside the bed. I have a great deal to tell you."

Uncomprehending but obedient, I did as he asked. With a slow, groping gesture that illustrated, if I needed any proof, how weak his physical condition really was, Father took my hand, but for some moments he was silent. He'd retreated so deeply into his thoughts that he might have been lost in another dimension. Finally he stirred, ever so slightly, and began to talk.

"It was so long ago," he said with a look that seemed to plead for my forgiveness. "I'd almost persuaded myself that it never happened. But it did happen, and I can't keep it from you any longer."

"Papa, I don't care about anything you may have done," I said quickly. "Don't fret yourself—"

"That's so like you, my darling," he interrupted me, "but this time I must pay the piper. There's no time for anything else." He braced his thin shoulders as if for a deluge, and began his account, slowly and with a dragging reluctance.

"It was nineteen years ago. The early spring of 1751. Your mother and I were driving through Champagne on our way to Paris. I'd had my usual indifferent luck at the tables in Strasbourg, and I was hoping—unwisely, as it turned out—that a change of scene might improve our fortunes. We couldn't afford to hire more than two horses, and we'd thrown a wheel earlier in the day, so we were hours late getting to Chaumont, where we intended to spend the night. It was already pitch dark, and under normal circumstances Sheila would never have spotted that stumbling figure beside the road, even though your mother always had the eyesight of a falcon. But, as it happened, there was enough light to see by. As we rounded a sharp curve in the road we were horrified to glimpse a tiny village half enveloped in flames. Frantic figures, outlined against the fiery sky, were attempting to keep the fire from spreading. Sheila and I tumbled out of our carriage to help a young woman who had staggered away from the burning village to collapse at our feet.

"She certainly needed help. She was far along in pregnancy, and even as we knelt beside her she began writhing in pain. 'Her time has come,' Sheila told me. 'We must get her to a doctor.' At the sound of your mother's voice the young woman opened her eyes and cried frantically, in an accent that was pure Scots, 'My husband—he's back there in the fire. Oh, please save my Marcel!'

"Well, of course," Father continued, "the young woman obviously needed our help more urgently than her husband. If this Marcel were still alive, the villagers were bound to rescue him. Disregarding the young woman's protests, I lifted her into the carriage and our postilion whipped our horses into a gallop. We stopped in the next town, a mere hamlet also, where by some miracle we located a midwife. The young woman's baby was born minutes after we arrived, in a bed-chamber of a miserable country inn. It was a little girl."

Father paused, his eyes reflective, as if he were reliving what must have seemed to him an exciting and adventurous evening. Caught up in the drama of the story, I asked eagerly, "What happened then, Papa? Who was the young woman? Was she really Scottish? Did she and her child survive? Did the villagers find her husband alive?" But even as I spoke, a warning bell sounded in the back of my mind. Why was Father telling me this story now?

"The child survived. The mother did not," Father said slowly. "The young woman lived until the next day, long enough to tell us her name and how she came to be at that burning village. Long enough to direct us to her carriage, abandoned by the roadside near the village the previous evening. I spoke to the villagers next morning; Marcel, whose parents lived in the little town, had died in a vain attempt to save them. I retrieved the young woman's belongings from the carriage. They included some letters and documents and jewelry. . . . "

"Which Major Cameron has just examined and pronounced to be genuine," I said with stiff lips. The warning bells were clanging more insistently. "Who was she, Papa?"

Father spoke even more slowly, the reluctance in his voice now almost palpable. "Her name was Fiona Cameron. She was the daughter of Alexander Cameron, Laird of Kildrummond and Earl of Carrickmore. She'd entered into a secret marriage with her French tutor, Marcel Lefevre. When she became pregnant and realized her condition would soon be impossible to conceal, she fled to France with Marcel, fearing that her father would attempt to have the marriage annulled. The young couple went to Paris, where Marcel tried vainly to find some kind of occupation—his tutoring skills in French were naturally of little use in his own country—and then after some time, their funds exhausted, they decided to go to Marcel's home village in Champagne, where his parents still lived. But as they drove near the village they were horrified to find Marcel's home and several other houses burning fiercely. Leaving Fiona in the traveling chaise, Marcel rushed into the conflagration to rescue his parents. He must have died almost instantly. His body was never found. That newborn baby girl had lost both her parents before she was a day old."

I was sitting rigidly erect now, the nails of my clenched fingers digging into my palms. I said tightly, "It was a tragedy that the baby was orphaned so early in life, but she wasn't alone in the world. She had a grandfather in Scotland. A wealthy and titled grandfather."

Father seized my hand again in a febrile grip, his eyes pleading for understanding. "The earl never knew he had a grandchild, Kirstie. I had every intention of notifying him about his daughter's death, naturally. But then Sheila persuaded me to allow her to keep Fiona's baby. Oh, I know it was wrong to keep the child, but Sheila convinced me the baby would be happier with parents who loved and wanted her than with a grandfather who might regard her as an embarrassing nuisance."

"But why?" I whispered. I had the oddest sensation that I was talking against an avalanche, trying with mere words

18

to hold back the torrent of disaster that was plunging toward me. My mouth dry, I added, "You said this happened in the spring of 1751. I'd just been born, or I was about to be born. Why would Mama want the responsibility for another baby? It wasn't as if Fiona's child was destitute or abandoned. No matter how much he disapproved of his daughter's marriage, the Earl of Carrickmore would hardly have repudiated her child." My eyes widened. "And what became of this Fiona's baby girl? Did she die, too?"

Hesitating, Father lowered his eyes, but of course I knew the answer to my question even before he finally found the courage to speak. "No, my darling Kirstie, she didn't die. You see, your mother and I had never been able to have a child. We took Fiona Cameron's baby and raised her as our own. You were that baby."

"No," I said, my voice rising shrilly. "No and no and no!" I jumped up from my chair and stumbled blindly to the door, tearing it open and rushing down the stairs to the parlor, still babbling my disbelief and scarcely aware of what I was doing. At the foot of the stairs Ian Cameron grabbed me, his iron fingers digging into my shoulders while he shook me so sharply that my teeth chattered. "Stop it," he said grimly. "Get control of yourself."

It was like being doused in an icy stream. Drawing several deep uneven breaths, I gradually forced myself into calm. I pushed against his chest, trying to free myself. "I'm quite all right now," I said dully. "Please let me go."

With a long curious look at my troubled face, he released his grip and moved back a step. "You seemed very agitated, Mistress MacDonell," he said, those glacial gray eyes probing.

"I'm quite all right," I repeated. Noticing Emily hovering behind him, her face troubled, I told her, "Please go up and sit with Papa. I'll be with you in a few moments." As soon as she went up the stairs, I gave Major Cameron a straight, hard look. "I think you can help me," I said abruptly. "My father's very ill, and his mind may be wandering, but he's just informed me that he and my mother were not my parents. He says my real mother was Fiona Cameron, the daughter of the Earl of Carrickmore. Is there any truth to this?"

"You really knew nothing of this story until now?" he asked. He sounded dubious.

I stared at him. "If I knew, why would I be asking you for information?" I snapped.

His lips tightened and his glance became even more frosty. "The Cameron family has believed for many years that Fiona Cameron died with her husband in a fire that destroyed Marcel Lefevre's home. At first the earl placed no credence in Mr. MacDonell's letter claiming that Fiona lived long enough to give birth to a child, whom your father had raised as his own. His lordship wasn't convinced by Mr. MacDonell's statement that he was revealing the truth now because he didn't have long to live and regretted leaving you destitute in a foreign land. Nevertheless, in all fairness, the earl decided to send me to France to investigate Master MacDonell's allegations. When I arrived here today, I examined some documents—a certificate purporting to be Fiona's and Marcel's marriage lines and a number of letters that presumably had passed between them—and some jewelry that Mr. MacDonell maintained had been in Fiona's possession at the time of her death. As I told your father—Master MacDonell—these documents and objects appear genuine to me. I think you may safely assume you are Fiona Cameron Lefevre's daughter."

I stared at Ian Cameron, my mind blank, unable to take in what he had told me.

"What's more," the dry, emotionless voice went on, "you are now the heiress to the estate of Kildrummond. Your Uncle David, Fiona's brother and the earl's only surviving child, died some months ago without issue. Since your grandfather's earldom is one of the few Scottish peerages that can descend in the female line, you will be the next Laird of Kildrummond and Countess of Carrickmore."

Chapter II

"Mistress Kirstie, come up here, quickly!"

Emily's urgent cry broke through the mental fog that had enveloped me at the dumbfounding news that I was the heiress to a Scottish estate. Rushing past Ian, I tore up the stairs to Father's bedchamber. During my short absence there'd been a terrifying change in his condition. His breathing was forced and erratic, and the right side of his face looked distorted. When he spoke his voice was so slurred I had difficulty understanding him. "My Kirstie," he whispered, "can you find it in your heart to forgive me?"

The crushing disappointment and resentment that I'd felt when Papa told me the circumstances of my birth faded away. No matter who my real parents had been, Calum Mac-Donell was the only father I'd ever known. Tears flooding my eyes, I took his hand, aghast to find that his right arm seemed to have lost all power of movement. "There's nothing to forgive," I whispered back. "Whatever you did, Papa, you did it for love."

I could hear a glimmer of the old insouciance in his voice as he murmured, "I never had any problems with love. It was all the other things that sent me off the beaten path." His face changed. "Kirstie," he muttered urgently, "I must see Père Chenvert. Ask him to come immediately."

That was a shock. My father hadn't attended church services in years. He thought of himself as a disciple of the Enlightenment, in the footsteps of Montesquieu, Voltaire and Rousseau. He liked our parish priest—as a matter of fact, they were old chess partners—but religion played no part in their relationship. If he now wanted to see Père Chenvert, it could only mean that Papa had no hope of recovery. Old gambler that he was, I surmised with a catch in my throat, he was hedging his bets.

I dispatched Emily to fetch the priest from his little house beside the church, a few yards away down the short village street. I followed her more slowly down the stairs to the parlor. Ian Cameron rose from his chair as I entered the room. "Your father is worse?" he asked politely.

I knew my nerves were on edge, more sensitive to imagined slights than usual, but I thought savagely that Ian Cameron might have been talking about the weather, for all the real solicitude I could hear in his voice.

"Yes, he's worse," I replied shortly, walking past him to the cupboard in the corner of the room. "I hope you've finished your business with Papa," I added with a touch of angry sarcasm, speaking over my shoulder. "I don't think he'll last the night. I've sent for the priest."

"I'm sorry to hear that," came the curt voice from behind me. "Fortunately, it won't be necessary for me to trouble Mr. MacDonell any further. My future dealings will be with you. Now, if there's anything I could do to help you . . . "

I gritted my teeth. "Nothing, thank you." I didn't need his cold-blooded offer of assistance. Why didn't he go? He was like a ghoul, waiting around for Father's soul to leave his body. Ignoring him, I rummaged in a drawer of the cupboard for the candles that Père Chenvert had blessed at Eastertime and took down the crucifix that Emily had placed on the wall over a small plaster statue of the Virgin. I headed back up the stairs without glancing at Major Cameron. By the time I had arranged the crucifix and the lighted candles

22

and a vial of holy water on a small table next to Papa's bed, Père Chenvert was entering the room.

Breathless from his hurried walk, the old priest patted my shoulder in sympathy. "I know it's hard, *ma chérie,* but try to draw a little comfort from your father's request to see me. You know I've been praying him back into the fold for many years! Now, then, I need to be alone with Monsieur MacDonell for a few moments, while I hear his last confession, and then you and your maidservant can come in."

After being anointed and receiving the Viaticum, Father seemed more at ease, though it was obvious his reserves of strength were rapidly waning. He even managed a shadow of a smile for me. "It will be all right for you now, my Kirstie," he whispered. My bruised heart a little comforted, I bent to kiss him and then turned to Père Chenvert with a word of gratitude on my lips. What I was about to say died unsaid. The kindly old priest appeared to be in shock.

"*Mon père,* are you ill?"

"*Non. Pas du tout.* You'll excuse me, my child. I must go."

Bewildered, I watched his burly form leave the room. What had come over the priest? This brusque leave-taking, this failure to remain even a few minutes to talk to me and Emily in the extremity of our grief, was so unlike him. In moments, however, the incident slipped from my mind. Suddenly, in the oppressive silence of the room, I became aware that Father hadn't taken a breath for several seconds. Then came a shuddering, difficult breath, and, after a longer interval, another. The seconds dragged by. He was gone.

The sound of the clods of earth falling on the coffin shattered the brittle shell of composure behind which I'd been sheltering. Trying to suppress the sobs of utter desolation that were racking my body, I swayed and would have fallen save for the steady arm that supported me and guided me away from the graveside.

"You'll feel better if you let yourself cry," said Ian Cameron quietly, and as if at a signal I collapsed against his chest in a storm of weeping. The hard-muscled arms held me securely but impersonally until I'd cried myself out. Moments—or minutes—later, I moved away from him, feeling as if a painful vise had relaxed its grip from around my heart.

Lifting my black veil and mopping at my tear-blurred eyes, I looked up at him, saying shakily, "Thank you. You were right. I do feel better." I tried to smile. "I—I hope I haven't ruined your coat with my waterworks display."

"Don't concern yourself about that. I was glad to be of assistance," he answered, ignoring my feeble attempt at humor. Staring at that impassive mask of a face, I felt a stab of resentment. Was there any conceivable happening that might bring a tear to Ian Cameron's eyes? Then a wave of guilt flowed over me. I was forgetting how the major had taken over the burden of arranging Papa's funeral, so quietly and so capably that I'd scarcely noticed what he was doing. I should at least be grateful to him for that.

"We'll have to discuss our plans in detail later today," he was saying, when Madame de Bassincourt came up to us, accompanied by a wide-eyed and subdued Marie Christine.

I managed a rather wan smile for my pupil. "I hope you've been practicing your cittern," I teased Marie Christine.

"I'll see to that until you're ready to come back to us, mademoiselle," the comtesse assured me. "Now, my husband and I would like you to ride with us to the château. Perhaps your cousin could take Monsieur le Curé in his carriage?"

I stared at her. With difficulty, I recalled that she and the comte had graciously invited the mourners to a collation at the château after the funeral. But as for the rest of her statement—"What cousin?" I asked blankly.

"Why, Monsieur Cameron, *bien sûr,*" Madame said, laughing. "Is it all that easy to forget you have a newfound relation?" She smiled at the major. "What a fortunate coincidence that you arrived for a visit, monsieur, just when *la pe-*

tite needed you most. My husband would have been happy to act for Mademoiselle Kirstie, but how much more suitable it was that a male member of her family was here to make the funeral arrangements. What are your plans? Will you be staying long?"

"No, madame, not long. A few days only."

"What a shame. Well, then, we must have a talk today at the château about mademoiselle's future. The comte and I have been putting our heads together and we have a little scheme. I'm sure you'll agree with us, monsieur, that a gently bred young woman shouldn't live alone. And so, my husband and I think that mademoiselle should become Marie Christine's resident tutor. We needn't decide this very minute, *naturellement*. Think about it, both of you."

As soon as the comtesse had gone off with Marie Christine, Ian said abruptly, "You and madame seem very close."

"Yes, she's always been most kind."

"Then why haven't you told her you're leaving France? She obviously thinks you're going to remain in her employ." He stared at my confused, telltale face. "You didn't tell the comtesse, close as the two of you are, that you're the heiress to Kildrummond, did you?" he said suddenly. "Why not? You do understand that you must return with me to Scotland?"

"I—I hadn't thought about it," I said, looking away. After a moment I turned back to him, saying in a rush, "I don't think I want to leave France. Bassincourt is the only home I can remember. The earl—my grandfather—needn't be concerned about my welfare. You heard the comtesse invite me to stay at the château. I'll be treated very much like a member of the family, and I'm sure Emily will be welcome to make her home there, too . . . "

"Good God, woman, are you daft?" he exploded. He paused, biting his lip. So Ian Cameron *did* sometimes allow his emotions to show. I heard clearly the clipped anger in his voice. Quickly recovering, though his Scottish burr sounded far more pronounced than usual, he said curtly, "I don't wish to be rude, but I don't think you've grasped the significance of your position. You say his lordship needn't be concerned about you. Altruism isn't the point here, or family affection, either. You should understand that your grandfather isn't so much concerned about you as a person—after all, he doesn't know you, never dreamed you existed until a few months ago—but as the last of his line, his only hope to see a Cameron of Kildrummond succeed him as Earl of Carrickmore. I must warn you, he's not a man to be thwarted. He won't accept your refusal to go to Scotland and neither will I, as his representative."

Stunned at his brutal frankness, I couldn't think of a rejoinder. After a moment, pinning me with that detached gray stare, he added, "I suggest you think about what I've said. I'll talk to you later." Nodding, he turned away, intercepting Père Chenvert at the gate of the cemetery, obviously to offer him a ride to the post-funeral collation at the château. To my bewilderment, the priest shook his head emphatically and walked off in the direction of the village. It was inexplicable behavior, an affront both to the Comte and Comtesse of Bassincourt and to me, and it increased the sense of desolation I felt at Ian Cameron's pronouncement. My world seemed to be collapsing around me. . . .

I placed the last of Father's clothing into a neat pile on his bed. I'd left his room for last, hoping, I suppose, to postpone for a little the realization that I'd never see him again. He hadn't possessed many clothes, and most of them were shabby, including the well-worn velvet coat and breeches he'd saved to wear for very special occasions such as his clandestine forays into the gambling dens of Caen. I was sure Père Chenvert would see that the articles of clothing reached someone in the village who could use them. Not the velvet coat and breeches, of course. I'd had Papa buried in his cherished finery.

My eyes fell on the miniature portrait that had always sat on the table next to Papa's bed. I picked it up, sitting down in a chair near the window to study my mother's face. She'd been so pretty when she was young, with her light brown hair and blue eyes, although in this formal portrait her soft curls were thickly powdered. I hadn't inherited her fragile, small-boned beauty. I looked like my father, tall and slender with regular features and dark eyes and hair.

I lowered the portrait into my lap, blinking against the sudden acrid sting of tears. What an idiot I was, allowing myself to hide behind reality again. My fancied resemblance to Calum MacDonell was a figment of my imagination. I wasn't his child. My dark eyes and hair came from Marcel Lefevre, Fiona Cameron's husband. My real father. I closed my eyes, recalling Marcel's face in the miniature painting in Fiona's brooch. He looked so young. His dark eyes were reserved and thoughtful, and his black hair, so like my own, was clubbed back severely from his face.

Rising abruptly, I stood at the window, looking down the street toward the weathered old stone church. Drowsing in the spring sun, the village looked as it always had, placid and drab, its only sign of life a small dog chasing its shadow. Illogically, I felt the place should have looked different, after these past five days, following Calum MacDonell's death, that had transformed me into another person and changed my life forever. And soon the village of Bassincourt would be only a memory for me. Tomorrow I was leaving for Scotland.

Emily came into the bedchamber, interrupting my reverie. "Mistress Kirstie, Madame de Bassincourt is here tae see ye. Aye, and the young ane, forbye."

I turned away from the window at the sound of Emily's voice. Motioning to the pile of Papa's clothing on the bed,

I said, "Put those things in the bundle of bed linens and curtains you're taking to Père Chenvert's housekeeper."

Emily stared at the clothing, a stricken expression clouding her usually stolid face. "It doesna seem right tae gie the Maister's belongings awa', mistress."

"Papa can't wear them anymore. Someone should get some use out of them," I said, patting Emily's arm. I walked slowly down the stairs. The comtesse and Marie Christine were sitting in the parlor, which now looked extremely bare with all the pictures and ornaments packed away and the curtains taken down.

"You seem well along with your packing, *ma chérie*," said madame, glancing around the room. "You'll have no need of the furniture in this house in your new home, of course, but will you be able to take everything else with you?"

"Oh, yes, even Papa's harpsichord." I nodded at the battered old instrument in the corner of the room. "I couldn't bear to leave it behind. Papa played on it every day almost to the very end. Major Cameron says we can send it to Scotland by carrier's cart."

"Mademoiselle MacDonell, please don't go to Scotland," Marie Christine exclaimed suddenly. Tears welling into her eyes, she went on, "If you'll only stay, I promise to practice the cittern *and* the harpsichord faithfully every single day."

"Hush, child, you mustn't make a sad occasion more difficult," her mother chided her. "Mademoiselle has an obligation to her family to return to Scotland."

I suppressed a smile. That was the voice of the *noblesse* of the sword speaking. Duty to king and country and family came before everything else.

"But mademoiselle doesn't want to go away, I'm sure she doesn't," Marie Christine burst out. "Don't her wishes count for anything?"

Giving her a quick hug, I tried to reassure her. "Your mother is right, you know. I'm the last in my family line. It wouldn't be fair to my grandfather not to go back. Of course I feel sad about leaving you and your parents and my friends in the village, but I'm also excited about meeting a family I never knew I had and seeing strange new places. If I didn't go to Scotland I'd always be wondering what I missed. You can understand that, can't you? And who knows, perhaps one day soon I can come back to visit you."

Marie Christine brightened somewhat at this little speech, but as I met her mother's wise, understanding eyes I knew the comtesse wasn't fooled. She was quite aware of the feelings of panic I was trying so hard to hold back. She was equally convinced, I was sure, knowing her patrician views, that I mustn't acknowledge my fears in any way.

Except to myself. My reluctance to go to Scotland was growing with each passing hour. I had a hollow feeling in the pit of my stomach at the thought of leaving Bassincourt, obscure and dull as it was, but where I could at least earn a modest living among people who were fond of me. I dreaded plunging into the unknown. I dreaded the prospect of living in that far-off northern land with aristocratic strangers with whom I had nothing in common, whose only interest in me was because of the accident of my birth, and who might well look down on me for my provincial ways.

"We mustn't take up any more of mademoiselle's time," madame told her daughter gently. "She has a great deal to do before tomorrow." She and Marie Christine made their last *au revoirs,* and then, as they were leaving—my pupil's eyes blinded with tears—the comtesse turned back to say quietly, "If ever you need anything, mademoiselle, don't hesitate to call on us."

After they were gone I lingered in the parlor for a few moments, marveling at how much madame's parting words had lifted my spirits. Of course I would never need her help in the future, but it was immensely comforting to know it was there as a last resort.

Still feeling a warming glow of comfort, I headed for the stairs to finish packing up my own belongings. It wouldn't take long. Like Father's, my wardrobe wasn't extensive: a few gowns of Indian cotton; my mother's shawls; my one claim to fashion, a dress of figured silk that the comtesse had insisted on bestowing on me. There would be plenty of room to pack my small library, my music and my cittern.

Halfway up the stairs I heard a light tap at the door, and hastened down to answer it. Bulky in his worn black soutane and shovel hat, Père Chenvert pushed his way into the room. *"Mon père,"* I exclaimed in delight, "I'm so happy to see you."

It had been such a sore point, the priest's failure to pay me a visit during the past three days. There were no secrets in a village as small as Bassincourt. He must have heard some version of the most exciting piece of gossip to circulate in years. He must have realized I was leaving France. He'd been so close to my father, and, I thought, so close to me, during all the years we'd lived here. Why hadn't he come to pay a farewell call? It was all of a piece with his abrupt withdrawal from Father's sickroom after administering the last rites, and with his refusal to go to Château Bassincourt to share a collation with the mourners after the funeral.

Today the laugh lines in his normally genial face looked more like age marks carved beside his mouth. "So, my child, they tell me you're leaving us," he said heavily, barely acknowledging my greeting. "Have you thought sufficiently about this? Do you think it's wise to go so far away from your home?"

"Mon père, I don't know how much you've heard," I faltered, "but Bassincourt isn't really my home anymore. You see, I'm not Calum MacDonell's daughter—"

"Oh, yes, I've heard the whole story," he interrupted. "I see what it is. You can't wait to shake the dust of this humble place and hobnob with your aristocratic new relations. Doubtless you'll have fine clothes and carriages, everything poor Monsieur MacDonell couldn't give you, and you'll be able to put on fancy airs and lord it over the common folk, but will this truly make you happy?"

I stared at the old priest in hurt surprise. Both his tone and his words were wounding. Deliberately so, it seemed to me. It was so unlike the kindly, affectionate man I'd always known. Swallowing my resentment, I said, "I don't think you understand. I'm my grandfather's only heir. Would you want me to be the cause of my family line dying out?"

"Better that than to live a life of idle luxury," he said sternly. "You do so much good here, my child, with your teaching. Think hard before you abandon such a vocation." Then, blessing me with a hasty sign of the cross, he stalked out of the cottage with a parting brusque comment, "I shall pray for you whatever you choose to do."

Caught up in my confrontation with Père Chenvert, I hadn't noticed that Emily had come down the stairs until I heard her voice beside me. "Mistress Kirstie, mayhap the auld priest ha' the richt o' it," she exclaimed, putting down a basket piled high with our castoffs. "Mayhap we should stay in Bassincourt."

"Don't be ridiculous," I snapped in sudden anger. "Of course we're not staying in Bassincourt." I couldn't allow Emily's doubts to reinforce the blow that Père Chenvert's strangely unfeeling remarks had dealt to my already sagging resolution to leave Normandy.

Emily persisted. "I've lived here sae lang, I dinna ken I could get used tae Scotland again," she said uneasily. A note of foreboding crept into her voice. "I'm getting a terrible bad feeling aboot this journey, mistress. Those Camerons, I've always heard they were a wild lot. And they live on the edge o' nowhere, smack in the middle o' the Highlands. We could manage here by oursel', ye ken, e'en though the maister's gone, ye wi' yer teaching, mysel' working i' the kitchens o' the château. Wha' do ye say tae that?"

Before I could answer her, Ian Cameron walked through the door that the priest had failed to close behind him. Every buckle and button on his uniform glinted with polish. His powdered hair was in perfect order beneath his fur bonnet. He gazed with approval around the bare room, noting Emily's heavily laden basket. "Good," he said briskly. "You've not much left to do here. I've ordered the horses to be put to at dawn tomorrow. I trust you'll be ready to leave then."

One look at that calm, arrogant face stiffened my backbone. He'd glimpsed my doubts and insecurities once before, at Father's funeral. For my own self-respect, I couldn't let that happen again. Ignoring Emily's snuffling, I said coolly, "We'll be waiting for you on our doorstep at the crack of dawn."

I seemed to be lying on something stationary. It felt like a proper bed, not a cramped bunk in a heaving ship's cabin. Cautiously I opened my eyes, blinking against the brightness of spring sunshine pouring in through the window of a small room with whitewashed walls. "I'm not on the ship," I mumbled to myself in a tone of discovery.

A chair creaked beside the bed and a moment later I could see Emily's anxious face hovering over me. "We're in Leith, mistress. In an inn beside the waterfront."

"Leith? The port of Edinburgh?" I repeated in awe. It was hard to grasp the blessed reality of being on dry land again, and at journey's end, too, in Scotland. The ship had barely cleared the harbor at Cherbourg before my stomach became queasy, and the violent spring storm that lashed the North Sea several days later had turned the voyage into a nightmare. I could recall only brief snatches of respite between bouts of nausea that made me want to die rather than endure one more minute at sea.

"How do ye feel, mistress?"

I pondered the question, lifting my head slightly to test the state of my stomach. "Human," I decided with relief. "I think I'll survive. When did we get here?"

"Late last even. The major carried ye ashore in a howling rain. I thought the both o' ye would be washed away i' the wet and the darkness."

I closed my eyes as the warm color suffused my face. I had a vague memory of being cradled in a vibrant embrace, feeling the strong, slow beat of a man's heart against my cheek. And not just on that one occasion in the driving rain. I asked suddenly, "Emily, did Major Cameron ever help you with my care while we were on the ship?"

"Oh, aye. He was sae guid. Many's the time he held ye steady, the whiles I tried tae pour a drop o' water down yer throat."

I kept my eyes closed, feigning drowsiness. Soon I heard Emily slip quietly from the room. But I didn't have the faintest desire to sleep. Instead, I was trying once more to solve the enigma that was Ian Cameron.

If I had expected us to become more friendly in the course of our journey to Scotland, I was soon disabused of the notion. After we left Bassincourt in the heavy berline with the Carrickmore crest on its panels, it took us three days of hard traveling to reach the port of Cherbourg, and we waited four more days for a ship. During that week, Ian remained as aloof, as self-contained, as he'd been in Bassincourt.

Not that I'd seen a great deal of him on this journey. He didn't travel with us in the berline. He preferred to ride beside the carriage, he said, and it would be far better if Emily and I could ride, also, because later, in Scotland, the roads would be impossibly rough. But Emily was no horsewoman, and I elected to ride with her in the berline. As a result I saw Ian only at the brief stops we made at posting inns to change horses and at mealtimes, where he spoke only when it was necessary to explain something about our journey, or in answer to a question. In Cherbourg itself he was absent from our inn most of the time, arranging for our passage.

I couldn't honestly accuse him of being either unfriendly or hostile. After all, in Bassincourt he'd removed from me the burden of Papa's funeral, and he'd taken me in his arms and urged me to cry out my grief. On board the ship he'd helped Emily to nurse me during the voyage. In general, though, his attitude remained polite but disinterested, giving a strong impression that he was acting merely as a courier. The Earl of Carrickmore had instructed him to escort me to Castle Kildrummond, and he was doing his duty. But for all the personal involvement he displayed, Emily and I might have been inanimate objects.

Logic told me I shouldn't expect anything more from him, simply because I'd suffered a recent bereavement and I'd had to leave my home and everything that was familiar to me. But I'd found that logic wasn't very comforting. A little human warmth would have done so much to blunt the edge of the aching loneliness that I was feeling during that first week away from Bassincourt.

At least, by the time we'd boarded ship, I'd learned a little more about him, by dint of direct questioning. Certainly he never volunteered information about himself during the brief intervals we were together.

The Black Watch, for example. "Was it difficult to get leave from your regiment to go to France to see my father?" I asked at one point as I was stretching my legs at a posting stop.

"Actually, I took indefinite leave from the Forty-second Foot several years ago," he replied.

"But why . . . ?" My voice trailed off. His wearing of the uniform had perplexed me from the first moment we'd met. The colorful kilt and fur headgear had made him the instant target of curiosity to every Frenchman who laid eyes on him. Not surprising, really, because it was only a few years since the end of a long and bloody war between France and England. "Why are you still wearing the uniform, then?" I asked bluntly.

He didn't answer for a moment. At length he said coolly, "You're exposing all my vanities. Are you familiar with the battle of Culloden?"

"Well, of course. The English defeated Bonnie Prince Charlie and the Highland clans there in 1745. Your own father—" I stopped short, biting my lip.

"Was hanged for treason and his estates were seized by the crown for taking part in the battle," he finished, an edge to his voice. "The English government also passed into law the Act of Disarming, which forbade Scotsmen to wear the kilt or to carry arms or to play the bagpipes. The Disarming Act posed a slight problem for the English, however. They wanted to retain the Highland Regiments to help fight their foreign wars for them, so it was necessary to compromise. The soldiers of the Black Watch can wear the kilt and carry the broadsword anywhere in the world *except* in Scotland. The moment we set foot on Scottish soil we're required to change into civilian clothes and hand over our weapons."

"Oh," I said in a moment of startled recognition. "You're simply making a point."

"Precisely." He smiled thinly. "By wearing my uniform at every opportunity outside Scotland I express my disapproval of the Disarming Act. Childish, but satisfying." The remark showed me another small facet of his character, a further indication that beneath that reticent façade there lurked some human feelings.

Another time, over a meal in the private parlor of an inn, I asked, "Why did you leave the army?"

"Before your Uncle David died, he was training me to become your grandfather's steward at Kildrummond."

"Steward?"

"Factor. Bailiff. I manage the estate, if you like."

"Then we'll be living near each other at Kildrummond?" I exclaimed in surprise.

"Not just near. With. I have quarters in the castle. It's convenient for the earl to have me close at hand, and not as unsuitable as it might be for someone who wasn't related to the family."

I gave him a startled look. "Madame de Bassincourt called you my cousin, but I thought she was just using a figure of speech. You and I are clansmen, but are we really related?"

"Distantly. You may recall my telling Mr. MacDonell that my father was chieftain of the senior sept of Clan Cameron." Casually he added, "We take the ties of blood quite seriously in the Highlands. When my father died, for example, your grandfather had me brought to Castle Kildrummond. I grew up there."

This revelation startled me even more. Obviously Ian Cameron's connection with the family at Kildrummond was much closer than I'd imagined. I took advantage of this insight, on one occasion during our stay at Cherbourg, to probe for information about the domestic situation at Kildrummond. Everything had happened so fast, Father's death and our departure from the village, that I had the bewildering impression that I was stepping into a void. I asked, "Besides my grandfather, are there any other members of the family living at the castle?"

"Yes. Your grandmother, the Countess of Carrickmore. Gwyneth, Lady Allendale, your Uncle David's widow. And, most of the time of late, your cousin Murdoch Graham, the son of the earl's younger brother."

"But . . . " I paused, my forehead wrinkling in perplexity. "But if this Murdoch is my grandfather's nephew in the male line, why isn't he named Cameron?"

"He would be if his birth had been legitimate. It wasn't. He goes by his mother's surname, Graham."

I would have been delighted to learn more about this Murdoch and the other members of the family. However, the conversation ended, as usual, with Ian giving me only the bare bones of information before politely excusing himself to go off on an important errand. In this case, to go down to the harbor to make the final arrangements for our voyage. Aboard ship, of course, I'd been so vilely ill that I'd have been hard-pressed to summon up any interest in the Second Coming.

A day on stable land, taking my meals in bed, and most important of all, enjoying the luxury of a steaming bath, made me feel like a different person from the bedraggled waif who'd been carried ashore at Leith. At daybreak the following morning I was ready to begin the final stage of our journey.

Hugging my cardinal—a three-quarter-length hooded cloak of scarlet cloth, which had once made me feel so fashionable but was now a little shabby—more closely around me against the brisk breeze blowing across the harbor, I walked out of the inn, narrowly avoiding a collision with a tall gentleman as I headed for the waiting berline. I murmured a hasty apology and walked on.

"Your servant tells me you're feeling more yourself this morning," said a familiar cool voice behind me.

I whirled, gaping at Ian Cameron in astonishment. He looked so different that I hadn't recognized him. He was wearing a fitted frock coat of dark blue cloth, doeskin breeches and half jack boots. A cocked hat covered his thick tawny-gold hair, unpowdered and uncurled and clubbed into a simple queue at the back of his neck. My heart skipped a beat, as it did so often when I looked at him, and once again I berated myself. It was another proof, if I needed one, of my abysmal lack of sophistication. Ian Cameron was the first attractive man of roughly my own age—I supposed he was about thirty—that I'd met since I ceased to be a schoolgirl, but that didn't excuse my fatuous response to his male good looks. Especially since he appeared to be thoroughly unimpressed with me.

"You've taken off your uniform," I said, collecting myself and stating the obvious.

"A precaution against being arrested," he replied drily. "I

told you the wearing of the kilt is outlawed in Scotland. Are you ready to go?"

"I—yes."

"You don't sound entirely certain."

Turning away from the harbor, I looked south, beyond the town of Leith, where, a few miles away, I could discern the outline of a low mountain. "Edinburgh's over there, isn't it?" I asked.

"Yes. Five miles from here. That hill is Arthur's Seat, in the park of Holyrood Palace."

"Could we—would it be possible to drive through the city on our way north?"

"I'm sorry." I didn't think he sounded especially sorry. "Your grandfather asked me to bring you to Kildrummond as soon as possible. I'd planned to catch the first ferry across the Firth of Forth this morning and be in Perth by nightfall."

Sighing, I bowed to the inevitable. But as Ian handed me into the berline I cast one last wistful glance in the direction of Edinburgh. It wasn't my birthplace, but it would have meant a great deal to see something of the city where my parents had lived for so long. And then reality intruded itself again. Calum and Sheila MacDonell weren't my parents.

Not allowing myself to brood, I concentrated on the first stage of our journey north, which took us, via the ferry at Queensferry, across the scant mile separating the two banks of the Firth of Forth and through the pleasant hills of Fife to Perth, the old capital of Scotland. There, at dinner in a snug inn near the ancient Parliament House, I commented to Ian, "You warned me that the Scottish roads would be very rough. Surely you were exaggerating? We must have covered a good distance today."

"We did," he acknowledged, draining his wineglass. "Over forty miles. Unfortunately, the next hundred or so miles to Fort William will be very difficult. Beyond Perth we'll be driving on military roads through largely mountain terrain."

"Military roads?"

"Roads built by the English army after the Fifteen and the Forty-five to make it easier to put down any future Jacobite rebellion," he replied with the familiar edge in his tone that surfaced whenever he spoke about English injustices. "Before that, in a country with very few roads of any kind, it was easy for the clansmen to evade capture once they'd slipped through the mountain passes to the Highlands."

Even after this further warning, I wasn't prepared for the difficult traveling we encountered after leaving Perth. The carriage's iron tires grated and slithered against the rutted, depressed surface of the roads, causing the berline to sway violently from side to side and leaving me with the distinct impression that my backbone was coming through my skull. One day it rained heavily, turning the road into a quagmire of slippery, sticky mud. Beyond the village of Pitlochry we began the long arduous climb through Glen Garry into the heart of the Grampians, where the coachman made frequent use of skid pans and rollers on the rear wheels to prevent the heavy carriage from either running over the team on the summit of a hill or from sliding backward on a slope.

The mountain scenery was magnificent, but as the tiring interminable journey wore on I was less and less inclined to appreciate it. It was bare, forbidding country, where the snow still lingered on the frowning peaks, even though we were in the month of May, and where for mile after wild lonely mile I couldn't spot a single sign of human habitation. Near the Pass of Drumochter, where we stopped for the night at a wretched inn that was little more than a hovel, my feelings came to a head.

As usual, I'd scarcely exchanged a word with Ian that day as he rode along beside the carriage, and, also as usual, he'd excused himself perfunctorily after the evening meal. Tonight I wasn't going to allow him to ignore me. I wasn't going to retire meekly to my bedchamber. I needed to talk with him, to bolster my slender store of confidence that was rapidly eroding under the numbing onslaught of this gray, inhospitable land.

I knew Ian had left the inn to go for a solitary stroll, as he often did of an evening, whether for exercise or to avoid my company, I wasn't sure. Slipping into my scarlet cardinal, I pulled the hood over my head to ward off the chill, even though it was still quite light. In these far northern latitudes, I'd discovered, the twilight faded slowly and the nights could be quite cold. Stepping outside the inn, I spotted Ian leaning against a large boulder, his arms crossed against his chest, staring into the distance toward the pass through which we'd be making our way tomorrow.

"May I join you?" I asked as I came up.

"Please do," he replied, as ever unfailingly polite. Pushing himself away from the boulder, he stood up to his full height. He was taller than I by more than a head, and I'd always thought of myself as a tall woman. "Are you sure you won't be chilled, standing out here?" he asked dutifully. "I apologize, by the way, for our accommodations. There's not another inn for miles."

"It doesn't matter. It's just for one night. Major Cameron—" I paused, then blurted, "It feels awkward to be so formal with each other. We *are* cousins. Would you mind if I used your Christian name?"

After a split second of dead silence, in which a sense of his reluctance was almost palpable, he stirred, saying smoothly, "Not at all. We should certainly be cousinly."

If there was a barb in his tone, I ignored it. "And I'm Kirstie, of course."

He bowed.

"Maj—Ian, could you tell me a little more about Kildrummond itself, and about my—my new family? Is the castle situated in country like this, barren and rocky and without any sign of human life?"

He looked startled. "Why, no. Kildrummond occupies one

40

of the most beautiful sites in Inverness-shire, beside a stream in a wooded glen running down to Loch Linnhe."

A little of the tightness left my heart. At least I wouldn't be living in an uninhabited desert. "What about the family?" I went on. Now that I had Ian in a position where he could hardly find a good excuse to take leave of me, I was going to take full advantage of it. "You haven't told me very much about any of them. My grandfather, for instance. What kind of a man is he?"

Ian shrugged. "The earl is about seventy, I suppose. Elegant, a man of the world. Fond of society. For years he didn't spend much time at Kildrummond. He and Murdoch, who are very close, preferred to live in Edinburgh or London."

"But I believe you said that both the earl and my cousin Murdoch are now in residence at Kildrummond?"

"It's a case of necessity. Gambling and horse racing are expensive pastimes. The earl has pretty much run through the fortune he acquired when he married your grandmother. She was Lady Elspeth Hamilton. A great heiress."

"Oh." I looked at Ian blankly. "That sounded quite harsh," I ventured. "You don't approve of my grandfather?"

He shrugged again. "It's not for me to approve or disapprove," he said indifferently. "I'm merely a hired servant."

"But . . . " I searched my memory. "Surely you're much more than a servant. Didn't you tell me that my grandfather brought you to live with him when—when your father died? You must have grown up as a member of the family."

Suddenly the gray eyes struck sparks. "Hardly a member of the family," he said harshly. "Alexander Cameron put food in my mouth and gave me a bed to sleep in and then ignored my existence for the next twenty years." He drew a deep breath and his lips clamped together as if to prevent another inadvertent word from escaping. "I think we'd better go inside," he muttered. "It's beginning to rain."

As he abruptly turned to go I caught at his arm. His mask was in place again, but I thought I'd detected a note of hurt

41

in his voice, and something impelled me to try to heal that hurt. "Ian . . . I didn't mean to pry, but I think I can visualize how a small boy might feel unwelcome, suddenly thrust into a house full of strangers. I feel a little like that myself! Isn't it possible, though, that you might have misinterpreted my grandfather's attitude?"

He jerked his arm away. It was darker now, and in the half light I couldn't see his face distinctly under the jaunty cocked hat, but there was no mistaking the throb of anger in his voice. "You're the new lady of the manor, and I work for your family, but there's nothing in the terms of my employment that requires me to discuss my personal affairs with you. Now that I've made myself clear, shall we go into the inn?"

My heart felt flayed, and there was no intelligent reason why I should have invited any more punishment, but I heard myself saying, "Ian, must we quarrel? Can't we be friends?"

"Friends? Oh, God." Suddenly he reached out for me, wrapping his arms around me in a bruising embrace while his lips ravaged mine in a kiss that ignited a torrent of unfamiliar fiery desire. I wanted him to hold me even closer, to explore my aching flesh with his hands, to meld his body to mine in an explosion of passion that I'd never even envisioned until this magic, chaotic moment.

He finally lifted his head, his breathing hard and uneven, his gray eyes no longer cold but alive with dancing flames. "I can give you this, any time you want it, but not friendship, Kirstie MacDonell Cameron. Friendship is between equals."

Chapter III

Wrenching myself out of Ian's grasp, I bolted toward the door of the inn, desperately trying to hold back the scalding tears that were stinging my eyelids. I brushed past a curious chambermaid and stormed up the stairs to my bedchamber, where I startled poor Emily by summarily ordering her out of the room. After she left I called on my pride and managed to restrain a flood of tears, but it was a small victory. I writhed in an agony of chagrin and humiliation. What must Ian Cameron think of me? I'd responded shamelessly to the searing embrace of a man who regarded me merely as an inconvenient encumbrance. He'd kissed me in what I supposed was a kind of desperation, because he literally couldn't think of anything else to do when I begged him for the friendship he wasn't prepared to give. And yes, he'd probably kissed me because he felt something of the rampaging physical desire that had coursed through my body. My face burned. He couldn't have failed to notice my response. How could I face him again? How could I face my own weak-willed self?

The following morning Ian took the matter into his own hands. When I walked reluctantly into the common room for breakfast—the inn didn't have such an amenity as a private dining parlor—Ian was already seated at the table. I murmured a low greeting without meeting his eyes as he rose and pulled out my chair for me.

"I'm afraid breakfast is even less edible than last night's dinner," he said. "The proprietor assures me that this peculiar-looking liquid is tea. At least it's hot."

"Thank you for your concern, but I'm sure I'm in no danger of starving," I replied stiffly, still avoiding looking at him. My throat felt constricted. It was hard to swallow the stale bread and the hardened bit of cheese that represented the innkeeper's idea of breakfast.

He said abruptly, "Will you allow me to apologize for my behavior last night, Mistress Cameron? I was—I was in a foul mood, which I had no right to inflict on you. I assure you it won't happen again."

There was just enough uncertainty in the normally confident voice to pull me out of the morass of self-doubt in which I'd been wallowing. From some deep reserve of self-respect, I summoned the poise to meet his eyes and say kindly, "There's no need to apologize. We all have bad moods now and again. You *have* forgotten something, though, haven't you, Ian? Last night we agreed to be cousinly and use our Christian names."

I could see a tiny muscle twitch in his cheek. "So we did. Thank you—Kirstie—for being so understanding."

It was a little thing, winning this skirmish. However, it stiffened my backbone enough to allow me to behave almost naturally toward Ian during the remainder of our journey to Fort William.

"Mountains and mair mountains, there's no end tae them. It's a fair benighted land, the Highlands," murmured Emily, gazing across the sparkling waters of the loch to the springing green hills of Ardgour. Emily was Edinburgh-born and bred, and had little enthusiasm for mountains. We were standing outside our inn in Fort William, waiting in the early morning light for the carriage to be brought around. "And there's anither, the one they call Ben Nevis," Emily added, motioning to the south with a resentful stab of her finger at the looming hulk of a great mountain.

"At least, these past two days, we've been traveling down hill, and we've actually spied a few trees and sheep," I reminded her. We'd arrived at Fort William, a small, unimpressive garrison town at the head of Loch Linnhe, the evening before, after a long and tiring drive through magnificent mountain scenery. This morning we would begin the final leg of our journey to Castle Kildrummond, and already, before I'd so much as set foot in the carriage, my stomach was churning with nervousness.

A flash of scarlet uniform caught my attention, and as I turned to look at the small fort, which I understood was the town's sole reason for being, a voice beside me remarked drily, "It was originally called Kilmallie. The fort was built by General Monk in 1655 to hold the men of Clan Cameron in subjection. It was renamed for our glorious King William."

I glanced up at Ian, resisting the impulse to let my eyes slide away from his face. It was still difficult for me to look at him without remembering the shattering encounter two nights ago outside that miserable inn at the Pass of Drumochter, when he'd made it so abundantly clear that there was nothing about me that interested him, except perhaps the temptation, firmly resisted, to engage in a casual sexual foray. It was still difficult, too, for me to speak to him without a sense of constraint.

As I watched a sentry present arms at the gate of the fort, I remarked with a spurious show of interest, "Is it really true that this fort was established to guard against the Camerons? You'll have me believing that my fellow clansmen have always been an incorrigible lot!"

The cool gray eyes looked at me, unsmiling. "It depends on how you look at it, doesn't it? The English certainly don't consider your grandfather incorrigible. No one could have declared more forcibly against Bonnie Prince Charlie. *My* father, on the other hand . . . " He bit off his words, closing the door, as he always seemed to do, against any display of personal feeling. "Here's the carriage. Shall we get started? It's not far, Kildrummond, about eight miles, but I must warn you that the going will be very rough."

He hadn't exaggerated. The jolting, rutted road leading south along Loch Linnhe soon disintegrated into little more than a rough track. It was beautiful country, thickly wooded and interspersed with a myriad of tiny, flashing streams, rising to a vista of wild and lonely mountains. But as Emily and I were bounced unmercifully from one side of the berline to the other, I barely noticed the scenery in my growing discomfort.

After what seemed hours of misery the carriage turned into a narrow glen, following a steeply inclined drive beside a foaming little river that rushed joyously downhill. And there, on an eminence several hundred yards away, at the point where the river suddenly widened and plunged into its final run toward Loch Linnhe, I could see rising the imposing outline of a large house built of silvery gray granite. In moments we rounded the curved drive encircling the house and stopped in front of the soaring portico. Ian appeared at the door of the berline to let down the steps. He held out his hand, saying, "Journey's end. This is Castle Kildrummond."

My heart was beating tumultuously, and it was hard to breathe. Despite the help of Ian's steadying hand I stumbled as I put my foot on the first step, and I fell hard against him. His arms closed about me automatically, convulsively, and I stared into his eyes, seeing again that leaping hot flame. Transfixed in a moment without time or boundaries, I was conscious only of the wild thudding of his heart and the bittersweet pain inflicted on my breasts by the metal buttons on his coat.

"Good day to you, Master Ian. So you've come home at last," came a sardonic voice from behind us, speaking in Gaelic. The spell was broken. With a sudden sharp exhalation of breath, Ian lowered me to the ground. We turned to face the tall young woman who stood in the driveway, skewering me with avidly curious eyes. She wore a mobcap over her reddish curls, and a neck cloth swathed the simple dark cotton gown with its skirt pinned up over a jaunty red petticoat. She had bright blue eyes and a sprinkling of freckles across her piquant little nose, but at the moment the pretty face was marred by an expression compounded of anger and some other emotion I couldn't quite place.

"Good day, Hallie," said Ian in English. "Yes, I'm home. I've brought the laird's granddaughter with me. Mistress Kirstie, this is Hallie Cameron, who works at the castle."

"I'm pleased to meet you, Hallie." I don't know what prompted me to speak in the Gaelic.

Both Ian and Hallie looked at me in surprise. Obviously they hadn't suspected that I could understand their language. The girl bobbed a brief curtsy. "Welcome tae Kildrummond, mistress. May ye be verra happy here," she said in broad Scots. To me, the provocation was quite deliberate. By refusing to answer me in Gaelic, Hallie Cameron was telling me that I was not to be admitted to the circle of those who belonged at Kildrummond. I felt chilled. I had just arrived at the castle, and already I'd discovered someone who didn't like me.

Apparently noticing nothing untoward in the young maidservant's manner, Ian briskly dispatched the carriage to the stables and sent Emily off with Hallie to meet the housekeeper and be assigned a place to sleep.

I looked up to see the great door under the portico opening. A liveried footman in a powdered wig appeared, bowing as we came up the steps. I found myself in a lofty circular hallway floored in marble. A shimmering crystal fire lustre hung from the ceiling, and directly in front of me rose a magnificent wrought-iron staircase. Advancing toward us was a slender, pretty woman who appeared to be in her late thirties, or perhaps her early forties.

"So you're back, Ian," she said. She sounded cool.

"As you see," he replied with equal coolness. There was little love lost here, I thought. To me he said, "Kirstie, your Aunt Gwyneth, Lady Allendale."

As I curtsied to her, she said with a smile, "My dear, I'm delighted you're here at last. We were beginning to wonder if you'd encountered a storm at sea, or had an accident to the carriage."

I studied my Uncle David's widow. Her manner was gracious, and she was saying all the right words, so why wasn't I more drawn to this woman? Why did I detect so little warmth when I looked into those violet eyes beneath the lacy cap? Then I chided myself for an overactive imagination. I was tired, I was insecure, I was feeling dowdy and unkempt beside this exquisitely dressed, elegant new relative, but I had no reason to think she wasn't sincere. "I'm happy to be here, Lady Allendale," I said.

Inclining her head, she went on, "I hope you won't mind not meeting the rest of the family immediately. His lordship is resting—perhaps Ian's told you that your grandfather hasn't been very well of late?—and Murdoch is off somewhere riding on the estate. We didn't know exactly when to expect you, you see. But what am I about, keeping you standing here? You must be exhausted after your journey. I'm always prostrate when I arrive here from Edinburgh after a long ride in that wretched coach. Come along, my dear. I'll show you to your bedchamber."

I turned to Ian, standing quietly behind me. "Thank you for escorting me all the way from France. I'll see you later this evening, no doubt?"

He bowed gravely. "Indeed. I take dinner with the family."

It was an odd way of putting it, I thought, but I had no time to reflect on the remark as I went off after Gwyneth.

Talking as she went, she escorted me, not up that beautiful staircase, but off to the side of the foyer, to a more modest flight of stairs leading to the second floor. "We use the state rooms on the first floor—they open into each other off the staircase—only for formal entertaining," she explained. "All our bedchambers are on the second floor, and we spend most of our time in the private family rooms on the ground floor. Your grandfather admired this type of room arrangement when he was visiting in London and Edinburgh, so he had the architecture copied when he had this house built thirty years ago."

"Only thirty years ago?" I exclaimed in surprise. "The house is called *Castle* Kildrummond, so I thought it must date from a much earlier time when fortified buildings were necessary in this area. I wondered if perhaps it had been remodeled from an earlier house on the site."

"Well, yes, there was an earlier building that your grandfather pulled down to make room for this one. However, Kildrummond takes its name from a real castle built in the thirteenth century, when, as you surmised, the Camerons had to defend themselves against all comers. You can still see the ruins of the gatehouse and the keep on the hill behind the house."

Still talking, she ushered me into a large, charming bedchamber furnished with graceful carved mahogany pieces, draperies and bed hangings of heavy silk and a Turkey pile carpet in muted shades of blue that harmonized with the draperies.

"What a lovely room," I said, adding frankly, "it's much grander than I've been accustomed to, Lady Allendale. My father—" I paused, choking back my aching sense of loss. "My foster father and I lived for many years in a tiny cottage."

"My dear, you mustn't be so formal. I'm your Aunt Gwyneth. Or simply Gwyneth, if you prefer. It makes me feel quite elderly to be an aunt to a tall young lady like you!"

Again, the voice and the sentiments were perfectly cordial, so why did I have this nagging sense that Gwyneth's welcoming charm was all on the surface?

"I expect it will take you some time to adjust to life at Kildrummond," she went on. "It will take time for all of us. Until a short time ago, after all, we'd never heard of each other. But it will come out all right in the end, I'm sure." She glanced around the bedchamber, as if checking to see that all was in order. "I'll leave you to rest now. We dine at five. A ghastly hour, I agree," she said as she noticed my eyes widen, "but we must be fashionable at all costs! Dining at two or three is considered impossibly dowdy in London these days, the earl informs me. Until five, then."

After Gwyneth left I removed my cardinal and placed it in the enormous wardrobe, where it looked curiously forlorn. My few articles of clothing wouldn't begin to fill the wardrobe, I thought uneasily, nor were most of my garments in the least fashionable. Well, there was nothing I could do about that now.

Aimlessly I wandered over to the window, which I soon realized overlooked the back of the house. It had rained, briefly and heavily, earlier in the day—a too frequent occurrence in the Highlands, I was soon to discover—but now a brilliant sun picked out in sharp relief the crumbling stones of the ancient pile looming forbiddingly from the height above the house. The original Castle Kildrummond, the place in which my newly found Cameron ancestors had lived for centuries. I shivered. Even in ruins, the castle had a menacing air. It was easy to imagine how safe its inhabitants must have felt behind those powerful walls.

I turned away from the window when Emily, looking ruffled, marched into the room, saying, "Ach, Mistress Kirstie, this hoose is sae much bigger than the château at Bassincourt, wi' all those wings and pavilions. The hoosekeeper gi'ed me directions tae find yer bedchamber, but still I lost mysel'. And the sairvants! There's a fair army o' sairvants i' this place. I dinna ken if we'll be verra comfortable here."

"I'm sure we'll get used to luxury, Emily," I reassured her. I wasn't going to admit to her that I was as nervous as she was about the grandeur of our new surroundings. Ahead of me was my meeting with my grandfather and my cousin Murdoch and my grandmother, the Countess of Carrickmore. My stomach felt hollow at the prospect.

There was a tap at the door and Emily admitted a pair of liveried footmen. One of them was carrying my two shabby portmanteaux and the other clutched a heavy old clock and my cittern in its case.

Closing the door behind the footmen, Emily said, "I'll juist pit yer things awa', mistress, while ye lay yersel' doon."

But I was too restless to take a nap, too apprehensive about meeting the other members of my new family. I needed something to occupy my mind, so I insisted on helping Emily unpack my meager belongings.

"Where shall I pit the clock, mistress?" asked Emily, her face dubious.

"Put it on the commode by the window," I said firmly, even though I acknowledged to myself how incongruous the battered, ungainly old clock looked atop the delicate chest japanned in gold and silver. However, I couldn't bear to hide the clock away. My mother had carried it with her all over Europe, a reminder to her, I supposed, of her childhood home in Edinburgh. Only, the thought returned with a pang, Sheila MacDonell wasn't my mother.

Another knock sounded at the door, and the maidservant, Hallie Cameron, whom I'd met when I first arrived at Kildrummond, came into the room with a pitcher of steaming water. "Will ye be wanting anything else, mistress?" she asked. Her tone was barely civil.

"No, I thank you, Hallie." I looked at her surly face, perplexed. I wasn't used to personal hostility, and this girl had apparently taken an acute dislike to me at first sight. "Have you been working long at the castle?" I asked pleasantly.

The bright blue eyes sparked. For a moment I thought she would ignore me. Then she said, biting the words off, "Ten years. I'm twenty-five, in case ye were thinking o' asking. Would that be all?"

"Yes, thank you." I lifted my chin. "You may go, Hallie."

With the briefest of curtsies, she flounced out of the bed-chamber. After she was gone I glanced at the tiny watch pinned to my shoulder and then at the pitcher of hot water on the washstand. Now I couldn't postpone the inevitable. It was time to dress for dinner.

"Ye look sae grand, mistress," Emily said admiringly a little later.

I *felt* grand in the gown of sprigged rose-colored silk with its wide paniers and frothing of ruffles at the sleeves. It had been a gift from the Comtesse de Bassincourt last Christmas, when she'd invited me to attend a fête at the château. However, it was the one fashionable garment I owned. If the occupants of Castle Kildrummond dressed grandly for dinner every evening I would soon become a depressingly monotonous sight to them, I reflected, and pushed the thought to the back of my mind. I could only cross one bridge at a time. Peering into the mirror on the dressing table, I adjusted a tiny lace-edged cap over my smoothly dressed dark hair. Several curls, tied with rose-colored ribbon, escaped from the coil at the nape of my neck to fall over my shoulder.

Taking a deep breath, I walked to the door of the bedchamber. I was as ready as I would ever be. And of course I got lost, just as Emily had done, in the labyrinthine vastness of my new home. Staircases seemed to sprout up and down every few feet, and there was a bewildering number of side corridors. Of the army of servants that Emily had spoken so feelingly about, I didn't spot a one to give me directions. Even the great central hall on the ground floor was empty of life when I finally found my way to it. I was standing beneath the shimmering chandelier, looking helplessly about me, when a laughing voice exclaimed, "Egad, a damsel in distress. And here I am, just the man to help her!"

Whirling around, I stared at the owner of the voice, a tall, slender man dressed in richly laced green velvet. His handsome mouth smiling, his blue eyes sparkling, he made me a graceful bow. "Mistress Kirstie Cameron, I presume? Allow me to introduce myself. I'm your cousin, Murdoch Graham. Or your half cousin once removed, to be more exact. Your grandfather and my father were half brothers. Did you get lost, as every visitor seems to do in this vast pile of a place?"

His friendliness was infectious, and I no longer felt quite so gauche. I smiled back at him. "I'm pleased to meet you, Cousin Murdoch. Yes, I did lose my way. I was trying to find the family drawing room."

"Right over here, to your left," he replied, tucking my hand under his arm and leading me toward a door to the rear of the grand staircase. "You'll soon become familiar with Kildrummond," he assured me as we walked together across the marble floor. Glancing up at him, I looked away, flustered, when I found his eyes fixed on me.

He burst into a laugh, stopping in his tracks. "Shall we stop being so polite and admit that we're curious about each other?" He gave me a long, close look. "You don't have the Cameron coloring," he said at last. "Most of us are blond and blue-eyed. I can see a hint of Fiona in you, but I think you really resemble your father."

"Oh, I do," I exclaimed without thinking, and then bit my lip, feeling the warm blush flooding my face. Would I never cease thinking of Calum MacDonell as my natural father? "That is, I have Marcel Lefevre's dark coloring," I went on hastily. "Did you know him well?"

He shook his head. "Not really. I saw him a few times in our house in Edinburgh, but I never noticed him particularly." He looked faintly embarrassed. "Well, there was no reason to notice him, you know. He was only—he was your mother's French tutor. No one in the family had any reason to suspect that Fiona and Marcel were interested in each other, let alone secretly married, until we found her note saying they'd eloped. But look, we shouldn't be talking about old, sad things on the day of your homecoming."

"No, please go on," I said quickly. "I'd like to learn more about my—my parents."

"Well, if you really want to know . . . " Murdoch shrugged. "It was nineteen, no, twenty years ago. The entire family was gathered at Kildrummond for the Christmas holidays, and we woke up one morning to find Fiona gone. Marcel, who we thought was in Edinburgh, if we thought anything about him at all, had slipped up here secretly to spirit her away in the middle of the night. We couldn't trace them. We think they must have had a boat waiting to take them down Loch Linnhe." Sighing, he added, "If only Fiona had had the courage to come to her father, she and Marcel might still be alive, and you, Kirstie, wouldn't have been a stranger to Kildrummond all these years. And the Earl of Carrickmore needn't have suffered the agony of believing his family line would come to an end when he died."

There was no reproach in his voice, but I found myself saying defensively, "My fa—my foster father said Fiona told him she was afraid the earl would have her marriage annulled."

"Oh, my uncle can be a little forbidding at times, I daresay. . . . " Murdoch smiled, tucking my hand under his arm again. "Now isn't the time to delve into the past. We can't change anything," he said firmly. "What matters is that you're here at last. Come along. We don't want to keep the earl waiting."

Gwyneth had spoken of the "family rooms" on the ground floor. If the large, richly furnished formal drawing room with its elaborately molded plaster ceiling was a good example of the private living quarters of the Camerons of Kildrummond, I could only speculate about the magnificence of the state rooms upstairs. The two occupants of the room rose as Murdoch and I entered.

Gwyneth came over to me, taking my hand. The elegance

of her saque gown of gleaming satin and the artistry of her high-dressed powdered hair immediately made me realize how far from fashionable I was in my sprigged rose-colored silk. "My dear Kirstie," she said, "pray allow me to present you to your grandfather."

"My lord." I curtsied deeply to the man standing before me.

The Earl of Carrickmore was a tall, handsome man whose erect frame and imperious blue eyes tended to obscure the telltale signs that he was old. There were deep age lines in his thin, aristocratic face and he supported himself, even if ever so carelessly, on a tasseled cane.

"How do you do, my dear." The deep voice was languid, the eyes hooded and expressionless. "Welcome to Kildrummond. I trust your journey here was not too uncomfortable?"

"No, I thank you, sir."

"Splendid." He walked slowly to an armchair and sat down. "Gwyneth, my love, perhaps my granddaughter would like a small glass of claret. And what delicacies, pray, is Cook preparing for us tonight?"

I must have looked as blank as I felt. Whatever I'd imagined about my reception at Kildrummond, I hadn't bargained on indifference. During the next few minutes, I listened with only half an ear while Murdoch kept up a steady amusing chatter and Gwyneth made polite small talk. My wineglass clutched in my nervous fingers, I kept stealing glances at my grandfather's distant inattentive face. He made no attempt to speak directly to me. He didn't ask me about my life in France, or about my father's—Calum MacDonell's—death. Nor did he talk about my mother, Fiona, or mention any pleasure he may have felt in discovering he had a granddaughter.

He has no real interest in me at all, I thought resentfully. I'm merely his last surviving hope of immortality. And then, of course, I remembered with a chilling clarity what Ian had said to me on the day of Calum's funeral: "You should understand that your grandfather isn't so much concerned about you as a person—after all, he doesn't know you, never dreamed you existed until a few months ago—but as the last of his line, his only hope to see a Cameron of Kildrummond succeed him as Earl of Carrickmore." Perhaps, in time, he and I might achieve a closer relationship. At the moment I didn't feel too sanguine about the prospect. I had the feeling that all the overtures would have to come from me.

My thoughts shifted. So Ian, with his customary cool-headed detachment, had been correct in his assessment of my grandfather's attitude toward me. And where was Ian? I wondered suddenly. Hadn't he told me that he dined with the family? I didn't quite know why I missed his presence. He was quite as indifferent to my charms as my grandfather seemed to be, but his face was at least a familiar one.

Ian finally made a tardy appearance as we were filing into the dining room. As he stood for a moment next to the earl and Murdoch, I could see the close family resemblance among the three men. They were all tall, slender and grace-ful, with well-shaped heads and strong-boned, handsome fea-tures. What color my grandfather's hair was—or what it had been originally—I couldn't guess, since he was wearing a wig, and Murdoch's hair was thickly powdered, but I suspected that both the earl and my cousin shared Ian's blond coloring.

"My apologies for being late," Ian murmured. His eyes rested on me briefly, and he gave me a slight, impersonal nod.

"No need for apologies, my dear boy," said my grandfa-ther. "We all know how conscientious you are in the per-formance of your duties. Doubtless estate problems have cropped up during your absence?"

"Nothing I can't cope with, sir." Though Ian sounded composed, even stolid, I didn't for a moment doubt that he'd caught the note of veiled provocation I'd heard in the earl's voice. A child could have seen that the two men disliked each other.

I'd been invited on several occasions to the Château de

Bassincourt, so I wasn't a complete stranger to formal dining, but even so, my eyes widened at the number of courses considered appropriate for a family dinner. Life at Castle Kildrummond was going to be very different indeed from my modest existence in Normandy.

It was an uncomfortable meal, at least from my standpoint. My grandfather and Gwyneth chatted languidly about inconsequentials—the weather, the lack of tenderness in the beef we were eating, the possibility of traveling to Edinburgh in the autumn—and Murdoch did his cheerful best to enliven the conversation and to draw me into it. I soon realized there was a bond between my grandfather and my cousin. The earl listened more attentively to Murdoch than to the rest of us, and my cousin could bring an occasional wintry smile to my grandfather's lips. Ian spoke only when spoken to. He gave the impression that he was present at the table simply because he was required to be. A stranger would never have guessed that he was a member of the family.

At one point, struck by a sudden remembrance, I glanced around the table and said, "But where is my grandmother? Is she ill?"

For several moments there was an odd, uncomfortable silence. Ian gave me a level, expressionless look and lowered his eyes. Finally Gwyneth said, "The countess is an invalid, Kirstie. She takes her meals alone, in her rooms."

"Oh, I'm sorry to hear that. Perhaps I could pay my respects to her after dinner?"

The silence became even more uncomfortable. Murdoch broke it, saying, "I don't think that's possible. The countess is a recluse. She rarely sees anyone."

"But surely she'd see me?" I said impulsively. "I'm her only grandchild, and we've never laid eyes on each other."

"My wife prefers not to have visitors. I must ask you to respect her wishes, my dear Kirstie," the earl cut in with a cold finality.

"Certainly. I wouldn't dream of disturbing her," I managed to say, hoping that the hurt I felt wasn't apparent in my voice. I added the Countess of Carrickmore to the list of people at Kildrummond who were not enthusiastic about my arrival.

I was relieved when the meal ended. As Gwyneth and I rose to leave the table, the three men stood up politely, and Ian said to the earl, "With your permission, sir, I won't stay to take port with you. I'm in arrears with my accounts."

The earl waved him off. "Far be it from me to undermine your admirable sense of industry." Again I could hear the silky barb beneath my grandfather's smoothly polite remark, but Ian appeared completely unruffled.

"Be it on your own head, Ian," said Murdoch, laughing. "There aren't many bottles of this excellent port left in my uncle's wine cellar."

Accompanying me and Gwyneth to the door of the dining room, Ian left us in the corridor with a bow and a brief good night. I trailed along after Gwyneth to the drawing room, where a footman brought us a coffee tray.

"I hope you won't be bored here," remarked Gwyneth, handing me my cup. "We're very quiet at Kildrummond these days. In the past, we spent a good part of every year in Edinburgh or London, but now . . . " She shrugged. "I think my father-in-law and Murdoch miss the gaiety and the stimulating company of the city even more than I do."

"Ian mentioned something about straitened circumstances," I ventured.

She looked at me sharply. "Ian said that? Well, it's true," she admitted after a moment. "You'd have found out soon enough that we're not very plump in the pocket at present. Reared as you've been, I daresay you have no idea how expensive it is to keep up an establishment in Edinburgh." She smiled indulgently. "Of course, it didn't help that the earl and Murdoch were so unlucky at cards!"

"Has my cousin Murdoch always lived at Kildrummond?"

"Virtually all his life. I suppose Ian told you Murdoch was

born on the wrong side of the blanket? His father, the earl's half brother, died shortly after he was born, and his mother not long after. Your grandfather looks upon him almost as a son. So much so that I do believe my husband was a little jealous of Murdoch to the day he died."

"So my grandfather reared the two boys, Ian and Murdoch, in addition to his own children, Fiona and David. That was generous of him."

Gwyneth startled me by the vehemence of her reply. "My dear Kirstie, you mustn't speak of Murdoch and Ian in the same breath. The two cases are nothing alike. Murdoch is the earl's nephew, and he's always given his uncle the love and respect of a son. Ian is a distant relative, the son of a man your grandfather distrusted and despised and who died a traitor's death. Nevertheless, the earl, because Ian was a member of the clan and family, took the child into his home as a five-year-old, nurtured him and educated him and gave him every advantage, and what did the earl get in return? Nothing but ingratitude and ill will. As soon as Ian turned eighteen he bolted from Kildrummond to enlist in the Black Watch, and I, for one, wish he'd never left the regiment."

"I see." Gwyneth's fondness for Murdoch was obvious. Perhaps it was more than fondness? Her dislike of Ian was equally obvious. "How is it, then, that Ian took leave from the Black Watch and came to work at Kildrummond?" I asked.

"That was my husband's doing," she replied shortly. "David, unlike your grandfather and Murdoch, was always interested in the day-to-day running of the estate, and acted as your grandfather's factor for many years. But David wasn't well the last three years of his life. He and I had no children and no prospect of any, and so, since Ian would inherit the property eventually in any case, David decided it would be best for the family if Ian left the army and came to Kildrummond to learn how to manage the estate."

There was a kind of roaring in my ears. "Ian the heir to Kildrummond?" I asked carefully. "How could that be?"

"He didn't tell you?" Gwyneth's lip curled. "That's like him. He's always ignored the unpleasant. Oh, yes, after David died and before you came along, Ian was the heir because he was the earl's closest legitimate male relative in the direct line of succession."

A pulse was pounding in my head and I suspected I would soon have a headache. All the puzzling fragments of my association with Ian Cameron were falling into place. In a dizzying reversal of fortune, I'd supplanted him as heir to the estate. Fiercely proud and independent and self-contained though he was, he hadn't been able to conceal from me entirely his feelings of chagrin and resentment. No wonder he'd said we couldn't be friends because we weren't equals. We would never be equals. When my grandfather died I would be the Master of Kildrummond and Ian would be my man, and I knew what it would cost his stiff-necked pride to accept that.

"Kirstie, are you well? You look a little pale."

I looked up in surprise to find Murdoch bending over my chair. I'd been so lost in thought I hadn't noticed that he and my grandfather had joined us.

"I'm very well, thank you. A little tired, perhaps," I murmured.

"It's been a long day for you," Murdoch said sympathetically. "Would you like to go for a stroll in the gardens? It might help you relax. It's still very light. Full darkness won't come for hours yet."

"Yes, I'd like that." Suddenly I yearned to escape from the drawing room. For the moment, at least, I didn't have the energy to engage in another stilted attempt at conversation with my grandfather, and if Gwyneth had any more unpleasant revelations, they could wait for another day.

"Good. One of the footmen will fetch you a shawl. You'll find our evenings can be chilly."

The formal gardens to the rear of the house were beautifully designed and well maintained—another of the expenses, perhaps, that had drained the family fortunes?—but they looked to my eyes mildly incongruous against the backdrop of wild mountain scenery in the distance and the hulk of the ancient fortress in the foreground. Noticing a gate in the rear wall of the garden, I asked Murdoch, "Could we see a bit of the old castle?"

"Well . . . It's in ruins, you know. There's nothing very much to see. It hasn't been occupied for over a hundred years, and it continues to crumble because the crofters keep robbing stones from it for their cottages. But if you'd really like to see what's left . . . "

"Oh, I would. It's where our family had its beginnings in the area, isn't it? In the thirteenth century?"

"That sounds right," Murdoch agreed as we passed through the gate and began the climb up the steep path behind the garden. Linking arms with me, he continued with a cheerful grin, "I'm not the one you should ask about these things. Ian's the family historian. When he was a lad, he used to play among these ruins with the crofters' children."

"Did you play with him?"

Murdoch looked surprised. "Oh, no. I'm older than he is, for one thing. Let's see. Ian came here right after the Forty-five and he was about five years old then. So he's thirty now. I'm thirty-seven. But in any case, we never had much to do with each other. I've scarcely seen him since he joined the Black Watch. Oh, he came home on leave occasionally, but he spent all his time with the tacksmen."

"Tacksmen?"

"I suppose you could call them the earl's chief tenants. They lease their holdings to subtenants. Most of them are related to the family in a loose sort of way. In bygone times they served as officers in the clan wars. Nowadays we don't see them socially, of course. Well, Ian visits them. He seems to prefer their company to ours. No accounting for tastes, I daresay. Or what one owes to the head of one's family."

So. Murdoch was making it unanimous. He didn't like Ian, either.

The path was rougher now, rounding a semicircular curtain wall flanked by two tall towers. "Careful," cautioned Murdoch as we approached the gatehouse on the eastern side of the wall. "These cobblestones are very rough. You don't want to turn your ankle."

Murdoch had been right. There wasn't much left to see of the original Castle Kildrummond. Inside the wide bailey, the crumbling remains of what had been a large two-story hall house occupied the straight side of the courtyard, and along the curving curtain wall I could make out the ruins of several smaller buildings. That was all. Suddenly I shivered. In the clear, lambent light of the slowly gathering twilight I could see nothing moving inside the bailey. Not even a breeze stirred the weeds growing around the foundations of the hall house. Nevertheless, I struggled against a sharp, stabbing fear that something alien, something threatening, was in the air around me.

"What is it, Kirstie? Are you chilled?"

"No." I hugged my shawl tightly around my shoulders. "Yes, just a bit. Can we go back to the house?"

"Yes, of course. I should have insisted you wear something warmer. You're not accustomed to our vile Highland climate." He tucked my hand solicitously under his arm and walked me out of the gatehouse and along the path bordering the curtain wall. In moments I lost the eerie sense of that alien presence. My shoulders slumped in relief.

We were about to round the last curve of the path before reaching the gate of the formal garden when Murdoch paused, motioning for me to stop. Almost immediately I realized why. A feminine voice called, speaking in the Gaelic, "Ian, I'm here, love, by the gate."

Raising an eyebrow, Murdoch moved back along the path,

pulling me with him. Soon we heard the sound of running steps, and a moment later Ian's voice saying, "This isn't very wise, Hallie. Someone might see us. What do you want?"

There was a low chuckle. "This." Then came the unmistakable sound of a kiss, and Hallie's voice saying tremulously, "Oh, Ian, you were gone so long. Much too long."

"Hallie, for God's sake, we can't stay here."

Again Hallie chuckled. "Then come with me, love."

I held my breath. Would they come our way, toward the ruins? But apparently Hallie had another place in mind. A long minute passed, and we heard nothing. Murdoch relaxed, saying lightly, "I think it's safe to go now. I never like to intrude on a private chat—" He broke off, eyeing my embarrassed face. "You understand the Gaelic, don't you, little Kirstie? Very well, I was fibbing. Our Ian wasn't merely having a private chat. Shall we just forget we overheard him? I must say, though, I thought he'd had put an end to that entanglement years ago—" He broke off again, looking embarrassed in his turn. "Please forget I said that, too," he said quickly.

"Consider it forgotten." But it was easier to say than do. Pleading weariness, I asked Murdoch to say my good nights to Gwyneth and my grandfather and escaped to my bedchamber, losing my way only once. I got rid of Emily as soon as I could, scarcely giving her time to place my sprigged silk gown in the wardrobe, and collapsed into a chair.

I couldn't let myself cry. Once started, I didn't think I could stop. I couldn't let myself think about Bassincourt, either, or mourn the loss of the love and simple affection and kindness I'd found there. The reality of my future was at Kildrummond, where only one person—my cousin Murdoch—had seemed even remotely happy to welcome me. Gwyneth and my grandfather were indifferent at best. My grandmother apparently would refuse to see me. The servant girl Hallie was openly hostile, and now, of course, I understood why. She regarded me as her rival for Ian's affection. The irony of that made me want to laugh and cry at the same time. Ian, who'd never displayed the slightest interest in me, who must feel that I'd robbed him of his birthright. Ian, who must never learn about the secret, shameful physical attraction I still felt for him.

All the thinking in the world wouldn't help me to change my situation, I reflected wearily, but a good night's sleep might make it easier to bear. I rose and walked toward the washstand, pausing to stare in bemusement at the folded bit of paper that had been pushed under my door. Slowly I bent to pick it up. Even more slowly I opened it and read the few lines of cramped writing it contained. "Why don't you go away?" it read. "You're not wanted here."

Chapter IV

I woke with a start, seized with an irrational choking panic. For a moment I was completely disoriented in the total darkness that surrounded me. Then my flailing outstretched hand brushed against a soft, slippery fabric, and I knew where I was. I was lying behind the heavy silken curtains of the great tester bed in my room at Castle Kildrummond. Memory came flooding back, and with it the sour taste of fear as I recalled the note someone had slipped beneath my door last night. "Why don't you go away? You're not wanted here," it had said.

I pushed aside the silken hangings and slid out of bed. It was still quite dark in the bedchamber, with only a glimmer of early dawn light coming through the window. I shivered in my loose white cotton night shift. Suddenly I longed to be outdoors, away from this great house where I felt so unwelcome and so unwanted.

Groping in the wardrobe for one of my simple cotton dresses and my shabby cardinal, I quickly dressed and stole out of the bedchamber and down the corridor, making several wrong turns as usual before I blundered into the flight of stairs leading to the foyer. If any of the servants were stirring as yet, I didn't encounter them. I left the house by the same rear door behind the grand staircase that Murdoch and I had used the night before. I paused in the formal garden, where a faint rosy glow on the horizon was bringing into focus the straight pathways, symmetrical flower beds and severely pruned shrubs. Glancing back at the house, I realized I could be seen by anyone who chanced to look out of one of those blank windows. The very person who'd written that note could be looking at me. That's the thought of a fearful child, I berated myself. Nevertheless, I turned on my heel and walked swiftly along the central path toward the gate in the far wall of the garden.

Trudging upward along the steep trail leading from the gate, I was soon out of sight of the house behind a screen of conifers and free to torture myself with the questions that had kept me awake half the night. Who disliked me so much, who resented my presence here so much, that he or she had felt impelled to write that poisonous message? And what should I do about it? I didn't intend to show the note to Emily. It would only frighten her. But shouldn't I tell some member of the family?

My mind churned uneasily. Whom would I tell? The writer of the note could be anyone in the house. Conceivably I could find myself pouring out my suspicions to the very person who'd sent me that spiteful message. Because, of course, the writer might even be Murdoch, the one person at Kildrummond who seemed to have any regard for me. I didn't think so, I didn't want to think so, but it was remotely possible, I supposed, that he was disguising some deep hatred of me beneath a friendly mask. The writer could be someone I hadn't even met yet. My grandmother, for instance. In the end, I decided against mentioning the note. I'd be making a blind accusation against a member of the household, and I already felt uncomfortable enough in this cold, unfamiliar place. Perhaps the note had been a random gesture of malice, one that wouldn't be repeated.

My light slipper caught on a stone outcropping in the rough path, causing me to stumble and startling me out of my black thoughts. Without thinking about where I was going, I'd arrived at the gatehouse of the old castle. I stood hesitating at the massive entrance, looking into the empty stretches of the bailey, where the first rays of the sun were now slanting in. A part of me shuddered at the prospect of going into the courtyard again. At the same time, I felt curiously impelled to enter the place.

Slowly, reluctantly, I walked into the great bailey, pausing in midstride as I glimpsed out of the corner of my eye a sudden movement near the left-hand corner of the hall house. Turning my head, I relaxed as I stared down a small brown Highland sheep, momentarily skittish at the sight of me, which quickly resumed its interrupted grazing. My relief lasted only a second or two. Almost immediately I sensed again that vaguely malign emanation that had so upset me the evening before. And something more. Although I knew I wasn't actually hearing sounds, I seemed to be aware of silent screams, piercing me to the heart with their unvoiced desperation and anguish. Trembling, I forced my leaden legs to move and scurried out of the bailey. The moment I stepped through the portals of the gatehouse, my feeling of terror vanished. Perhaps, I told myself, what I was experiencing was some kind of folk memory. Generations of my family had lived and died, fought and suffered in the old castle. Wasn't it possible that something of their spirit remained there, imprisoned in the crumbling stones? It was ridiculous to suspect that some supernatural evil was stalking me.

Having at least partially reassured myself, I became aware that I was hungry and thirsty and chilled, and started back toward the house. At a fork in the path, where Murdoch and I had overheard Ian and Hallie speaking the evening before, I paused, wondering—and feeling guilty and prying for wondering—where Ian and Hallie had gone for their twilight tryst. Putting that idea hastily out of my mind, I gave in to the specious argument that I really ought to explore the environs of Kildrummond if I was going to live at the castle. I turned down the secondary path, which meandered through a stand of birch trees before descending prosaically to the walled stable area behind the mansion.

As I pulled open the heavy wooden gate and stepped into the courtyard, several stable hands, evidently beginning their morning's work, stared at me curiously. So did Ian, who paused as he was about to mount his horse. His gray eyes chilly as always in his impassive face, he put his hand to his hat, saying, "Mistress Cam—Kirstie, you're up and about early."

"Yes, I was out walking. I used to walk a great deal at Bassincourt. You're an early riser, too."

"I like to start my work as soon as possible in the morning. Did you enjoy your walk? I noticed you came from the direction of the castle ruins."

His tone was perfunctory. We were back to our old impersonal relationship, I thought. Behind Ian's polite veneer, he was probably calculating how many more dutiful remarks were required of him before he could take his leave of me. I decided not to let him off that easily.

"Gwyneth told me the castle is centuries old," I remarked. "I suppose it has many colorful stories attached to it."

"Colorful?" He frowned. "That's hardly the word I'd use to describe massacres and pitched battles and bloodthirsty feuds. For example, in—oh, I think it was about 1590—a cattle feud erupted among the clans in this area. A delegation of MacLeans from Ardgour arrived at Kildrummond to parley about some stolen cattle. Actually, 'lifted,' instead of 'stolen,' is the term we prefer to use in the Highlands. The MacLeans seemed sincere enough in their desire for a truce. However, after accepting Cameron hospitality, they turned on their hosts in the middle of the night and tried to murder them. When the fighting ended, all the MacLeans were dead or wounded, and there was hardly a single one of the defenders left uninjured. But it was a long time before the Camerons of Kildrummond had any more cattle lifted by the MacLeans."

As Ian spoke, his eyes began to sparkle, and his voice rang with excitement and pride. Once again I was seeing proof that the man did have emotions beneath that frozen facade. At the very least, he cared for his country and he cared for his family traditions and history.

I said impulsively, "Gwyneth told me something else last night. She said you were considered the heir to Kildrummond until my grandfather learned that Fiona had borne a child. I've been wanting to tell you I'm sorry it turned out this way. I know how disappointed you must feel. This news must have changed all your plans for the future."

The mask came down over Ian's face. "Why are you sorry? Would you rather your existence hadn't been discovered? Are you thinking of renouncing your new position?"

"Well, no, of course not. . . . "

He shrugged. "Then I think you'll agree that my feelings, whatever they might be, are beside the point. Would you excuse me? I have a great deal to do this morning."

I watched him ride out of the stable yard, erect and graceful in the saddle, his back uncompromisingly straight, and I reflected rather drearily that I'd emerged from yet another conversation with him feeling unsettled and off balance. But why on earth had I expected him to change his attitude toward me? I was still the interloper who'd cut him off from his inheritance.

The household was stirring by the time I returned to the house. On the staircases I encountered a number of the servants, each of whom greeted me respectfully but with a second, slanting glance that told me quite plainly what he or she thought of my worn, serviceable garments and my generally unfashionable appearance. I bit my lip. A more unlikely "lost heiress" to the grandeurs of Kildrummond would be hard to find!

"Mistress Kirstie, ye're back," Emily Robertson exclaimed in relief as I entered my bedchamber. "I was sae worried aboot ye. I couldna understand where ye could ha' gone at this hour o' the morning."

"I went out for a stroll, you goose. What could possibly happen to me on the grounds of the estate?" My eyes shifted from Emily to the figure standing in rigid immobility in the center of the room, her bright black eyes fixed on me with an unnerving intensity. She was a tiny woman with a seamed, ancient face and a bone structure as delicate as a bird's. She wore an enveloping white apron with a large bib, and her straggling white hair escaped over her forehead from a starched white cap tied under her chin.

"Be ye really Mistress Fiona's bairn?" she whispered. "Come tae us like a miracle frae across the water?"

Something about her intonation told me that Scots-English wasn't her primary tongue. I said in the Gaelic, "Yes, I'm Fiona's daughter."

"God be praised! That I should live tae see this day!" She rushed to me, her sticklike arms enclosing me in a convulsive hug while she crooned endearments in the Gaelic. I looked over her head, raising a questioning eyebrow to Emily.

"She's yer mither's auld nurse, Mistress Kirstie," Emily murmured. "Janet Cumming's her name."

At last old Janet raised her head, holding me off with those fragile arms as she peered into my face. I had the oddest sensation she was comparing my features, one by one, with another face she could see only in her memory.

"Ye havena the look o' my Fiona," she said after a long moment, lapsing into English.

"No. I resemble my father, Marcel Lefevre."

The faint expression of disappointment faded from her face. She nodded, her lips curved in a tremulous smile. "My Fiona's French tutor. I never knew the laddie, but she told me aboot him, that last Christmas she was here. She loved him so, he must ha' been a guid mon. She would ha' been happy tae know that ye look like yer faither."

"Sit down and tell me about my mother, Janet," I said,

motioning to a settee. "I never knew her, and no one here seems to want to talk about her."

"Ach, ye must call me Nanny, as yer mither did," Janet said, settling down on the settee. "My Fiona, she was sae bonny, sae bright and loving. She had hair the color o' ripe grain and the bluest eyes. She lit up a room when she passed through it. She loved everyone, and everyone loved her. Even the auld laird couldna resist her, his only daughter. That's why they willna talk o' her. They miss her still."

How strange, I reflected. Emily and I talked constantly of Father—of Calum MacDonell. As long as he was in our thoughts and in our words, he was still with us. But apparently reserved, intensely private people like the Camerons— especially that stiff old autocrat, my grandfather—handled grief differently. With them, the loss was easier to bear if they locked it deep inside themselves. Perhaps now, with this new insight from Nanny, I could deal more understandingly with my new family.

"Thank you, Nanny. Now, what about you? Do you still work at the castle?"

"Nay. I'm auld noo, and there havena been any bairns tae care fer these many years. I live by mysel', in a snug cottage the laird gi'ed me years agone. Ye maun come visit me one day, mistress. It will almost be like ha'ing my Fiona again."

"I'd be happy to. What do you do with your days, Nanny? Do you have a garden?"

"Aye, I ha' a wee garden. But mostly I reads the cards. Or palms, I dinna care which. And sometimes I heal, but I canna charge fer that, ye ken."

I stared at Nanny. Her comment had sounded perfectly matter-of-fact. Perhaps I'd misunderstood her. "You tell fortunes, and tend the sick?"

She laughed at my puzzled expression. "My mither was a Gypsy, mistress. I've always ha' the knack o' fortune-telling, and forbye I can tell ye aboot yer dreams. As fer the

71

healing, they call me a charmer, but I canna tell ye more than that."

Suddenly she reached out for my left hand. "Be ye right-handed, noo? Aye, sae I thought." She studied my left palm carefully, murmuring to herself. "A beautiful Fate Line, sae strong, sae lang. And here's yer deepest Marriage Line, next the line o' yer heart. Guid, guid." She looked up with a beaming smile. "Ye'll ha' great power and position, Mistress Kirstie, and soon ye'll ha' yer true love, too."

Thanks to *Père* Chenvert's influence, I've always found it hard to take superstitions seriously. Our old parish priest in Bassincourt had an aversion to anything smacking of witchcraft, and he'd always preached against such things as fortune-telling and spells against the Evil Eye. However, I couldn't hurt the old nurse's feelings. I thanked her for reading my palm, saying with a laugh, "I certainly hope I needn't wait too long to meet my true love. I'm nineteen years old already, almost on the shelf!"

After Nanny had gone, renewing her invitation to visit her cottage and promising to return to see me soon, Emily said with an air of disapproval, "I dinna think very highly o' *that* fortune, Mistress Kirstie. Great position, indeed! Ye already ha' a grand position. Ye're the heiress to Kildrummond!"

"Oh, you know I don't put any store in fortune-telling, but I'm glad Nanny came to see me." Sitting at the dressing table while Emily arranged my hair for the day, I thought with satisfaction that the old nurse was my first real link to my mother, the first person I'd met who'd been able to transform Fiona Cameron from a tiny portrait in a brooch to a living, breathing woman. Now, after talking to Nanny, I almost felt that I'd known Fiona.

After my hair was arranged in its usual simple style, and after I'd drunk the chocolate that Emily brought from the kitchens, it was still very early, not yet eight o'clock in the morning. Breakfast, Gwyneth had told me, was at half after nine. But after I'd eaten breakfast, the rest of the day would then stretch emptily ahead of me. In Bassincourt, I'd scarcely had a free moment. Tutoring Marie Christine, helping Emily with her housekeeping, caring for Father—for Calum—had filled my days completely.

I stood at the window of my bedchamber, gazing down at the formal gardens, feeling restless and uncertain. Heiress to Kildrummond. I grimaced. How empty that sounded. Oh, some day I'd be Countess of Carrickmore, after my grandfather died, and then I'd have estate duties to perform, I supposed. If Ian would let me, that is. My grandfather apparently believed it was best to leave everything in Ian's capable hands. But in the meantime, how was I to fill my days? I was too accustomed to being busy and useful to contemplate a life of idleness. I squared my shoulders. Certainly I'd never discover what avenues were open to me if I stayed shut up here in my bedchamber like a shy and awkward mouse.

I wandered down to the ground floor, glancing into the family drawing room and the dining room. They were both unoccupied. Evidently all the members of my new family were late risers, except for Ian. I crossed the foyer to the wing opposite the family quarters, where a succession of closed doors faced me blankly. I lifted my hand to the handle of the first door on my right and dropped it again, feeling like a curious intruder. Don't be an idiot, I berated myself. This is your home now. Some day you'll be the mistress of it.

Drawing a deep breath, I forced myself to walk down the corridor, opening doors and peering into a succession of rooms. A well-stocked library. A billiards room. A room which, from the open ledgers on the untidy desk, I guessed might be Ian's study. And finally, to my delight, a small music room. Facing me as I entered was a large harpsichord with two manuals, and leaning against it, as if they'd only recently been set down, were a Spanish guitar and a recorder. I sat down at the harpsichord, depressing several keys at random, quickly discovering the instrument was in perfect tune. From memory I played a little air by Couperin—"The Nightingale in Love," a favorite of my father—and then drifted into a Handel partita.

"Oh, it's you, Kirstie."

I turned around with a start. Gwyneth was standing in the doorway. With one part of my mind, I noticed she looked elegant even in her half dress, a simple open saque worn with an embroidered apron.

"I heard the sound of playing as I was coming down the stairs," she said, advancing into the room. "I couldn't imagine who it might be at this hour of the day. You play very well. Murdoch will be pleased. He likes to play duets. He has a very fine voice, too. Perhaps you could accompany him."

Again I heard the special note that crept into Gwyneth's voice when she spoke of Murdoch. I wondered if her obvious affection for him was more than cousinly-by-marriage. It wouldn't be an unsuitable match, I presumed. They were close in age—Gwyneth appeared only a few years older than Murdoch—and they seemed to be on the best of terms.

She broke into my thoughts. "Come and have breakfast."

There were only the two of us at the long table. "The earl never comes down to breakfast," Gwyneth explained. "Your grandfather rarely stirs from his rooms before early afternoon. But Murdoch—oh, there you are," she smiled, as Murdoch strolled into the dining room, looking well turned out in his plain frock coat, tight breeches and buckled shoes, his thick hair powdered and curled.

Helping himself to tea and toast and a rasher of bacon, Murdoch sat down, saying, "I trust you're fully recovered from your journey, Kirstie. We must find something amusing for you to do. Do you ride?"

"Not very well. Madame de Bassincourt insisted I learn to ride so her daughter could have a companion on her daily outings. However, I never considered myself a very apt pupil."

"The only thing that matters is that you don't fall off,"

said Murdoch cheerfully. "Would you care to go riding with me this morning?"

"Oh, I think not this morning, Murdoch," Gwyneth interjected. "I'm sure Kirstie would like a tour of the house. After all, she's the new mistress of Kildrummond. She'll want to see how the household is managed before she decides on any changes she might wish to make."

Gwyneth's remarks came as a great shock. How could I have been so obtuse? I'd been so puzzled by her lack of warmth toward me. Now I understood. With my grandmother a recluse, Gwyneth had been the undisputed mistress of domestic matters at Castle Kildrummond for many years, probably since the time of her marriage to my Uncle David. Naturally she resented being supplanted by a newcomer. I couldn't blame her. Possibly also she saw ahead of her a string of sterile, meaningless years in which she'd be a mere hanger-on in the place where she'd once exercised so much authority.

"Oh, please," I said, distressed. "I'm sure the castle is run most efficiently under your direction, Lady Allendale—Gwyneth. I'm hardly in a position to suggest changes. You must remember that my previous home was a four-room cottage! I'd like a tour of the house very much, though, and if there's any way I could be helpful to you I wish you'd tell me. You see, I'm not used to being idle," I added with a touch of apology. "I was thinking, for instance, that I might give music lessons to the children of your tenants. In Bassincourt I directed the children's choir at the church."

"Oh, music lessons would be far beyond the capacity of the crofters' children," exclaimed Gwyneth, looking shocked. "And really, my dear, you must know it wouldn't be suitable for one in your position." Now that I'd informed her I had no intention of usurping her duties, she seemed to unbend a little. "You mustn't worry about being idle. We'll do our best to keep you busy and interested."

"Indeed we will," said Murdoch, his eyes glinting with amusement. "And so, little Kirstie, you're a musician."

"Well . . . I play the harpsichord, and the cittern."

"Capital. We'll have some musical evenings. What did I tell you, Gwyneth? This dull old pile will brighten up a bit with Kirstie around."

Gwyneth smiled, but it was obviously an effort. She'd unbent a little, but she was still far from enthusiastic about me. "If you're finished, Kirstie, perhaps we could start our tour."

I followed Gwyneth up the exquisite sweeping wrought-iron staircase, dividing into two at the top of the stairwell, into a series of richly furnished state rooms leading one into the other in a circular plan. "The earl was a guest at a house in London many years ago," Gwyneth observed, "where he admired the arrangement of the public rooms so much that he hired the architect to design the same kind of house at Kildrummond."

We made the circuit of the state suite, starting in an antechamber in white and gold, through a card room with walls of red damask to a large formal music room equipped with a gilt-trimmed harpsichord and a golden harp. It had the sterile look of a room that was little used. I suspected that the smaller, cozier room downstairs was the real center of musical activity at Kildrummond. After the music room came a vast formal drawing room hung with tapestries, which led into a dining room capable, to my provincial eyes at least, of seating a regiment, and thence back out to the stairwell.

"The suite is beautifully adapted to entertaining," Gwyneth said with a sigh, "but we've done precious little of that in recent years. The earl and Murdoch were away so much, and David didn't really like to entertain."

Her voice sounded wistful, as if she was picturing those great rooms thronged with guests. Life had probably been dull for her these past few years during her husband's illness and the long absences of Murdoch and the earl. But I was just as happy that my grandfather's poor health and strait-ened financial circumstances had curtailed the social life of Kildrummond. The magnificence of the carved and gilded furniture and the sumptuous wall hangings of the state rooms was overwhelming to someone who'd been reared in a cottage with occasional visits to the modest splendors of Château Bassincourt.

From the state rooms we went to the basement floor, where a pleasant-faced housekeeper showed us through the various storerooms and the servants' hall. In the kitchen, a vast and cavernous space with an enormous fireplace, long work tables and dressers piled with gleaming copper utensils, the cook and her helpers stopped work when we entered, standing respectfully at attention as the housekeeper, Mistress Forsyth, introduced me. I was sure the introduction was superfluous. They all knew who I was. Probably I'd been the object of long and thorough discussion. From behind one of the long tables, a pair of unfriendly eyes in a familiar face stared out at me.

"Hallie!" said Mistress Forsyth sharply.

Hallie Cameron shifted her hostile gaze from me to the housekeeper. "Ma'am?"

"I've told you this before, Hallie. Her ladyship doesn't want children underfoot in the kitchen, or anywhere in the house where you're working."

I caught my breath as I looked at the child who'd just crawled from beneath the table, pushing a crudely carved wooden toy. I guessed him to be five or six years old. He was a beautiful child, with classically regular features, blond hair and gray eyes the color of sunlit ice.

"My mither isna well, ma'am," said Hallie defensively. "She couldna care for the bairn, and I didna like tae leave Gavin tae his own devices."

"Gavin is entirely your responsibility, Hallie. If his care interferes with your work here, then perhaps we should make some changes."

A look of alarm crossed Hallie's face. "Please, Mistress Forsyth. Ye know how much I need the work, tae put food in the bairn's mouth."

The housekeeper's expression didn't soften. "Then you'll pay heed to the rules."

"Yes, ma'am." Hallie lowered her head in submission, but I didn't for a moment doubt that those bright blue eyes were sparking with resentment.

Gwyneth had remained silent while the housekeeper disciplined Hallie, but after we left the kitchen she remarked approvingly, "I'm glad to see that Mistress Forsyth is firm with Hallie. The girl's a trial, I understand. A good worker, but so often she seems to verge on the disrespectful, and then she has to be put in her place. The problem is, of course, that she doesn't know her place, because of—" She stopped, looking faintly embarrassed.

"Because of the child?" I asked. My voice was quiet, but I felt a little quiver of hurt in my heart.

"You noticed, then." Gwyneth sounded relieved. "I didn't quite like to speak of it to you so soon, but . . . Yes, it's the child. Murdoch tells me that Gavin is the exact image of Ian at the same age."

"Is—does Ian acknowledge the boy?"

"Oh, no. However, it's always been taken for granted. Well, who else could the child's father be?"

"Who is Hallie? The daughter of one of your tenants?"

Gwyneth seemed mildly surprised at my interest. "Why, no, nobody of that much consequence. She's the daughter of a crofter. What you'd call a subtenant, I suppose. Someone who leases a tiny plot of ground and tries to raise a family on it." Her voice took on a note of disdain. "Ian's never kept a proper distance between himself and the tenants and the crofters. Apparently he took up with Hallie on one of his visits home from the Black Watch. It didn't—couldn't—mean anything, naturally. Another young man's fling. But Hallie's apparently always thought she should be treated differently

78

from the other servants. As if she were the only crofter's daughter on the estate who'd borne a Cameron by-blow!"

I cringed inwardly. Oh, I wasn't completely naive, even though I'd spent most of my life in a tiny Norman village. I knew quite well that girls of inferior station who dallied with gentlemen of quality did so at their own risk. Take the woman I'd always considered my mother. Sheila MacDonell, a tavern keeper's daughter, had been one of the lucky ones. Instead of having an affair with her, Calum had fallen in love with Sheila and married her. But the cold indifference in Gwyneth's voice troubled me. Whatever Hallie's mistakes and surliness of disposition, she was a real person, with real feelings and real sufferings. Gwyneth's attitude seemed to make Hallie a little less than human.

I could feel my face grow warm as I thought about Ian and Hallie. Was he really the father of her child? Had he loved her once, or had she simply been a convenient partner when he came to Kildrummond on his infrequent military leaves? How did he feel about her now? Last night Murdoch had seemed convinced that Ian and Hallie had resumed their affair, but I wasn't so sure. Ian certainly hadn't sounded like a lover when he greeted Hallie yesterday on our arrival at the castle. Of course, my presence might have inhibited him. Last night, though, when Hallie accosted him on the path above the castle, he couldn't have known he was being overheard, and still he'd sounded more harried than ardent.

I drew a quick, dismayed breath. I was rationalizing Ian's actions. What did I know about how he expressed his emotions? Suddenly I could feel again the rough, urgent pressure of his lips on mine. That hadn't been love, or anything approaching it. Perhaps Hallie and I were sisters under the skin. Perhaps we both aroused physical desire in Ian and nothing more.

"So you'll inform Mistress Forsyth?"

"What?" I stared at Gwyneth. I didn't know how long she'd been talking to me.

"I said, will you please tell the housekeeper if Hallie is ever less than respectful," repeated Gwyneth with an edge of impatience. "Now, shall we have a look at the second floor?"

Under Gwyneth's capable guidance, I began to have a clearer picture of the floor plan of the vast house. I doubted I would ever lose my way again in that maze of corridors that connected the central block with the wings and terminal pavilions. Most of the family, it seemed—my grandfather, Murdoch, Ian, Gwyneth herself—occupied apartments in the east wing. My bedchamber and sitting room were at the southern end of the west pavilion, overlooking the formal gardens and the looming hulk of the ruined castle beyond.

"I'm a little overwhelmed, having a whole pavilion to myself," I laughed.

"Well . . . That's not quite true. Your grandmother's rooms are at the opposite end of your corridor."

"Oh. I see." I looked down that long dark corridor of silent doors, and I wondered again at the odd note of reluctance that seemed to underlie any mention of the Countess of Carrickmore. Why didn't the family want to talk about my grandmother? Why was she a recluse?

Quickly changing the subject, Gwyneth said, "Perhaps you'd like to see your mother's bedchamber." She opened a door midway along the corridor and ushered me into a charming room, furnished with pieces in dark Virginian walnut and a silk Persian carpet in muted shades of soft blue that matched the bed hangings. The bedchamber was in perfect order, but it also looked unlived-in. There were no toilet articles or trinket boxes on the dressing table, no letters or invitations scattered over the neat little desk, no favorite books beside the bed. The room had a curiously static atmosphere, as if time had stood still since the young Fiona Cameron had stolen away in the middle of the night with Marcel Lefevre. I knew I wasn't being merely fanciful when Gwyneth remarked, "From the day the earl learned about Fiona's death in France, he gave orders that everything in this room was to be left exactly as it was on the night she eloped with your father. No one else was ever to occupy the room."

I stood still, remembering my talk with old Nanny early that morning. She'd said, "My Fiona, she was sae bonny, sae bright and loving, even the auld laird couldna resist her . . . " My grandfather had apparently made this room into a shrine for my mother. It was hard to comprehend how the cold, aloof man I'd met yesterday could be afflicted by such terrible, long-lasting grief, but perhaps it was the key to his seeming indifference to me. Perhaps the hurt of his loss was still so raw that he couldn't bear to be reminded of Fiona by my presence.

Gazing around the bedchamber, I tried to evoke some sense of my mother. This was the room, after all, which she'd probably occupied since her nursery days—the same furniture, the same color scheme, the same pictures on the walls. But the bedchamber gave back no echoes of Fiona Cameron to me. I picked up a pair of miniatures in a double ebony frame from the desk. The woman's face, delicate featured and blue eyed, with powdered hair drawn smoothly back from her forehead, reminded me of the miniature of the girlish Fiona in my brooch. The man, handsome, imperious, was a younger, more virile version of the Earl of Carrickmore. "My grandparents?" I asked Gwyneth.

She nodded. "I believe the earl had the double miniature made for Fiona's sixteenth birthday. Murdoch once told me it was one of her most prized possessions."

"But . . . " I looked down at the two painted faces. "But why didn't Fiona take the miniatures with her, then, when she eloped?"

Gwyneth's forehead creased in a puzzled frown. "Why— I don't know. Perhaps Fiona felt guilty? Didn't want to have her parents' reproachful eyes watching her, even from a portrait? Because she must have known how much she'd be grieving the earl and the countess by running off to marry a—a—"

"A nobody?"

Gwyneth flushed. "I'm sorry, but there's no use trying to disguise dirty linen. Your mother's marriage *was* a mesalliance."

"Yes," I said quietly. "I know you all think so." I put the double miniature carefully back on the desk and gave a final glance around the room. "Shall we go?"

As I came out of Fiona's bedchamber a few steps ahead of Gwyneth, I nearly collided with a woman carrying a tray. "Pray excuse me," I said in some confusion. "I hope I didn't make you spill anything—" I paused, faintly unnerved by the unblinking stare from her deep-set black eyes. She was a tall, thin woman in early middle age, with stolid, expressionless features. She was dressed in severe black. A mobcap with kissing strings tied tightly under her chin hid all but a trace of wiry black hair streaked with gray. Completely ordinary-looking, one would have said, except that one of her shoulders was decidedly higher than the other, causing her to look deformed, and her face was deeply scarred with pockmarks.

"Kirstie, this is Maura Fraser, your grandmother's companion," said Gwyneth. "Maura, I'm sure you've heard that Fiona's daughter has come home at last."

"Welcome to Kildrummond." Maura Fraser dropped me an abbreviated curtsy. I felt a familiar sinking feeling. The woman was polite, but only barely so. There was no warmth, no real welcome in that low harsh voice. Was Maura still another of the residents of Kildrummond who looked upon me as an interloper?

"Have you been my grandmother's companion for a long time?" I asked, grasping at words to distract the disconcerting stare that continued to rake my features.

"Thirty-five years." Maura's lips closed firmly after the clipped reply.

"Is—is my grandmother well?"

"As well as usual."

"Lady Allendale tells me that my grandmother doesn't receive visitors," I went on, in a floundering attempt to strike some kind of a chord of empathy with this frozen-faced woman.

"She does not."

Before I quite realized what I was saying, I blurted, "Well, do you think I might see her for just a few moments? I'm her only grandchild. . . . " Beside me, Gwyneth inhaled her breath sharply, and my voice trailed away.

Maura stiffened. "The countess isn't up to visits, even from the family. Would you excuse me? She'll want her tea."

Watching Maura walk down the corridor in the direction of my grandmother's rooms, Gwyneth murmured, "As I told you at dinner last evening, your grandmother never sees anyone."

I could hear the veiled note of reproach in her voice. Suddenly irritated, I went on the offensive. "I gather Maura Fraser makes very sure of that. She's like a dragon, guarding the fortress."

"I daresay she is rather like that," said Gwyneth, looking startled. "She's fiercely attached to your grandmother. And with good reason. She's the countess's distant cousin, you know. She grew up in a family that had no money, and who had little thought or care to bestow on an unattractive young woman who had no chance to marry well. If your grandmother hadn't taken Maura under her wing, she'd have ended up as the family drudge, at best. Since she came to Kildrummond, the countess has been her whole life. I don't think she cares a whit for any of the rest of us. Well, except for Ian, perhaps. She seemed to take a fancy to him when he was brought here as a child, after Culloden. At any rate, she sees more of him than the rest of the family."

As I went off to my bedchamber to dress for my ride with Murdoch, I reflected on the oddity of a friendship between Ian and Maura, and then I realized it wasn't odd at all. The pair had a common bond. They were both outsiders, even more so than I was. While I was a newcomer, and seemingly not a very welcome one, I was an immediate member of the family, and they had only the most distant claim on the Camerons.

I enjoyed my ride with Murdoch much more than I'd anticipated. Dressed in one of Madame de Bassincourt's castoff riding habits—a collared jacket designed like a man's, worn over a long full petticoat—I'd felt both awkward and dowdy, but Murdoch's unaffected charm soon put me at ease. Nor was my limited riding skill tested too severely, since Murdoch vetoed a ride into the upper glen. "The trails are rough up there, and there's nothing to see anyway," he remarked. "Crofters' cottages and black cattle and a few sheep. We'll ride along the lakeshore."

It was a lovely bright day, with the sun dancing off the rippling cascades of the river as it scampered down to join the waters of the loch. As we rode along the lakeshore, I drank in the panorama of wooded hills and bare peaks and breathed deeply of the perfume from the banks of bluebells nestled among the trees. "It's so lovely," I murmured to Murdoch. "Do you come here often?"

"Yes, I ride every day, but not for the sake of the scenery, I fear." He grimaced. "I'm trying to ward off the effects of terminal boredom from the dullness of life at the castle. If I could choose where I wanted to spend most of the year, it wouldn't be Kildrummond, I assure you. However, being in a state of penury, I can't choose."

"Penury?" I looked at his exquisitely tailored clothes, at the diamond winking in his cravat, and smiled.

"Yes, penury," he said with a laugh. "Hasn't Gwyneth told you that the earl and I wasted our fortunes on riotous living and were forced home to Kildrummond on a repairing lease?" Sobering, he added, "Of course, my uncle's health has deteriorated so much that he probably would have been obliged to retire to the country in any case."

"Riotous living sounds quite dashing," I said, lifting an amused eyebrow.

"Oh, well, I was exaggerating a bit. You see, times have changed in the Highlands. It used to be that the great clan leaders were content to live in isolated splendor on their lands. Now many of them, like your grandfather, have become more civilized, and they want to savor some of the pleasures of living in Edinburgh and London. And there's the rub. Most of them can't afford to maintain a double establishment, primarily because the typical Highland estate is still run on feudal lines instead of modern business practices."

At my blank expression, he smiled, saying, "That's enough of serious talk. I'll warrant you won't hear me complaining of boredom anymore, now that you're here! Shall we have some music tonight after dinner? There's a Scarlatti piece I'd like to try, and perhaps you could play your cittern for us?"

When I came down to the family drawing room before dinner that afternoon, the earl and Gwyneth and Murdoch were already assembled there. It was the first time I'd glimpsed my grandfather that day. He motioned me with a languid wave of his hand to sit down beside him. "Have you had a pleasant day, my dear?" he inquired, with the same deadly, disinterested politeness he'd shown me yesterday.

"Yes, thank you, sir." I gazed into that high-bred, impassive old face, wondering if we'd ever achieve any degree of intimacy. How could I reach him? "Gwyneth kindly showed me my mother's bedchamber today," I remarked off the top of my head.

"Indeed." Was I mistaken, or had the air between us suddenly grown colder?

I plunged ahead. "I admired the double miniature of you and the countess so much. Since it was a gift to my mother, do you think I might keep it in my bedchamber? At least for a while? To remind me . . . "

No doubt about it. My grandfather's eyes were charged with frost. "I'd prefer my daughter's room to remain exactly as it is."

I kept my eyes fixed on my clasped hands, fighting back the stinging tears at the back of my eyelids at this latest rebuff. To my relief, Ian's entry into the room distracted attention from my distress. Apparently he didn't often join the family before dinner.

"Well, this is a pleasant surprise," drawled the earl. "To what do we owe this honor, my dear Ian?"

"Shall we say, to your fine claret, sir?" Ian lifted his glass to me. "The stable boys tell me you went riding today. I hope you enjoyed it."

"Very much, thank you."

"Yes, indeed, Ian, while you were being the industrious ant, Kirstie and I were playing grasshopper," said Murdoch. "You should learn to play a little. You lead far too serious a life."

"That's what his lordship pays me for," said Ian calmly. He glanced at the earl. "Two of Jamie Dowd's crofters got into a scuffle today. It might have caused a deal of unpleasantness, but I think I've managed to smooth it over."

"Oh, my uncle knows he can always depend on you," exclaimed Murdoch with that faint undercutting of mockery that both he and the earl seemed to employ habitually when they talked to Ian. "I was just telling his lordship and Gwyneth that we have a musical treat ahead of us this evening. Kirstie and I are going to play together. Perhaps you'll join us, instead of poring over those infernal ledgers."

Ian bowed slightly.

Turning to the earl, Murdoch said, "Now that Kirstie's been reunited with us, I think we ought to consider how we might entertain for her. At the very least she'll want to be introduced to our neighbors."

The earl nodded. "An excellent suggestion. A small ball, perhaps, to initiate the festivities?"

"Oh, please," I exclaimed involuntarily. "I don't have a suitable wardrobe for any grand occasions."

"Then you must have a suitable wardrobe," said Murdoch.

"Gwyneth, I think we should take Kirstie to Edinburgh. What's the name of that modiste in the High Street you like so much?"

Before Gwyneth could answer, Ian cut in. "A trip to Edinburgh for any reason is out of the question, and that includes purchasing an expensive new wardrobe," he said curtly. "I informed you months ago that if I'm to drag the estate out of insolvency you must all cut expenses to the bone."

There was an appalling silence. I longed to sink through the floor. Finally my grandfather said, curling his lip, "So be it. We've allowed you to make our beds, Ian, and now we must lie in them."

Dinner was a horribly uncomfortable affair. Ian ate in silence. The rest of us barely exchanged a word or a look. I was glad to escape to the drawing room while the men drank their port. "Well, my dear," said Gwyneth drily when we were alone, "it hasn't taken you very long to learn that Ian holds the purse strings at Kildrummond."

"I don't quite understand. . . . "

"It's quite simple. Neither the earl nor Murdoch has a head for business, and after my husband died someone had to take over management of the estate. Ian refused to take the position of steward unless the earl gave him full control over all income from the estate."

I shivered. I could understand better now the latent antagonism that seemed to underlie all of Ian's dealings with the family. They apparently needed him, to rescue Kildrummond from financial chaos—caused mostly, apparently, by the financial extravagances of the earl and Murdoch—but they deeply resented the authority they'd had to grant him to effect that rescue.

Ian didn't join us in the little music room on the ground floor during the interval before supper, and I was glad of it. It made for a much less tense atmosphere, and I was already nervous enough at the thought of playing for my new relatives. But Murdoch, as usual, smoothed my way. He pulled out several music books from a cabinet in the corner, saying, "I'd like to sing several of these, if you'll accompany me." "These" included Scarlatti's "O cessate" from "Pompey," and a Purcell song from "The Tempest." Murdoch had a fine tenor voice, and I had no difficulty accompanying him on the harpsichord. Afterward I brought out my cittern and played and sang several old English songs—"And Would You See My Mistress's Face" and "Gather Ye Rosebuds,"—that I'd sung so often with and for Calum MacDonell in Normandy. As I finished, I suddenly became aware of another presence in the room. I glanced up. Ian was leaning against the wall just inside the doorway, his arms crossed his chest, his eyes locked into mine. Catching my breath, I recognized the quick hot flame that momentarily lighted that glacial gray gaze. However I might fight against it, I realized that some kind of bond, purely physical or not, existed between us.

When I finally trudged up the stairs to my bedchamber that night after supper, I felt inexplicably exhausted. I didn't know why. In comparison with my busy daily round at Bassincourt, I'd done nothing that day except indulge myself. Perhaps I was weary from all the conflicting emotions that had buffeted me throughout the day.

Emily rushed at me as I opened the door of the bedchamber. "Mistress Kirstie! Look!"

Articles of my clothing were strewn over the carpet. My treasured family Bible lay sprawled on its spine, several torn pages scattered over the floor.

Bending to pick up one of my shifts, Emily stared at it helplessly. "I'd juist brought up yer things, all freshly laundered. Who could ha' done this, Mistress Kirstie? Why?"

I couldn't answer her. I didn't know who'd entered my bedchamber and scattered my possessions. I only knew it was someone who hated me, who wanted me gone from Kildrummond.

Chapter V

At breakfast a week later, I was still vacillating about telling the family about the damage to my belongings.

"Come back to us, Kirstie. You're off somewhere miles away."

I looked up from my plate, startled out of my thoughts by Murdoch's teasing remark.

"You've hardly uttered a word since you sat down at the table," he went on. "Nothing troubling you, I trust?"

"No . . . " I hesitated. I'd had an argument with Emily this morning. At the time it happened, a week ago, she'd urged me to report the minor upset that had occurred in my bedchamber. It troubled her, as it did me, that someone in the household had felt impelled to creep into my room and tear pages out of my family Bible, rummage through my clothing and toss it on the floor. It was so petty, and yet so malicious. Last night, watching me try to mend the torn pages of my Bible with a rough paste of flour and water, Emily had renewed her entreaties to report the incident. This morning we'd had a sharp set-to about it.

Was I being weak-willed for not wanting to make my problem public? Not necessarily, I defended myself. My hesitation sprang from the same argument that had prevented me from telling anyone about the unpleasant warning message I'd received on my first evening at the castle. I had no proof.

I didn't know who'd sent that first message, or who had scattered my possessions and ripped apart my family Bible, and I was deeply reluctant to make a blanket accusation. In some cowardly recess of my mind, I suppose I didn't want to know who disliked me so much. On the other hand, while I'd been harassed, I hadn't actually been harmed, and nothing alarming had happened for a full week. Perhaps my unknown tormentor had vented his spite sufficiently and wouldn't trouble me again. Balancing the arguments, I took a quick decision to keep the matter to myself. "Why, no, nothing's troubling me," I said calmly to Murdoch.

"Good," he said, reaching over to pat my hand. "We want you to be happy here at Kildrummond. Isn't that so, Gwyneth?"

"Oh, of course," Gwyneth murmured. She sounded dutiful but not enthusiastic. Those words summed up the attitude of my aunt by marriage. I suspected that behind her beautiful, elegant manners she wasn't really reconciled to being supplanted as the mistress of Kildrummond. However, we were more at ease with each other now, although I doubted there would ever be a genuine fondness between us.

"Well, what shall we do today?" Murdoch inquired. "After our morning ride, that is. Do you care to take me on at chess again? I warn you, I'll *never* allow you to beat me!"

Gwyneth shot a quick look at me and lowered her eyes. For the first time, it occurred to me to wonder if she was jealous of the time Murdoch spent with me. Surely she must realize he was merely being kind. In any case, she didn't care for riding, and she was an indifferent musician. Why should she begrudge Murdoch the pleasure of sharing those activities with me?

I smiled at Murdoch. "No chess today, I fear. This afternoon Janet Cumming—Nanny—is coming to escort me to her cottage. Poor old thing, she seems to feel that my mother would want me to visit her home."

Gwyneth sighed. "The housekeeper told me Nanny came

to see you. I hope you weren't put off by her oddness. She's very fey, to put it charitably. Of course, we're accustomed to her ways, and make allowances for her. She's always been a fixture here, since before my time. As you know, she was Fiona's nurse, and my husband David's before that. The earl has always seen to it that she was well provided for. However, I'm grateful she hasn't been frequenting the castle very much in recent years. I find her odd ways a little hard to stomach. Did you know her mother was a Gypsy?"

"Yes. She told me about her mother and her own ability to tell fortunes and read palms. I don't believe in such things myself, but it sounded quite harmless."

"Oh, if that were all! I daresay she didn't tell you she's also a witch!"

"Don't be alarmed, Kirstie," said Murdoch, grinning. "Gwyneth is talking fustian. Old Nanny considers herself a charmer, or white witch, as opposed to the other kind, who steal milk from cattle, or sink fishing boats with magic spells, or cause illness or injury by sticking pins into clay images of their victims. Nanny believes she's helping people, rather than harming them."

"The Almighty keep me from such help," Gwyneth retorted. "The crofters are convinced Nanny can say an *eolas* or charm over water and create a magic potion that will cure everything from the toothache to miscarriage. The poor benighted creatures are also partial to Nanny's braided colored cords that can allegedly restore a cow to health if you tie the cord around the cow's tail. Utter nonsense."

"Not if it cures the cow," Murdoch joked. "Don't be so stiff-necked, Gwyneth. Kirstie is right. Nanny's potions and spells are quite harmless. And that's enough about witchcraft, white or otherwise! We have more important things to talk about. Kirstie's ball, for example."

I hunched my shoulders resignedly. During the past few days there'd been continuous talk about the necessity of giving some kind of entertainment to introduce me to the ranks of local society. Feeling as provincial and awkward as I did, I shrank from the thought of being put on display as the long-lost heiress to Kildrummond. However, although he didn't seem to derive much pleasure from the prospect, my grandfather apparently was convinced it was his duty as head of the family to launch me on a social career. It was probably a reversion, I thought, to the old days, when his ancestors had been the autocratic patriarchs of Clan Cameron of Kildrummond, men whose absolute authority went unquestioned.

Murdoch's voice lapsed into discontent. "It would be far more fitting to present Kirstie at a ball in the Edinburgh house, after you, Gwyneth, had seen to it that she had an appropriate wardrobe."

"Now, Murdoch, you know that's quite impossible. Ian—"

Murdoch's handsome face turned grim. "Don't remind me," he interrupted Gwyneth. "I realize our domestic tyrant has spoken, but I needn't be resigned to it. By Jove, sometimes I wonder why we all stand for his dictatorial ways. I only hope my uncle doesn't have cause to rue the day he took Ian Cameron into his house."

I gaped at the unaccustomed savagery in Murdoch's voice. Gwyneth merely shook her head at him with a gently chiding smile. Probably she'd heard Murdoch express similar sentiments many times before. At the moment, her mind was obviously elsewhere. She said, frowning, "Could I ask a favor, Kirstie? Would you allow your abigail to show me your wardrobe? I'm quite certain you'll need new clothes if we're to entertain for you, and I'd like to know what we have to build on."

"Which is precious little," I replied, flushing. "Gwyneth, I honestly don't see how I could be turned out in the latest mode without great expense. And even supposing I—we—all of us were in funds, it's dead certain there are no fashionable modistes in Fort William!"

"No, but we have a substitute here who will do," Gwyneth

said, looking a trifle smug. "It came to me a few minutes ago. Our talk about Nanny reminded me that she's a deft seamstress. She made several of Fiona's gowns for her come-out year. Nanny hasn't any sense of style herself, but she can copy any garment. As it happens, I have several swatches of material laid by, and recently I received a number of moppet dolls from a friend in Paris. I'll warrant Nanny will be able to copy one of them very well. As for the rest of your wardrobe, I have several gowns that could easily be altered to fit you."

I was frankly skeptical that my mother's old nurse would be able to sew anything remotely fashionable, but Nanny, when she arrived that afternoon to escort me to her cottage, had no doubts at all about the project. She fairly bubbled over with excitement at the thought of sewing a festive gown for her beloved Fiona's daughter. "Ye say her ladyship ha' some material laid by? A nice bit o' tabby, now, or a silk damask, might it be?" She paused as we were walking across the formal garden in the rear of the house, giving me a long, considering look. "A fine piece o' fabric is ane thing. Forbye, it maun be richt in color," she fretted. "Ye canna wear my Fiona's pale blues and soft pinks. Fer ye, a deep, rich blue, mayhap, or a rose-pink like the color of a spotted orchid."

"I'm sure Lady Allendale will choose a becoming color," I said firmly to soothe her anxiety. The lined old face brightened.

Chattering happily again about my new ball gown, Nanny led me through the rear gate of the formal garden and turned right at the path that I knew came out by the stables. I breathed a sigh of relief that we weren't following the higher path that led past the ruins of the old castle. I'd fallen into the routine of taking an early morning walk, familiarizing myself with the paths that crisscrossed the area above and below the house, but I'd been carefully avoiding the vicinity of the ruins. Memories of that forbidding place continued both to draw and repel me. Something atavistic deep within me wanted to go there, to that ancient place of my family. At the same time, I dreaded any further exposure to the eerie sense of evil I'd felt there, though I freely conceded that the emanations were most probably the product of my own fanciful imagination.

Above the stables, as we approached a rather makeshift wooden bridge that spanned the river, I paused, my attention caught by a fuzzy, tawny bundle mewing piteously beside the path. I picked up the tiny kitten, its eyes barely open, and cuddled it to my breast. "Where's your mother?" I murmured. "How did you get up here all by yourself?"

"'Tis juist a stable cat, mistress," said Nanny disapprovingly. "Set it doon. Its mither will find it. Or, if not, no harm done."

"Oh, I can't leave the poor helpless little thing here. I'll take her—him—to the stables myself."

Still cuddling the shivering kitten, I trudged after Nanny up a steep path winding through thick stands of larch and silver birch. Nanny's cottage sat snugly in a small clearing. It was built of stone and thatched with straw interspersed with turf rods to bind the roof. Inside, Nanny showed me the single room of the cottage, floored in deal with plastered walls. It had a built-in fireplace and was furnished with a wooden table and benches, a boxbed in the corner and several cupboards.

Nanny seemed blissfully proud of her home, but I was rather appalled by it. It was far smaller and more primitive than the little cottage in Normandy I'd shared with Calum MacDonell and Emily. I wondered why my grandfather hadn't provided more suitably for the old nurse. Later on I realized how fortunate Nanny really was. As I learned more about the estate I'd one day inherit, I became very familiar with the hovels inhabited by the crofters. Their dwellings had no deal floors, no plastered walls, no fireplaces. Only an open fire in the middle of the earthen floor, spewing soot over the residents and the livestock who shared their home.

A knock sounded at the door, and when Nanny walked over to open it I looked past her figure to the waiflike creature standing outside. She was a woman of indeterminate age, her eyes large in a thin, wan face, dressed in a dirty striped petticoat with a ragged shawl swathed around her head and shoulders. After a moment of murmured conversation, Nanny went to a cupboard, taking from it one of the tiny glass vials ranged neatly on a shelf, and returned to the doorway to hand the vial to the woman. Closing the door, Nanny made no reference to her visitor. Though I was curious, I didn't ask any intrusive questions. However, remembering my talk with Gwyneth about the nurse's reputation as a "white witch," I surmised that the shawled woman—a crofter's wife, perhaps?—had come to request a magic potion to cure some ailment afflicting her family.

"Do you have some milk for the kitten?" I asked. After the little creature was lapping happily from the saucer Nanny reluctantly provided, I took a closer look at the interior of the cottage.

It soon dawned on me that at least a part of the little dwelling was a shrine to Fiona. Arranged on a shelf in one of the cupboards was a collection of objects connected with my mother. "Fiona had this painted specially fer me," Nanny said, showing me a small portrait. It was rather primitive, probably the work of some itinerant artist, but it was unmistakably the face of the girl in my brooch. An inexpensive copper bracelet, a simple string of beads, an enameled sewing box, were all gifts to her old nurse from Fiona. There was also a sampler, yellowing now with age, which displayed such delicacy of execution that it gave me one more tiny insight into my birth mother's character.

Gazing lovingly at her treasures, the old nurse murmured, "She isna really gang awa', ye ken. She's somewhere near, only I canna see her."

I felt a pang of pity. How sad to grow old and have no

one to call your own, except the memory of a little girl you'd helped to blossom into a brief and tragic womanhood.

Later, after I'd consumed a cup of tea and a freshly baked scone she pressed on me, Nanny said anxiously as I rose to leave, "Ye'll come again? Ye'll no fergit auld Nanny?"

I thought for a moment. Was there any possibility that Nanny was seeing me as a projection of Fiona? And if so, should I guard against it? Somehow I couldn't bring myself to dampen the devotion in her old eyes. "I couldn't forget you if I wanted to," I laughed, patting her shoulder. "You're going to make me the most beautiful ball gown in the world, remember? We'll be seeing each other often."

Bundling the drowsy, satiated kitten into a corner of my shawl, I assured Nanny I was perfectly capable of finding my way back to the house without her, and started down the wooded path to the bridge. There, my eye caught by a flash of brilliant deep blue, I paused with delight to drink in the beauty of the wildflowers edging the stream. Taking off my shawl, I wrapped the kitten in its soft folds and placed it on the ground, and then knelt down on the grass to enjoy the flowers at eye level. I recognized a variety of violet, and some yellow and blue flowers that resembled the pansies in my garden in Bassincourt, but the delicate pinkish bells on their long slender stalks and the white, yellow-veined blossoms that smelled faintly of honey were new to me.

"Are you hurt? Can I help you?"

I looked up in surprise to see Ian several yards away, about to dismount from his horse. I'd been so lost in the beauty of the flowers that I hadn't heard the sound of his horse's hooves on the trail leading down from the upper glen.

"Why, no, I'm fine," I replied, rising and shaking out my skirts. I felt as shy and flustered as a schoolroom miss. I hadn't been alone with Ian since that brief unsatisfying encounter in the stable yard, the morning after my arrival at the castle. We'd scarcely exchanged a word for a week, not since he'd so bluntly reminded me and the rest of the family that he controlled the purse strings at Kildrummond and there was to be no extraordinary expenditure for my come out, if such it could be called. In fact, I'd seen very little of him for days. He appeared only at dinnertime, ate largely in silence, and then disappeared, whether to his ledgers or to some other occupation, I had no idea.

As he approached me, leaving his reins looped around a thorn bush, I had to fight back the enticing thrill of excitement I always felt at the sight of that austerely beautiful face with the lean classical planes and the remote gray eyes. It galled me to be so attracted to a man who'd done his best to ignore me from the first moment we met. It had helped some—not much, but some—to remind myself that the attraction was only physical.

"I thought you might have fallen and turned your ankle," Ian remarked as he came up to me.

"No, I was only looking at the flowers. They're so lovely. Most of them I don't really know. Those over there, for example. They look and smell like bluebells, but they're white."

"Sometimes Scottish bluebells *are* white. Or pink."

"I never knew that. What are these white flowers with the yellowish veins?"

"That's Grass of Parnassus. The purplish-red flowers are marsh cinquefoils."

"And these beautiful violet blooms?"

"Ah, now that's an interesting plant." Ian bent down to pick one of the flowers, complete with leaves, and showed it to me. "The butterwort, beautiful as it is, is an insect trap. See the ant caught on the sticky leaf?"

I looked at his face, warm and alive and interested now that he was immersed in something he cared about. Before I realized what I was doing, I placed my hand on his arm. "Ian?" I said softly. "Can't we talk?"

His arm tensed under my touch, and when I looked up into his eyes I saw that their clear wintry gray was darkening like an ocean sky before a storm. "Talk about what?" He made a slight, instinctive gesture, as if to pull away.

I tightened my fingers on his arm, moving closer, until I could almost feel the heat of his body. Of course I knew, in one sane, sedate corner of my mind, that I was playing with fire, but I couldn't seem to help myself. "About us," I breathed. My voice sounded husky. "Ian, why must we go on treating each other like strangers? We're cousins, we're living in the same house, we're eating at the same table. Can't we be at least a little friendlier?"

He stared down at me, his breathing deepened and erratic, his eyes completely darkened except for the pinpoints of flame like the glowing embers of a fire. He bent his head. For a moment shivering arrows of delight scintillated through my body like shooting stars as I closed my eyes and waited, mesmerized in a drowning flood of sensual expectancy, for the remembered pressure of his lips on mine.

Then rough hands pushed me away. I opened my eyes to find Ian standing several feet from me. His face was a frozen mask except for the muscle that twitched in his cheek. "I'm sorry. We talked about this once before, remember? I told you then that there were no grounds for friendship between us. I'm still your family's hired servant."

My face flamed in an agony of embarrassment. I remembered all too well what he'd said that night at the Pass of Drumochter. Did he think I was asking him now for the sexual gratification that was all he was prepared to give me?

Trembling with hurt and humiliation, I whirled away from him, muttering, "I've been unpardonably dense. I assure you, it won't happen again." As I started down the path to the bridge, my eyes were filmed with angry tears. I missed my footing and crumbled to the ground with one foot twisted beneath me.

Instantly strong slender fingers grasped my arms, helping me to my feet. "Are you all right?" Ian asked, hearing my quick gasp of pain.

I shrugged off his hands and stepped back, putting my weight gingerly on my left foot. With relief, I told him, "I'm quite all right, thank you. I've only turned my ankle slightly. Please don't concern yourself. I'm perfectly able to walk." I heard the composure in my voice and felt rather proud of myself. The few moments that had elapsed during the incident had given me the breathing space I needed to stiffen my backbone. Never again, I vowed silently, would I give Ian Cameron the satisfaction of knowing he had the power to start my heart pounding, to turn my limbs to jelly, by the lightest touch of his fingers.

"There's no need for you to walk. You can ride my horse back to the castle."

"I wouldn't dream of troubling you," I replied distantly. Cutting off my nose to spite my face, I thought. The ankle wasn't broken, or even seriously sprained, but it *was* painfully tender. The walk back to the house would be uncomfortable. The next thing I knew, Ian had effortlessly hoisted me into the saddle. Secretly rather glad he'd taken the initiative, I glared at him nevertheless, trying vainly to pull down my skirts to cover my legs.

Eyeing my rucked-up skirt, Ian said, "I'm sorry you'll have to ride astride. Under the circumstances, I can't offer you a sidesaddle. Unless you'd want me to ride behind you?"

"No, thank you. I can manage." The very thought of being in such close proximity to Ian, our bodies intimately touching with each movement of the horse, made my heart strum painfully.

"Good enough. Is that your shawl on the ground over there?"

"Yes. Be careful," I called suddenly, when he bent over to pick up the shawl. "There's a kitten in it."

His face looked bemused as he walked over to me, handing me the bundled kitten with careful hands. "I found the poor little thing abandoned by the path," I explained at his faintly questioning expression. "Nanny said it probably belonged to one of the stable cats."

"It's more than likely," he nodded. "It's even likelier, you know, that the mother cat is dead."

"Oh." I glanced down at the minuscule pointed ear that was all that was visible of my tiny ball of fluff. If her mother was dead, what would become of the little creature? It dawned on me that I'd just acquired a pet. I wondered what Gwyneth would say. Were there housekeeping rules about bringing animals into the house?

Ian walked ahead of me, leading the horse across the bridge and down the hill toward the house. He made no attempt to talk. I was glad of it. After what had happened—or didn't happen—between us, I couldn't have thought of any polite, inconsequential remarks. However, the interval gave me a little more time to recover from my hurt and confusion after my latest rebuff at Ian's hands. By the time we arrived in the stable yard, I'd become quite calm. However, there was one awkward moment. Sliding down from the horse overly hastily to avoid exposing my limbs to the gaze of the stable boys working in the yard, I grabbed at Ian's steady arm to keep my balance. I moved away instantly, wondering if he, too, had felt that sudden jolt of electricity at the contact, hoping he hadn't noticed my quickly drawn breath.

If he felt anything, he wasn't showing it. He asked gravely, "Does your ankle hurt?"

"It's complaining a little," I admitted. "Nothing to worry about." Smoothing my skirts with one hand while holding fast to the kitten with the other, I looked up at him with a pleasant, polite smile. "Thank you for the ride."

He replied, equally formally, "I'm happy to have been of service."

With a nod, I turned away. I was limping slightly. After an initial curious glance as I passed, each of the stable hands kept his eyes fixed so assiduously on his task that I was quite certain my return home astride Ian's horse would soon be gossip fodder in the servants' quarters.

Inside the rear hallway leading from the stables, I ran into Emily, who stared disapprovingly at the shawl bunched up in my arms. "Ye'll catch yer death, Mistress Kirstie. 'Tis nippy oot there. Why aren't ye wearing yer shawl?"

"This little thing needs it more. Look, Emily. Isn't she adorable?"

Emily looked at me with a resigned expression. "Dinna tell me. Ye're planning tae keep yon beastie in yer bedchamber."

"She needs me. She's lost her mother. See if you can find a little basket for her to sleep in, and a—a box for the necessary, I suppose. And some milk."

"I've been looking for you, Kirstie, wondering if you'd returned from your visit to old Nanny. Well, well, what have we here?" said Murdoch, strolling up from the direction of the foyer. He put out a finger to stroke the kitten. "Planning to start a menagerie? Gwyneth doesn't like cats, you know. Don't worry about it," he added at my look of alarm. "Just keep the animal out of her sight. Look, why don't you let your abigail take charge of the kitten? I've been making a duet arrangement for harpsichord and cittern of that Couperin piece you like so much, and I'd like to try it out."

I handed the kitten to Emily. "Here you are. Take good care of Daffodil. The name suits her, don't you think?"

"Sae it might, Mistress Kirstie," said Emily drily, after a brief inspection of the kitten, "save that she's a he, ye ken."

"Well, we'll call him Daffy, then," I replied, making a face at Murdoch when he erupted in a whoop of laughter.

The quiet hour I spent in the music room with Murdoch was very soothing, coming on the heels of the unsettling encounter with Ian. It was good to know that at least one person at Kildrummond enjoyed my company. We broke off reluctantly to go up to dress for dinner.

As I emerged into the corridor leading to my bedchamber

in the west pavilion, I paused in surprise when I saw Ian there, talking to my grandmother's companion, Maura Fraser. Like Murdoch's, Ian's rooms were in the east wing, and I'd never seen him in this part of the building before. He and Maura were standing close to each other, deeply absorbed in conversation. As I watched, I saw Ian place his hand on Maura's shoulder, giving her a smile of such radiant sweetness that my heart turned over. A moment later, bending to brush her cheek in a farewell kiss, he left her and began walking toward me as I stood hesitating at the angle of the corridor. His face once more closed and remote, he didn't stop to talk to me, merely inclining his head as he murmured "Kirstie" in a brief acknowledgment of my presence.

My grandmother's companion was already halfway down the corridor when I called out, "Good day, Maura. How is the countess today?"

She turned back to me, reluctance written all over her figure. She was no more cordial, no more accessible, than she'd been when I'd first met her, shortly after my arrival at Kildrummond, although we saw each other at least once every day. "The countess is about as usual," she replied, biting off her words. It was her invariable response to my requests for information about my grandmother's condition, and usually it ended our encounter. It was so obvious she was unwilling to talk to me, and I wasn't inclined to force my company on someone who didn't want it.

Today, however, I stubbornly continued our conversation. "You and Ian seem to be very good friends," I ventured.

She clamped her lips firmly together, and for a moment I thought she wouldn't answer. "He's a good boy," she said finally.

"Gwyneth told me you befriended Ian when he first came to Kildrummond," I went on. "It must have been lonely for a five-year-old boy to come live among strangers."

A flash of angry resentment crossed her unprepossessing, pockmarked face, the first show of emotion I'd seen in her.

"Aye, strangers, that's what they were," she snorted. "That child might have been invisible, for all the attention they paid him. When he came here, he'd just lost both his parents, his mother in childbirth, his father on the gallows, but did they show him a scrap of human kindness? No, they handed him over to a slut of a nursemaid and the earl and his entire household forgot about the lad. He could have died of neglect—he almost did—and they wouldn't have cared a whit."

"But why?" I asked, perplexed. "Because his father had died in disgrace, his lands forfeited, for supporting the prince? Wasn't Ian, even at so young an age, even if he were landless, still considered the chief of the senior sept of the clan? Wasn't he my grandfather's closest relative after his own immediate family? I can't believe the earl would treat a child so uncaringly, for no reason at all. . . . "

Apparently my remark touched some kind of nerve. Suddenly I was overwhelmed by a torrent of words, breaking through the barriers that had probably blocked off the bitter feelings she'd been harboring for years. "I see you don't know very much about the Earl of Carrickmore," Maura sneered. "Why would he mistreat Ian? I can give you reasons. Because he'd always hated Ian's father, Alastair Cameron of Inverloch, since the day they both started courting the same woman, and Alastair won. Because the men of Clan Cameron idolized Alastair as much as they disliked him, the chief of their clan, and he was jealous. Because, and most important, the earl has never cared for anything except his own comfort and pleasures, and he's always been willing to sacrifice whoever gets in his way."

I stared at Maura, appalled. What a venomous, utterly devastating opinion she had of my grandfather. And how one-sided, I reminded myself. Gwyneth and Murdoch obviously wouldn't agree with her. Ian? Well, obviously there was no love lost between him and the earl, but Ian had never accused my grandfather of gross neglect or outright abuse. What about my grandmother? Cautiously I asked, "Was there nobody at Kildrummond, except for yourself, who would take Ian's part? Of course, my Uncle David and Gwyneth weren't married yet, and Murdoch was only a boy, but my grandmother—"

Maura's eyes glinted. "The countess never failed anybody," she interrupted me. "But she was seldom at Kildrummond at that time, immediately after the battle of Culloden. The earl insisted on those grand stays in Edinburgh and London, where he could mingle with his high and mighty friends. And Fiona was a little girl, and often ailing, and she needed her mother."

She sounded defensive. Too much so. Something of what I was thinking must have shown in my face. "You'll not be at Kildrummond much longer before you learn that nothing happens here without the earl's connivance," Maura said angrily. "Oh, it did my heart so much good when Ian became the heir, after David died. How it must have galled the great Laird of Kildrummond to realize he'd be succeeded by Alastair Cameron's son! And then you came along."

The voice flattened into a monotone and she stopped short. She'd been stripping away the protective shell guarding her innermost emotion, and suddenly she knew it. "I must go to the countess," she muttered, and turned away.

As I walked slowly to my bedchamber, I wondered what my grandfather had done to make Maura Fraser hate him so much. Oh, granted, Alexander Cameron of Kildrummond was a cold, haughty, undemonstrative man. Look how he was treating me, the granddaughter whose belated coming would ensure the continuance of his family line. Could it be that he was simply incapable of close personal feeling? No, that couldn't be true. He'd adored his daughter Fiona so much that he still couldn't bring himself to talk about her. He seemed fond of Gwyneth and Murdoch, and they of him, and he'd provided for old Nanny. For that matter, whether or not he realized how much Maura Fraser detested him, he'd certainly retained her as his wife's companion for many years now.

I tried to put the enigma of Maura Fraser to the back of my mind. Perhaps she was a little unbalanced, a little warped, from all those years of living in deep seclusion with my recluse grandmother.

In my bedchamber, I broke into a laugh at the sight of Emily on the floor, carefully tucking a scrap from one of my old shifts around the somnolent form of my new kitten in his little basket. "I thought you didn't approve of cats in the bedchamber," I teased her.

"Ach, Mistress Kirstie, sae lang as we maun ha' the wee beastie here, yon Daffy might as well stay warm," Emily replied with dignity.

As she was helping me into the inevitable rose-colored sprigged silk, I thought wistfully of what Gwyneth had said about Nanny's abilities as a seamstress. If the ball gown was a success, perhaps Nanny could also make me a dress or two to vary the monotony of my appearance at the daily family dinner table. Or she might remodel one of the dresses Gwyneth had offered to me.

A knock sounded at the door. "Come," I called.

Hallie came into the room carrying a package swathed in a coarse cotton material. "Her ladyship said ye were tae ha' this."

"This," when I'd removed it from its wrappings, turned out to be a length of delicate, feather-light taffeta, the color of the first tender leaves of spring. "Oh, how lovely," I breathed, running a caressing finger along its silken surface. Turning to the cheval glass, I held a piece of the material to my face. The pale green set off my dark hair and eyes, and gave my skin the translucent glow of apple blossoms faintly tinged with pink.

"Isn't the material exquisite?" I asked Hallie, who had, rather to my surprise, lingered to watch me open the packet.

"Nanny's going to make a ball gown for me out of this lovely stuff."

"Aye, 'tis bonny." The words were respectful, but the bright blue eyes were boring into me with a hot, barely restrained hostility. I sighed. Had the servants' grapevine already told Hallie about my encounter with Ian this afternoon? It might be reassuring to her, I thought sardonically, if I told her that he'd once more thrown my friendship back in my face.

A little later, giving Daffy one last pat as he woke up mewing querulously for another saucer of milk, I left my bedchamber to go to dinner. Halfway down the corridor I paused, struck by a bright gleam of late afternoon sun slanting in on the carpeting from a partially opened door. The corridor was usually deep in shadows even during full daylight, with all the doors leading off it kept firmly closed.

It was the door of Fiona's room that was ajar. It had looked so immaculate on the day I'd visited it with Gwyneth that I knew it must be dusted and swept regularly. The maidservant who cleaned it today must have neglected to close the door when she left.

Hesitating, feeling oddly intrusive, I pushed the door open and walked into the room. It looked the same as it had on my first visit, pretty, charming, sterile. I stood with my eyes closed, hoping to evoke some illusive, gossamer sense of what my unknown mother had been like when she last occupied this bedchamber over twenty years ago.

I opened my eyes at the sound of a light footstep behind me, but before I could turn around a pair of strong hands encircled my neck, cutting off my breath in a cruel, choking grip. Frantically I tore at those clawlike iron fingers digging into my throat, but my attacker hung on grimly. In the silent room I could hear plainly the macabre, gasping breathing that told me how much effort my assailant was expending in trying to kill me, and the sound was more chilling than any shouted obscenities could have been. As the desperate

106

seconds ticked by and I failed to dislodge those murderous hands, I began to lose consciousness. . . .

"My throat hurts," I croaked.

"Don't try to talk, Kirstie. It's all right now."

Unwillingly I opened my eyes. It was Murdoch's voice speaking. I was standing in the circle of his arms, clasped tightly to his chest. The room seemed to be full of people, all of them talking at once. Gwyneth was there, half dressed, and Maura, and a handful of servants. And Ian in his shirt-sleeves, holding fast to a struggling, babbling old creature, straining to prevent her from injuring either herself or me.

"Is that—?" I whispered.

"Yes, Kirstie," said Murdoch gravely. "This is your grandmother."

My mouth dry, my throat aching, I stared at the Countess of Carrickmore. Tiny and fragile, with disheveled pure white hair and great haunted blue eyes in a wasted face, she didn't much resemble the exquisitely beautiful woman in Fiona's double miniature. As I looked at her, she gradually quietened. The wild muttering died away, and she sank limply back against Ian's steady arm.

"But . . . Why was my grandmother trying to kill me?"

"She wasn't responsible, Kirstie," said Ian levelly. "Don't you understand? She's quite mad."

Every head in the room turned as a new voice barked, "What's this? I heard screams loud enough to wake the dead, and the sound of running feet. What are you all doing in this room—? In God's name, Elspeth?"

My grandfather was standing in the doorway, leaning on his cane. He was elegantly dressed for dinner, every curl of his wig in place. His face turned ashen beneath its patches and dusting of rouge as he looked at his wife.

Gwyneth hurried over to him, placing a supporting hand on his arm. "We don't quite know how it happened, sir. The first I knew, Maura came bursting into my bedchamber, screaming that the countess was trying to strangle Kirstie and she couldn't stop her. Murdoch and Ian rushed out of their rooms then, and a mob of servants appeared, as if out of the woodwork, and we all dashed for the west pavilion. By the time I got here Ian had dragged the countess away from Kirstie, who'd fallen into a swoon."

His color returning to normal, the earl glared at Maura, who had taken her mistress's unresisting form from Ian's arms and was holding her, murmuring words of endearment and comfort.

"You've been remiss in your duties, Maura Fraser," the earl roared. "My orders are that my wife is never to be left unattended. Why was she allowed to roam about the house? You see the result of your carelessness. My granddaughter was almost killed."

Maura looked subdued and frightened at the earl's vehemence. "I just stepped out to get some fresh linen. The countess has been so quiet for weeks now, I saw no harm in leaving her alone for a few moments. You see, the serving girl who usually helps me was down with the toothache—"

"Pray refrain from giving me your miserable excuses," said my grandfather coldly. "If such an incident ever occurs again, I'll be obliged to dismiss you."

Maura blanched. "You wouldn't—you couldn't. . . . "

"I could, and I would. Please take my wife to her bedchamber."

"Allow me, sir." Ian stepped forward, lifting my grandmother and cradling her frail form gently. Her head fell back against his shoulder and she closed her eyes. "Come, Maura."

After they'd gone, the earl lifted his quizzing glass to his eye, surveying the rest of us. "Do you have no duties?" he inquired of the gaping servants, and they disappeared with astonishing speed. He went to the door, turning to say with a chilly imperturbability, "Now that the excitement seems to have diminished, shall we go down to dinner?"

I caught Murdoch's arm as he prepared to follow Gwyneth

and the earl out of Fiona's bedchamber. "Please, Murdoch. I must know about my grandmother. Why didn't the family tell me she was mad? How long has she been like this? And why did she attack me?"

Murdoch looked at me compassionately. "We didn't want to burden you. You see, Elspeth was prostrated by the news of Fiona's death. They were very close, even for a mother and daughter. Elspeth turned in on herself, brooding constantly over the loss of Fiona, refusing to see her friends. Gradually she slipped into periods of madness. She becomes a little worse every year, I think. By now she's ceased to recognize the members of the family, and we've stopped visiting her, sad to say." He shrugged. "It's heartrending to speak to someone who doesn't know you. We've managed to keep the truth about Elspeth's condition from being generally known. Most people think she's an eccentric recluse, no more. I'm sorry if we've hurt you. We simply thought it would be kinder not to tell you about Elspeth."

"No, I think it's better to know," I murmured. "Is—is she often violent? Is that why she came after me?"

"No, she's normally very quiet, almost comatose, if you will. Tonight she was left unattended, which I don't suppose has ever happened before, and she chanced to wander into Fiona's bedchamber. I can only conjecture that she thought you'd gone there to steal some of her daughter's possessions, or even to injure Fiona."

"Injure Fiona? What do you mean?"

Murdoch hesitated. "Well, she takes queer notions into her head occasionally. Sometimes she thinks Fiona is still alive."

Dinner that afternoon was a cheerless, silent affair. The tragic overtones of what had happened hung over us in an almost visible cloud. The earl sat immersed in a brooding gloom, hardly looking up from his plate. Ian bolted from the table as soon as the barest civility would allow him. Even Murdoch's bright spirits were dampened. He suggested we try out some new duets in the interval between dinner and

109

an early supper, but neither of us could summon much enthusiasm for music. I was glad to escape finally to my bedchamber, where I discovered that the trials of this interminable day were not yet over.

As soon as I entered the room, Emily silently pointed to the shimmering pale green mound in the middle of the carpet. Someone had shaken out the folds of the material for my new ball gown, thrown it down on the floor and stamped on it. The marks of a dirty boot were plainly visible in several places. Worse, an ugly slashing cut had almost severed one corner of the fabric from the rest of it.

"Weel, Mistress Kirstie? This time, will ye no' tell the laird or her ladyship wha' is happening tae ye?"

"No," I replied dully. I stared at the fabric, hoping the damage was reversible. Surely Emily and I could clean the marks from the material, and perhaps we could simply snip away the torn fragment, so that it wouldn't be necessary to report the incident. Because I thought I knew now who my enemy was. I remembered the simmering rage and jealousy in Hallie's eyes when I'd draped that gleaming length of pale green over my shoulder. She'd heard I'd been out riding with Ian this afternoon, and she hadn't been able to bear the thought that I'd bedazzle him, dance with him, in a gown made from that lovely material.

Yes, I knew, or thought I knew, who'd damaged my green taffeta. But I'd rather be flayed alive than reveal that a jealous serving girl was persecuting me because she fancied I'd stolen the affections of a man who was totally indifferent to me.

Chapter VI

On an afternoon two weeks later I walked toward the west pavilion and my bedchamber to dress for my coming-out ball. If the person who'd damaged my green taffeta had hoped to prevent me from attending the ball, he or she was disappointed. Emily had skillfully removed the stains from the material, and Nanny had sewed me a lovely gown.

As I walked along, I heard a sudden burst of laughter from behind one of the closed doors on the corridor. Several moments later I paused to exchange a smile and brief greeting with a pair of young ladies strolling toward me.

"La, Mistress Cameron, we're looking forward so much to the dancing tonight," said one of the two girls, who were obviously sisters. They were MacDonalds from Moidart, I recalled, but I'd met so many people today and yesterday that I couldn't be sure. She went on, "It's been weeks since we had the pleasure of attending a ball."

"I hope you'll enjoy the evening as much as I intend to." I smiled. After I left them, it occurred to me, for the very first time, why my grandfather had built such an enormous residence in the wilds of the Highlands. He needed the extra space for important social events.

Tonight all those vacant bedchambers in the huge house were occupied by Hendersons and MacLeans and Stewarts, by Livingstones and Campbells and MacDonalds. Those of our guests from such nearby areas as Lochaber and Ardgour would be returning to their homes tonight after the ball was over, some of them going by boat along Loch Linnhe. However, many guests were coming from the more remote parts of Morvern, Benderloch and Sunart. To them, it was necessary, because of the poor or nonexistent roads in this primitive country and the lack of public lodgings, to offer the overnight hospitality of Kildrummond.

Now that the ball was actually upon me, I found that much of my nervousness had disappeared. I'd been a little overwhelmed to meet so many people—and I'd be meeting many more of them tonight as they arrived for the dinner and the ball—but everyone had been kind, putting me at my ease. If they displayed a bit of curiosity about the lost heiress of Kildrummond, that was understandable.

As a matter of fact, I admitted, laughing at myself, I was beginning to anticipate the brilliance and excitement of my first formal ball with a great deal of eagerness. So much so, that, although it was only midafternoon, here I was, heading for my bedchamber to dress for the festivities.

A sudden thought struck me as I neared the west pavilion. I paused, then turned left, instead of right toward my own rooms, and walked to the far end of the corridor. There I stood irresolutely for a moment before the door of my grandmother's apartment. It wasn't the first time I'd come here since that terrifying occasion when the Countess of Carrickmore had attacked me and I'd discovered she was mad. The very next day, I'd insisted that Maura allow me to see my grandmother. . . .

"Why do you want to see the countess?" Maura flared, her voice filled with angry suspicion. "To satisfy your curiosity? It's better for her ladyship's peace of mind not to see people."

"She's my grandmother, and I have a right to see her," I'd repeated stubbornly. In the end, of course, she had to give in. In her position as servant and companion, she couldn't really hold out against me. I was the daughter of the house.

She made one last try, her black eyes staring at me with a kind of perverse satisfaction. "Remember what happened in Fiona's bedchamber."

If she was trying to frighten me away, she wasn't successful. Somehow, I wasn't afraid, even though I recalled clearly the grip of those talonlike fingers yesterday around my neck, and my throat was still bruised and sore from the assault. On the other hand, I wasn't really sure why I'd come. Murdoch had said the family had stopped visiting Elspeth because she no longer recognized them. I felt in my bones that was wrong. It seemed to me that to make no attempt to reach Elspeth was to leave her in her madness. And then—perhaps my imagination was playing tricks on me—but I believed I'd glimpsed a forlorn, indescribably sad expression in the depths of the countess's blank blue eyes, as if somewhere, far below the level of consciousness, a part of her mind was desperately trying to make contact with other human beings. . . .

Today, standing before Elspeth's door, hesitating to knock, I had to admit I'd probably been fanciful. Certainly during that first visit and the ones that had followed every other day or so during the past two weeks, my grandmother hadn't responded to me in any way. So why, then, was I back again? I didn't know the answer. I only knew that something was impelling me to break through the prison of my grandmother's madness. I tapped lightly on the door.

"Oh, it's you," said Maura when she opened the door. She sounded unfriendly as always, but she stepped aside to allow me to enter.

The tiny creature who sat in a chair by the window, wrapped in a fleecy shawl, her white hair confined neatly under a lacy cap, looked the same as she had on my previous visits. Not in the least violent. In fact, her stillness, her complete apathy, were more alarming than violence would have been, because that at least would have indicated she had some awareness of her surroundings. She stared straight ahead of her, her eyes registering no change in their blank blueness when I moved into the angle of her vision. She didn't know I was there, obviously. I could have dematerialized into the air, and there'd have been no reaction.

"Good day, Grandmother," I said softly. "I hope you're feeling better today." No response. I'd been saying a few words to her on each visit, hoping that the sound of my voice, rather than the sense of my words, would penetrate the fog that enveloped her mind.

"It's useless, you know," said Maura. "She doesn't hear you."

I sighed. It probably *was* useless. Why did I think I could reach Elspeth, when Maura and the other members of the family hadn't been able to do so?

Glancing about the room, so beautifully and comfortably furnished, I guessed it was a matter of pride to the earl that his wife's apartment should reflect her social standing and her family's solicitude, even though she appeared oblivious to her surroundings. In a far corner of the room was an instrument case I hadn't noticed before. "Is this a cittern?" I asked, walking over to it.

"Yes. The countess was very musical. She and Fiona liked to play together."

"May I?" I picked up the case and started to open it.

"Go ahead," said Maura grudgingly. "It hasn't been played for years."

That was obvious, I thought, as I lifted the pear-shaped instrument, its neck terminating in a carved grotesque, and sat down with it in a chair to examine it. The four courses, or pairs of wire strings, were limp on the fingerboard. Cautiously I tried tightening the pegs. The strings didn't break. Without attempting to tune the instrument, I ran my fingers gently across the courses. Something prompted me to lift my head. My grandmother was looking at me, really looking at me. For one electrifying second, her vacant-eyed stare sharpened. A fleeting sanity gleamed in the old eyes. Then the familiar wrenching blankness returned.

I put the cittern back in its case and rose. My mind was working busily on the details of a plan I wasn't going to divulge to Maura until I'd given it more thought. "Good-bye, Grandmother," I said to Elspeth. "I must go now to dress for the ball tonight." To Maura, I said, "I'll be back soon."

"Suit yourself. I don't know what you think you'll accomplish."

As I came out of Elspeth's room, closing the door behind me, I saw Ian coming down the corridor, bound, I presumed, on one of his visits to Maura. Walking toward him, I nodded, preparing to pass by without speaking. Since the day we'd met near the bridge and he'd made it so abundantly clear he didn't want my friendship, I'd seen little of him, except at the dinner hour. When I did see him I'd made it a point to behave as distantly, as coolly, as he did. If I could help it, he'd never again have any grounds for suspecting I was pursuing him.

He put out his hand, catching my arm as I passed. "Could I speak to you for a moment, Kirstie?"

"Certainly." I halted, unobtrusively disengaging my arm. I willed my treacherous senses to ignore the sudden leaping thrill I felt at his touch.

"Maura tells me you've been coming to see the countess. Might I ask why?" The gray eyes expressed only a chilly disinterest. Had Maura prompted him to talk to me?

I was strongly tempted to tell him my doings were none of his affair. Instead, I said coolly, "Do I need a reason to visit my own grandmother?"

"No, but you might consider whether it's in the countess's best interests. She was driven into a frenzy at the sight of you not so long ago."

"She's shown no further signs of violence. I think she's

been left too much to herself over the years. More outside contacts might help her to recover her sanity."

Ian's lips tightened. "And they might also make her condition worse. Does the rest of the family know you've been seeing the countess?"

"No," I replied, lifting my chin at him. "I don't consider I'm under any obligation to report my actions. To anyone," I added pointedly. "Is there anything else you wish to discuss?"

"Nothing, thank you." He bowed, stepping aside for me to pass.

Well, for once I held my ground, I reflected as I walked toward my rooms at the other end of the corridor. So why didn't I feel a greater sense of satisfaction? I had, after all, demonstrated to Ian that I was my own woman. He, of all people, should appreciate that. He'd certainly made independence the touchstone of his own life.

My mind wandered back to a conversation at the dinner table two days ago. We—or rather, Gwyneth and the earl—were discussing the seating arrangements for the gala dinner that would precede the ball. It seemed to be a matter of intense importance to them. Gwyneth was saying, "Ian, you'll sit opposite Mistress Campbell of Aird—"

He looked up from his plate and interrupted her. "You'll have to find Mistress Campbell another partner. I won't be attending the dinner or the ball."

The earl had impaled Ian with a haughty stare. "Doubtless you have a good and sufficient reason for such a statement?"

"None that I care to give, sir."

"And none that I would accept," the earl snapped. "I'm officially presenting my granddaughter to local society two days hence. You, as a member of this family, will take your part in entertaining my guests."

"Is that an order, sir? Not to a member of your family—that, if we're all being honest, describes me only by stretching the meaning of the term—but to your steward?"

The effrontery of the question, delivered in a cool, conversational tone, deprived my grandfather of breath for an instant. Then he replied, his lip curling in disdain, "Call it what you wish. I expect you to be present at both the dinner and the ball, and to conduct yourself as a gentleman and a member of this household."

"Very well, sir," Ian had said indifferently, and resumed eating. But he'd made his point. He was my grandfather's steward, and he had no interest in joining the inner family circle. He'd appear at my gala dinner and ball only because he was ordered to.

Pushing open the door of my bedchamber, I put Ian and his appearance or nonappearance at my ball out of my mind as I looked with surprise at Emily and Nanny on their knees on the carpet. Emily was shuffling a pack of playing cards which she proceeded to lay out in three neat piles. The kitten Daffy was doing his best to swat at the cards with his tiny claws.

Emily glanced up, looking flustered. "Mistress Kirstie, I didna expect ye sae soon." A guilty note crept into her tone. She knew how I felt about fortune-telling. "Nanny's reading the cards fer me."

I hesitated for a moment. Then I said indulgently, "Well, why not use the desk in my sitting room? You look so uncomfortable on the floor."

"We need a bit o' room tae spread out, mistress," said Nanny. She reshuffled the piles of cards together and then laid them out on the carpet. "There, Emily. Choose ten."

Piqued by a mild curiosity, I dropped down on my knees beside them, swooping up Daffy, who settled down peacefully in my lap. Nanny was laying out the cards Emily had chosen in front of her in a definite pattern: one card in the middle, face up, covered by another face down, flanked by four other cards to top and bottom and right and left. To the side were four cards in a row. I picked up the remainder of the deck, noting that the suitmarks were totally different from the ones on the playing cards I'd used in France. Instead of hearts, trefoils, pikes and squares, these suitmarks consisted of swords, wands, coins and cups. I looked inquiringly at Nanny.

"'Tis a tarot deck, mistress. I've heard tell the Gypsies first brought the tarots tae these parts frae far away i' the East. This deck belonged tae my mither." Her voice dropping to a monotone, her brow furrowed in concentration, Nanny examined the cards in front of Emily. "Well, noo, the card in the center is yersel', Emily, yer 'significator,' the Queen o' Swords. On top o' it is Number Two, yer obstacle card. Above it is Number Three, showing yer ideals—"

Emily drew an abrupt, frightened breath. "Nanny, look at Number Six. Isna that the death card? And doesna it foretell wha' will happen tae me soon?"

In spite of myself I shivered when I glanced at that macabre card in the position to the left of the "significator" card. It showed a medieval knight on horseback, his visor drawn back to display the grinning head of a skeleton.

"Aye, Emily," said Nanny quickly. "'Tis the death card, but dinna fash yersel'. It doesna ha' tae mean death. Forbye, it can mean change, or birth, or transformation. Many things."

Emily shook her head. "Mayhap 'tis true, but I've no' the heart tae ha' my fortune read this day."

I said hastily, "Another time would be better, Nanny. Now I must dress for the ball in that beautiful gown you made for me."

Pride in her handiwork battled briefly with Nanny's disgruntlement at having to cut short Emily's reading, and pride won out. In a moment she joined happily with Emily in helping me into the lovely gown she'd copied so faithfully from the Parisian moppet doll Gwyneth had given her. The open saque gown of lustrous green taffeta with a matching underskirt trimmed with pleated self-material had lace-edged gauze ruffles at the neck and sleeves and a tiny bouquet of silk flowers at the bodice. Around my neck I wore a small lace ruff tied with matching green ribbons.

Emily arranged a powdering cloth around my shoulders and sat me down before the dressing table. Dressing my hair high, with curls at the side and back, she applied a bit of pomatum and then, using a tiny bellows, she puffed a white powder scented with orange flower over my coiffure.

When I stood before the cheval glass for a final inspection, I didn't recognize the tall slender creature in misty green with high-piled white curls. It simply wasn't me.

"Oh, Mistress Kirstie, ye're sae bonny," sighed Emily, standing in blissful admiration.

Nanny was more practical. "Ha' ye no' a fine trinket or twa tae set ye off?" she inquired.

"I've nothing very grand, I fear. There's this gold bracelet that belonged to my—to my foster mother." My eyes misted. I remembered so well how much Sheila MacDonell had valued the bracelet, one of her few possessions that had survived Calum's gambling ways. Clearing my throat, I added, "I also have a cameo bracelet that belonged to Fiona, and this brooch. Do you know it, Nanny? It belonged to Fiona, too. See, it opens to display her miniature, and Marcel's. I've often wondered if he gave it to her."

"Nay, I dinna think I ever saw my Fiona wearing it." Nanny held out an eager hand. "Could I ha' a wee closer peek at it?" Taking the brooch, she studied the pictured faces of Fiona and Marcel, and then, before my horrified eyes, she gave a piercing scream and sank in a faint to the floor.

Instinctively I bent over her, only to have Emily thrust me back. "Ye maun be careful o' yer gown, mistress." She dampened a cloth in cold water at the washstand and knelt down beside Nanny, gently applying the cloth to the old nurse's face and wrists. In a few moments Nanny stirred, opening her eyes in a blank stare that turned almost immediately into a look of sheer terror. She lifted trembling hands as if to ward

119

off a danger that only she could see, muttering some incoherent words in the Gaelic.

Emily helped the old creature to her feet and put her arms around her, crooning, "Hush, noo, Nanny. Ye've no reason tae be affeared."

I shook my head, thoroughly bewildered. What could have sent Nanny into such a state? Gwyneth had once described her as fey. Murdoch called her a "white witch." She was also very old. Who could say what had set her off? I said to Emily, "Nanny should be put to bed. Take her to the servants' hall by the back stairs and ask the housekeeper to find her a room for the night. I don't think she's fit enough to go back to her cottage alone."

Shortly after Emily left, tenderly supporting Nanny's frail frame, Murdoch knocked at my door. He was in full evening dress in a suit of gold velvet with ruffles at neck and wrists, his thick hair precisely curled and powdered. His eyes lighted up when he saw me. "Turn around, let me have a good look at you," he commanded. "Egad, I never would have believed it. Gwyneth was right, Nanny was able to copy that moppet doll perfectly. Kirstie, you're beautiful!"

"I certainly look different," I said with a nervous little laugh.

"You're beautiful," he repeated. "You'll turn every head, capture every heart." He extended his arm. "Come. It's time to go to your triumph!"

Suddenly my stomach felt hollow, and my hands were icy cold. However, Murdoch continued his reassuring, amusing chatter as we mounted the great wrought-iron staircase leading to the state rooms, and by the time we reached the white and gold antechamber, with its graceful arabesques and convoluted plaster ceiling, I'd become reasonably composed.

My grandfather and Gwyneth were waiting for us in the antechamber. My aunt gave me an approving glance, while the earl, magnificent in lavishly laced maroon brocade, examined me closely. "Very fine, Kirstie," he said with one of his wintry smiles.

The room started filling with dinner guests. My head soon ached from trying to remember which splendidly dressed lady or gentleman belonged to Clan MacLean, or Clan Stewart or Clan MacIntyre. And I'd have it all to do over again later when the guests invited only for the ball began to arrive. At length, as I strolled about with my grandfather, speaking a few words with each guest, Gwyneth came up to us, murmuring, "It's almost time to go in to dinner. Where is Ian?"

"Pray don't concern yourself, my dear. I trust we can survive without his presence," said the earl coldly.

"Well, yes, but my table arrangements . . . "

Gwyneth broke off. Ian had just entered the antechamber. In a moment, the sound of conversation died away. Every head in the room turned. Ian looked as he had when I first saw him. He was dressed in the red coat and green tartan kilt of his Black Watch uniform. His hair was curled and powdered, clubbed behind in a queue. He looked magnificent, and magnificently out of place.

Walking over to us, Ian bowed. "Good evening, sir, Gwyneth. Kirstie, your gown is charming."

Not a shade of emotion showed in the earl's face, but his tone was venomous as he said in a low voice, inaudible to his guests, "What's the meaning of this, Ian? You're in contravention to the Disarming Act. By law, no Scotsman is allowed—"

Ian cut him off. "No Scotsman is allowed to wear the kilt, or to bear arms or to play the pipes. However, as you can see, sir, I'm not wearing my broadsword, nor do I have with me a set of bagpipes, which in any case I'm unable to play. I'm merely dressed in the uniform of His Majesty's Fortysecond Foot. A crime, perhaps, but surely a very minor one."

Murdoch emerged from the crowd to stand beside my grandfather. "Sir, you're never going to permit—"

My grandfather's eyes glittered with anger. He muttered,

"I'll take care of this, Murdoch." To Ian he said, "You're playing games with me, but don't think I don't know what you're up to. I'm not going to order you to leave, only because such a request would draw even more attention to your disgraceful behavior. But count yourself lucky if someone doesn't report you to the commanding officer at Fort William for infraction of the Disarming Act."

"I'll take my chances, sir." Ian bowed again to the earl and turned to Gwyneth. "If I'm to take Mistress Campbell of Aird in to dinner, will you point her out to me? I don't believe I know her."

"She's the tall thin woman near the fireplace, dressed in primrose satin."

Ignoring the curtness in Gwyneth's voice, Ian went off to introduce himself to Mistress Campbell, and Murdoch moved close to me, saying with suppressed fury, "Be damned to Ian Cameron. How can my uncle stomach him? Oh, I daresay it was better not to force him to leave. Doubtless Ian would have enjoyed that. You realize he deliberately wore that infernal kilt to spoil your party, don't you?"

"No," I said, startled. "What do you mean?"

"Oh, come, Kirstie. Your grandfather saw through that little ploy. Our Ian wanted to show the world his contempt for the stranger who's supplanted him as the heir to Kildrummond."

My heart skipped a beat. I'd assumed Ian had worn the kilt out of pure defiance after my grandfather had ordered him to take part in tonight's entertaining. It hadn't occurred to me that his appearance in Black Watch uniform might represent a deliberate gesture to embarrass me and show how little he regarded my presence at Kildrummond. Could it possibly be true? Ian wouldn't have been human if he didn't resent my usurping his place, but, despite his cold indifference to me, I'd never before seen any sign of pettiness in him.

I tried to put the hurtful thought out of my mind, gazing around at the guests to see how they were reacting to Ian's appearance in the forbidden kilt. To my surprise, after the first moment of shock, there seemed to be very little reaction at all. I noticed more than one understanding stare, more than one secret smile of amusement. None of these people present tonight had flocked to the standard of Bonnie Prince Charlie, as Ian's father had done, but many of them probably had a soft spot in their hearts for the clansmen who did. Perhaps my grandfather and Murdoch had made too much of the incident. Perhaps Ian had acted on pure impulse, after all. Perhaps . . .

It was after the many-coursed dinner for forty guests was over and the orchestra had begun to play in the enormous drawing room, now cleared for dancing, that I really began to understand how perfectly suited was this suite of state rooms for formal entertaining. The magnificent furniture and rugs, the exquisite paintings and tapestries, the diamondlike beauty of the crystal fire lustres, formed a fitting backdrop for the elaborately dressed and bejeweled men and women who danced and talked and flirted and played cards in the circuit of rooms grouped around the head of that graceful staircase.

When Murdoch led me out for the first dance, I was light-headed from nervousness. In the old days at Bassincourt, I'd learned the steps of the minuet and the folk dances with Marie Christine when the dancing master came to the château to give her lessons. I'd also attended several small informal balls at the château, but I knew nothing of the Scottish dances that Murdoch informed me would take place during the evening. Several practice sessions with Murdoch in the family music room, with Gwyneth at the harpsichord, hadn't given me much confidence. As the evening wore on, of course, I was to discover that enthusiasm went a long way toward minimizing a lack of skill while dancing the reel and the strathspey.

The first dance was a minuet. I'd always loved the slow and graceful movements and curtsies, the pauses filled with witty phrases and compliments, and with Murdoch as a partner I quickly gained confidence. As we sank to the floor in a final bow and curtsy, exchanging the time-honored kiss, Murdoch broke into a chuckle. *"Magnifique,* Kirstie," he murmured. "See how foolish you were to be nervous? I'll be fortunate to have another dance with you. Your swains will be standing in line!"

Well, that was an exaggeration, but not by much. I was literally the belle of the ball that night, for the first time in my life. A heady feeling for a provincial nobody. Several would-be partners besieged me for every dance, and I managed to acquit myself reasonably well, not only in the frisky movements of the folk dances but in the skipping and stomping steps of the reel and fling.

Of course there was a fly in the ointment. Ian. He, too, danced every dance. His partners were the prettiest girls in the ballroom. I'd never seen him as he was tonight, smiling, attentive, brimming with charm, obviously enjoying himself. And he never came near me. Was he pointedly ignoring me to show all my new acquaintances how little he regarded me?

Toward the end of the evening, he walked up to join the circle around me as a minuet was about to start. "May I have the honor, Kirstie?" He sounded different. In a moment I realized why. A large sideboard in the dining room had been set out with spirits of every kind, and a number of the men present had been imbibing freely. So, obviously, had Ian. The smell of whisky was strong on his breath, though he wasn't yet unsteady on his feet and there was only a faint slur in his voice. He smiled—though the smile didn't extend to his eyes—and extended his hand. "Shall we satisfy the amenities? Your grandfather seems to feel we ought to dance together."

I stiffened, restraining the hand I'd been about to place on Ian's arm. "Pon rep, you must have misunderstood the earl," I said carelessly. "Surely he can't believe that your duties as the family's steward should include dancing with his granddaughter. Especially since I'm not lacking for partners, and you and I haven't the slightest desire to dance with each other."

Ian's lips tightened. A quick spark of anger ignited in the depths of his gray eyes. "As you will. I'll leave you to more congenial partners, then." He bowed and walked away.

An answering anger enabled me to get through the next minuet and the following reel, though my feet were moving independently of my seething thoughts. *Boor*, I thought fiercely. Even if my grandfather had actually ordered him to ask me to dance—and I wasn't sure I believed that—Ian had gone out of his way to make sure I knew he was acting under duress. Why had he bothered? He'd already made his indifference abundantly clear to me. Perhaps there was some streak of cruelty in him that I'd never noticed before. Or perhaps Murdoch had been right. Ian *wanted* to spoil this gala night for me.

A little later, during the interval, I was left with no further doubt about Ian's motives. I was sitting in a secluded corner of the card room, waiting for Murdoch to bring me a glass of ratafia and a bite of supper, when another couple entered the room. Ian and one of the two vivacious MacDonald sisters from Moidart were carrying plates and glasses and were obviously looking for a convenient place to settle down to eat. Since as many additional guests had been invited to the ball as had been present at dinner, seats were at a premium.

"There's a space over there, Major Cameron. Draw up another chair." From the sound of Mistress MacDonald's voice, I guessed she'd allowed her dancing partners to fetch her one too many glasses of ratafia. Ian pulled his chair next to hers. Laughing and flirting, they were so absorbed in each other that they didn't notice my presence.

I couldn't help overhearing them. "La, Major, it's been an age since I last saw you," said the MacDonald girl. "It was at a ball here at Kildrummond, just before your cousin David, Lord Allendale, died, remember?"

"Yes. The earl hasn't entertained here since then."

"That's understandable. Lord Allendale was his only son. Lord, when I think how fast a person's life can change! A year ago you were the heir to Kildrummond. Now . . . " Mistress MacDonald drank half a glass of ratafia and began to giggle. "You can easily recoup, you know. Why don't you marry Kirstie Cameron-Lefevre, or whatever her name is? You'd be the next Laird of Kildrummond in all but name."

Involuntarily I jerked my arm against the small table next to my chair, causing a china figurine to crash to the floor. Both Ian and his partner lifted their heads, staring at me. Then Ian rose and walked over to my chair. Leaning over me, he murmured, "Don't be concerned, Kirstie. I have no designs on you. Marriage is really too big a price to pay, even for Kildrummond."

I couldn't help myself. I couldn't sit tamely, waiting for Murdoch, while those cruelly bitter words were ringing in my ears. I jumped up from my chair and half walked, half ran into the adjoining antechamber and out to the landing of the staircase. Blinking my eyes against the tears stinging my eyelids, I plunged down the stairs.

"Kirstie, wait," came Ian's urgent voice behind me and the sound of his quick steps. I ignored him. As I reached the foyer, Ian grabbed my arm. "Kirstie, will you please listen to me? I didn't mean—"

"I don't care what you meant," I flared. I shook off his hand. "Leave me alone." I spun on my heel, but before I could get away he reached out to grasp my shoulder.

"Let me go," I said contemptuously, tearing at the long slender fingers that bit into my shoulder. "Do you want me to call for help?"

"Damnation, you'll hear me out—" Ian broke off. A pair of footmen, carrying trays of clean glasses, came into the foyer, their eyes avidly curious in their wooden faces as they walked past us to the staircase. "We can't talk here," Ian muttered. "Come along." Before I quite realized what he was doing, he'd dragged me across the foyer and into the small family music room on the adjoining corridor. Closing the door, he stood with his back to it. "I want to apologize to you," he said, biting off each word as if he was unwilling to let it go. "I saw how much I'd hurt you when I made that cloddish statement about marriage being too big a price for Kildrummond. It was the whisky talking, and resentment against your grandfather. I had no right to say that to you."

"You can keep your apologies. I don't want anything from you, Ian Cameron. I'd die happy if I never had to see you or talk to you again." I drew a long, steadying breath and walked over to him. "Please step away from that door so I can leave."

He stared down at me, the glacial gray of his eyes melting into a spreading flame, his body tensing like a watch spring. Slowly, reluctantly, he put out his hand to touch my face. "You look so beautiful tonight, Kirstie," he whispered. "You're irresistible, like a Circe. You make me ache to touch you, to hold you like this. . . . "

Suddenly he pulled me into his arms, tightening his grasp until I could feel the pounding of his heart and the pressure of his hard thighs through the fragile taffeta of my gown. His breath coming in ragged gasps, he kissed me with a savage urgency, forcing open my lips so that his rapacious tongue could plunder my mouth. Touched by the same raging passion that was consuming him, I couldn't find the strength to resist him until, lifting his head at last, he said huskily, "I want you, Kirstie, I want all of you. Come with me. . . . "

A scalding color flamed in my face. I felt used, I felt dirty. Pushing violently against him, I caught him by surprise and managed to stumble away from him. "You told me once you could give me only one thing, Ian Cameron. I don't want it. Don't ever try to touch me again."

"Kirstie . . . " Whatever Ian had intended to say, he never got a chance to say it. His back was still against the door, and at that moment it crashed open, throwing him to the floor.

Murdoch strode into the room, his face like a thundercloud. "Catriona MacDonald told me Ian had come chasing after you, and then one of the footmen—" He stared at me, aghast. I knew I must look a sight. My coiffure, over which poor Emily had labored so lovingly, had collapsed, and the lovely silk posy at my bosom was a bedraggled ruin. Turning on Ian, who had just risen to his feet, looking somewhat dazed, Murdoch snarled, "You attacked Kirstie, you miserable poltroon," and hurled himself at his cousin.

It was a messy fight. Neither man had a weapon, fortunately. I learned later that both of them were expert fencers and good shots. It was obvious from the start that Murdoch was no pugilist. And Ian was half drunk. They lurched back and forth across the room, flailing at each other with their fists, inflicting bruises and bloody noses but no real damage. I saw no way to stop them. When, however, Murdoch got in a lucky blow and sent Ian crashing against my cittern case, which rested against the harpsichord, I screamed. Loudly. "Stop it, you idiots!"

"I couldn't agree more, my dear." My grandfather, standing in the open doorway, calmly closed the door in the face of several interested gentlemen who seemed to have accompanied him, and advanced into the room. With a deft flick of his wrist, he laid his cane against a surprised Murdoch's throat, stopping him in his tracks. The earl tossed Ian, struggling to his feet, a look of disdain, and said coldly, "If there is any conceivable explanation for engaging in a common brawl, I'd be interested to hear it. Kirstie, my dear, will you leave us?"

Chapter VII

On the morning after my ball, I stood with my grandfather in the great foyer of Kildrummond, saying good-bye to our guests.

"Thank you for honoring us with your presence. May you have a safe journey home," said my grandfather to Sir Graham Henderson, repeating the gracious farewell he'd extended to each of his guests as they left. Sir Graham and his family were the last to leave. As they went out the door, my shoulders sagged in relief.

Standing beside the earl, flanked by Murdoch and Gwyneth, I'd envied my grandfather his air of serene composure. For better than half an hour, I'd had to keep digging my fingernails into my palms in order to force myself to meet the eyes of these people with whom I'd danced and dined the evening before. Not one of them had said a word to me about what had happened, but I was convinced there wasn't a soul among them who didn't know that Ian and Murdoch had battled over me at the ball. Within days, I supposed, the tale would be all over this corner of the Highlands, embellished and amplified and becoming more titillating with each telling.

A fresh wave of anger swept over me. It was all Ian's fault. It was bad enough he'd alternately ignored me and insulted me at the ball, destroying all my pleasure in it. He'd made matters worse by forcing his attentions on me so publicly that Murdoch had been goaded into attacking him and my grandfather had become aware of the incident. Worst of all, though torture wouldn't have wrung the admission from my lips, I'd nearly succumbed once again to Ian's sheer animal appeal. What was this perverse thing that kept drawing us together, despite the fact that I'd come to despise him for his unyielding resentment and boorishness, and he wanted nothing to do with me? Except, apparently, when we inadvertently came into physical contact with each other, and he couldn't keep his hands off me.

Murdoch took me aside, saying in a low, urgent voice, "Kirstie, we must talk about what happened last night. If Ian has been trying to—" He broke off, his lips pressed together in an ugly line. He didn't sound like himself, and he didn't look his usual elegant self, either. His nose was somewhat swollen, and there was a cut over one of his eyebrows.

My grandfather strolled over to us. "You can speak to Kirstie later, Murdoch. First, I'd like to have a few words with her in private."

I glanced at the earl apprehensively. Sooner or later, I knew, I'd have to discuss the fight between Ian and Murdoch and what had led up to it, but I hadn't anticipated seeing the earl until later in the day. Normally he never came down from his rooms until the middle of the afternoon. His health wasn't strong and he needed a great deal of rest. I followed him across the foyer and down the corridor past the family music room to his study, situated next to Ian's estate office.

"Sit down, my dear," said the earl, settling into a chair behind his desk. I guessed, from the lack of papers on the desk and the absence of ledgers and account books, that my grandfather spent little time here. Probably he used the room only to sign documents and give a routine approval to plans that Ian had already drawn up.

The earl picked up a slender paper knife with a handle of raised enamel and balanced it between his forefingers as he gazed at me with those hooded, penetrating blue eyes. "I should like to know the cause of the unseemly incident that so nearly disrupted your ball," he said. "I spoke briefly to Ian and Murdoch last night. Ian wasn't very communicative, Murdoch only slightly more so. May I now have your version of what took place?"

I hesitated. If I could possibly help it, I wasn't going to reveal to anyone the details of my humiliating encounter with Ian. But I was hampered in what I could say because I didn't know what Ian and Murdoch had already told my grandfather. Oh, if only I could consign everything that happened last night into oblivion, so I'd never have to talk about it or think about it again!

"There isn't much to tell, sir," I began with a dry mouth. "Ian and I quarreled about something—something very unimportant, and Murdoch assumed, incorrectly, that Ian had—had attacked me. I regret very much anything I might have done to cause such an embarrassing scene."

"You and Ian quarreled over something unimportant," repeated the earl in a musing tone. "Was it really that unimportant? According to Murdoch's story, Catriona MacDonald saw you bolt out of the card room in obvious distress after Ian made a remark to you. Later, a footman told Murdoch he'd seen Ian literally drag you into the music room."

"The footman was exaggerating," I said hastily. "Truly, sir, Ian and I merely had a silly argument."

My grandfather looked at me for a long, appraising moment. "I'm sorry Kirstie," he said at last. "I'm not able to believe you, not when I recall your appearance in the music room after your 'silly argument' with Ian." The earl leaned suddenly across his desk. His voice rasped like a whiplash. "Did Ian make an improper advance to you? Is that why you ran off? And when he caught up with you, did he assault you sexually?"

The shock of the question hit me like a blow. "No. No, of course not," I protested. "Oh, he kissed me, but that

131

was . . . He was angry, that's all. He wasn't trying to—" I couldn't bring myself to use the word, "rape." I went on, "He wasn't trying to harm me. You see, sir, Ian and I have never been friendly. For some reason, it only takes a trifle to put us at each other's throats."

"That was all? You're sure?"

"Yes, sir. I'm very sure. I think we should all put the incident behind us and not discuss it anymore. That includes Murdoch. He still seems so angry with Ian. . . . "

"Oh, I'll see to it that there's no more brawling," my grandfather assured me. "And I quite agree with you that we needn't discuss the matter any further, now that we've established that Ian was guilty of no more than his usual loutishness." The earl shook his head. "Bad blood, my dear. It always tells. Ian's family, the Camerons of Inverloch, were a surly lot, feckless and disloyal, a disgrace to the rest of the clan, and I fear Ian's proving no exception. If I didn't have such strong feelings about kinship . . . But there, we've talked enough about Ian, unless—" He paused, looking thoughtful. After a moment he said, "You're aware he was my heir until we learned Fiona had borne a living child?"

"Yes." My voice must have reflected the slight surprise I felt. He'd never previously mentioned the subject to me.

"Well, then, has it ever occurred to you that Ian may be attempting to recoup his fortunes in the only way open to him? By marrying you?"

My face flamed with embarrassment. "Ian's the last man in the world I'd want to marry," I blurted. "And he feels the same way about me. I told you. We dislike each other."

"I'm happy to hear it. I can't think of a more objectionable match. May I suggest, however, that you give some thought to the subject of marriage itself? One day you'll be Laird of Kildrummond. But after that, unless you marry and provide an heir to succeed you, our line will die out."

"Oh—there's no need to think of that now, surely. Not right away. I'm only nineteen, there's plenty of time. . . . "

"At nineteen, many girls are already married." He paused again. Then he said abruptly, "What would you say to marrying Murdoch?"

I gaped at him, speechless for once in my life. My vocal chords felt paralyzed.

"You seem surprised," said the earl. "I wonder why? I've observed that you and Murdoch like each other. You have similar tastes. You're related, but not too closely. Nor should the fact of his illegitimacy disturb you. His father's relationship with his mother was an honorable one, even though they weren't free to marry."

At last I found my voice. "You can't mean what you're saying. Murdoch and I are friends, yes. He's been very kind. But he's never even hinted that he might want to—to . . . "

My grandfather said calmly, "Perhaps he doesn't realize it himself yet, but I believe my nephew is very much in love with you." He smiled faintly at my confusion. "You can rely on my discretion. I'll not say a word to Murdoch. However, when he does come to realize how he feels, I want you to know that the match has my entire approval. Run along, now. I daresay I've given you more than enough to think about for the time being."

I closed the door of the earl's study behind me and stood, hesitating, in the corridor. So much had happened in less than twenty-four hours. I felt buffeted by conflicting emotions, unable to sort out my chaotic thoughts. Almost automatically, I headed for the music room, taking refuge, as I had so often in times of trouble, in a familiar solace.

I sat down at the harpsichord, playing snatches of melody at random, an obbligato to my thoughts. For the first time since my arrival at Kildrummond, I'd spoken seriously and at length to my grandfather, and he'd unleashed a thunderbolt. Marry Murdoch! I had to rearrange my thinking to consider him in a romantic sense. He was older, for one thing. Only in his middle thirties, I reminded myself. Not too old for a girl of nineteen to marry, not by any means, I supposed.

133

We were also close kin. Wasn't he almost an uncle? Well, no, not really. His father and the earl were only half brothers. He was Fiona's cousin, or was it half cousin, so he and I were cousins, too. First cousins once removed? No, that didn't take into account the fact that Murdoch's father and the earl weren't full brothers. . . .

I shook my head in frustration. None of this mattered, except that from now on my easy friendship with Murdoch was bound to be different. I'd always be wondering if my grandfather was correct in his assumption that Murdoch was falling in love with me. It wasn't hard to understand why the earl approved of the idea. Murdoch was like a son to him, and Kildrummond had always been Murdoch's home.

"Kirstie, I heard you playing . . . "

I hadn't heard the door open. My fingers struck a discordant chord as I twisted away from the keyboard and stood to confront Ian. He, too, bore the marks of a scuffle. One cheekbone was badly bruised, and the knuckles on his right hand were scraped.

"Kirstie, could I speak to you?"

"I thought we said all there was to say last night."

"Not quite all. Why wouldn't you accept my apology?"

I couldn't help myself. "Why should you care?"

His lips tightened. "Because I've got some pride. I don't make gratuitous cruelty a practice, and I don't want you to think I do."

Perhaps it was the note of sincerity I thought I detected in his voice, perhaps it was the stiff way he held himself, as if he expected a blow from me and was doggedly prepared to let me deliver it without defending himself, I don't know. But something led me to say, "Very well. I accept your apology."

"Thank you." The stiff shoulders relaxed. He hesitated. "Will you also let me make amends of a sort? Will you come riding with me this afternoon? I'll be going to the upper glen. Perhaps you'd like to see something of your future estate."

I hesitated. Dangerous, I thought. This was a different Ian Cameron, but I didn't know why he'd changed. If he really had. We weren't good for each other, I did know that. I heard myself saying, "I'd like to see the estate. What time this afternoon?"

After he left the music room, I stood for a moment, castigating my weak will. I tried to convince myself I was doing something meritorious in riding about the estate with Ian. In all my rides with Murdoch we'd never ventured into the upper glen. Too rough, he'd said. Nothing to see except crofters' cottages and black cattle and Highland sheep. But as the future mistress of Kildrummond, didn't I have the duty to familiarize myself with the way my tenants lived?

Well, mistake or no, I'd agreed to go. As I was about to leave the music room, my eye hit upon my cittern case, knocked awry last night when one of Murdoch's random blows had sent Ian reeling against it. Hurrying over to the case, I opened it, observing with relief that the instrument hadn't suffered any damage. I stood quietly for a moment, looking at the cittern. Then, making a sudden decision, I closed the case, picked it up and walked out the door with it.

Maura Fraser viewed me with her usual jaundiced stare when she opened the door of my grandmother's apartment. "Why did you bring that thing, then?" she asked suspiciously when she saw my cittern case.

"I'm going to play for my grandmother. I remember you told me she used to enjoy music. Didn't she play duets with my mother?"

"I don't hold with this, Mistress Kirstie. It's not good for the countess to be disturbed."

"Well, we can't know if she'll be disturbed by my playing until we try it, can we?"

Maura lowered her defiant eyes and stepped aside. My grandmother sat in her usual place in a chair by the window, staring vacantly into space. She didn't move a muscle when

I came into the room, not even when I pushed a chair beside her and sat down, softly tuning my cittern.

I played and sang several old English folk songs—"O Mistress Mine," and "Gather Ye Rosebuds," and a favorite French song, *"L'Amour de Moi."* I might have been singing to the wind, for all the notice my audience of one took of my performance. Elspeth's empty old face didn't register even a shade of emotion. All but resigned to the failure of my scheme—I'd hoped my playing would touch my grandmother in some place deep within her, where mere words couldn't reach—I drifted into the strains of a song my father—Calum—had loved, "The Lament of the Border Widow."

> "My love he built me a bonny bower
> And clad it a' wi ' lilye flour;
> A brawer bower ye ne'er did see
> Than my true love he built for me."

Elspeth's great haunted blue eyes opened wider. She leaned forward, smiling. "That was lovely, darling," she whispered dreamily. "Now be a good girl and play 'The Bonny Earl of Murray.' "

I had the eerie feeling she was talking to a person she knew well, someone very close to her. Fiona? A chill crept over me. Obediently my fingers strummed the opening bars of "The Bonny Earl of Murray," but before I could sing, "Ye *Highlands* and ye *Lawlands,* Oh! where ha'e ye been," the curtain had descended again over my grandmother's eyes. The tiny window of—not sanity, perhaps, but awareness—had shut. She sat in her familiar unmoving lethargy.

I stood up, restoring my cittern to its case. "You saw that, didn't you?" I asked Maura anxiously. "I didn't imagine her response?"

"She's not a vegetable," said Maura shortly. "She can hear, you know. But whether she understands . . . " Her voice changed, became almost pleading. "Mistress Kirstie, I daresay you mean well, but you must think ahead. As likely as not, the next time you play and sing for the countess, you may set off one of her violent moods. She might suspect, for example, that you'd stolen Fiona's cittern and attack you in a frenzy of protectiveness, as she did awhile back when she found you in Fiona's bedchamber. You see, I've cared for her for a great many years now, and I've found it's best to keep the atmosphere around her as quiet, as soothing and relaxing, as possible."

"It sounds like a living death to me. If I were my grandmother, I'd far rather feel *something,* rather than nothing. No, Maura. I'll come back. I believe I reached the countess today, even if it was only for a single moment."

"You won't heed what I've said?"

I hesitated, fumbling for the right words. "No. I don't like to oppose you in this, but—oh, it's hard to explain—I *know* it's right to do what I'm doing."

"Very well. Then I must do as I think best, also."

Which probably meant, I thought, as I walked away from my grandmother's apartment to my own rooms at the other end of the corridor, that Maura would appeal to—no, not the earl; I'd gathered she preferred to have as little to do with my grandfather as possible—to, most likely, Gwyneth, in an effort to stop my visits. I sighed. Both of us, Maura and I, wanted only what was best for my grandmother, and yet we were locked in dispute.

When I entered my bedchamber, I found Nanny there with Emily. "Are you feeling better today, Nanny?" I asked. "I was worried about you last night. I thought you might have hit your head when you fell."

Emily flashed me a warning glance, moving her head slightly from side to side. Without turning her head in my direction, Nanny began mumbling in the Gaelic. I caught only a few words. "My poor Fiona . . . Pain, such pain . . . Screams, oh the screams to raise the dead. . . . "

I walked over to her, placing my hand gently on her shoulder. "What is it, Nanny? What's troubling you?"

She looked up then. Her eyes seemed unfocused. Suddenly her face contorted with fear and she struck my hand away. Obviously at that moment she didn't know who I was. Then, the brief spurt of energy having dissipated, she shifted her gaze and resumed her incoherent muttering. She made no objection when I took her arm again, leading her to a chair and settling her into it.

Turning to Emily, I murmured, "What on earth could have happened to set her off like this?"

"I dinna ken, mistress. She seemed her usual sel' when she came tae yer bedchamber this morn. Oh, a wee bit daft, the way she always is, now I think on it. No' anything tae concern me. She wanted tae look at yer brooch again, the one wi' the pictures o' yer mither and yer faither. I saw no harm i' it. But the moment she took yon brooch in her hands, she turned pale, and I was afeared she'd faint again, but then she began asking me about the fire that killed Marcel—yer faither—and shocked Fiona intae gie'ing birth tae her bairn ahead o' her time. But I couldna tell Nanny verra much aboot that terrible night. Maister Calum and Mistress Sheila and I, we saw only the flames that destroyed half yer faither's village, and Fiona stumbling away frae the fire."

I glanced at Nanny, frowning. She still seemed dazed, though she'd stopped muttering. I said to Emily, "I don't understand it. You say she seemed quite normal until she handled my brooch. She was normal last night, too, until I handed her the brooch."

"Recall her mither was a Gypsy," said Emily slowly. "The sairvants here at Kildrummond, they say she ha' the gifts o' healing and foretelling wha' is tae come. They also say she needs only tae touch an object belonging tae someone, e'en a complete stranger, and she can tell ye all aboot that pairson."

I swallowed hard. The rational side of my nature didn't

believe in the occult, and yet . . . Unwillingly I voiced the dark suspicion I could see forming on Emily's lips. "You think, don't you, that Nanny felt some kind of powerful emotion emanating from the brooch that had belonged to Fiona, forcing her to feel the same pain and anguish that Fiona felt on the night of the fire."

"Aye, mistress, that is wha' I believe."

Despite myself, I was shaken. Into my mind, unbidden, came the memory of the eerie sense of "otherness" I'd felt during my two brief visits to the ruins of the old castle. No more then than now had I wanted to believe in malign spirits or other occult influences at work around me. I'd told myself that places and objects might well retain vestiges of the suffering and tragedy originally associated with them, that there might be phenomena in the universe that we didn't perfectly understand. The explanation had reassured me then. It did the same now. With more confidence, I said to Emily, "I think you should take Nanny home. She'll feel better in the familiar surroundings of her cottage."

When I entered the stable yard that afternoon, Ian was already waiting for me. Holding the reins of two saddled horses, he stood watching me as I walked across the cobblestones toward him. "I thought you might have changed your mind about coming with me." He spoke with his usual unsmiling gravity, but there was something different about him. For the first time since I'd known him, the gray eyes seemed direct and open. There wasn't a trace of the slight wall of reserve he'd always erected between us.

"Why would I change my mind? I told you I wanted to see the estate. Murdoch—"

"Murdoch's not much interested in the details of how the estate is run," said Ian. He sounded quite matter-of-fact. There was no animosity in his tone. Another change in him, certainly. He extended his hand to help me into the saddle.

139

Soon we were crossing the rickety wooden bridge across the river above the stables, heading upstream along the thickly forested banks. Murdoch had been right. The riding was much rougher here.

Gradually the glen widened out, until, as we approached the shores of a small lake, I could see a stretch of green and level ground extending for a mile or more to either side and on into the distance, where the river curved around the flanks of the mountains that enclosed the valley. The trees that apparently had once covered the slopes of the mountains were gone now, except for scattered plantations high up in the hills.

"This is more a strath than a glen," Ian said. "The valley is wider than most. Those little streams coming down from the hills have created their own miniature glens. Our chief tacksman lives in the nearest one to your left. We'll go see him later."

"Is this all Kildrummond land? It seems to go on and on," I exclaimed in awe.

"There are larger estates, but Kildrummond is a very satisfactory size. The earl owns forty thousand acres."

It was hard for me to comprehend an estate of that size. I'd always considered Bassincourt a large holding. Compared to Kildrummond, it was quite modest.

We rode slowly along the path beside the river. The land here was a haphazard-looking mosaic of small plots of cultivated ground and pastures, all of difference sizes, interspersed with small cottages. Crops appeared to be planted in long rows. Ian explained that this method of farming was called "runrig." Some of the more prosperous tenants held the rights to several of these strips of arable land, which often were not contiguous, while others held only one strip.

"It seems a rather wasteful method of farming. Wouldn't it be better if the strips were consolidated into a single plot?" I asked.

"Of course. And under the terms of the original leases,

many of these holdings were larger. But over the generations each tenant felt the need to provide his children with a bit of land, and this hodgepodge of separate strips is the result."

"Well—you're the steward. Can't you do something about this?"

Ian smiled rather grimly. "If a custom has persisted long enough, your average clansman thinks of it as a fiat from the Almighty. We're a stubborn lot, we Highlanders."

He seemed to get along well with the tenants, I thought. He stopped frequently to greet one or another of them, or to discuss a current problem. Usually he introduced me as the earl's granddaughter. They responded to him with what appeared to be respect and even liking.

As we moved away from the area near the river, the land appeared to be less fertile, the plots smaller, the cottages more nondescript. At one point, in a rocky section halfway up the slope of the mountain, Ian paused to talk to the tenant of a small log and stone hut, roofed in turf. Even a cursory glance told me the dwelling didn't compare with Nanny's snug cottage. Like most of the men we'd encountered, the tenant was dressed in a rough coat and a long shirt worn loose over a pair of ragged breeches. He had no shoes or hose. He was unprepossessing with his sunken, unshaven cheeks and his shabby, grimy clothes.

As Ian stood talking with the man, I sat on my horse, watching the two children who had just emerged from the windowless hut and were relieving themselves in full view of their father and Ian and me. A scrawny brown sheep and a goat wandered past them to enter the hut. The children's appearance appalled me. Both were quite naked. I might have reserved judgment, because they were very young and standards of modesty needn't apply. Possibly, too, the family had little money for clothing. However, even though it was the month of June, the temperature was chilly, and the children were shivering. They were also very thin and quite filthy, as if they'd climbed down a sooty chimney. Remembering the sturdy, rosy-cheeked peasant children on the Bassincourt estate in Normandy, I felt my heart contract.

Waiting until Ian had finished his conversation and remounted his horse and we were moving away from the hut, I burst out, "You must do something about those poor children. They look half starved."

"There are many more like them, Kirstie. We had a very hard winter here. They'll look better when the kale and potatoes come in, and the cow gives a little more milk."

I stared at him. "You mean this family isn't an isolated example? There are other people on this wealthy estate living in poverty? Why, at Bassincourt the comte would have—"

"This isn't Normandy," Ian cut in. There was a definite edge to his voice. "Land tenure in the Highlands is the result of a process going back for centuries. The proprietor leases land to tacksmen, who subleases to tenants, who often lease in turn to subtenants, the crofters. That was a crofter family you saw just now. They subsist on a tiny strip of arable and the grazing rights for one or two animals. That's not enough land to support themselves. Even in good times they can't produce enough to feed their families. In a bad winter, like this year's, they live on cakes made out of boiled beef blood and a bit of oatmeal. And why do you suppose those children looked so dirty? All the members of the family *and* their livestock live in that one-room hut. It has an earthen floor with a fire hole in the middle of it, and when the rain leaks through that turf roof the soot pours down on everyone inside."

"But then, why don't you—?"

"Why don't I wave a magic wand and make all the Kildrummond crofters healthy, happy and prosperous?" Ian said savagely. "Because it takes time to change life in the Highlands. Because I can't push too hard without doing more damage than good. Because, in the end, I don't own Kildrummond. I'm the Earl of Carrickmore's . . . " Ian bit off his reply, clamping his lips together. I knew he'd been about to say "the Earl of Carrickmore's hired servant." He was silent for a moment, obviously trying to tamp down the angry frustration he felt. Finally he said, "There's someone on the estate who feels as you do, and he's done something about it. Come meet Jock Cameron."

As we slowly rode back toward the entrance of the glen, Ian surprised me by talking about my life in Bassincourt. He'd never done that before, not during his short stay in the village at the time of Calum's funeral, nor during the long journey from France to Kildrummond. I wondered why he was doing it now. He asked me questions about Calum and Sheila, listening with apparent interest when I told him how they'd ended their wanderings about the Continent from one gambling center to another in order to give me a more stable home life. He laughed with me as I described Calum's periodic binges in Caen when he could no longer resist his gambling urges. Ian asked me, too, about Calum's last years, and how he'd been so fearful about leaving me unprovided for that he'd finally decided to risk losing my love by confessing the truth to my grandfather about my parentage.

"I know it's foolish and unrealistic, but sometimes I find myself wishing that Papa—Calum—had never written to the earl," I blurted. "Oh, I know I gained a new family and a new identity. Also, quite literally, I lost the memory of a father and a mother I'd known and loved."

"And exchanged them for stranger parents you never knew, who were dead and in their graves before you were a week old," said Ian. "I understand."

I glanced at his austere profile, startled. He *did* sound understanding. Not a bit like the martinet Black Watch officer who'd informed me curtly at Calum's funeral that my wishes didn't matter, that I had no choice about going to Scotland, that my duty to my family's lineage was all important.

We left the valley to turn into the glen that had been formed in the folds of the hills by a small tributary of the main river. This area was still well wooded in its lower reaches, and when we arrived in the arable part of it I noticed that the cultivated plots were larger and that the sheep grazing in the upland pastures were not the small, hairy brown creatures I was accustomed to seeing. They were larger, black-faced sheep with a heavier fleece.

Jock Cameron, the chief tacksman of Kildrummond, welcomed us to his house, his comely, buxom wife by his side. He was a tall, powerful man in early middle age with grizzled hair and keen eyes that gazed at me searchingly when Ian introduced me. His face relaxed in a smile as he said, "Meggie and I were wondering how it would be if the next Laird of Kildrummond was a lady. Now we've met you, we shan't have any more worries on that score, isn't that so, Meggie?"

His wife replied with a shy smile, "Aye, Jock, Mistress Kirstie will do just fine, I'm sure."

"Thank you both, I promise I'll do my best. However, I hope I won't become the laird for a long time to come," I replied, warmed by their kindliness.

Although they didn't speak in the broad Scots of the castle servants or of their own tenants, Jock Cameron and his wife didn't pretend to the ease and elegance of dress and manner of the earl and Gwyneth and Murdoch and Ian himself. Still, they were obviously people of standing. I recalled what Murdoch had once told me. In the old violent days before the defeat of the Jacobite cause, a clan chief's tenants were also his standing army. The tacksmen, or principal tenants, were often related by blood to the chief and acted as his officers in battle. In other times, I mused, the ancestors of Jock Cameron would probably have been frequent guests of their chief. That, of course, would have been before the Lairds of Kildrummond had become ennobled, married into wealth and spent their days in the drawing rooms of Edinburgh and London. I was quite sure that Jock himself had never been invited to Kildrummond except on estate business.

The tacksman's house was a square, stone-built structure that looked solidly comfortable, though by Kildrummond standards it was modest in the extreme. His wife Meg ushered us into a neat-as-a-pin parlor and offered tea to me and a small glass of whisky to Ian.

"I was telling Kirstie that you've made improvements to your leasehold, Jock," said Ian. "Tell her about it."

"Well, now, 'tis no great thing," began Jock. And indeed the changes he described seemed quite simple, though I couldn't mistake the pride in his voice. Most of his tenants farmed on joint leases; he'd persuaded them to throw their acreages together, to sow and harvest collectively and to graze their animals on a common pasture. "So ye see, mistress, my tenants make bigger profits and so do I, when I raise their rents! I must admit it's helped to bring in some Black-faced Lintons. They winter better than our Highland sheep and give better wool and three times as much meat."

Jock Cameron paused, looking toward the door. A small boy with gray eyes and blond hair stood on the threshold, looking wistfully at the delicately browned shortbreads Mrs. Cameron had served to us. "Does your grandmother know where you are, laddie?" Jock said severely. The boy hung his head. "Well, no harm done, I suppose," the tacksman added, his tone softening. "Come have a biscuit, and then you must go home."

Rising, Meg took the boy's hand and led him over to the table. "Take four biscuits, Gavin, two for you and a taste for your grandmother. And you must greet Master Ian and the young lady who's our guest. Mistress Kirstie Cameron from the castle."

Gavin swiftly tucked a handful of shortbreads into the pocket of his shirt. Afterward he shot Meg a puckish, questioning look. Suppressing a smile, she didn't comment on the number of biscuits he'd taken. Well over four, by my reckoning.

I glanced surreptitiously at Ian as the boy walked over to us, bobbing an awkward little bow. Seeing him with Ian, no one could have failed to notice the resemblance between them. Gavin's fair hair hadn't yet turned tawny, his straight

145

little features hadn't yet developed into the austere beauty of Ian's face, but it was impossible to doubt their relationship.

Ian's expression registered merely a careless friendliness when he greeted the little boy. "Good day, Gavin. Are you enjoying the bilbocatcher?" he asked, glancing at the contraption in Gavin's hand. It consisted of a cup and ball joined together by a string. I recognized it as a *bilboquet,* a popular toy with the children of Bassincourt.

Gavin seemed torn between painful shyness and a blissful pleasure in this meeting with Ian. The boy's eyes were shining as he half whispered, "Aye, Maister Ian. 'Tis a grand toy. My mither says ye fetched it all the way frae—frae—"

"From France, that's right. I'm happy you like it."

Reluctantly Gavin turned his attention from Ian to me. "Ye be the lady who's gae'ing tae be our next laird? My mither says ye came frae France wi' the maister."

So, Hallie had discussed me with her son, I thought, feeling mildly annoyed though not really surprised. "Yes, I did come from France with Master Ian, Gavin. Don't forget, though, I'm a Scotswoman, too."

The exchange appeared to exhaust Gavin's powers of conversation. However, he continued to stare at me curiously. His steady gray gaze disconcerted me momentarily. It was so reminiscent of someone else!

Meg intervened. "Run along now, Gavin. Your grandmother will be worried about you." I suspected she wanted to prevent the boy from repeating any further gossip he may have heard from his mother.

Later, when Ian and I were leaving, Meg said shyly, "Thank you for coming, mistress. Please come again if you've a mind to." I promised myself silently that I would. Even during these brief few minutes I'd felt more comfortable with Meg than I ever had with Gwyneth.

As we were riding away from the house, Ian remarked, "I wish we had more tacksmen like Jock. If your Uncle

David had paid heed to Jock and his ideas years ago, Kildrummond would be far more prosperous today."

"Yes, he appears to be very efficient," I murmured rather absently. My mind was on another matter entirely. "Do I gather that Hallie's father is one of Jock Cameron's tenants?"

"He was. He died some years ago. However, Jock has always allowed the widows of his crofters to stay on in their cottages. Hallie's mother was a 'grasswoman' for a while, I believe—she did some herding for Jock. Now, mainly, she takes care of Gavin."

I hesitated. "The Camerons seem to be very indulgent employers," I ventured. "It's not usual, is it, to allow the child of one of your crofters to wander in and out of your house?"

"Oh, well, Jock and Meg are fond of Gavin. They haven't any children of their own, you know. I've often thought they might offer to take Gavin if Hallie marries. It would be a good solution for all of them. Probably Hallie wouldn't agree, though. I believe she's genuinely attached to the boy."

For several seconds I was too flabbergasted to speak. Ian was discussing Gavin from the standpoint of an outsider. No one hearing him would have suspected he had any personal interest in the child, let alone that he was Gavin's father. It was hard for me to believe, knowing his intense nature, that Ian didn't feel any responsibility for Gavin's existence. Oh, I could understand that he wouldn't choose to marry Hallie, because of the difference in their stations, especially if theirs had been merely a casual affair during one of his leaves from the Black Watch. It might be impossible, too, because of the legal ramifications, to acknowledge paternity officially. However, it sounded downright unnatural for him to display so little interest in a matter as important as Jock Cameron's adoption of his own son.

The puzzle of Ian's attitude toward Gavin engaged my mind during the rest of our ride, so much so that I didn't notice how silent I'd become. When we dismounted in the stable yard, he stood looking down at me, his eyebrows raised. "You've scarcely said a word since we left Jock's house. Regretting that you came out with me today?"

"Oh, no. I enjoyed the ride very much."

"I, too." Ian cleared his throat. "Kirstie, I realized today that it's been very uncomfortable to be at odds with you. You don't need to tell me who's responsible for any disagreements we've had," he hastened to add, and then fell silent again. I could sense the effort he was making to break through the prickly reserve that had always guarded his emotions. Finally he said, "Could we make a try at being friends?"

"I'd like that, Ian."

"Good." He smiled his rare, difficult smile. "Let's go riding again soon."

I presume, after I left Ian in the stable yard, that I went into the house and climbed all those stairs in the usual way, but all I remember is a distinct sensation of floating on air.

When I entered my bedchamber to dress for dinner, Emily looked up from her position in a chair by the window, where she was trying to combine a spot of knitting with her daily reading of the Bible. At her feet, the kitten, Daffy, was rapidly turning a ball of yard into a Medusalike snarl. "No need tae tell me ye enjoyed yer ride," Emily said drily. "Ye look as happy as Mademoiselle Marie Christine used tae look, when ye told her she needn't practice the cittern a minute longer." She bent down to retrieve her yarn. "A pox on ye, Daffy," she grumbled. "Ye maun leave off stealing my yarn. Ye're mair trouble than ye're worth."

I laughed, picking up the kitten. "I can tell Daffy believes every word you say. You're frightening him to death." I settled down on the bed with the kitten, stroking his wispy fur until he relaxed in a purring ball. I felt like purring myself. At this moment, I was happier than I'd been since that terrible day when Calum died and I learned I wasn't his daughter. I didn't allow myself to analyze my feelings too closely. Nor did I probe into Ian's reasons for wanting to be friends. It was enough that we could start again after the wretched beginning we'd made together.

Emily broke into my thoughts. "I thought ye pasted all the pages back intae the Holy Buik," she remarked.

"What?"

"I juist noticed, Mistress Kirstie. All the pages wi' the births and the deaths and the marriages, they're gone."

Emily was right. The pages recording the vital statistics of my mother's—Sheila MacDonell's—family, going back almost a hundred years, had been ripped out of the Bible. Had the vandal who'd defaced the book carried the pages away with him? If so, why? Or had he—she—come back later to finish his work? Or had someone else entirely entered my bedchamber to despoil my possessions?

I closed the Bible. My euphoria over my afternoon with Ian was rapidly fading. On the whole, I preferred to believe that the original vandal had for some reason taken away the missing pages, and Emily had only now discovered their absence. I'd already faced the shock of that first incident. Nothing alarming had happened during the past few weeks and I'd hoped that my unknown tormentor's malice had been satisfied. If not, or if still another person was involved . . .

Chapter VIII

As I picked up my cittern and started for the door of my bed-chamber, I glanced at Emily, who was clearing away the remains of my early morning chocolate, and paused. Her mouth was turned down in an expression of stern disapproval.

"You don't think I ought to visit the countess, do you, Emily?"

"'Tis no' fer me tae say."

"Perhaps not, but that usually doesn't stop you," I retorted. "Out with it, Emily."

"Weel, I ken ye're trying tae help the countess wi' yer music, but ye've played fer her sae many times this past week. Is she no' as daft as ever she was?"

"I did arouse her once, remember? She really heard the music, I'm sure she knew I was playing just for her. It's true she hasn't responded since then. I keep hoping she will. I don't want to give up yet."

Emily looked skeptical. "And if ye should rouse the countess? Ye shouldna fergit how the puir auld lady attacked ye."

Perhaps it was foolhardy of me, I reflected, as I walked down the corridor toward my grandmother's apartment, but I hadn't the slightest fear that the countess would fly into a frenzy and attack me again. Actually, I'd have welcomed some strong show of emotion. On that occasion a week ago—

it was the day I'd gone riding into the upper glen with Ian—
my playing of the "The Lament of the Border Widow" had
seemed to strike some chord in Elspeth, and she'd smiled and
spoken to me. Only a word or two, but she'd spoken. Since
then she'd remained deep in her apathy, unresponsive to my
overtures. I didn't want to consider the possibility that she
might not respond again. Against all logic, I clung to my belief that deep in Elspeth's buried consciousness there lurked
a glimmer of sanity that I could reach if only I tried hard
enough.

"Well? Haven't had enough of this foolishness yet?" de-
manded Maura, dour and unwelcoming as always when she
opened the door of my grandmother's apartment.

I shrugged, pushing past her. I'd learned not to waste my
time arguing with Maura. I took the cittern out of the case,
tuned it quickly and sat down in my usual chair opposite Elspeth. The June sun poured in through the window, bathing
her face and figure in light and warmth, of which she seemed
to be unaware. She was as stonily unmoving as the effigy on
a tomb. I shivered at the analogy, quickly beginning to play
and sing. I rambled through my repertory of songs, Scottish,
English and French, glancing at her hopefully as I finished
each one. Elspeth's blank blue eyes continued to stare unsee-
ingly at the far corner of the room. Finally I slipped into an
old Gaelic melody I'd never sung to her before, *"Cuir, A
Chinn Dilis"*:

"O, cuir, a chinn dilis, dilis, dilis,
Cuir, a chinn dilis tharam do lamb . . .
(O sweetest and dearest, fairest and dearest,
Take me, my darling, now in thine arms) . . . "

A hand reached out to take the cittern from me. "My darling, your playing is becoming very careless," Elspeth said
disapprovingly. "Your third course is tuned too low." She
was right. While I'd been playing, my third set of strings had

slipped out of tune. Her eyes intent on the instrument, Elspeth quickly corrected the tuning, and then, while I scarcely dared to breathe, she softly strummed the opening bars of *"Cuir, A Chinn Dilis."*

The sudden burst of awareness lasted only a moment longer. Even as she sang the first words, "O sweetest and dearest, fairest and dearest," her voice faltered and the cittern slipped from her fingers. As I reached out to save the instrument from falling to the floor, she began to cry soundlessly, unnervingly, the tears streaming down her face in a hopeless torrent of grief.

Maura rushed to throw her arms around the countess, cradling her like a child. "Hush, now, hush my dear." Maura glared at me. "Go, Mistress Kirstie, before you do any more harm."

"I don't understand. She was so normal for an instant. . . . " I paused. "Except that—Maura, do you think my grandmother could have believed she was talking to Fiona? Murdoch told me there are times when the countess is convinced Fiona isn't dead."

My grandmother was still crying those dreadful silent tears. A baleful look on her dark, ugly face, Maura screamed at me, "Oh, just go. We don't want you or need you here!"

The malevolence in her voice shook me. I quickly put my cittern in its case and left the room. As I walked back to my own bedchamber to put away the instrument before I went down to breakfast, my elation at achieving what I believed to be a real breakthrough with my grandmother was tempered by the memory of the sad aftermath. Yes, I was troubled by Elspeth's inexplicable outburst of grief, but not enough to abandon my attempts to help her.

In my bedchamber, I was about to tell Emily what had happened when she forestalled me. "Mistress Kirstie, I was juist straightening out yer dressing table. Yer brooch is missing frae yer trinket box," she announced.

"Missing? Don't you mean mislaid?"

"I dinna mislay yer things, mistress."

"No, of course not. Let's see, when's the last time I wore the brooch?"

" 'Twas on the nicht o' yer ball. I took it frae yer gown and placed it back i' the box."

I frowned. I hadn't worn the brooch since that night. At the family dinners my usual ornament was a little gauze ruff tied about my throat with ribbons. "Are you suggesting someone stole the brooch?"

"Nay. I think auld Nanny took it," Emily replied bluntly.

After the first moment of shock, I was inclined to agree with her. Since my arrival at Kildrummond, Nanny had come to visit me almost every day. During the time she was sewing my ball gown, she'd been in my rooms almost constantly. Now it occurred to me that I hadn't seen her since the morning after the ball. She was still acting strangely then, as she had the night before, when my mother's brooch apparently touched some kind of occult nerve in her. If someone had taken the brooch it was most likely Nanny. Which meant that she must be more disturbed than I'd realized. I felt vaguely guilty. After the first few days, when Nanny didn't reappear, I should have sent Emily to check on her.

"Don't worry about the brooch," I told the old servant. "If Nanny has it, there won't be any difficulty about getting it back. Meanwhile, we won't talk of it. I don't want to cause an uproar over it."

I glanced at my mother's—Sheila's—old clock in its place of honor on the ornate chest japanned in gold and silver. It was time to go down to breakfast, although I hadn't needed to check the clock to know that. My stomach told me it was time to eat. In my few short weeks at Kildrummond I hadn't yet learned to shed my country ways. I still rose very early every morning. After a brisk walk around the grounds, I had plenty of time to read, write letters, play with Daffy and enjoy a cup of chocolate before the breakfast hour. By that time, of course, I was always ravenous.

For once, this morning, I wasn't the first to arrive in the dining room. Gwyneth was already seated at the table. As I walked into the room, she looked up, her face grave, and said, "We must talk, Kirstie."

After I selected some ham and cheese and rolls from the sideboard, I sat down with an inquiring glance at Gwyneth, who wasted no time coming to the point. She said accusingly, "My dear, Maura Fraser came to see me this morning. She told me you'd been paying frequent visits to the countess."

So, Maura's finally made good on her threat. She must have gone to Gwyneth immediately after I left my grandmother this morning. I gazed at Gwyneth warily, thinking how ironic, and yes, how sad, it was that Elspeth's closest relatives should have so little contact with her that they didn't know about my visits to my grandmother until it was reported to them by a servant. Even as I thought this, I knew I was being unfair. According to Murdoch, they'd stopped visiting Elspeth because she no longer recognized them.

"I'm sure you mean well," Gwyneth continued, "but I must tell you I'm appalled by your conviction that you have the power to cure the countess's insanity by playing and singing to her!"

"I don't believe my grandmother is completely mad," I protested. "I think that some part of her is trying to return to reality, and I'd like to help her. On at least two occasions I've reached her. This morning—"

"This morning, Maura informed me, the countess had a very bad spell while you were present," Gwyneth interrupted me.

"What's this about the countess?" Murdoch inquired as he came into the dining room. "Is she ill?" He paused on his way to the sideboard, while Gwyneth told him about Maura's complaint, and then sat down at the table without helping himself to any food. With a troubled frown, he said, "I fear you're being very unwise, Kirstie. We in the family have resigned ourselves to the fact that the countess is hopelessly mad. I realize it must hurt you to see her in such a state, but truly, it's kinder to leave her in her madness. You can't bring her out of it, except perhaps to provoke her into some kind of mindless violence. And that would be to risk both your safety and hers."

Murdoch sounded so reasonable, so logical. Nevertheless, I said stubbornly, "I can't give it up just yet. I don't know how I know, but I'm convinced there's still a tiny spark of sanity deep in my grandmother's mind. I think I can fan it to life."

Gwyneth's expression hardened. "Rubbish! Dangerous rubbish. If you won't listen to us, Kirstie, we have no recourse. Murdoch, we must go to the earl. He'll stop Kirstie's visits soon enough."

"I forbid you to do that," Murdoch said sharply. "It would only upset my uncle. Even worse, he'd probably fly into a rage with Kirstie."

Gwyneth's porcelain cheeks turned a dull red. "And of course we mustn't allow the future mistress of Kildrummond to be upset," she snapped. Pushing back her chair, she swept out of the room.

"Oh, dear." I looked at Murdoch, feeling acutely uncomfortable. I'd sensed Gwyneth's jealousy before, although she'd never displayed it so openly. "Thank you for defending me, Murdoch. I hope I haven't caused a quarrel between you and Gwyneth. She has a point, you know. She's as concerned about the countess as I am, and she has a right to inform my grandfather about my visits."

He smiled, reaching out to pat my shoulder. "Don't worry about Gwyneth. I'll have a word with her." He got up to serve himself from the sideboard and sat down again with his plate. "The thing is," he said, after he'd chewed a mouthful of ham, "there's no need to roil the waters with my uncle. I fancy your own common sense will soon tell you you're being unwise. Consider this: after so many visits to the countess, you still can't say positively that she has any awareness of reality. In my opinion, she's merely responded several times, by pure instinct, to a snatch of melody. She always loved music. On the other hand, what worries me is the possibility that, if you persist, you may arouse her into attacking you again." He took my hand, pressing it gently. "Promise me you'll think about what I've been saying."

I was touched by Murdoch's evident concern for me, and grateful to him for not bludgeoning me with his disapproval. "I will," I said. "I really will think about it. I promise."

He patted my hand again and then proceeded to eat a hearty breakfast. As he finished his second cup of tea, he took out his watch and announced, "I'm off. I promised Archie Henries I'd be with him at noon. I told you about him, didn't I? Old friend of mine, down from Edinburgh for a few days. I'm eager to hear the latest town gossip."

"Mind the time. Don't forget we're invited to a ball tonight."

"By Jove, yes, the Fort William garrison ball. I won't forget."

I wasn't unhappy to see Murdoch go off by himself. While he was in the castle he tended to monopolize my time, with chess, or music or rides along the shores of the loch. It was only natural, of course. He'd become bored with his enforced stay at Kildrummond, away from the pleasures of the city. But today I had other plans, which didn't include Murdoch.

I went up to my bedchamber to change into my riding habit. Before I left the room to go to the stables, I delved into the old chest I'd brought from France, which contained some small mementoes of my life in Bassincourt. From it I extracted a small carved and painted box, tucking it into the "pocket" tied around my waist under my skirt.

As I trotted away from the stable yard, uphill in the direction of the glen, I thought rather smugly of how much I'd improved my riding skills since I came to Kildrummond.

Now I had no qualms at all about starting off on a solitary ride. Crossing the river by the wooden bridge, I tethered the horse to a convenient birch tree and began climbing the steep slope to Nanny's cottage in the woods.

The closer I came to the cottage, the more my steps slowed, and the more my reluctance increased. I didn't want to go to the cottage, for fear of an embarrassing scene with Nanny. Yet I felt obligated to go, if only to make certain she wasn't ill. I had an idea that no one in the castle ever bothered to check up on the fey, independent old lady in her lonely cottage in the hills. And I had to find out if Nanny had taken my brooch, one of my few mementoes of my real mother.

In the clearing in which the cottage stood, I knocked on the door, waited briefly, and knocked again. No answer. Nanny wasn't home. Giving in to a guilty relief, I was about to leave when my inconvenient conscience reminded me that Nanny might be lying ill inside the cottage. Or, if she'd stepped out, she might be back at any moment. I pushed open the door and walked in.

Nanny wasn't there. The embers in the fireplace emitted a slight warmth, however. She hadn't been gone long. Feeling like an intruder, I stood in the center of the room looking around me, my eyes inevitably drawn to the cupboard where Nanny kept her treasured memories of Fiona. Slowly I walked over to the cupboard. There in the place of honor on Fiona's "altar," as I'd known it would be, was my brooch. I reached out my hand, then dropped it to my side. I didn't like to take away the brooch without first confronting Nanny. Wouldn't that, in its own way, be a form of theft, too?

However, as I paced back and forth across the room and the minutes lengthened into the half hour and crept toward the hour, I became impatient. After all, the brooch was my property. Even if Nanny had only intended to borrow it, it didn't excuse what she did. I squared my shoulders. Picking up the brooch from the cupboard, I slipped it into my pocket and left the cottage. I'd come back and talk to Nanny another time. On my way out of the clearing I encountered a thin, shabby woman, swathed in the folds of an old shawl. A crofter's wife or daughter, probably, come to obtain a charm or a curing potion from Nanny. I paused to greet the woman and say to her, "If you see Nanny, please tell her Mistress Kirstie was here to visit her." There, I thought, as I walked down the hill to the bridge, now I don't feel quite as furtive about taking away the brooch.

Mounted again, I headed for the glen, leisurely following the river. It was a bright, smiling day. Since my arrival at Kildrummond the weather had been surprisingly fair, according to Murdoch, who once told me gloomily that it usually rained every day in the Highlands, and sometimes twice. There was little breeze today, so I had to brush away several midges, but nothing like the horde of insects that would have been attacking me had the weather been damp.

As I rode along, my thoughts reverted to the day, a week ago now, that Ian had taken me on a tour of my future estate. I still found it hard to believe how much his behavior had altered during those few short days. He'd shed, I hoped forever, his armor of aloofness. When he looked at me, there wasn't a hint of ice in the clear gray depths of his eyes. We were simply friends, or at least on the way to becoming friends.

I saw more of him now. He'd actually taken to joining us in the drawing room before dinner, never saying very much and ignoring the lack of warmth on the part of everyone except myself. On several occasions he'd appeared after dinner in the music room when Murdoch and I were playing duets, listening intently to the music and expressing a quiet word of appreciation before going off to his office and his eternal ledgers.

What would happen to our relationship in the future? I didn't know, wouldn't allow myself to speculate. I only knew that now, as of this moment, I was content with my life.

After I emerged into the glen, I encountered several of the

tenants I'd met during my previous visit with Ian. They interrupted their round of chores—hoeing, herding, mucking the byres, fishing in the stream—to duck their foreheads and smile a shy hello. Some day, I thought with a sudden queasy feeling, I'll be responsible for every soul in this valley.

Turning off to the left, I rode up the little glen where Jock and Meg Cameron had their home.

"Please to come in, Mistress Kirstie." Meg's shy smile couldn't entirely conceal her surprise at seeing me. Probably Gwyneth, or Elspeth before her as mistress of Kildrummond, had never set foot in Jock Cameron's house. Gradually Meg's slight air of constraint faded as she showed me her buttery and her storerooms and her knitting. Over a cup of tea we were soon chatting like old friends. She reminded me a little of Madame de Bassincourt, who, despite her distinguished ancestry, had the common touch, the knack of putting people at ease.

"You've known Ian a long time?" I asked at one point.

"Since he first came to Kildrummond," she replied, nodding. "Poor bairn, set down in this strange place, with his mother dead and his father shamed on the gallows, he got precious little sympathy from—" She broke off, blushing. At last she continued, saying, "He used to sneak away from the castle to follow Jock on his daily rounds. That's when he learned to love Kildrummond, and everything about the running of the estate. Later, after he joined the Black Watch, he'd come to see us when he had leave. He seemed to regard us as family, for all he was our next laird and far above us in station."

I had a sudden memory of my first night at Kildrummond, when Murdoch and I had strolled through the gardens and up to the old ruins. "When Ian comes home on leave," Murdoch had said, "he spends all his time with the tacksmen. He seems to prefer their company to ours. No accounting for tastes, I daresay. Or what one owes to one's family."

How strange, I mused, how two versions of the same event

could be so different in tone and substance. Nevertheless, I was sure both Meg and Murdoch were speaking sincerely when they recalled the circumstances of Ian's infrequent leaves from the Black Watch.

"How is Gavin?" I inquired a little later. "I thought I might see him today."

Meg's face clouded. "He's not very well. He fell into the burn several days ago and caught a chill. His grandmother's been keeping him to his bed."

"I'm sorry." I hesitated. "Could you tell me where he lives? I've brought him a little gift." Reaching into my pocket, I brought out the painted box and opened it. Inside was a set of worn and well-used wooden dominoes. "These were my father's—my foster father's. He taught me how to play when I was very small. During his last illness we had a game every evening after supper."

"I've no doubt Gavin will be enchanted with the dominoes, mistress. But do you not have a great regard for them because they belonged to your foster father? Are you sure you wish to give them to Gavin?"

"Oh, yes. The dominoes are just objects. It's my memories of my foster father that are important."

The hut where Hallie and her son and her mother lived was a short distance up the little glen from Jock Cameron's house. Next to it were a small patch of kale and a plot of potatoes, and a single goat was tethered far enough away to prevent it from eating the young plants. I dismounted and walked to the house, hesitating in the open doorway. The cottage seemed to be larger than the crofters' huts in the valley, consisting of at least two rooms. Instead of an open fire in the floor of the principal room there was a raised fireplace.

A middle-aged woman with a worn, tired face turned away from the hearth as my figure darkened the doorway. "Yes, mistress?" she said rather uncertainly. Though I was wearing the shabby riding habit Madame de Bassincourt had given me, she obviously recognized me as a member of the gentry from beyond the glen.

"I'm Kirstie Cameron. I've come with a little gift for Gavin. I hear he's been ill. Could I see him?"

A flicker of surprise, and yes, some other emotion I couldn't identify, crossed her face. "He's in there, mistress," she said, pointing to the inner room.

Gavin was lying on a pallet in the tiny room, which had just enough space in its windowless interior to accommodate a large box bed and a crude cupboard. He looked up as I entered. He obviously had a fever. His gray eyes, so like Ian's, were overly bright, and his cheeks were flushed.

"Hello, Gavin," I said, kneeling down beside his pallet. "Mistress Cameron tells me you aren't feeling well." I handed him the painted box. "Here's a set of dominoes. I used to enjoy playing with them when I was your age."

He opened the box, fingering the wooden oblongs, clearly pleased by the attention, but dubious, too, about the purpose of the strange spotted objects.

"I'll show you how to play the game when you're feeling better," I assured him. "I think you'll enjoy it. Dominoes is a favorite with French children."

"Ye'll come back soon tae show me the game?" he inquired. An intensely shy expression settled over his flushed face. "Mayhap Maister Ian would like tae play."

"Oh, I fancy Master Ian might be too busy for games," I said quickly. I felt my heart constrict. Hallie must have told Gavin that Ian was his father. Nothing else would account for the boy's look of suppressed yearning. Also, in the ordinary course of events, a crofter's child would hardly have expected any attentions from someone of Ian's rank.

When Gavin had a bad coughing spell I cut short my visit, promising to return soon. As I was about to mount my horse, Hallie came up the path to the cottage. She stopped short when she saw me.

"Good day, Hallie," I said. "I expect you're here to check on Gavin."

"Aye, mistress. The housekeeper is verra kind tae allow me tae come home fer an hour." Hallie's words, as usual, were unexceptional. Her grudging tone was another matter. With Hallie, I always had the impression she was smothering an intense anger whenever she spoke to me.

"I was sorry to hear from Mistress Cameron that Gavin was ill," I said to her. "I hope he's better soon." Nodding, I climbed into the saddle and rode off. I had the uncomfortable sensation that Hallie's hostile eyes were boring into my back, and I had to prevent myself from glancing around to see if she was looking at me.

Perhaps I shouldn't have given into impulse and visited Gavin, I thought uneasily. Not only because I should have realized Hallie would feel resentful, but also because it might be unwise to get too close to the boy. What if I were unable to keep up the contact? Gavin would believe I'd snatched my friendship away. And I knew in my bones that my grandfather and Gwyneth and Murdoch and possibly Ian himself would disapprove of any relationship with Gavin, both because of the chasm of rank that separated us and because it might cause gossip, especially among the other tenants.

"Sae I was i' the richt," said Emily. "Nanny had yer brooch." Her deft fingers paused in the arrangement of my hair, and her eyes met mine in the mirror of my dressing table. "Wha' will ye do aboot it?"

"I don't know. Nothing, I think. I simply can't bring myself to accuse her of theft. My grandfather might actually decide to evict her from her cottage. And I really don't think she's entirely responsible for her actions."

"Aye." Emily nodded. "Puir auld soul, she may be turning a wee bit daft like yer grandmither." Returning to my coiffure, she tucked two of Fiona's jeweled ornaments into my

163

hair, saying, "There, now, mistress, I've finished. Ye look bonny. Lady Allendale's gown suits ye fine."

I glanced down with a pleased smile at the sack back dress of shot silk in an amber yellow with a matching petticoat and stomacher, lavishly trimmed with pleated silk brocaded with tiny multicolored flowers. It had been necessary for Nanny to unpick the back pleats and rearrange them to bring the gown into the mode. Fortunately Nanny's handiwork had caused no damage to the delicate fabric. Like most gowns meant for formal wear, Gwyneth's dress had been stitched with large running stitches, specifically to allow for later re-modeling.

"Ye'll be the bonniest and the best-dressed lady at the ball," Emily said with satisfaction. "All those officers in their red coats will swarm aboot ye like bees around a honey pot!"

I laughed, shaking my head. "I daresay nobody would accuse you of being prejudiced." I bent down to pick up Daffy, who was finding the delicate silken trimmings on my gown, fluttering gently with each slight movement of air, well-nigh irresistible.

"Be careful o' that dratted beastie's claws, mistress. Ye dinna want him tae put a rent in yer gown," said Emily as she went to the door to answer a knock.

"I maun speak tae the mistress," came Hallie's voice.

As she stepped into the room, one glance at her tightly compressed lips and her rigid shoulders led me to say, "You can go, Emily. I'll see Hallie alone."

After Emily left, I remained seated in my chair, stroking a purring Daffy. A contemptuous flick of her eyes showed me what she thought of a grown woman fondling a kitten. "Well, Hallie? What is it?"

She'd been holding one hand behind her back. Now she brought the hand forward. "I came tae gi'e ye this." She handed me the painted box of dominoes.

"The dominoes were a gift to Gavin," I said, looking straight into her angry eyes.

"I dinna want ye tae give Gavin gifts."

"Why not?"

"Because we dinna need yer charity. Gavin and me, we can take care o' oursel', wi'out any help frae ye, and we dinna need yer friendship, forbye."

I winced at the raw emotions in her face and voice. Bitterness, anger, jealousy, she was eaten up with them. "Very well, Hallie, you're Gavin's mother. I can't force you to allow him to accept the dominoes."

She nodded curtly, sketching a curtsy, and turned to go. As she opened the door she came face-to-face with Ian, standing outside in the corridor. He was wearing a black velvet coat and breeches laced in gold. A three-cornered hat was tucked under his arm and his hair was powdered and curled. He looked, quite simply, breathtaking.

"Good day, Hallie," he said, his eye slipping away from her after a casual glance. "Is Mistress—? Oh, there you are, Kirstie," he added, walking past Hallie into the room. "I came to tell you it's time to leave for the ball. The carriage is waiting."

"I'm ready to go." Still holding the kitten, I stood up, shaking out my silken skirts.

"You look beautiful, Kirstie. That color becomes you." He came closer, reaching out his hand to stroke the kitten. "Daffy's grown since the day you rescued him by the bridge," he observed. Laughing, he added, "Have you noticed that your gown is almost exactly the same color as Daffy's fur? Hallie, isn't that so?"

"Aye, Maister Ian. Sae they be," Hallie replied stolidly. "Ye'll excuse me, mistress?" She stalked out of the bedchamber.

Ian didn't seem to notice anything unusual about Hallie's behavior, or, if he did, he didn't say anything. However, I'd caught the expression of desolate rage on her face when she'd glanced from Ian in his black and gold magnificence to me in my amber-colored ball gown.

* * *

The road between Kildrummond and Fort William was every bit as rough as I remembered it from the day of my arrival at the castle. Murdoch and Ian cannily elected to ride, leaving me and Gwyneth to commiserate with each other as we were bounced from one side of the carriage to the other.

"I daresay by the time there's a civilized road along Loch Linnhe, I shall be in my grave," Gwyneth muttered between clenched teeth. "I pray every day that Ian will miraculously clear up our financial affairs so we can get away from this place for a little while."

If the carriage ride was a trial, the warmth of our reception at the ballroom of the Fort William garrison more than made up for it. The huge room, lit by a myriad of candles, was dazzling in its brilliance and color, the silks and velvets and brocades of the civilian guests contrasting with the scarlet coats of the officers. And when I was surrounded by a circle of junior officers, all clamoring for a dance, I was reminded of Emily's analogy of the bees around the honey pot. I set myself to enjoying every minute of my newfound popularity.

Before starting out for Fort William, I'd had a few uneasy moments, wondering if I'd be the object of curious glances and muttered comments in the aftermath of the quarrel between Murdoch and Ian at the Kildrummond ball. Many of the officers and their guests had been present at the ball. However, to my relief, I wasn't aware of any gossipy attention as the evening wore on. Perhaps the sight of Murdoch and Ian, squiring me in at least surface amiability, had put an end to the speculation. My grandfather had apparently instructed Murdoch not to continue the quarrel, and he'd obeyed. He and Ian had been observing a wary truce when they were in each other's company.

"Do you realize I practically had to challenge Lieutenant Mainwaring to a duel in order to snatch this dance with you?" Murdoch complained toward the middle of the evening as he led me out for a folk dance. "You're becoming entirely too popular, Kirstie. I believe I'll suggest to the earl that we keep you hidden away in the castle before one of these young sprigs tries to spirit you away from us!"

"I haven't the slightest intention of eloping to Gretna Green with anyone, if that's what you have in mind," I retorted.

At the end of the dance, Murdoch whisked me off the floor and out the door of the ballroom.

"Murdoch!" I protested. "Where are we going? I've promised the next dance."

"Whoever he is, he can wait a bit." Holding my hand fast in his, Murdoch led me down the corridor, looking first into one room and then another. "Card room's full of idiot gamblers," he muttered. "Ah, here we are. Now for a little privacy."

"Murdoch, what on earth . . . ?" We were in a tiny room containing a battered desk and several cabinets. The regimental adjutant's office, more than likely.

Murdoch smiled at me. He was so handsome in his green brocade, his height and bearing reminding me, as I'd been reminded before, of the basic resemblance among himself and Ian and my grandfather. "I opened my mouth a bit ago, Kirstie, trying to be amusing, and ended up like Saint Paul on the road to Damascus, seeing the light."

I gazed at him, thoroughly bewildered.

"Remember my little joke about keeping you shut up in Kildrummond to prevent one of your admirers from eloping with you? Kirstie, what a blind idiot I've been. I love you. I've loved you for a long time. I just didn't realize it. If you elope with anyone, it had better be with me!"

He put out his hands to me and I backed away. "No, please, Murdoch, don't say anymore. You're my friend, my kind, caring friend, but not my lover. I've never thought of you that way."

He caught my hand. "But you'll think about it now? You'll

see, it'll come to you, as it did to me, like a thunderclap. One moment you were my sweet, amusing companion, the next, I knew I was head over heels in love with you." He shook his head, smiling whimsically. "At my age, too! It never happened to me before."

"Murdoch, listen to me," I said, gently pulling my hand away. "I'm very fond of you, and I always will be, but I'm sure I'll never be in love with you. Let's not talk about it anymore. Come, I think we should return to the ballroom."

I walked to the door and opened it. Murdoch caught up with me as I stepped out into the corridor. "Kirstie, is there someone else?" His eyes widened. "It's not Ian?"

"Ian!" I could feel my cheeks burning. "Of course not. Why would you say such a thing?"

He laughed, putting his arms around me. "I'm sorry, love. I was being stupid—and a bit jealous." He bent his head to kiss me. His lips were warm and experienced and ardent. The difference between his kiss and Ian's was the difference between sitting in cozy comfort beside a hearth fire and being plunged into the flames.

I pulled away from him, saying breathlessly, "Murdoch— someone will see us," and stared straight into Gwyneth's eyes. She'd turned a pasty white beneath her carefully applied paint, and her mouth was working, though she didn't say anything. I pushed past her in the direction of the ballroom, walking faster and faster until I realized that people were staring at me in my blind haste. Then I slowed down.

"Kirstie, what is it?"

I looked up at Ian in surprise. I hadn't realized he was anywhere near. "Nothing, nothing," I muttered.

He glanced down the corridor, his lips compressing as he saw Murdoch and Gwyneth coming toward us. He tucked my hand under his arm, saying, "I hope you haven't forgotten this is my dance."

My fingers tightened on his arm. I felt my agitation vanishing. "No, I hadn't forgotten."

It was my first dance with Ian, ever. It was a minuet. In a dreamlike state, I walked through the slow, graceful, intricate figures, conscious only of the close, compelling clasp of his hand, the intensity of his gaze when we looked at each other during the stately pauses. If we spoke, I don't remember what we said. We had no need for charming compliments and well-turned phrases. At the end of the dance, when we sank to the floor in a last bow and curtsy, our lips met in the formal kiss. And met again and clung, until I heard the ghost of a laugh from somewhere behind me and hastily drew away. I looked about me. No one had observed me and Ian, I thought, except the merry-faced woman moving away on the arm of her partner, who smiled and put a playful finger to her lips in a silent promise of discretion.

After I'd placed the amber-colored ball gown in the wardrobe, I put on my night shift and sat down at the dressing table to brush the powder out of my hair. Knowing we'd be very late coming back from the officers' ball at Fort William, I'd ordered Emily, against her objections, not to wait up for me.

My hand paused in its slow brushing. I looked into the mirror, smiling at the telltale glow in my face. Murdoch's proposal, with all its possibilities for future embarrassment, and Gwyneth's latest fit of jealousy couldn't cloud the joy I felt tonight. Without words, Ian and I had drawn closer together. Whatever happened in the future, this was the happiest night of my life.

I heard a faint tap at the door, and the sound of hurried footsteps. When I opened the door, I looked down at the steaming cup of milk in its saucer and began to laugh. Emily! She never disobeyed orders, but she usually found a way to get around the ones she didn't approve of. I'd told her not to wait up for me. This was her way of showing me what she thought of that.

Picking up the milk, I shut the door and headed for my comfortable chair by the window. Daffy intercepted me, brushing against my leg and mewing hungrily. "You've got a bottomless pit instead of a stomach," I said severely, bending down to pour some of the milk into his saucer. "Mind now, it's hot."

I sat down, placing the milk on the table next to my chair, and stretched out comfortably. Before I could raise the cup to my lips I heard a choking sound. I turned my head to see Daffy's tiny body in convulsions.

Chapter IX

Early the next morning, before the household was awake, I brought Daffy back to the place where I'd found him, beside the bridge over the rushing little river. Wrapping him snugly in my old shawl with its many pulled threads from his tiny claws, I put him into the shallow hole I'd dug out with a sharp piece of rock. I patted the damp earth firmly over him and then placed on the little grave a bunch of march marigolds that matched almost exactly the tawny yellow of Daffy's fur.

The flowers blurred as the scalding tears started to flow. I buried my face in my hands, mourning for Daffy, yes, but also for myself.

Daffy was dead, and so would I have been, if I hadn't given him some of the milk that was meant for me. I had to face a sickening truth: someone at Kildrummond hated me enough to want me dead, and I believed I knew who it was.

I thought back over the scattered acts of malice that had dogged me since my arrival at the castle. The warning note that first night: "We don't want you here. Why don't you go?" My clothing scattered over the floor. The pages torn out of my Bible. The damage to my lovely green taffeta. The incidents hadn't been life threatening. Unpleasant, frightening, yes. It had unnerved me to realize I was the object of an unreasoning dislike from the moment I arrived at Kildrummond, but from the first I'd seen the persecution as the act of petty spite on the part of someone who didn't dare to express his or her feelings openly.

Almost from the first I'd suspected Hallie. Anyone with eyes in his head could see she worshiped Ian. Apparently she'd sensed, at her first sight of us together, that there was some kind of a bond between Ian and me.

Whoever had committed those minor acts of vandalism had to be someone who lived in the castle and whose appearance in or near my rooms wouldn't have to be explained. Hallie. Her duties took her frequently to my bedchamber. Yesterday, for example. I drew a sharp breath. She'd burst in on me, smarting with anger and resentment, in order to thrust back in my face the set of dominoes I'd given Gavin. While she was in my room, Ian had arrived to escort me to the officers' ball at Fort William, the kind of glamorous event that Hallie had never been able, and never would be able, to attend. In front of Hallie, Ian had told me I looked beautiful, and then, with a few casual remarks, he'd hinted at the growing intimacy between us. "Daffy's grown since that day you rescued him at the bridge," he said, and "Have you noticed that your gown is almost exactly the color of Daffy's fur?"

Already angry and jealous, brooding for hours after Ian and I had left for the ball, Hallie had crept to my door in the dead of night with the poisoned milk that I would probably assume, and did assume, had been left by Emily.

The sky had been overcast with dark clouds when I'd crept out of the house this morning to bury Daffy. I hadn't wanted Emily to see his stiffened little body. I planned to tell her I'd found the kitten dead, apparently of natural causes, when I woke up. Now a fine drizzle began to fall as I sat on the riverbank, but I didn't get up. Drawing up my legs, I pulled my shawl over my hair and rested my head on my knees, while I tried to fathom the enormity of what Hallie had done and decide what I should do about it.

Although I'd sensed her hostility from the outset, it had

never entered my head that she might try to kill or injure me. It still seemed out of character, almost the act of a mad-woman. Wait. My forehead furrowed with the intensity of my thoughts. Was it possible that Hallie had put a nonfatal potion in my milk, hoping merely to make me wretchedly ill? A potion that wasn't strong enough to kill me, a grown woman, but which had been lethal to Daffy's tiny body?

Very well. Supposing, then, that Hallie hadn't intended to kill me. What she'd tried to do was cruel and irresponsible enough. What was I to do about it? I had no proof. Without that, my grandfather could hardly turn her over to the authorities, although, knowing him, I thought it likely he'd ask Jock Cameron to throw Hallie off his leasehold. My sense of justice rebelled against that. Gavin would suffer, for one thing. For another, there was that small chance that Hallie wasn't guilty, that another person had poisoned my milk. Above all, reporting Hallie would cause a terrible scandal, not only at Kildrummond but throughout the countryside. On the other hand, did I have the right to ignore her conduct completely? Her continuing jealous resentment might prompt her into still more dangerous attempts on me.

While I was still wrestling with my dilemma, the fine cold drizzle turned into a heavier rain, which I ignored. After an interval I heard a familiar voice above me, near the bridge.

"Dinna keep blethering at me, woman, I canna help ye," Nanny was saying impatiently.

Another voice spoke, indistinctly. Then came the sound of a scuffle, followed by a sharp cry of pain. Jumping to my feet, I scrambled up the bank to the path. Nanny was walking rapidly away from me across the bridge. Behind her, a shab-bily dressed woman—a crofter's wife or daughter, I presumed; she looked vaguely familiar—lay sprawled on the ground, clutching at her arm. "She pushed me, auld Janet pushed me," the woman muttered. "My arm hurts. I only wanted ane o' her potions, but she wouldna even speak tae me."

173

I knelt beside the woman, running my hand over her arm, which didn't appear to be broken. Probably she'd fallen on it, bruising or spraining it, when Nanny pushed her. "I think you'll be all right," I told the woman. "Do you need help getting home?"

"Nay, mistress, I thank ye."

I ran across the bridge, catching sight of Nanny's slight figure ahead of me on the path leading to the stables. "Nanny. Janet Cumming," I called. She didn't turn her head. I hurried after her, catching up with her at the curve where the path made its last plunge to the stable area. "Nanny, I want to talk to you," I said, placing a hand on her arm.

She whirled, her face so twisted with fury that I recoiled. There was no trace about her of the gentle, wistful creature who'd welcomed her beloved Fiona's daughter to Kildrummond with such joy. "Dinna touch me, ye wicked woman," she said fiercely. "Ha' ye no' done harm enow?"

Trying to keep my voice soothing, I said, "Are you talking about my mother's brooch, Nanny? You know I took it from your cottage, don't you? I'd planned to come see you about that. Now, of course, you'd like to have the brooch as another remembrance of Fiona, but you must realize, surely, that it belongs to me, and—"

"Haud yer wheesht. I willna speak tae ye aboot my bonny Fiona, after wha' ye did." She turned on her heel, and when I again put out my hand to stop her, she gave me a violent shove, causing me to lose my balance and fall. I wasn't hurt, I was merely too surprised for a moment to get to my feet. When I did rise, I stood watching Nanny's departing figure, making no attempt to follow her.

What had come over the old lady? Was she growing senile, so much so she'd convinced herself that the brooch was hers and I had stolen it? My flesh began to creep. Could Nanny have poisoned my milk with one of the potions she was always concocting from herbs and weeds and other ingredients too ghastly to think about? Toads came to mind. I shuddered.

When she returned to her cottage yesterday, she must have missed the brooch, and if the crofter woman I'd met as I was leaving the clearing had delivered my message, Nanny knew well enough who'd taken it. Had she come to my bedchamber last night while I was at the ball, looking for the brooch? And when she didn't find it—because I was wearing it—had she determined to take revenge by doctoring my milk to make me ill, or worse?

I began walking slowly toward the stables, ignoring the rain that had replaced the drizzle, while I sorted out my dark thoughts. It was no less distressing to think that Nanny, rather than Hallie, might have tried to harm me, but on the whole I found it easier to believe. My mind had balked at the idea that Hallie had gone to such an extreme. I'd always sensed her anger and resentment and jealousy, and I still believed she'd torn the pages out of my Bible and damaged that lovely length of taffeta, but underneath her roiling emotions there was a core of common sense. She was spiteful, but I doubted very much that she was a killer. You simply didn't murder a woman you suspected of stealing your lover's affections. But Nanny . . . Nanny'd become irrational during the past few days, since the evening of the Kildrummond ball when she'd fallen into that terrifying trance.

"Good God, Kirstie, where've you been?"

I stared blankly at Murdoch. While I'd been so preoccupied, my feet had carried me through the rear entrance of the house behind the grand staircase and into the foyer.

"You're wet through," Murdoch went on, removing the soggy shawl from my shoulders. "Your abigail and I have been worried about you. When you didn't appear for breakfast, I went up to your bedchamber. I wanted to talk to you. Your abigail—Emily, is that her name?—told me you must have gone out at the first light of dawn and hadn't returned. Kirstie, is there anything wrong?"

"No," I said. The lie came fairly easily. Once again I'd retreated to the position I'd taken after I received that first warning note. I had no proof that Nanny or Hallie had tried to harm me or intimidate me, and I wasn't going to accuse either of them. "I don't understand why you and Emily were concerned," I continued. "I went out for my morning walk and lost track of the time."

"But it's raining!"

"I like rain. I'm famished now, though. I wish I hadn't missed breakfast."

Murdoch smiled indulgently. "I daresay Cook can find something for you. First, though . . . Kirstie, you didn't go tramping out in the rain because you were upset with me, did you?"

"Why would I—oh," I exclaimed, startled. The events of last night at the Fort William ball had slipped from my mind. I hadn't once thought of Murdoch's proposal. "No, I'm not upset with you."

Murdoch looked relieved. "I was afraid I'd offended you when I kissed you. I couldn't help myself. You're irresistible, you know."

"Murdoch, I told you last night—"

"I know what you said last night." He placed his hands on my shoulders and looked down at me with an expression compounded almost equally between hope and uncertainty. "You may not want to make a decision about marriage at this moment, but I'm quite willing to wait. Well, I'm sure you've guessed I'm a gambling man! I'm gambling you'll come to love me as much as I love you."

"Good heavens, Kirstie, you look as bedraggled as a scullery maid. A visitor would think you *were* a scullery maid!"

At the unexpected sound of Gwyneth's voice I stepped back from Murdoch, hoping my face didn't register the twinge of guilt I felt when I saw the pinched look on her face. If she'd meant her comment to be light and teasing, she hadn't succeeded. That look and the unguarded expression in her eyes gave her away. There was no reason for me to feel guilty. I had no designs on Murdoch, and Gwyneth had no grounds for her jealousy. However, I could hardly tell her that without plunging both of us into a hideously embarrassing scene.

"I apologize, Gwyneth," I said. "I must look a sight. I've been foolishly walking in the rain. I'll go right upstairs and change before anyone else sees me."

As I approached my corridor in the west pavilion, I was resigned to finding Emily waiting for me, primed for a scold when she saw my damp garments. However, making the turn into the corridor, I came to a dead stop. I'd caught a fleeting glimpse of Nanny as she opened the door of my bedchamber and went inside. I didn't move. I didn't want another confrontation with Nanny so soon after the last one. Coming to a quick decision, I slipped into one of the vacant rooms along the corridor and waited for the old nurse to leave my bedchamber.

Afterward I realized I hadn't been thinking clearly. Nanny had refused to talk to me only a short while ago. Therefore, she hadn't come to my rooms for any kind of conversation. But that didn't occur to me as I waited in the empty bedchamber with the door slightly ajar, thankful that I wouldn't have to talk to her just yet. It was only when she passed by the door, weeping softly and fondling an object in her hands, that it dawned on me why she'd come to my room. She'd come to steal back my mother's brooch.

Conscious of a sudden stab of anger, I opened the door and stepped into the corridor. "Nanny, wait a moment. I want to talk to you," I called. She ignored me completely, neither turning her head nor slowing her steps. It didn't occur to me that she might be so immersed in her tormented, irrational thoughts that she literally wasn't conscious of those around her.

Really angry now, I started after her, determined to take back the brooch. To my surprise, she didn't take any of the staircases to the lower floors. Instead, she made a quick turn into a narrow staircase leading to the floor above, which housed, so far as I knew, only the servants' bedchambers. Why was she going up there? Not to visit one of the servants, surely. They'd all be busy elsewhere in the house at this time of day.

My curiosity piqued, I started up the stairs after her. She was already out of sight when I reached the head of the staircase, and I looked about me uncertainly, wondering where she'd gone. Then I noticed still another stairway on my left, which probably led to the top floor of the house and the attics.

I crept up this stairway, emerging to find myself in a very narrow dark corridor lined with closed doors. Except for one, from behind which, as I approached, I heard a low-voiced muttering and the sound of heavy objects being moved.

Cautiously I approached the open door and peered into a large room, lit only by a pair of tiny, cobwebbed windows high in one wall. The room appeared to be a storeroom filled with discarded furniture and trunks and portmanteaux of various sizes. Nanny was moving about the room, pushing aside a chair here, a battered chest there, to gain access to the row of trunks ranged along the far wall. I stepped over the threshold, standing quietly near the door as I watched her, expecting at every moment she'd notice my presence. She didn't.

Keeping up a steady, monotonous murmuring, Nanny opened one trunk after the other, reaching deep within each one to pull out part of the contents. She then stuffed the items haphazardly back into each trunk and slammed the lids shut. Toward the end of the row, she apparently came upon a trunk or portmanteau that was locked. Looking wildly around her, she lurched over to one of the chests, picking up an object which I couldn't see clearly in the dim light, and proceeded to pound on the locked trunk with it. She was obviously trying to break the lock, or, most likely, to wrench it from its hinges. The pounding went on and on, and I wondered where the frail old lady was finding the strength to keep it up.

Suddenly she stopped, dropping something with a heavy thud—whatever she'd been using to pound with, I supposed—and heaved up the cover of the trunk. She began pulling out the contents, and then, suddenly, she sank down on the floor, leaning her head against the trunk. The sound of her desolate sobbing filled the room.

At length Nanny rose to her feet and began walking toward the door. I tensed as she approached me, but from the groping movements of her arms I guessed that the flood of tears pouring down her face had half blinded her. At any rate she apparently didn't see me. She passed within inches of me and went out the door.

I took a hasty step toward the doorway and then paused. Nanny was in such great distress. I knew I ought to go after her. However, my curiosity overcame my scruples. What had the old nurse been looking for? I made my way through the obstacles of old furniture to the row of trunks against the wall. Narrowing my eyes to see better in the poor light from the cobwebbed windows, I opened several of the trunks. They seemed to be filled with castoff clothing. Nanny had been careless in returning the garments to their proper places. The skirt of a gown protruded from beneath the lid of one trunk, the sleeve of a mildewed velvet coat from another. On the floor beside one of the trunks was an old-fashioned full-bottomed wig, in a style that was out of date by at least fifty years.

My foot brushed against an object on the floor. It was a massive pewter candlestick, heavy enough to rip the hinges from the lock of the trunk in front of me. Raising the lid, I saw that this piece of luggage, like all the others, was filled with clothing. I knelt down beside the trunk. I pulled out a motley collection of garments: a long cloak lined with fur, several gowns of brocade and silk, an embroidered petticoat with built-in paniers, a small lace shoulder cape, or pallatine,

179

some linen shifts. The same type of old-fashioned clothing that filled the other trunks. Mystified, I replaced the garments and stood up. What on earth had Nanny been searching for? Whatever it was, she hadn't found it. The locked trunk at the end of the row had apparently been her last hope, and when it, too, failed her she'd fallen into a fresh paroxysm of grief.

I sensed rather than heard a movement behind me. There was a flash of excruciating pain and then I plunged into oblivion. Moments—minutes?—later I opened my eyes to find myself supine on the floor of the attic room. Something hurt. It hurt like fury. I lifted my fingers to the back of my head and felt a patch of wetness.

I pulled myself to my feet by catching at the side of the trunk beside me. Bracing myself against a chair, a chest, a settee, I tottered slowly across the room to the door. My thought processes seemed glutinous. Ideas kept slipping away. But one thing I knew: Nanny must be losing her mind. She'd come back to the storeroom, found me kneeling beside one of the trunks, and promptly attacked me. Why? She didn't need a rational reason. Perhaps she simply resented the fact that I'd followed her into the attics. She was probably dangerous, either to herself or to others. I had to get to her.

Running my hand against the wall of the corridor for support, moving largely by instinct, I inched into the staircase leading from the attics, reached the third floor and the servants' quarters without encountering anyone and headed down the stairs to the family rooms on the second floor.

"There you are, Kirstie. I must talk to you about Nanny."

I blinked, trying to focus. There seemed to be two Murdochs. I croaked, "Nanny . . . ?"

"Yes, Nanny. I just met her in the gardens. She was wild, talking gibberish. Something about settling scores, whatever that might mean. Kirstie, she had this."

I stared blearily at the object in his hand. I was looking at my brooch.

180

"It's yours, isn't it? I was sure I recognized it. What was Nanny doing with your brooch?"

"Murdoch, you ass," came Ian's incisive voice. "Can't you see Kirstie's hurt?" I sagged gratefully against his chest. Even in that moment of extremity I noticed his distinctive clean masculine odor. He gently touched the back of my head and drew a quick breath. "What—who did this, Kirstie?"

"Nanny . . . I think she hit me." I bit my lip to keep from fainting. "She took my brooch."

Murdoch's voice sounded incredulous. "She hit you? Oh, God, I suppose we should have known it would come to this. All those spells and charms, and the reading of the cards, and her belief she merely had to touch an object to know all about the owner . . . she must have started to believe in her own powers, and now she's gone queer in her attic. Well, it makes no difference that she was devoted to Fiona. We've put up with enough from her. I'll go see my uncle immediately. We'll have her transported, or better yet, clapped into a madhouse."

"Murdoch, wait," I said weakly as he charged off down the corridor. Before I could say any more, a wave of faintness swept over me. The next thing I knew, I was lying in a bed. My own bed, I thought, opening one eye enough to glimpse my familiar bed hangings. My head felt as if it had swollen to twice its normal size.

"Hold still, Kirstie," came Ian's quiet voice. "I'll try not to hurt you, but I must see if your injury is serious." I winced as he rubbed the back of my head with something cool and damp. He was removing the caked blood from my wound, I supposed. Then I felt the careful touch of his fingers, probing the area around the contusion. "It's all right, I think," he said with relief. "The skin is broken, that's all, and your head may ache for a while. Don't move too quickly," he cautioned, as I turned my body from one side to the other so I could look up at him as he stood beside the bed.

My mind was much clearer now, though a hammer deep

181

inside my head was pounding insistently. There was something I had to do. I caught at Ian's hand. He eased himself to a sitting position on the side of the bed, clasping my hand closely. "What is it? You needn't talk about what happened until you feel better, you know."

"Might I inquire, Ian, what you're doing in Kirstie's bedchamber?"

At the icy sound of my grandfather's voice, Ian rose to face the door. The earl was standing on the threshold, flanked by Murdoch and Gwyneth, who looked as if she'd been interrupted while dressing for dinner. Her hair, usually so perfectly arranged, hung limply on her shoulders.

"Kirstie fainted, sir," said Ian quietly. "I brought her to her bedchamber. Unfortunately, her abigail wasn't here."

"I'll send for Emily immediately," Gwyneth assured the earl. Nevertheless, she lingered, as if mesmerized by the drama of the situation.

"Kirstie fainted?" said the earl sharply. "Murdoch said something about Nanny attacking her. I didn't realize . . . Are you badly hurt, Kirstie? Shall we send for the surgeon from Fort William?"

"I don't think that's necessary," said Ian. "The wound's not serious. Kirstie simply needs rest."

"Doctor Cameron, is it?" Murdoch glared at Ian.

"No, I'm not a surgeon, Murdoch, but I've seen a good many wounded men on the battlefield. Kirstie shows no signs of a bad head wound."

"I'm happy to hear it," said the earl. He walked over to my bed. "I came here to learn the details of this attack, my dear Kirstie, but that can wait until you're feeling stronger. We'll talk tomorrow. However, before I go, I want you to know that Janet Cumming will be punished, and punished severly, for what she did." He patted my hand perfunctorily. "And now I think we should leave you to your rest. Come along, all of you."

"Ian, please stay for a moment." The words slipped out of me involuntarily.

If a pin had dropped in the ensuing silence, the sound would have been perfectly audible. At length my grandfather said coldly, "As you wish, my dear. Ian, I trust you won't stay too long."

After the earl had left with Murdoch and Gwyneth, Ian brought up a chair next to the bed and sat down. His face was still, but the gray eyes were no longer cold. "Can I help, Kirstie?"

My fingers clutched Ian's arm. "Don't let my grandfather and Murdoch punish Nanny," I begged. "She wasn't responsible for what she did. She was upset and angry over the brooch and she lashed out at me. I was angry, too. Now that I'm thinking more clearly, though, I know she never meant to hurt me. She cared too much for my mother. I'm sure she'll be herself again soon. She's not mad, or criminal, either. She's disturbed. Please, will you help her?"

He took both of my hands in his. "I won't let anything bad happen to old Nanny," he murmured. "You believe me, don't you?"

I nodded my head mutely. My tension and even most of my pain seemed to disappear. It felt so normal, so natural, to have Ian sitting beside me, holding my hands and assuring me that everything would be all right.

Chapter X

I stayed in bed for two days after Nanny attacked me with the pewter candlestick. On the third morning, feeling quite well except for a tender spot on the back of my head, I disregarded Emily's protests and went to visit Elspeth, taking my cittern.

I played several songs for her, and then my fingers trailed off the strings of the cittern in a discordant chord. My grandmother made no sign that she'd heard me. She remained limply in her chair, her head sagging against the backrest, her eyes closed.

My eyes filled with tears. If I hadn't seen the slight rise and fall of her chest, indicating that she was breathing, I could easily have assumed she was dead. Never in all the visits I'd made to her had she seemed this divorced from reality. It was a crushing blow to see her like this, especially since I'd arrived this morning so full of anticipation, remembering how she'd responded on my last visit, only a few days ago. She'd spoken to me, she'd actually played a few bars of *"Cuir, A Chinn Dilis."* I'd dared to hope I was getting through to her.

I brushed away the film of tears with the back of my hand and rose, putting the cittern in its case. "It's one of her bad days, I fear," I said to Maura Fraser. "Perhaps she'll be feeling better the next time I come."

"Mayhap she won't," Maura replied sourly. "Have you considered it might be your visits, with you plunking away at her with that silly cittern, that have put her into this state?" The familiar note of hostility was in her voice, and something else I couldn't quite define. It couldn't be satisfaction. Why should she be pleased that my grandmother had regressed to a comatose state? Surely she didn't resent my visits so much that she preferred to see her beloved countess totally unresponsive to her surroundings?

I shook my head, swallowing against the lump in my throat, and left the room without replying. It was useless to argue with Maura. *But I'll be back,* I vowed, walking along the corridor to my bedchamber. *I won't give up yet.* Somehow my protestations had a hollow ring. It was more difficult than usual this morning to keep my spirits up. For one thing, I'd developed a dull headache.

"Ye look sae pale, Mistress Kirstie," said Emily, peering at me anxiously as I entered the bedchamber. "Ye should spend anither day in yer bed."

"Nonsense. I'm perfectly fit." I put the cittern case in its usual place beside the wardrobe. As I turned away, my foot brushed against the little basket. My voice broke slightly as I said, "Emily, please take Daffy's bed away."

"Aye, mistress." The abigail's long bony face was expressionless. She knew me very well, she must have wondered why I'd crept out at dawn to bury Daffy, not to return for hours. She'd been appalled, too, to learn about Nanny's mysterious attack on me. Uncharacteristically, however, Emily hadn't deluged me with questions. Evidently she'd realized I was deeply affected by something I couldn't bring myself to talk about. With a completely un-Emilylike forbearance, she'd kept silent.

Actually, I thought, going down the stairs to my first family breakfast since my enforced stay in bed, I was less agitated than I would have been had my initial suspicions been correct. If I'd continued to believe that Hallie had deliberately tried to murder me, I'd now be in a state bordering on frenzy. I'd be going about in fear of my life, unable, or unwilling, to accuse Hallie because I had no proof, convinced that at any time, without warning, she might launch another attack. It was easier, and curiously more comforting, to think that Nanny, in a fit of temporary derangement, had struck out at me. Of course it wouldn't happen again. Nanny would soon revert to her normal self. And Hallie might continue to play her spiteful tricks on me, but they weren't life threatening, and perhaps I could find a way to spike her guns.

Gwyneth looked up with an air of surprise as I came into the dining room. "Oh. Kirstie. You're feeling more the thing today?" She was merely going through the motions of civility. During my brief spell of invalidism, she'd visited me every day. Her manner then had been chilly, too. Basically she'd reverted to the dutiful, distant politeness of my first days at the castle. Her attitude was wrongheaded and exasperating, but there was nothing I could do about it. She'd fixed it firmly in her head that I was her rival for Murdoch's affections.

"I feel very well, thank you, Gwyneth." I helped myself to tea and rolls at the sideboard.

When Murdoch appeared a few moments later, he was effusive in his greetings. "You're recovered, Kirstie! I know you said last night you planned to get up today, but I was convinced that your abigail would never allow you to leave your bed. What an ogre that woman is!"

"Oh, Emily tried her best," I said, laughing. "I had to be firm with her, though it's difficult to argue with someone you've known from your cradle." I was suddenly reminded of Nanny and her years of devotion to Fiona. "Murdoch, did you hear anything of Nanny this morning?"

His pleasant face turned grim. "No. She still hasn't returned to her cottage. Don't worry. This is the only home she has. Eventually she'll come back, and then we'll deal with her."

I opened my mouth to protest and closed it again. Ian had promised me to keep Nanny from harm. I trusted him to do it.

"Well, now, Kirstie, what shall we do today?" said Murdoch, about to raise a forkful of cold ham to his mouth. "Would you like to ride? No, I daresay that might be a bit strenuous. We'll have a game of chess, and after that we can polish that little French madrigal."

"Oh, Murdoch, I'm sorry. It sounds very pleasant. Perhaps another time? Last night Ian invited me to ride into the glen with him today, and I accepted."

"Oh. I see. I would have thought it was too rough a ride. . . . Of course, you must please yourself." His face wooden, Murdoch concentrated on his breakfast. As he got up to leave, he said, "I almost forgot, Kirstie. I looked in on the earl before breakfast. He gave me a message for you. If you feel up to it, he'd like to speak to you this morning."

"This morning?" I looked at Murdoch doubtfully. "He never comes down from his rooms until the afternoon."

"He wishes to see you in his sitting room. I daresay he won't keep you long. You'll be in good time for your ride with Ian."

After Murdoch left, Gwyneth remarked, "You and Ian seem to have become very friendly of late. I recall a time when you barely spoke to each other. Apparently his rough edges don't grate on you anymore."

I gave her a composed look. "Sometimes initial impressions are wrong. If Ian has any 'rough edges,' I haven't noticed them."

"Really?" Gwyneth raised an eyebrow. "How odd. You must see a side of Ian that's concealed from the rest of us." I thought I heard a note of smugness in her cool voice. Perhaps it had occurred to her that my growing friendship with Ian might distract me from any interest in Murdoch.

Later that morning, having changed into my old riding habit, I stood before my grandfather's door, nervously tapping my riding crop against my hand. What did this unexpected summons by the earl mean? I'd never before set foot in his apartment. His valet answered my knock. He ushered me into a large sitting room, rather overfurnished with heavy old-fashioned furniture. My grandfather, wearing a splendid brocaded banyan, was sitting in a wing chair beside a small table that held his breakfast tray. "There you are, my dear," he said. "Please sit down. I'm pleased to find you looking stronger." He motioned to his valet. "You may take the tray away."

As I looked at the earl's high-bred, expressionless face, I thought back to our first meeting on the day I'd arrived at Kildrummond. I'd been devastated then by his apparent lack of personal interest. In the weeks that had followed, I'd grown more at ease in his company. However, at this moment, sitting opposite him in the privacy of his sitting room, I felt no closer to him than I had in the beginning. I had no sense of a strong family tie binding us together. We were still well-mannered strangers.

The glittering object in his hand caught my attention. It was a slim, wicked-looking dagger, the hilt of which was thickly encrusted with diamonds and emeralds. He smiled at my obvious interest, handing me the weapon for a closer inspection. "It's beautiful, isn't it? It once belonged to a Mameluke sultan of Egypt."

"Yes, it's very beautiful," I replied. But I quickly handed the dagger back to him. Its cold glitter filled me with distaste.

"Collecting old and valuable weapons is one of my hobbies," my grandfather said, motioning to a glass cabinet at one side of the room. "Swords, daggers, pistols. I have something of everything." He put down the dagger and said, glancing at my habit, "You must be feeling recovered indeed, if you're about to go riding. Take my advice and don't overdo on your first day out of bed. However, I'm sure that Murdoch won't allow you to overtax your strength."

My face must have registered my confusion. "Have I said something wrong?" he inquired.

"No, not at all. It's only—I won't be riding with Murdoch today. Ian is taking me to see the upper glen."

"Ah." My grandfather's hooded eyes remained fixed on me for an instant. "Speaking of Murdoch, I hope you won't be embarrassed if I tell you my nephew has confided to me that you refused his offer of marriage."

"I don't mind," I said after a pause. "I know you and Murdoch are very close." Whether I was embarrassed or simply annoyed, I suspected, would count for very little with my imperious grandfather.

"I must confess your refusal rather mystified me. You haven't forgotten our recent conversation? I believe I told you then that I would look most favorably on such a marriage. Murdoch hasn't done anything to offend you?"

"No, not at all." I looked him squarely in the eyes. "I declined Murdoch's offer because I'm not in love with him."

"Love?"

If the word had been an object, I could have visualized it being held distastefully between my grandfather's thumb and forefinger like a noxious piece of vermin.

"Love?" he repeated. "What, pray, in our station of life, does love have to do with marriage? Surely you realize that most marriages in our class are arranged by the families, in the interest of the families? A responsible parent arranging such a marriage will, of course, ensure that respect, liking, a certain affinity, are present. As they seem to be with you and Murdoch."

Anger began to build up in me. I tried to keep it out of my voice and still make my point. "Everything you say is doubtless true. However, much as I'd like to be guided by your wishes, in this matter I prefer to make my own decision."

The hooded eyes registered no emotion. He shrugged, saying, "I assure you I have no desire to coerce you. I do urge you to consider Murdoch's proposal very carefully. You may well decide to change your mind. I hope you do." He lifted a languid hand in dismissal. "Thank you for coming to see me."

I stood up, curtsying. As I turned toward the door, I stopped in midstep. "Grandfather, there's something—"

"Yes?"

"It's Nanny. She hasn't returned to her cottage yet, as you probably know. When she does—"

"When she does, Janet Cumming will be prosecuted to the limit of the law."

"But, sir, she's an old lady, I don't think she meant to harm me. . . ."

"My dear Kirstie, this is what comes of being a romantic. You aren't thinking realistically. Janet Cumming stole a valuable brooch. She physically assaulted a member of my family. Don't you know that a man can be hanged for stealing a cow? Transported for life for pilfering a loaf of bread? Why should Janet Cumming be treated any differently?"

I said no more. I hoped Ian would be able to change my grandfather's mind. It certainly seemed beyond my powers.

I must have looked unusually pensive as I entered the stable yard a few minutes later. When I came up to Ian, he said quietly, "What is it?"

I told him about my conversation with my grandfather, omitting any reference, of course, to Murdoch's proposal.

"I think I can bring the earl around," Ian assured me. "He's angry with Nanny now. When he's calmer, he'll realize the family will be the object of undesirable gossip if the story gets around that his daughter's old nurse tried to kill his granddaughter. If I can't persuade the earl to be reasonable, I'll simply send Nanny into hiding for a while."

"Where?"

"The same place she's in now, unless I miss my guess. Somewhere not far from here with her Gypsy kin. You remember her mother was a Gypsy? Maura Fraser once told me that Nanny used to disappear for a short time in the old days whenever a band of Gypsies came into the area. I heard last week there was an encampment of Gypsies near Glen Carnoch. Depend on it, that's where Nanny is. So don't worry about her. She's perfectly safe for the time being. Now, shall we start on our ride?"

By the time we cantered across the wooden bridge, the specter of old Janet, on her way either to the gallows or a madhouse, had faded, and I was becoming more cheerful.

"Are you sure you feel up to a long ride today?" Ian inquired. "I'd planned to go as far as the pass and the *Lochan na Fola.*"

"*Lochan na Fola,*" I repeated, and shivered. "The little lake of the blood."

"Oh, it won't be as gruesome as it sounds," Ian replied, grinning. "You'll see. Shall we go? Or do you think you might get too tired? You just got up from a sickbed this morning."

"I'm perfectly healthy. I wouldn't have stayed in my bedchamber yesterday if Emily hadn't insisted. She's a tyrant."

We were now approaching the point where the glen widened into the broad green acres of the arable. As we emerged from the wooded area bordering the stream bed, Ian muttered a curse under his breath. "Trouble, I think," he said, motioning to his right, where, far across the fields, a large crowd of people had gathered around what appeared to be a crofter's hut. "Will you wait for me here? I'd best go over there."

"Could I go with you? They're my people, Ian. Or they will be, some day."

"Well—all right. Perhaps it's not serious." He didn't sound hopeful.

The people crowding around the hut stared stolidly at us as Ian and I rode up and dismounted. Nobody said a word. Ian handed his reins to me. "Stay here, please." As I watched, he walked into the mass of people, pausing to talk to several individuals in turn. Then he entered the hut.

The silence, and the tension I could almost see, began to unnerve me. And yet, I couldn't discern the slightest clue as to what might have happened. The hut, situated on the less fertile ground sloping up to the mountains, was no meaner or more decrepit than the other crofter's houses I'd seen. A single goat was tethered to a post to keep him out of the kale patch. Several scrawny chickens scratched in the dirt. The potato plants were coming up. I didn't see any children. . . . My heart started to race. When Ian emerged from the hut and started toward me, I already had an inkling of what he'd found in the hut.

Ian's gray eyes were glacial in his drawn face. "Kirstie, you'd better ride over to Jock Cameron's house while I attend to this. Meg is expecting us, as you know."

"If that's what you think best. What happened?"

He hesitated, not meeting my eyes. "Something terrible, something you might not want to hear about."

"Did it involve a child?"

"How did you know?" he gasped.

"I didn't. I guessed. Tell me."

"The woman who lived in that hut delivered a baby prematurely early this morning. Her husband had gone to fetch the midwife. By the time he returned, his wife had smothered the new baby and stabbed to death their other two children. Then, before he could stop her, she turned the knife on herself."

"Oh, God. . . . Why? Why would she do such a thing? Did she leave a note?"

He glared at me as if I were a driveling idiot. "A note? The woman couldn't write. Her husband can't read. She didn't have to leave a note. She killed herself and the children because she had no way to feed her family. She and her husband received a notice of eviction yesterday."

"I don't understand," I stammered. "Who evicted them?"

"The tacksman, naturally. The man who leases this property from your grandfather—" Ian broke off as a tall, burly man walked up the slope toward us.

"Guid day, Maister Ian," said the man. He gave me a jerky bow. "My son juist brought me the sad news. I dinna ken how the woman could do sich a terrible thing. Her ane bairns! Puir, puir Robbie! Noo he hasna a wife nor bairns neither."

Keeping his voice pitched low so that it was inaudible to the silent, watching crowd near the hut, Ian snarled, "Don't pitch that gammon to me, Kennedy. You know better than anyone why Robbie's wife committed murder and suicide. You'd just condemned her and her family to starvation. Why did you evict Robbie? At this time of year, when his kale and potatoes were already in, and without any notice beforehand. Where did you expect him to go?"

Kennedy's face reddened, and he shifted uneasily from one foot to the other. Nevertheless, he tried to bluster, saying, "'Twas my richt. Robbie wasna a guid tenant. He was lazy, and shiftless. . . . "

"Yes, and yesterday he told you what he thought of you for raising his rent and squeezing him dry so that he couldn't have fed his family through the winter even if you allowed him to stay on his miserable plot. You don't like to hear the truth about yourself, so you evicted him. Robbie hopes you'll rot in hell for what you did. So do I."

The tacksman had turned a pasty white. "Lookit here, Maister Ian, ye canna talk tae me like that, fer all ye're the Kildrummond steward. The auld laird's son, Lord Allendale, when he was steward, he never found any fault wi' me. He knew I always pay my rents on time and in full."

"Don't count on being able to do that in future," snapped Ian, turning his back on the man. "Kirstie, I can't do any more here. Let's go." He helped me to mount and swung into the saddle himself.

As we rode away, I said hesitantly, "Why didn't the crofter—Robbie, is that his name?—why didn't Robbie come to you when that man Kennedy threatened to evict him? He must have known you'd try to help him."

"I couldn't have done anything for him, and he knew it. I have no authority over Kennedy, or any of the tacksmen."

"But—you're the steward. This is my grandfather's estate."

Ian exploded, his words cutting like a whiplash. "Damnation, Kirstie, you're a grown woman, why don't you use the wits God gave you?" At my look of hurt bewilderment, he cut himself short, biting his lip so hard he drew blood. "I'm sorry," he muttered. "I've no excuse for taking my foul temper out on you. You see, it's really quite simple. Kennedy has a lease. He can do anything he likes with the property, provided he pays his rent promptly. Robbie, and all the other crofters, are merely tenants-at-will. They can be evicted at any time, for any reason."

"So Kennedy could evict someone else tomorrow, and your hands would be tied."

"Yes. For now. In a year's time, though—less than a year now—Kennedy will be out of the glen. That's when his lease expires." For a moment Ian's face brightened with a savage joy. Then he lapsed into a morose silence. I knew he must be thinking of Robbie's dead family and how powerless he'd been to avert their fate.

When we rode into the courtyard of Jock Cameron's house, the tacksman came out to meet us, smiling his usual cheerful smile. "So you're off for a ride up the valley. You have a fine day for it. Meg's packed that basket you asked for, Master Ian." Pausing at the sight of Ian's set face, Jock said to me, "Mistress, perhaps you'd like to join Meg in a cup of tea? Master Ian and I will be along in a moment."

Meg greeted me with her usual shy pleasure and chatted casually until she'd poured the tea and pressed a biscuit on me. Then, glancing out the window of the parlor at her husband and Ian talking in the courtyard, she said quietly, "Master Ian looks troubled." She broke into soft cries of distress when I told her about the tragedy of the crofter's family. "I can't say I'm entirely surprised," she said at last. "Zack Kennedy's a warm man, and a mean one. Oh, that poor woman." After a moment she added, "I've no doubt Master Ian feels this strongly. Will he still be of a mind, I wonder, to go riding up the glen?"

I'd been wondering the same thing. A pall had been cast over what had promised to be an enjoyable afternoon.

"And you, too, mistress," Meg ventured. "Are you up to it? We heard that you—we heard you'd had an accident."

I had no doubt at all that every tacksman, tenant, subtenant and servant on the Kildrummond estate knew exactly what kind of an "accident" I'd had. I hoped their loyalty to the family would prevent the gossip from spreading beyond the estate. In the old days, the Highland chieftains had had the power to administer justice in their own private courts. Now the judicial power for this area was vested in the sheriff at Fort William, who might come looking for Nanny if the rumors about the attack came to his ears.

When Ian finally joined us in the parlor, I was relieved to see that he'd recovered much of his composure. "Robbie will be taken care of," he told me. "Jock needs a grassman, and he tells me there'll soon be a cottage open as well. One of his old widows won't last much longer. And Jock will see to the funerals, too."

"Thanks to you, Master Ian," Jock said, patting his pocket.

Ian looked embarrassed. "Anybody can give money," he mumbled.

"Can but won't," Jock retorted. A pleasantly expectant look settled over his rough-hewn face. "Do ye suppose Zack Kennedy has any idea his days at Kildrummond are numbered?"

Meg interrupted him, saying to Ian, "Your basket is all ready. I put in that bottle of French wine you brought."

For a moment Ian looked uncertain. I thought he was

about to postpone our ride to another day. Then he smiled at me, saying, "Remember that red wine we had at the inn in Cherbourg? I bought half a dozen bottles. This is the last. I imagine it will taste even mellower in the open air, taken with a pick-nick lunch."

"I'm looking forward to it," I said demurely. "No doubt I'll need a restorative after you tell me the story of 'Blood Lake.'"

The Camerons burst out laughing. "Oh, Master Ian," said Meg, wiping the corner of her eye with her apron, "that reminds me of years gone by. You couldn't hear that tale often enough when you were a lad."

Shortly afterward, as I rode with Ian out of the Camerons' courtyard, I spotted a small figure trudging down the path from the crofters' cottages farther up the hill. Reining in, I called out, "Hallo, Gavin, how are you feeling?"

The child quickened his steps, pausing beside Ian's horse to murmur shyly, "Guid day, Maister Ian." Ian returned the greeting gravely.

Gavin walked over to me and bobbed his head in a jerky little bow. He was barefoot and his shirt was grubby, but he seemed healthy again, if a little pale. He'd evidently made a quick recovery from the fever during the past four days. Staring up at me with those clear gray eyes that were so startlingly like Ian's, he said, "Guid day, mistress. I wish tae thank ye fer those d—dom—"

"Dominoes."

"Aye, dominoes. I hope ye werena angry that I couldna keep them. My mither . . . " His voice trailed off. His cheeks reddened. Obviously he felt too much loyalty to Hallie to reveal what she'd said to him about my gift.

"I understand, Gavin. Your mother probably thinks you're too young to play the game."

"Aye, that's it," he replied, seizing quickly on the excuse. He glanced curiously at the basket hanging on Ian's arm, the

197

neck of a bottle protruding from one end of it. "Ye and Maister Ian are gae'ing on a journey, mistress?"

"A very short one. We're riding to the end of the glen."

Gavin's eyes lighted up. "Sae far? The grassmen, they talk aboot gae'ing up there tae the hill shielings in the summer."

The note of yearning in his voice was unmistakable. I looked at Ian, sitting his horse in composed silence, waiting for me to finish the conversation, and said impulsively, "Couldn't we take Gavin along with us, Ian? I'm sure there's plenty of food."

The familiar chill settled into the gray eyes. I could almost see the word "No" forming on his lips. It must have been Gavin's expression, a blend of eagerness and an unchildlike resignation to the buffetings of fate, that decided Ian. "Very well, Gavin," he said. "You may come with us if your grandmother gives us her permission." There was little real warmth in his voice, although Gavin, who was jumping up and down with squeals of joy, apparently didn't notice.

There was little warmth, either, in the face of Gavin's grandmother when we rode up to her cottage to make our request. It was clear she would have preferred to refuse us. Probably she dreaded having to deal with Hallie's displeasure. However, when Ian said curtly to her, "You needn't fear for the boy's safety while he's in my care," she gave in. I understood why. Ian was the laird's steward. For nearly all the inhabitants of the valley, he was the only visible sign of the earl's authority. The woman looked on with a morose expression as Ian reached down his hand and Gavin clambered happily onto the horse behind him.

During the first part of the ride, which took us farther into the cultivated part of the glen, Ian said very little. Was he still brooding about the suicide and murders in the crofter family? Perhaps he was merely resentful that I'd asked him to allow Gavin to join us. Short of acting like a curmudgeon, there'd been no graceful way to refuse me. And why did he seem to have so little feeling for the child who resembled him so closely? I began to wish I hadn't given in to impulse. It was hard to see how the afternoon could be salvaged.

Before long, however, Gavin's bubbling good spirits began to wear away at Ian's taciturnity. The child seemed to enjoy every passing moment, asking questions, calling attention to a miniature waterfall, an elusive red deer, the soaring flight of a peregrine falcon. Soon Ian was responding readily, giving every indication he was enjoying Gavin's company.

Gradually, as the river and the valley curved around the flank of a jutting mountain, the landscape changed. The peaks became higher and more forbidding, the soil thinner and rockier, carpeted with scrawny grasses and heaths and thickets of gorse and occasional growths of fir trees. High on the crests of the mountains the fir plantations were thicker. There were no cottages here and no cultivated strips, and yet the area had a wild and austere beauty. Ian pointed out some of the more prominent landmarks. *Dalness,* the field of the waterfall. *Meall Dearg,* the round red hill. *Inverrigan,* the wooded confluence, where three little streams came together. And, as we neared the narrowing end of the valley, the Devil's Staircase, a narrow path climbing precipitously up the stony slopes of the towering mountain that closed in the glen, and, at its foot, a sparkling little lake. *Lochan na Fola.* The little lake of the blood.

After the long ride, it felt refreshing to dismount and stroll along the shores of the lake. Gavin and I vied with each other to see which of us could discover more varieties of wildflowers. Soon we had a variegated bouquet of wood anemones, dog violets, sweet-scented bog myrtle and spotted orchids, interspersed with the pink and white of bogbeans and the flaring yellow of celandines.

"What are you going to do with your posies?" Ian asked, grinning.

"Take them home and put them in a vase, of course, what else?" I took a second look at my bouquet. Some of the flowers were already wilting. "Oh. They won't last until I get to Kildrummond, will they?"

"I fear not."

"Gavin, we shouldn't have picked the flowers," I told him. "Wildflowers should be enjoyed where they grow." I ruffled his fair hair. "Never mind. We'll know better next time."

"Next time? We'll come back again, mistress?"

"Oh— Yes, I hope so." As I spoke, I felt a stab of guilt. It was wrong to raise the child's expectations. Very likely, if Ian ever asked me to return to this place, he wouldn't include Gavin in the invitation.

"I'm hungry," Ian announced. Leading the way to a level dry spot a short distance from the boggy lakeside, he unfolded the white cloth tucked around the contents of Meg's basket and spread it out on the ground. There was ample food for all of us. Gavin's eyes widened at the sight of the sliced mutton, the whole roasted chicken, the wheel of cheese and the freshly made scones. Poor mite, I thought, remembering what Ian had once told me about the meager diet of the crofter families.

While Gavin dove enthusiastically into the food—Ian and I were more restrained, since we'd be obliged to present ourselves at the family dinner table later that afternoon—Ian finally satisfied my curiosity about "the little lake of the blood."

"Many many years ago," he began, "when Fergus the Red was chieftain of the Camerons of Kildrummond—"

Gavin piped up, "How many years ago, Maister Ian?"

"More years than you can count. This happened before the Forty-five, before the Fifteen, before King Jamie went to London and we no longer had our own Scottish king." At Gavin's bemused look, Ian laughed, saying in broad Scots, "Dinna fash yersel', laddie. You'll learn your country's history in good time, I hope. Just remember Fergus the Red. See the Devil's Staircase over there?" Ian pointed to the steep path up the mountain. "After a desperate battle on Achnafeadh Moor, on the other side of the mountain, Fergus and a band of his men came scrambling down that trail one night, driving a herd of black cattle before them, and with a small army of Hendersons in close pursuit."

"Now, wait," I said. "Aren't you leaving out something? These cattle you mentioned. They were 'lifted' from the Hendersons, weren't they?"

The corners of Ian's mouth curled in a quirky grin. "You have a good memory for words. Yes, Fergus had 'lifted' some Henderson cattle. Quite a few of them, in fact. Unfortunately, he was caught out, and during the fight that followed several of his men were seriously wounded. When they reached this point in the glen, the wounded could go no farther. Fergus decided to make a stand by the lake. The Hendersons greatly outnumbered them. Soon all the men of Kildrummond were down except for Fergus, standing defiantly with his back to the lake, his bloody claymore raised high. Two of the Hendersons rushed him, one engaging his sword while the other plunged a dagger into his chest. With his last ounce of strength, Fergus threw his claymore deep into the lake, shouting, 'Ye'll ne'er take the sword of Cameron of Kildrummond!' Then he fell dying, his blood crimsoning the water. The Hendersons spread the tale of their gallant foe far and wide, and so, forever after, the little lake has been called *Lochnan na Fola.*"

Gavin sat staring at Ian, his eyes like saucers, so mesmerized by the story that he'd stopped eating. After a few moments, he asked, "This Fergus, Maister Ian. He were yer great-grandfaither, mayhap?"

"Something like that." To me, Ian said, "I believe one of Fergus's grandsons became the first chief of the Camerons of Inverloch. He was my great-grandfather."

Gavin inquired, "Did they ever find yer great-grandfaither's claymore?"

"No. The loch's small, but it's very deep."

Looking abstracted, Gavin rose and began walking toward

the lake. Watching him go, Ian murmured, "It's odd Gavin should ask that. When I wasn't much older than he is now, my ambition in life was to find Fergus's claymore. I used to inveigle Jock Cameron into taking me out here. The water in the loch is very clear, you see, and contains little vegetation. I was convinced I could recover the sword by making dives into the middle of the loch. Jock put a stop to that after I nearly drowned."

Gavin was standing on the shore of the loch. I said uneasily, "You don't suppose that child is thinking of diving in to find the sword?"

"I doubt he can swim. See, he's moving away from the loch." Ian called out, "Gavin, don't go too far."

Gavin called back, "I were juist gae'ing tae climb a wee bit up the Devil's Staircase."

"Very well. Be careful." Ian assured me, "It'll be all right. We can easily keep him in sight from here." He picked up the bottle of wine. "Now, then, shall we finish this off?"

I sipped my wine, enjoying the fragrance of growing things and dreamily watching the breeze ripple the surface of the little lake. It was an unusually warm day for the Highlands, where I'd found a light wrap was often necessary for comfort even in the summer. Ian removed his three-cornered hat and his coat, closing his eyes and lifting his face to the sun. I sat quietly, looking at him. I liked looking at him. His sharply angled features had the antique beauty of a face on a Greek coin. Wisps of his thick tawny hair had escaped the severe queue and were curling damply on his temples. I could sense the controlled grace and power of his body beneath the fine linen of his shirt, and a vagrant thought crept unbidden into my mind: he'd look magnificent stripped to the . . . Hastily I said, "You know a great deal about our clan history, don't you?"

He opened his eyes. "Yes, I suppose I do." He hesitated, then began to speak slowly, almost as if he was explaining his thoughts to himself. "When I first came to Kildrummond, I was—I was quite lonely. Lonely and frightened. They told me my father was dead, killed in some loathsome way. I didn't see how I could ever fit in with your grandfather's family. So I clung fiercely to the only things that belonged to me, the memories of my home in Inverloch, and the stories my father used to tell me about the old days. I could escape to the glories of the past whenever the present threatened to overwhelm me. Later Jock Cameron told me even more of the clan history. It was a bond between us."

Slowly I released the breath I'd been unconsciously holding. This was the first time since I'd known him that Ian had opened his heart to me to reveal the hurts and insecurities of his childhood. Since the time he was Gavin's age, he'd lacked the wholehearted parental love given to me so unreservedly by Calum and Sheila MacDonell. I leaned across the space between us, placing my hand over Ian's. "I'm glad you found Jock and Meg," I said softly. "Every child needs friends."

For a moment he seemed faintly startled. Then a diamond-like flame ignited the gray eyes. His fingers twisted beneath mine, and he lifted my hand to his mouth. A quick warmth curled through me as his lips brushed my palm and I felt the hint of roughness from the beard that had begun to grow since his early morning shave. "You have such soft skin, Kirstie," he murmured. He reached out, placing a hand on either side of my head to frame my face. "It feels like satin, like rose petals," he whispered, as his lips glided caressingly along my cheeks, across my closed eyelids. "Your mouth is soft too. . . ."

My lips responded to those gentle, clinging kisses, which gradually became harder and more insistent. Suddenly Ian's arms closed around me, and in a single fluid movement he pushed me back against the soft grass, his mouth seizing my lips in a devouring, bruising kiss. His breathing was gasping and erratic, and his heart seemed to be thudding out of control. A raging torrent of desire was sweeping over me, leaving me conscious only of the power of Ian's enticing maleness. I put my arms around his neck and strained against him. A shudder ran through his body and he lifted his head, groaning, "Oh, God, Kirstie, you can't realize what you're doing to me. I don't know if I can—"

"Maister Ian!"

Gavin's shocked little voice was like a douche of ice water. Abruptly releasing me with a strangled curse, Ian rolled away from me and stood up. His eyes were the color of chilled granite and his voice rasped like a file. "We're leaving now, Gavin. Wait for Mistress Kirstie and me where the horses are tethered."

"But, Maister Ian, shouldna I help ye pack up the basket?"

"No, we don't need your help. Just leave. Can't you see where you're not wanted?"

Gavin blinked against the tears filling his eyes. He wheeled about and ran down the slope toward the horses.

"Ian, you shouldn't have spoken to Gavin like that." The reproachful words escaped me before I thought.

"The boy's been raised like a savage," Ian muttered, avoiding my eyes. "No manners, no consideration for other people's privacy."

"I'm sure he didn't mean any harm when he—when he interrupted us." I bit my lip. "For that matter, we shouldn't have been—we should have been more circumspect in public."

A muscle twitched in Ian's hard, impassive face. "As I told the child, it's time to go." He knelt down on the turf, quickly packing away the food, the empty wine bottle and the white tablecloth. He got up, holding the basket. I moved close to him, putting my hand on his arm. "Ian, don't be so hard," I pleaded. "He's such a little boy. And he's your son."

Ian jerked away from me, as if my hand were a burning brand on his arm. He burst out, "Don't call him that. He's not—" His mouth working, he was silent for a moment. Then the dam seemed to break. "He could be my son, yes. He could be anybody's son. More specifically, he could be your cousin Murdoch's son."

I took an involuntary step backward. "Murdoch? Murdoch was Hallie's lover, too?"

The momentary flare of passion died out of his face. He sounded cold, level, indifferent, like the Ian Cameron I'd first met in Normandy. "That surprises you? I must say, it surprised me, more than a little. I first learned of it one night when Hallie and I were in bed together in my bedchamber and Murdoch paid me an unexpected visit. He thought it was very amusing. 'My God, Ian,' he said, 'is the slut planning to bed all the men in the family? Shall I tell my uncle he's next in line?' "

Ian may have thought he'd kept the emotion out of his voice. He hadn't succeeded. He couldn't hide completely that long-ago hurt. Now I understood why he'd always held Gavin at arm's length. I understood, too, why he'd reacted so harshly to the little boy's intrusion. It must have seemed to Ian that the past was repeating itself. Murdoch had once interrupted Ian's lovemaking with Hallie. Now Murdoch's son—or the child who might be Murdoch's son—had invaded Ian's privacy with me.

Chapter XI

I went riding with Murdoch several days later. I must have been a very poor companion. My thoughts were so full of Ian and that disastrous pick-nick that I virtually ignored Murdoch.

"Perhaps we should go back, Kirstie."

"What?" My hand paused in midair in its futile attempt to ward off a cloud of midges.

"You haven't been listening to a word I've been saying," Murdoch accused me. "I suggested we should return to the house if the midges were too much for you."

It had rained almost constantly for the past several days. Driven into boredom by inactivity, Murdoch had seized upon the first sign of clearing skies this afternoon to propose a ride along Loch Linnhe. But, although the midges were more of a nuisance than usual because of the increased moisture in the air, they weren't responsible for my preoccupation, of course.

"No, I can bear the midges if you can, Murdoch," I said, swatting away at a renewed onslaught by the insects. "I'm enjoying being outside. I was getting restless, having to stay in the house until the rains stopped."

"Well, then . . . Is something amiss? Is it the countess? Gwyneth tells me you're still visiting your grandmother."

I hadn't been thinking of Elspeth, but Murdoch's comment reminded me of the renewed disappointment I'd felt this morning when my visit had again failed to elicit the faintest response to my overtures. If anything, my grandmother appeared to have sunk even deeper into the comalike state in which she'd been immersed for well over a week. And, as before, I'd gone away puzzled by Maura Fraser's stolid reaction to the situation. When I'd failed again to get through to Elspeth today, Maura had seemed—well, not pleased, exactly, not triumphant, either, though I thought I'd detected a trace of both sentiments in her manner. Her entire life revolved around the countess. Why wasn't she displaying more concern for her mistress's deteriorating condition?

"Kirstie, I don't like to see you troubled. Hasn't the time come when you must admit that you can't help your grandmother?"

I didn't resent Murdoch's gentle question. I'd been asking myself much the same thing. Possibly Elspeth's few brief moments of lucidity had been a fluke and would never be repeated. Should I give up my dream of bringing my grandmother back to reality? "Perhaps you're right," I murmured. "I'll think about it."

"Good." He shot me a keen look. "Have I annoyed you in some way?"

I raised my eyebrows in surprise. "No. Why do you ask?"

"Oh—it's hard to explain. . . . You've seemed a little distant lately. I *must* have done something to offend you."

"You're imagining things," I said hastily. I looked away, hoping to conceal the flush of embarrassment I felt rising in my cheeks. Murdoch's intuition must be very keen. In some subtle way, my manner toward him must have altered during the past few days. He'd certainly been in my thoughts, not because he'd done anything to annoy me, but because my mind had been dwelling almost constantly on my pick-nick excursion with Ian and Gavin.

Each time I recalled the shattering ending to that picknick, I'd felt a fresh shock. I'd been forced to dissect everything I knew about Ian and Hallie and Murdoch and Gavin and put the pieces back together in a totally different way. "Gavin could be anybody's son," Ian had said. "He could be Murdoch's son." And, " . . . one night when Hallie and I were in bed together, Murdoch paid me an unexpected visit. He thought it was very amusing. 'My God, Ian,' he said, 'is the slut planning to bed all the men in the family?' "

No wonder Ian had always seemed to be both attracted to, and repelled by, Gavin. He hadn't dared to give his heart to the child who was universally considered to be his son, but whom he might not have sired. It made no difference that Gavin so closely resembled him. Gavin also looked like Murdoch. As I'd so often noted, Ian and my grandfather and Murdoch shared a strong family resemblance. It made no difference, either, that Hallie seemed to be in love with Ian. She'd also apparently slept with Murdoch, and had done so at approximately the same time as her affair with Ian. Otherwise, Ian wouldn't have had any doubt about Gavin's parentage. Whether there'd been any affection on the part of either Hallie or Murdoch was beside the point. Perhaps Hallie herself didn't know who Gavin's father was.

It's not fair to judge Murdoch more harshly than Ian, but that's what I've been doing, I thought suddenly. Murdoch had evidently sensed my uneasiness. Oh, I'd accepted that society was governed by certain rules, one of which was that men lived their sexual lives according to a different standard of conduct than women. So if I'd condoned, however reluctantly, Ian's relationship with Hallie, shouldn't I do the same for Murdoch? Both men had apparently had affairs with the same compliant servant girl. Murdoch was no more guilty than Ian, if guilt there was. But I couldn't rid myself of my distaste for what Murdoch had said: " . . . my God, is the slut planning to bed all the men in the family? Shall I tell my uncle he's next in line?" Somehow, no matter what the provocation, I couldn't imagine Ian talking like that.

Ian. I couldn't keep my thoughts from him. I felt a burning

sensation deep in my loins. What would have happened, the day of the pick-nick beside "the little lake of the blood," if Gavin hadn't innocently interrupted us? Was there any use in speculating about it? Judging by Ian's behavior, the incident was closed. Leaving the lake that day, we'd ridden to Gavin's home in a forbidding silence that reminded me of Ian's behavior during our earlier interminable journey from Normandy to Kildrummond. Poor Gavin. He'd looked so subdued, so miserable, when we dropped him off at his grandmother's cottage. Ian helped him down from the saddle without saying a word.

I'd hoped that Ian and I could clear the atmosphere once we were alone. We didn't. During our ride out of the glen to the stables, Ian never referred to what had happened beside the loch. Instead, calmly and impersonally, he treated me to a lecture on the relative importance of kale and potatoes in the Highlander diet. I understood perfectly why he'd retreated behind the mask of his reserve. He'd allowed me inside the innermost core of his being, where all the old hurts and insecurities lurked and festered, and now he regretted it. Apparently he'd continued to regret it. I'd had nothing but impersonal contacts with him since the day of the pick-nick. . . .

Once more Murdoch broke into my thoughts. "Well, Kirstie? If I haven't offended you, what *is* wrong? For a good five minutes you've simply been staring into space." Usually so urbane, he sounded a bit exasperated.

"I'm sorry I've been such a dull riding partner." I smiled at him. "You see, I have a great deal on my mind. Such as, what shall I wear to Donald Stewart's birthday dinner next week? And why haven't I received a letter recently from my friend the Comtesse de Bassincourt?"

He laughed. "I'll forgive you this time for being so inattentive. I can see you're burdened down with cares. These abominable creatures"—he slapped vigorously at a swarm of midges—"aren't helping matters, either." He glanced at the little jeweled watch he took from the pocket at the front of his breeches. "It's later than I thought. We should be getting back to the castle. It will soon be time to dress for dinner."

As we rode back along the loch, we saw a heavy traveling carriage moving slowly toward us from the direction of Fort William. We reined in our horses at the turnoff for the castle, waiting for the berline to come abreast of us. Carriages were a comparative rarity at Kildrummond. The Highland roads were so dreadful that people traveled only by necessity, or to attend a gala social event.

The coachman halted the carriage near us and jumped down to open the door and let down the steps. A middle-aged man emerged from the berline. He wore a plain bagwig on his head, and his sober dark garments had no pretension to fashion. He removed his hat and bowed to Murdoch. "Could ye tell me, sir, if this is the turning fer Castle Kildrummond?"

"It is."

The man hesitated. "Do ye live here, sir? Might I ask yer name?"

"Certainly. My name is Murdoch Graham. I'm the Earl of Carrickmore's nephew."

"And I am Andrew Crawford, at yer sairvice, sir."

Murdoch inclined his head. "Master Crawford. You have business at Kildrummond?"

Did I imagine the faint air of surprise in Andrew Crawford's manner? "Oh—aye. I'm here tae see his lordship."

"I see." Murdoch looked at the man appraisingly. "Drive straight up the hill, then. The servants will take care of you."

There it was again. I thought I detected a flicker of bewilderment in Master Crawford's face. He cleared his throat. "Verra well, sir. I thank ye most kindly."

After he'd climbed back into his carriage and the coachman had driven off, I said curiously, "I didn't know my grandfather was expecting a guest. Gwyneth didn't mention it."

"A guest! The fellow had cit written all over him. He must be a tradesman of some kind."

A tradesman? How odd. Andrew Crawford obviously hadn't come from nearby Fort William. His carriage and the coachman's clothing were thick with the dust and dried mud of a long journey. Could he be my grandfather's tailor or jeweler, come all the way from Edinburgh to deliver the latest order? I smiled to myself. Perhaps he was bringing the earl another of those exquisite enameled snuffboxes he so doted on. Or an antique weapon, another jeweled dagger, perhaps, to augment his collection. My grandfather was quite capable of such an extravagant gesture. Ian would have something to say about *that*, no doubt.

The little mystery continued to engage my attention while I rode to the stables with Murdoch, and afterward, as I climbed the staircase to my rooms. "Here I am, Emily, back in good time—" I paused in surprise.

It wasn't Emily who was waiting for me. It was Hallie. Evidently she'd brought up the freshly pressed linen stacked in a pile on my bed. "I want to talk to you," she said, without any pretext at civility.

I sighed. Hallie had learned about the excursion to "the little lake of the blood." I supposed it was inevitable. Even if her free days, when she went home to visit her mother and her son, were infrequent, the grapevine of estate gossip would bring her the news soon enough. My only real concern was Gavin. What, if anything, had he reported about my romantic interlude with Ian? I stared warily at Hallie. "Yes? What is it?"

"Ye'll please tae stay awa' frae my son, mistress. No mair gifties, no mair wee rides tae the end o' the glen. Juist leave the laddie alone."

Of course I knew better than to argue with Hallie. She was beyond logic. For Gavin's sake, however, I tried. "Hallie, I know you dislike me, but why deprive Gavin of a few inno-

212

cent pleasures? I'm not trying to take the boy away from you—"

"Take Gavin awa' frae me? I'd kill ye first," she blazed. Oh, she'd talked to Gavin, all right. "Dislike ye? I hate ye, mistress. I've been wanting tae tell ye that fer a long time, and I dinna care if ye carry tales about wha' I've said tae Lady Allendale and his lordship."

"Do you feel better, now you've told me what you think of me, Hallie? Don't worry, I've no intention of tattling to Lady Allendale or the earl. If that's all you have to say, will you go, please?"

Even though I'd kept my composure in front of Hallie, the incident left a bad taste in my mouth. Her hatred for me must be overwhelming. Otherwise, she'd never have risked her position at the castle, her very livelihood, and Gavin's, too, for the satisfaction of venting her feelings to me. My heart ached for Gavin, and for me, too. I was so drawn to the boy that I really didn't care who his father was. However, it might be better for the child if I stayed away from him. There was no telling what violence Hallie might be capable of if I provoked her again.

When I went down to the family drawing room before dinner, I was still feeling subdued. I glanced around the room quickly to see if Ian was there. He wasn't. Since the pick-nick, he'd fallen into his old habit of joining the family for dinner only at the last moment, when we were about to file into the dining room.

Someone else was there, however. My eyes widened at the sight of Andrew Crawford, sitting in a chair next to my grandfather. He'd put on a shirt with ruffles down the front and on his cuffs, but he still looked like a tradesman. The contrast between him and the earl was ludicrous, he in his plain, utilitarian garments, my grandfather like some exotic peacock in his gold lace and velvet.

Gwyneth, elaborately dressed, powdered and patched, came forward to greet me. "Kirstie, my dear, we have a

213

guest," she said. "Allow me to present to you Master Crawford, from Galloway. Master Crawford, his lordship's granddaughter, Mistress Kirstie Cameron."

Crawford bowed. I curtsied. "Ach, the young lassie frae France," he said with a broad smile, clapping me heartily on the shoulder. "His lordship, noo, he's been telling me wha' a bonny lass ye are, and forbye I ken he was in the richt. Welcome, noo, tae Scotland."

At this familiarity on Crawford's part, a look of pain crossed Murdoch's face, but quickly disappeared. The bright, artificial smile faded from Gwyneth's lips. My grandfather's normally granitic expression didn't change. However, I noticed that his hand suddenly tightened on the knob of his tasseled cane. I glanced rather helplessly from one to the other of them, not really knowing what was expected of me in dealing with Master Crawford. How on earth had this common little man obtained an invitation to dine at Castle Kildrummond? From his appearance and manner he would have been far more at home in the servants' hall.

Determined not to appear impolite, I said, "If you've come from Galloway, Master Crawford, you've had a long journey."

"Oh, aye, 'twas that. I was afeared my old bones wouldna stand sich a bouncing and a racketing aboot. But here I am, all i' ane piece, thanks be tae the Almighty."

"You have business in the Highlands, perhaps?"

Crawford looked at the earl and broke into a chuckle. "Indeed and indeed, mistress. Yer guid grandfaither and mysel', we've agreed tae raise sheep taegether."

I opened my mouth in stupefaction, but not a word came out. I was literally speechless. Murdoch intervened. "Master Crawford, you're going a bit too fast for my cousin," he said with a genial smile. "Kirstie, do sit down. Let me bring you some tea, and then we have some very exciting news to share with you."

A little later, putting down my teacup, I said expectantly, "Well? What is this exciting news?"

Murdoch glanced at the earl, who nodded, as if to make his nephew his spokesman. "Well, I'm sure I don't need to tell you that we've been in straitened circumstances here at Kildrummond. Near paupers, as near as makes no difference."

I wanted to laugh. Murdoch sounded so solemn. However, it struck me as ridiculous to speak of paupers and poverty when one lived in an enormous mansion, waited on by an army of servants, eating and drinking the finest of food and wines. My old friends the Bassincourts, in a far more modest establishment, considered themselves very well off. "I know you're not in cash at the moment," I agreed. "It's a temporary situation, though, isn't it? Ian says that good management—"

"Bother Ian," flared Murdoch. "We've had more than enough of him and his ideas."

"Murdoch is quite right," my grandfather cut in. "This discussion involves only the immediate family."

I was growing more confused by the minute. Something important was afoot, that was clear. The air of tension in the room was almost palpable. Gwyneth's hands were clenched tightly in her lap. Murdoch shifted nervously from one foot to the other, like a fencer poised for combat. My grandfather sat in expectant stillness, not moving a muscle. Could I have heard correctly? A partnership between the earl and Master Crawford to raise *sheep*? And how did it concern me?

Murdoch continued. "As I think you know, Kirstie, my uncle lived in Edinburgh or London for most of every year until fairly recently, when your Uncle David died. The earl has become more familiar with the day-to-day workings of the estate since he took up a permanent residence here, and he's come to the conclusion that the management of the property, as it's been conducted for hundreds of years, must change to modern methods. I believe you've made several tours of the glen with Ian. You must have seen something of the inefficiency and waste of our present system of tenantry: runrig farming, where tenants cultivate long narrow strips of land, often at a distance from other holdings; overcrowding, with many of the crofters unable to support families on inadequate holdings; the poor quality of the livestock."

I nodded. Murdoch was repeating opinions I'd already heard from Ian and Jock Cameron.

"So my uncle has decided on a new course for Kildrummond. He won't renew the leases of his tacksmen as they fall due," Murdoch went on. He was speaking very carefully and slowly, as if it was important that I understood every word. "Once the old leases are cleared, my uncle will grant the entire leasehold of Kildrummond to Master Crawford, who has had great success in raising sheep in the Lowlands."

"Black-faced Lintons, mistress," Master Crawford interjected. "They gie three times more meat than black cattle, on the same range. Forbye, they're much hardier beasties than those scrawny hairy brown sheep o' yer Highlanders. My Lintons, they'll not sicken and die during the harsh winters i' these parts. And fer the future, I ha' my eye on a new breed, the Cheviots. The Great Sheep, they call them i' the Borders. Better'n my Lintons, sae they tell me."

His eyes sparkling, Murdoch exclaimed, "It will transform Kildrummond, Kirstie. The income from the estate will triple, quadruple, in a few years' time. We'll move out of the Middle Ages at last and into the modern world." He paused, gazing at me expectantly. "Well? What do you think?" His eyes narrowed. "You don't approve?"

"Oh, I don't think my opinion matters," I said quickly. I looked straight at my grandfather. "You're the owner of Kildrummond, sir. You'll of course make your own decision. There's one thing, though, I'd like to ask you about—"

The earl interrupted me. "Oh, but your opinion does matter. It's a question of the terms of my agreement with Master

Crawford. He's informed me that he wants a long lease. Twenty years, I believe you said, Master Crawford?"

The sheep farmer nodded. He no longer looked so genial, so eager to please. "Fair's fair, yer lordship," he said crisply. "Ye're asking me tae bring thousands o' my Lintons north tae yer glen. I wouldna wish tae be forced tae remove the beasties in a few years' time."

"And indeed, I see your point." The earl bowed his head graciously. "On the other hand, my dear Kirstie, I think Master Crawford understands my position. Supposing I should become dissatisfied with his management of the property? An unlikely prospect, certainly. Master Crawford has a superb reputation in his field. Still. Conceivably we could fall out, and then both of us would be locked into a long lease. So I've proposed a compromise term of ten years. Master Crawford has agreed to accept a shorter lease, provided he has the assurance that my heir shares my vision of a new direction for Kildrummond."

Four pairs of eyes were glued on me. It felt unnerving.

"I think Kirstie is a little confused, sir," said Murdoch. He sat down beside me, taking my hand. "Naturally, we all hope that my uncle will continue to enjoy good health for many years to come, and that he'll be perfectly capable of making his own decisions about leases. However, should the worst happen, Master Crawford merely wants to be certain that you're sympathetic to my uncle's plans. If, as Laird of Kildrummond ten years hence, you disapproved of using the estate exclusively for raising sheep, you wouldn't be inclined to renew Master Crawford's lease."

"I know so little about estate matters . . . " A sudden memory of my rides into the glen with Ian flashed through my mind. "What will happen to my grandfather's tenants if you clear the glen for sheep?" I asked Master Crawford. "Of course, you'll need a certain number of shepherds—"

His lips compressed into a straight, angry line. "Nay, mistress, I'll no' permit any ignorant, shiftless Highlanders tae come near my Lintons. I'll bring my own shepherds wi' me frae Galloway."

"But . . . " I glanced around me in bewilderment. "Where will they go, the tacksmen and the tenants and the crofters? What will they do? Ian says these families have farmed the glen for generations."

"And of course we won't just turn them out," Murdoch assured me. "Have you ever heard of the Honorable Society of Improvers? The Improvers have led the way in other parts of Scotland in modernizing agriculture. Their solution to the problem of workers displaced by the new methods is to increase nonagricultural employment. Landowners all over the country have founded villages where these workers can pursue such activities as fishing, kelping, brewing, sack-making, saddlery, weaving—all the occupations necessary for a well-rounded economy. Cuminestown in Aberdeenshire, for example; when the landowner founded it some years ago the town returned only a few pounds in rent. Now it's so prosperous that the owner receives a hundred and fifty pounds a year in rentals."

I thought about the way of life among the crofters I'd observed in the course of my rides with Ian. The miserable cottages with the open fire in the middle of the dirt floor. The naked, dirty children. The shoeless, shabbily dressed adults. The mother who'd killed herself and her children because her family had been evicted. I thought about the horror tales of near starvation in a hard winter. I thought of Gavin, and how little chance he'd have for a secure future.

I said to my grandfather, "I'm not opposed to progress. And I think it would be an excellent thing if Kildrummond produced a larger income, but not at the expense of our tenants. On the other hand, I've seen with my own eyes that many of the crofters on the estate are merely subsisting. It seems to me that almost any other kind of life would be preferable to what they have now. They'd be much better off in these villages Murdoch spoke of. Do you really think there's a good possibility of providing for our people in this way?"

My grandfather's eyes turned chilly. "Certainly. We wouldn't have broached the subject if it weren't possible. Any such undertaking would take time, naturally. But then, it will take time to clear the leases and for Master Crawford to complete his plans."

"I understand." I looked boldly at Andrew Crawford. "I didn't agree with your blanket condemnation of our people as ignorant and shiftless. I think some of our tenants would make excellent graziers. You should consider hiring them."

Murdoch turned on the sheep farmer. "What do you say to that, Master Crawford?"

Obviously nettled, the Lowlander pursed his lips. "I'll think on it. Mair I canna promise."

"Fair enough." Murdoch gave me a challenging look. "Well, Kirstie?"

"If you really want my opinion . . . "

The earl said with a trace of irritation, "We have said so, my dear."

"Then, based on what I've heard during the past few minutes, I have no objection to raising Black-faced Lintons at Kildrummond," I said quietly.

My grandfather nodded to Crawford. "There you have it. My heir and I are in agreement. I look forward to our partnership."

"Ye'll no' regret striking a bargain wi' me, yer lordship. Now, as tae those deeds and estate maps ye mentioned earlier—"

The earl waved his hand. "Those are matters you must discuss with my steward. Murdoch, will you ring for that champagne I asked you to order? We'll drink to our new undertaking."

As Murdoch walked to the bell rope, Gwyneth turned to the earl, her face glowing. "May we drink also to opening the Edinburgh town house for the next spring season?"

"You may indeed. You might also start thinking of new wardrobes for yourself and Kirstie."

"And perhaps a jaunt to London, eh, sir?" said Murdoch, grinning.

"Not out of the question, not out of the question at all. I must say, it's been far too long since I played a game of whist at White's." My grandfather's face was more animated than I'd ever seen it. Obviously he was convinced that his venture with Andrew Crawford would allow him to resume his old way of life.

A few minutes later, as the footman was carrying around the tray of glasses filled with champagne, Ian entered the drawing room. Taking a glass from the tray, he looked around inquiringly, his eyes resting for a moment on the face of the stranger. "This seems to be a gala occasion," he remarked. "May I ask what we're celebrating?"

"Nothing less than a new beginning for Kildrummond, my boy," said my grandfather. "I must introduce our guest to you. Master Crawford of Galloway. Sir, my steward, Ian Cameron."

Slowly Ian lowered the glass he'd been about to put to his lips. His eyes narrowed. "Crawford the sheep farmer?"

"Aye, that I am, Maister Ian," said Crawford, stepping forward and bowing. "I see ye've heard o' me. . . . "

"Oh, I've heard all I care to know about you," said Ian, his eyes raking Crawford with a contemptuous glance. He confronted my grandfather. "What's the meaning of this, sir? What's this man doing at Kildrummond?"

Crawford recoiled, his face reddening. I exclaimed involuntarily, "Ian! Master Crawford is a guest!"

Ignoring me, Ian continued to stare at the earl. "Well, sir? I should like an answer."

"Which I give you willingly, despite your display of boorish manners. Quite simply, I've agreed to grant Master Crawford the leasehold of Kildrummond for a period of ten years, during which time he will make use of the property to raise his prize Black-faced Linton sheep." Although the earl's expression remained as impassive as ever, there was no mistaking the faint note of malicious triumph in his voice.

Ian's face hardened. "So it comes to this, you've decided to break your solemn word."

Murdoch stood up, his fists clenched. "I won't allow you speak to my uncle like that."

"Be still, Murdoch. My quarrel isn't with you—yet," Ian snapped. He turned his eyes to the earl. "One year ago you showed me a letter from this Crawford, offering to lease Kildrummond for the raising of sheep. I told you then I'd resign as your steward if you persisted in such a scheme. I also warned you that when I succeeded to the estate, I'd refuse to renew any lease you might negotiate. At that time you promised—oh, very reluctantly, but you did promise—to abandon your proposal to clear Kildrummond of its people and replace them with sheep."

"And now I've changed my mind," the earl replied with a chilly indifference. "That *is* my prerogative, I believe. As of now, I'm still Laird of Kildrummond. And you, my dear Ian, are no longer my heir."

Drawing a quick, shocked breath, Ian swung around to face me. "No, I'm no longer the heir, Kirstie. *You* are. Do you know about this agreement with Crawford?" He saw the answer in my face. "And you approve?"

"Yes," I replied with stiff lips. "I've seen for myself how poorly some of our tenants live. I think they'd be infinitely better off living in these villages Murdoch has been telling me about—"

"You needn't say any more. I see Murdoch has converted you."

I winced at the savage anger in his voice. I was utterly confused. Why was Ian so intolerant? Didn't I have the right to disagree with him on a matter affecting the future of the estate? And why hadn't my grandfather and Murdoch informed me that Andrew Crawford had made his first offer to lease Kildrummond a year ago? For that matter, why had Murdoch pretended to be unfamiliar with Crawford's name and his occupation when we met the man a few hours ago at the entrance to the estate? It took very little thought to answer the last two questions. There really wasn't much of a mystery. Murdoch and the earl knew I'd become increasingly friendly with Ian and that I'd discussed estate matters with him. Doubtless they feared I might automatically look with disfavor on Crawford's proposal if I knew beforehand that Ian was opposed to it. And, as the heir, my approval of the plan seemed to be essential both to my grandfather and to Crawford. I sighed. They'd been a little devious, Murdoch and the earl. Perhaps they'd felt justified because of the antagonism that had always existed between them and Ian.

Enmeshed in the welter of my thoughts, I'd lost the thread of the conversation. I came back to the situation at the sound of Ian's voice. He was obviously trying to rein in his temper. "You gave me five years to turn the estate around," he was saying to my grandfather. "At the end of that time, I hoped the family would be enjoying a higher income and the tenants would have made a start on a better way of life. I'm asking you not to go back on your word."

The earl shook his head. "I don't want to wait five years for an insignificant amount of progress. Master Crawford proposes to fill my purse now."

Ian's eyes blazed with a sudden fury. "Then you'll turn Kildrummond into one vast sheep farm without my help!"

"As you will," replied the earl, shrugging.

"But, Ian, must you be so hasty?" I faltered. "Kildrummond needs you. It will be difficult for all the tenants to make an adjustment to such different conditions. Besides, where would you go?"

Murdoch laughed, saying, "My dear Kirstie, Ian has a profession, remember? I daresay the Black Watch will be happy to have him back. There's bound to be another war starting somewhere or other."

After his outburst, Ian had himself in hand again. Tossing Murdoch a glance of utter contempt, Ian said to the earl, "I've never claimed to be indispensable. Doubtless you'll easily find a new steward more to your liking. I will, of course, remain in my position until you've replaced me. However, I think I should warn you that you or your new steward will face certain difficulties. There is, for example, the question of the tacksmen's leases."

"Those leases will be coming due within the year, and will not, naturally, be renewed. Under the circumstances, I presume that most of the tacksmen will be happy to surrender their leases even sooner in return for a cash payment."

Ian smiled grimly. "Not Jock Cameron. He has a seven-year lease, which won't expire for another three years."

"Three years!" Master Crawford looked horror-stricken. "I canna wait three years. I maun ha' the lease o' yer entire estate noo, my lord."

In a rare display of emotion, my grandfather struck the floor angrily with his cane. "Why wasn't I informed of this?"

His lip curling, Ian stared back at the earl without speaking. A faint flush showed in my grandfather's face beneath the dusting of rouge. He knew well enough why he wasn't aware of the length of Jock's lease. For years now, he'd left estate matters entirely to his stewards, first to his son David and then to Ian.

"Oh, we know you and Jock Cameron are cronies, Ian, but you had no right to give him special treatment," exclaimed Murdoch furiously. "Did he give you a bribe to extend his lease?"

"He did not. He had no reason to do so. It was your cousin David who granted Jock that seven-year lease. David recognized, as I do, that Jock's methods were making his tack more profitable with each passing year. David hoped that Jock's example would show the way to the other tenants."

Turning away from Murdoch, Ian said to my grandfather,

"Now that you're aware of Jock Cameron's long lease, you might wish to reconsider your plans."

"I'll do nothing of the sort," snapped the earl. "We'll deal with Jock Cameron. Offer the fellow a generous enough sum and I'll warrant he'll be happy to shake the dust of Kildrummond from his feet."

"You don't know your man," flared Ian. "In my opinion, Jock would suffer the tortures of the damned before he'd take a ha'penny from you. But we'll see who's right, won't we? Be sure I'll be encouraging Jock every step of the way." He turned on his heel and stalked toward the door of the drawing room.

I jumped up from my chair. "Ian, wait," I called. I caught up with him outside the door. "Don't go," I pleaded, clutching at his arm. "Please come back to the drawing room and discuss this sheep-raising proposal with my grandfather. There *are* two sides to every argument, you know." I felt his arm tensing beneath my fingers and added hastily, "At least talk to me. . . . "

He jerked his arm away. "There's nothing to talk about, Kirstie. You've joined the enemy."

Chapter XII

When I returned to the drawing room, my face must have reflected the shock I felt at Ian's bitter parting words.

Murdoch exclaimed, "Good God, Kirstie, what's the matter?"

"Ian. He said I'd gone over to the enemy," I repeated. My mind was in a daze.

Gwyneth exclaimed, "Enemy, indeed? His own family!" Her face registered a kind of perverse satisfaction. "Well, Kirstie, you can't say I haven't tried to warn you about placing any trust in Ian. Now perhaps you understand why he's succeeded in alienating himself from all of us."

"My dear Gwyneth, I'm sure we're all gratified that Kirstie's eyes have been opened to the kind of man Ian is," said my grandfather, waving his hand impatiently. "At the moment, however, we have a more important matter to consider: Jock Cameron's seven-year lease."

"Aye, my lord, we canna proceed wi' our agreement afore the question o' that lease is settled," said Master Crawford.

"Oh, the devil," Murdoch exclaimed. "There's no reason for us to be concerned about Jock Cameron. We'll simply offer him a sum of money large enough to make it worth his while to surrender his lease. It will cut into our profits, but that can't be helped."

"Don't be so sure you can buy off Jock Cameron," I blurted. Four pairs of astonished eyes bored into me.

"Buy off?" repeated the earl, as if I'd used a vulgar word.

I said slowly, "Jock's invested so much time and effort in improving his property, I'm not sure he'd be willing to give up his lease for any amount of money."

Murdoch snorted, "You're an innocent. The fellow has his price. We just have to find out what it is."

"Be quiet, Murdoch," ordered my grandfather. He gave me an appraising stare. "Am I to understand, my dear, that you're acquainted with this Jock Cameron?"

"Yes. That is, I've visited him and his wife several times. I liked them very much. They were most gracious to me."

"Kirstie! You've been consorting with these people behind our backs?" Gwyneth bristled with disapproval. "You forget your position! The heiress to Kildrummond doesn't call on her future tenants!"

"My dear." A look from the earl silenced Gwyneth. He turned his gaze on me. "No doubt this Jock Cameron and his wife were impressed by your condescension. I think you should visit them again, Kirstie. You might well be able to persuade the fellow to see reason in the matter of his lease."

Dismayed, I exclaimed, "Oh, I don't think I—"

My grandfather interrupted me. "I should like you to visit the man as soon as possible. Tomorrow, let us say."

The next morning I walked to the stables with dragging feet. Murdoch had offered to accompany me to Jock's house, but I'd refused. He'd have been so grotesquely out of place in Meg Cameron's neat parlor. What could he and the Camerons possibly find to say to each other? I think Murdoch was relieved not to be going with me. I envied him. I'd never approached any errand in my life with more reluctance.

The groom was waiting with my horse when I entered the stable yard. As he gave me a hand to mount, I detected a fleeting expression of avid curiosity in his face. Servants, I thought resignedly. In some fashion they'd learned about Crawford's proposal to raise sheep at Kildrummond, and probably they were also aware of Ian's opposition to it.

Had the news spread already to the valley, too? I wondered as I cantered slowly out of the stable yard and up the hill to the old bridge spanning the river. Did Jock and Meg know about Crawford? And how would they react to my errand? I felt wretchedly uncomfortable about the prospect of offering Jock money to abandon his tack. Whether or not he welcomed the offer, I wasn't the proper intermediary. I was merely the heiress presumptive to Kildrummond. In a matter of such importance, my grandfather, or Ian acting as his agent, should have been involved.

As for Ian . . . My shoulders slumped. He'd been so angry yesterday, so obstinate and stiff-necked in his refusal even to listen to any arguments against his position. What would happen if Jock accepted the earl's offer and Crawford obtained the leasehold to the estate? Would Ian persist in his refusal to act as steward? If he went off to rejoin his regiment, would I ever see him again?

Jock came to his door to greet me as I dismounted in the courtyard and handed my reins to a waiting groom. "Mistress Cameron," he said gravely. "Please to come in." He'd heard about Crawford, that was obvious. Did he also suspect the reason for my visit?

Meg's pretty face looked vaguely troubled as she bustled about her parlor, pressing a cup of tea and a freshly baked scone on me. She said nothing, however, and I ate and drank in silence, grateful for the respite the refreshments allowed me. I still had no idea how I was going to broach my grandfather's offer.

Jock smoothed the way. "You have a visitor at the castle, so we hear, mistress."

I put down my cup. "Yes. A Master Crawford. A sheep farmer from the south."

"Ah."

I said abruptly, "Jock, have you seen Ian today?"

"Ian? Nay."

"Oh, I thought . . . Jock, I'm here on estate business on behalf of my grandfather."

His face calm, he waited for me to go on.

"It's about your lease. My grandfather is prepared to offer you—"

A harsh voice interrupted me. "To offer what? A larger bribe, I trust, than Murdoch accused Jock of making to me."

Jock and Meg and I turned our heads. Ian stood in the doorway of the parlor, staring at me with an expression of barely restrained fury.

"Ian," I faltered. "I wouldn't—you must know it's not a question of a bribe."

"No? What would you call it, then?"

"Master Ian." Jock's voice held a quiet authority. "This is a matter that concerns me. I'd like to give Mistress Kirstie the courtesy of speaking her mind."

Ian bit his lip. "I'm sorry, Jock," he muttered. "Do you want me to go?"

"Nay. You're welcome to stay."

Ian walked into the parlor, standing apart from us, his shoulder braced against the mantel. He was outwardly calm, though I could sense the whipcord tenseness in his tall form.

"Now, then, Mistress Kirstie," said Jock.

Stumbling over my words, acutely aware of Ian's unfriendly gaze, I told Jock about Crawford's plan to raise sheep at Kildrummond and how much my grandfather was prepared to give Jock to terminate his lease. Meg uttered a little gasp at the size of the amount.

"That's a deal of money, mistress," Jock said slowly. "More than I've seen in my lifetime. Enough to buy a nice property anywhere I choose."

"But, Jock," Meg whispered, "it would mean leaving our home. . . . "

"Aye, love. And leaving our tenants forbye." I couldn't tell from Jock's matter-of-fact voice and manner whether he was disposed to accept my grandfather's offer or not. He gave me a keen look. "Do I gather that you favor this Crawford's proposal?"

"I do, yes."

"And have you thought about what will happen to your grandfather's people if the glen is cleared for sheep?"

"Yes, I have," I replied eagerly. "Many of our tenants are living such hard lives, one step away from starvation. I'd like to help them. My cousin Murdoch has been telling me about special villages that have been set up in other parts of Scotland to settle tenants displaced by newer methods of agriculture. I remember Murdoch's mentioning one very successful village. Cuminestown, I think it was called." A flicker of recognition crossed Jock's face. "You're familiar with this place?"

"Oh, aye. But Ian can tell you more about it than I can."

Ian walked over to us. "Cuminestown is in Aberdeenshire," he said curtly. "That's rich farming country, and the town was established mainly to provide an outlet for the excess produce of the estate. In any case, the owner poured a fortune into that village, and it was years before he saw any return. We have a totally different situation here in the Highlands. Poor soil, harsh climate, lack of transportation. A village like Cuminestown would have no chance of success here. You'd end up with starving, landless peasants with no place to lay their heads. And even under the best of conditions, our people wouldn't want to leave the glen to work in a fishing village far from here, or in a community of weavers or flax-makers. They've lived here for generations and they feel they belong here. This is their home."

"But if they have only two choices, either to stay here and starve, or to go elsewhere and learn new skills," I began.

"There's a third way," he said levelly. "I thought your grandfather had agreed to let me try it. We'd follow Jock's example. Proceed slowly and gradually. Leave our tenants in possession. Persuade them to join their holdings, not to continue cultivation with the inefficient runrig system, but to raise better livestock. Provide them with capital to purchase small flocks of sheep, urge them to use a common herdsman, accept rent payments in kind—wool and meat."

As Ian spoke, his eyes kindled into warmth and his face took on a glow of enthusiasm. It was the familiar transformation that always came over him when he was talking about something that really mattered to him.

I hesitated. Now that we were talking again, I didn't want to disrupt the tenuous flow of communication between us. "Ian . . . Wouldn't this plan of yours take a long time to put into practice? Wouldn't it cost a great deal of money, all of it coming out of my grandfather's pocket, without any guarantee you'd be successful? And I'm not sure our tenants are capable of taking on such responsibility. Master Crawford has such a poor opinion of our people that he doesn't even want to hire them as graziers for his prize Lintons."

His mouth hardening, Ian said with a quiet savagery, "The earl must be proud of you. You're an apt pupil. When you succeed him as Laird of Kildrummond, you'll know how to wring the last penny of profit from the estate without a moment's care for your tenants. Of course, by that time there won't be many tenants. You and your grandfather will have turned them out of the glen to rot away from starvation and disease." Ian looked at Jock. "Old friend, I'm going now. You'll make your own decision about your lease, but if you want my opinion later, I'll be very happy to give it to you." Wheeling, he strode to the door.

"Ian!"

He ignored my cry. We heard his quick steps receding down the corridor.

I gulped down the lump in my throat. "Meg, how could Ian talk to me like that?"

"Mistress." Meg put a gentle hand on my shoulder. "Master Ian was angry. You know how much he loves Kildrummond."

"Oh, yes, I know that." I swallowed hard again. "What I don't understand is why he doesn't seem to realize that I love Kildrummond, too." I straightened my hat and picked up my riding crop. "Jock, I've given you my grandfather's message. I won't press you now. You'll want to talk to Meg. Will you send your answer to the castle when you've come to your decision?"

"Aye, that I will."

As I rode away from Jock's house, I was struck again by the fact that I had no idea how the tacksman would reply to my grandfather's offer. As Jock himself had said, the earl's money would enable him to buy or lease a property anywhere he chose to settle. However, he would also be obliged to leave Kildrummond, where his family had lived for generations, and to which, I'd always thought, he was as deeply attached as Ian.

I cantered slowly down the valley toward the entrance to the glen, trying to sort out my muddled thoughts. How strange, that Jock's decision might change my life at Kildrummond forever. For one thing, if Jock accepted the earl's offer, if Crawford turned the estate into a vast sheep farm, I'd probably be spending little time at the castle in the future. Most of the year, I guessed, I'd be staying in Edinburgh, where my grandfather and Murdoch and Gwyneth much preferred to live. And, in all likelihood, I'd never see Ian again. Because his mind would be made up for him. If Crawford's proposal became a reality, my grandfather would neither want nor need Ian's services as he had in the past.

As I crossed the old wooden bridge on my way back to the stables, I glanced up the steep path leading to Nanny's cottage. So much had been happening recently that it was some days since I'd thought of Nanny. She must still be with the Gypsies. If she'd come back to Kildrummond, Murdoch would surely have learned of it. I hoped she'd stay on with the Gypsies for a while, until my grandfather's anger had cooled and until she no longer nourished any irrational suspicions of me. Then she could return to her little cottage and . . . I felt a pang of misgiving. What would happen to Nanny if all the tenants at Kildrummond were resettled in special villages? Would there be any place there for a "white witch?" Was there any real reason why Nanny couldn't continue to live in her own cottage? I'd speak to my grandfather about it.

But not now, I decided, as I rode into the stable yard. The thought of the earl and Murdoch and Gwyneth and Crawford waiting impatiently to hear the result of my visit to Jock was suddenly unbearable. They'd convinced me that accepting Crawford's proposal was the right course for all of us at Kildrummond, family and tenants alike, and they wouldn't notice, or care, that the conviction was tearing me apart. It had opened a chasm between me and Ian, and I saw no way of bridging it. No, I needn't report to the earl just yet. Jock hadn't made his decision. It wouldn't hurt my grandfather and the others to wait awhile longer for the negative news.

I waved off the groom who came running out to take my horse. "I've changed my mind about returning to the house just now. It's such a lovely day, I believe I'll go riding along the loch."

"Will ye be wanting me tae gae wi' ye, mistress? Maister Murdoch, he usually—"

"Oh, no, thank you. I won't need you. After all, I can hardly get lost."

My spirits began to rise soon after I reached the loch. It was almost impossible to nourish gloomy thoughts in the midst of such lushly beautiful scenery. I reined in my horse and sat for a long time looking out over the rippling blue waves of the loch to Inverscaddle Bay on the opposite shore, flanked by the undulating hills of Ardgour. The interplay of sunlight and water exerted a mesmerizing, soothing effect on me. I was able to put Black-faced Lintons and Master Crawford and even my unhappiness over Ian out of my mind, at least for a while. Even the midges were no problem. A brisk breeze was blowing off the water.

Finally, rousing myself, I turned my mount to the right, in the direction of Fort William. I rode along, pausing frequently to enjoy the wealth of wildflowers growing along the banks of the loch or to raise my eyes to look with awe on the gaunt soaring peak rearing above the trees far to my right. Ben Nevis. The highest mountain in the British Isles, where snow lingered throughout the year.

Suddenly I chuckled as I remembered a story Ian had once told me. He'd sworn it was true. A certain Cameron of Glen Nevis held his lands by virtue of a charter granting him tenure only as long as there was snow on Ben Nevis. So a winter in which little snow fell was followed by the hottest summer in memory, and poor Cameron was forced to erect a tent over a patch of snow on the mountain to keep it from melting.

As I meandered along I glimpsed ahead of me, next to a large boulder on the edge of the water, the deep purple glimmer of a plant that was unfamiliar to me. A variety of orchid, I thought. If I dismounted, it might be tricky to get back into the saddle unaided. No, I'd take my chances. I was determined to see those flowers, which I suspected might be marsh orchids. Dismounting, I was bending to examine the plants when I heard a faint moaning sound. I straightened, listening intently. In a moment the moan was repeated. It seemed to be coming from the other side of the boulder. Animal? Human? Slowly I edged around the huge mass of rock, stifling a scream when I recognized the crumpled little figure lying there.

Throwing myself down on my knees on the boggy ground, I reached out my hand to him. "Gavin, Gavin, what's happened to you?"

He moaned again, a sliver of a sound, entirely involuntary. Deeply unconscious, he was beyond answering me. There was an ugly bruise, caked with congealing blood, on his temple. More alarming was the sight of his right leg, twisted beneath him at a grotesque angle. I glanced up at the boulder beside us. If I knew Gavin, he'd climbed the rock, or tried to climb it, losing his balance and falling. When he hit the ground, he'd evidently struck his temple against the jagged piece of rock now lying beside his head. Which injury was more serious I couldn't know. I suspected, however, that it was no common fracture that had caused Gavin's leg to bend at such an angle.

What was he doing here, miles from his grandmother's cottage? It must have taken him hours to trudge this distance on his six-year-old legs. It didn't matter why he was here, I reprimanded myself. It only mattered that he was badly injured. What was I going to do about it? How was I to help him?

I stared down at Gavin's face, deathly white except for the darkly red gobs of blood on his temple. He had a terribly injured leg and he might have an equally serious head injury. It would probably be dangerous to attempt to move him. In any case, move him or not, I wouldn't be able to mount both of us on my horse.

Then what should I do? Leave Gavin and go for help? What if he should recover consciousness while I was gone? My heart constricted. He'd awaken frightened, bewildered, in agonizing pain. He needed someone familiar to hold him and comfort him until help arrived.

But if I didn't go for help, he might die. Travelers passed along this rough road infrequently. I couldn't depend on someone passing through to carry a message to Kildrummond, especially since it was already late afternoon. If I were at the castle I'd already be thinking of dressing for dinner.

Crouched beside Gavin, listening to his occasional faint moan, hoping and yet fearing that at any moment he would open his eyes, I tried to force myself to do what was right, to choose the lesser of two evils. In the end, I decided I had to leave this helpless child alone and go for help.

Slowly I rose, reaching for my docile horse's trailing reins. I looked about me for a convenient rock to use as a mounting block. Then, from around a bend of the path behind me, I heard the welcome sound of hooves. In a moment Ian cantered into sight. "Kirstie, are you all right?" he called. Quickly dismounting, he walked toward me, saying, "One of the grooms informed me you'd gone riding by yourself along the loch, and he was concerned that you'd hadn't come back yet. He thought you might have been thrown from your horse—"

"Oh, Ian, I'm so glad to see you," I burst out. "It's Gavin. He's badly hurt."

His eyes followed my shaking finger to Gavin's limp form. He uttered a strangled, "Oh, my God," and sank down on his knees beside the child. Catching his breath in dismay at the sight of the crumpled leg, he turned his attention to the boy's head wound. Ian's long sensitive fingers probed gently into the caked blood and hair on Gavin's temple. At last Ian rose to his feet, his face drawn with anxiety. "It's bad, Kirstie."

"Ian! He's not—he's not dying?"

He hesitated. "The blow to the temple may not be serious. I couldn't feel any fracture," he said finally. "In fact, the head injury may be a blessing. While Gavin's unconscious, he can't feel any pain. But the leg . . . It's the worst fracture I've ever seen. We must get the child to a surgeon immediately to have the bone set. There's a regimental surgeon at Fort William, a friend of mine. He'll treat Gavin. But even then . . . " Ian shook his head. "The boy could be crippled for life."

My heart turned over. That beautiful child, never to race over the moors again? "If you'll stay with Gavin, I'll ride back to the castle for help," I said urgently. "I'll bring back a carriage—"

Ian interrupted me. "It would take too long. The boy needs treatment immediately. And a jolting ride in a carriage on this rough road would jostle the leg unbearably." He thought

235

for a moment. "Kirstie, between us we can get Gavin to Fort William, if you think you can hold the boy securely in front of you as you ride. I'll walk beside you, leading your horse and mine, supporting Gavin's leg as much as possible."

"Yes, of course, I can do that," I exclaimed in a surge of relief. "Here, give me a hand into the saddle." Once mounted, I waited, scarcely daring to breathe, as Ian lifted Gavin slowly and carefully and reached up to deposit the little figure in my arms. During the transfer, Gavin groaned heavily and partially opened his eyes. *Oh, God,* I prayed frantically, *make him unconscious again.* The eyelids fluttered shut.

We were some six or seven miles from Fort William at this point. It normally took well over an hour to reach the town on horseback over the wretched road, longer by carriage. However, it felt more like sixty or seventy miles as we inched along the rutted roadway, with Ian walking at a snail's pace at the horse's head, carefully guiding the animal around the roughest patches in the track while he kept one hand firmly but gently beneath Gavin's mangled leg.

Three hours later, prone on a table in the regimental surgery at Fort William, Gavin groaned sharply as Doctor Smithson was putting the finishing touches to the splints on his leg. "Don't let him move, Major Cameron," the surgeon ordered Ian brusquely. Ian, tense and perspiring, tightened his grip on Gavin's shoulders and upper torso, but it wasn't necessary. The child had lapsed into unconsciousness again.

"Will Gavin be all right, Doctor?" I asked, as the surgeon moved away from the table and smoothed down his shirt-sleeves.

He looked at me compassionately. "I can't guarantee he won't limp. I believe he'll be able to walk. Frankly, the head injury concerns me more at the moment. I don't think there's a fracture. Concussion, now, that's a possibility. I confess the prospect worries me. The child's been unconscious for—well, for some hours. We don't know for how long. Never a good sign. His skin feels somewhat cold and clammy, too, and his respiration isn't as strong as I'd like to see it. For the present, he should be kept warm and quiet and flat on his back, and he should be watched very carefully. You'll be staying in Fort William tonight, of course?"

"Yes. At least I will," said Ian. He glanced at me and then at his watch. "Kirstie, I'm planning to take Gavin to that inn where we stayed the night on our journey from France, remember? It's not much past eight o'clock yet. It won't be full dark for several hours. Do you think you could ride back to Kildrummond by yourself?"

"I'd be delighted to escort Mistress Cameron to her home," offered the doctor unexpectedly. He grinned at me. "You were surrounded by so many cavaliers at our regimental ball that I'm sure you don't recall meeting me, but I must tell you I deeply resented not being able to claim a dance with you."

I returned his smile dutifully, but my attention was on Ian. "I don't want to leave Gavin," I told him. "Please let me stay. I've had experience with sick children. I helped nurse many of the village children while I was living in Normandy."

"Mistress Cameron has the right of it, Major," the surgeon spoke up. "Four hands—especially when two of them are female!—will be more useful than two if that child has a crisis in the middle of the night."

"Please, Ian. I couldn't rest tonight if I didn't know what was happening to Gavin."

"We'll see," said Ian noncommittally. Wrapping Gavin in the coarse military-issue blanket the surgeon found for him, he lifted the boy, carrying him to the door, where he paused, saying, "I'll send you a message, Doctor, if Mistress Cameron decides to return to Kildrummond and requires your services as escort."

A few minutes later, trotting along beside Ian as we passed the sentry at the gate and began walking the short distance that separated the fort and the inn, I said, "I'm not going back to Kildrummond, now or later. You need me."

"Kirstie, be reasonable. No one at the castle knows where you are. Murdoch probably has a search party out after you."

"You can send one of the inn servants to Kildrummond with a message."

"Yes, I can do that, I suppose."

"Well?"

"Oh, the devil. Have you thought it might cause gossip if you and I stay unchaperoned at a public inn to nurse a child who everyone for miles around considers my bastard?"

"I'm your cousin, remember? Which makes Gavin my cousin, too. Which makes the situation utterly respectable. I'm staying."

Ian shrugged, making no further effort to dissuade me to leave. I peered sideways at his grim, set features as we walked together in the gathering twilight. His anger toward me hadn't cooled, that was obvious. It was going to be an awkward evening.

When we arrived at the inn, Ian acted with his usual competence, reserving the private parlor for our use, requesting that a cot bed be installed for Gavin, giving instructions for stabling our horses, ordering wine and a light meal. Before I went to the parlor, I scribbled a quick note to Gwyneth, telling her about Gavin's accident and asking her to notify Hallie, and dispatched it to Kildrummond by one of the tap boys.

After we'd put Gavin carefully onto the cot, piling him with blankets, Ian and I sat across from each other at a small table, drinking some wine and pecking at the food that neither of us seemed to want. "What do you think Gavin was doing on the Fort William road?" I asked suddenly. "I daresay he'd never been that far away from home in his whole life."

Ian compressed his lips together. For a moment I thought he wasn't going to answer. At length he said levelly, "It was probably my fault. I shouldn't have talked to him as I did on the day of our pick-nick at the loch. I saw his grand-mother today while I was making my rounds. She hadn't laid eyes on the boy since early morning, and she was growing concerned about him. When I pressed her, she admitted that Gavin had been very low in his mind since our excursion to the end of the glen. Apparently he told his mother something of what had happened at the pick-nick, and she flew into a rage with him. I beleive she told him she wished he'd never been born."

"Oh, poor mite! He was running away, Ian."

"I believe he was. Six-year-olds have very literal minds." There was no emotion in Ian's voice, but the hand holding the wineglass tightened so convulsively that the knuckles showed white. He left the table abruptly and walked over to Gavin's cot, staring down at the still form. He was blaming himself for the boy's injury and I couldn't absolve him of all responsibility. I'd long suspected that Hallie had hinted to Gavin that Ian was his father. Probably the child had been daydreaming that one day Ian and his mother would be united and they'd all go to live together at Kildrummond. Then on the day of our trip to the loch Ian had turned on Gavin so savagely that the child's hopes had been shattered.

Without putting our intentions into words, Ian and I alter-nated the watch over Gavin that night. The hours wore by, and the child's condition remained about the same. Toward midnight, I noticed with a lurch of fear that he was shivering slightly. I touched his skin. It had felt chilled and clammy; now it had the coldness of death. And the little pulse in his throat was fluttering wildly.

"Ian," I called. He left his chair by the fireplace, where he'd been sitting, half dozing, and stood beside me. "He's worse," I whispered. "This is what the doctor was afraid of. Isn't there anything we can do?"

He shook his head. We stood there together, not touching,

keeping the vigil that dragged on and on with the slow ebbing of a child's life.

Suddenly Gavin moved his arms. He opened his eyes, fixing them on us in an unfocused stare. "I'm gae'ing tae be sick," he gasped.

I put my arm under his shoulders, saying, "Ian, the washbasin." Gavin was royally sick, and no sooner had he stopped vomiting than he clutched at me, crying out in agony, "My leg, my leg. . . . "

Trying to restrain his threshing limbs before he reinjured his leg, I said to Ian, without looking up, "It's time to use the laudanum the surgeon gave us. Put some of it into a little wine mixed with water. It will ease Gavin's pain."

I heard the quick intake of Ian's breath. Placing his hand quickly on Gavin's splinted leg to prevent the boy from trying to move it, he muttered, "I'm not sure we should give him the laudanum yet. We don't want him to lapse into unconsciousness again. He might have a concussion. We should keep him awake for a while longer."

I was panting from my efforts to keep Gavin still. "He's suffering," I snapped. "Give me that laudanum."

After a long irresolute moment, Ian moved away, returning with a glass that he forced against Gavin's lips. "Drink this, lad, it will make you feel better," he said softly.

The child stilled, apparently recognizing the voice of authority even in his suffering. He swallowed obediently. In a short while, his eyes closed and he relaxed against my arm.

Carefully laying Gavin back against his pillows, I sat watching him, observing with a growing relief that he was sinking deep into a natural sleep. After a few minutes, I disengaged my arm and rose, moving away from the bed. "Thank God," I murmured.

Ian stared at me out of haunted eyes. "We shouldn't have given him the laudanum. Not yet. You heard the surgeon. He told us that some patients with severe head injuries die without recovering consciousness."

"Yes, I heard the surgeon," I retorted. "It's you who wasn't listening. Dr. Smithson also said that patients recovering from concussion often feel nauseated and complain of pain from their wounds. Gavin's come through the crisis. He's going to be all right."

Ian looked at me for a moment, his mouth working. Then, wheeling away from me, he strode to the fireplace, where he stood against the mantel with his face buried in his folded arms. He made no sound, but I could see his shoulders heaving.

I walked over to him, placing my hand lightly on his back. "Please believe me. Gavin's going to recover."

Ian drew a deep breath. "I know," he muttered, his voice muffled in his arms. "It doesn't console me very much. If it wasn't for me he wouldn't be lying there with a shattered leg."

"Don't blame yourself too much. You spoke harshly to Gavin, but every father does that sometimes, saying things he really doesn't mean."

He lifted his head and stepped away from the mantel. His face looked haggard. "Not every father denies his parenthood. Gavin would have overlooked any remark I made in anger if I hadn't also rejected him as my son."

"Ian, you've never actually done that. It's just that you weren't sure . . . "

"Don't make excuses for me. It shouldn't have made any difference who his father was. I loved the boy. I should have told him so."

"Oh, Ian." My cheeks felt warm. I knew I must be radiating joy. "Aren't you glad you've admitted this to yourself at last? Now you can love Gavin without any regrets."

Suddenly he reached out for me, folding me in his arms. Pressing his face against my hair, he murmured, "You've always done that, haven't you? You've always loved him for himself." Hesitating for a moment, he tightened his arms

241

around me. "Could you love me that way, Kirstie?" he half whispered. "No regrets, no reservations?"

I was trembling from the onslaught of the fiery stream that had begun to flood through my veins. I leaned into his embrace, and my thudding heartbeat gave him his answer. His mouth claimed mine, his lips gentle and clinging at first, the pressure gradually deepening in an insatiable demand that bruised my mouth and left me gasping for breath. Slowly, relentlessly, he forced my lips open to allow his devouring tongue to caress the interior of my mouth. At the same time he lifted me slightly, grinding against me so that I became achingly aware for the first time in my sheltered life of the overwhelming power and enticing danger of a man's sexual arousal.

I felt myself being swept away into the terrible beauty of Ian's love, and then, instinctively I put my hands against his chest and shoved.

Gradually his arms relaxed. He looked down at me, his eyes dazed, his breath coming in short, panting gasps. "God, but I love you, Kirstie," he muttered. "I want you. Body and soul I want you." His arms were drawing me against him again and I pulled away.

"I want you, too," I whispered. "But not here. Not now. It's too soon. You must give me time."

The passion and the strain and the uncertainty gradually faded from his face. He smiled, taking my hand and leading me to a settee next to the fireplace. He sat down beside me, laying his arm across my shoulders and resting his cheek against my hair. "I've never met a woman like you," he murmured. "When I touch you, my bones melt and my blood turns to fire. I can't be with you without wanting to possess you." He laughed softly. "Do you remember what we were taught in the catechism about avoiding the occasions of sin? You'll have to marry me to remove me from temptation, because I can't resist you."

Startled, I turned my head to look into the gray eyes, no

longer cold, dancing now with amusement. "Be assured I don't want to marry you merely to sanctify our carnal relations," he grinned. "I also happen to love you with every part of my being." He paused, gazing at me with a trace of uncertainty when I didn't reply. "Kirstie? You do love me, don't you? You want to marry me?"

Feeling giddy with a quicksilver rush of happiness, I threw my arms around his neck, my lips fluttering against his mouth as I said, "You idiot. Of course I love you. Of course I want to marry you."

His mouth responded instantly in a lingering kiss that held all the sweetness and none of the desperate urgency of his earlier caresses. "When, love? How long must I wait for you?" he whispered.

"Oh." Regretfully I ended the kiss, leaning back against his shoulder. "I don't know . . . I suppose we should talk to my grandfather first."

Ian was suddenly very still. "Why?" he asked after a moment.

"Well—he's the head of my family. I'm his heir. It's only right I should consult him. And you forget I'm not yet of age. I need his consent to marry."

"Not in Scotland."

"I see." I thought for a moment. "That doesn't alter anything. My grandfather would never forgive us if we married against his wishes. I'd be estranged from him and all the rest of my family. We'll have to win him over."

Taking both of my hands in his, Ian said, "My darling, that will never happen. The earl has despised me since I was five years old. He'd rather see you married to the lowliest grassman on the estate than to me."

"But—"

Ian gave me a level look. "You'll have to choose. Your grandfather or me. Think about it."

I did think, for all of five seconds. Then I raised my hand, running my fingers along the lean chiseled planes of his face.

"It's an easy choice," I smiled, touching my forefinger first to his lips and then to mine. "I want to spend the rest of my life in your arms."

He wound his arms around me, crushing me in an exuberant hug. "Oh, Kirstie, you'll never regret it. It will be a wonderful life you and I will have at Kildrummond! I can't wait to see the high and mighty Earl of Carrickmore's face when we come to him and tell him to send Crawford packing."

"What?" I pushed away from him. "What do you mean, send Crawford packing?"

"Why—you must know I couldn't act as Laird of Kildrummond if Crawford had a lease to clear the estate for sheep farming."

Something was squeezing my heart. My throat was so dry it was hard to force the words out. "You'd be my husband, Ian, not the laird. *I'm* the next Laird of Kildrummond."

His mouth tightening, Ian said, "Well, of course, but I'd assumed I'd be running the estate. . . . "

Whatever it was, was squeezing even harder. "You will be running the estate, but under my orders. I want Crawford to have that lease."

Ian rose abruptly and stood looking down at me under drawn brows. "I won't consent to that."

"Won't? You've nothing to say about it."

He drew a hard breath. "Then it comes down to this: you can have Crawford, or you can have me," he said brutally. "If you want me as your husband, you'll send Crawford packing."

So that was it. How could I have been so blind? Ian's feelings for me hadn't changed since the day he made his arrogant way into Calum MacDonell's house in Bassincourt. He'd disliked and resented me then for usurping his position as my grandfather's heir, and he still did. I should have remembered what he'd said to me as recently as the estate ball: "Marriage to you is too big a price to pay, even for Kildrummond." Since then, however, he'd apparently realized he could still lay claim to his inheritance if he could persuade me to marry him. And so, little by little, he'd begun to ingratiate himself with me. The rides in the glen. The introduction to Jock and Meg Cameron. The attentions he paid to me at the officers' ball in Fort William. The pick-nick excursion to the "little lake of the blood."

I felt sick. I felt used. Blinking back the tears scalding my eyelids, I said, "I'm glad we had this little talk now rather than later, before we wasted time making elaborate wedding plans. I should have listened to my grandfather. He told me once you'd try to get your hands on Kildrummond by marrying me. I didn't believe him then. Now I do. I don't want you as a husband. I can't conceive why I ever thought I did."

Not a flicker of emotion showed in his face. "In that case, there's nothing more to be said, is there? I think you've made the right decision about marrying me. We wouldn't suit."

Gavin uttered a faint cry then, and I brushed past Ian to go to the child.

Chapter XIII

We left the inn at Fort William very early the next morning. There'd been a light rain during the night, but now it had stopped. In the stable yard the ostler gave me a hand into the saddle as Ian emerged from the inn with Gavin, closely wrapped in blankets, in his arms. The innkeeper had offered us the loan of his battered chaise, but Ian and I had agreed—in one of our few exchanges of words since the middle of the previous night—that Gavin and his heavily splintered leg could be transported back to Kildrummond more comfortably by horseback.

With the utmost care, Ian lifted Gavin to saddle height and deposited him in my arms. The boy stirred during the transfer, opening his eyes briefly and smiling drowsily at me before settling back against my arm. Minutes before, I'd given him another small dose of laudanum. I hoped the drug would keep him quiet and free from pain until we got him safely home to his grandmother's cottage.

Ian looked up at me. His face was a mask, his eyes a familiar glacial gray. "Are you ready?" he asked.

I nodded.

Without another word he started off, leading my horse, the reins of his own mount looped over his arm. We went even more slowly than we had the previous day, because the rain had left a coating of mud on the rutted road. What the journey would have been like in the innkeeper's ancient chaise I didn't like to think about. Poor Gavin would have been jolted unmercifully.

During the three hours it took us to reach the turning for the castle, Ian didn't speak as he trudged along at my horse's head, guiding the animal past the worst of the ruts. Occasionally he turned his head to glance at Gavin. He never met my eyes. He'd maintained this silence—except to confer tersely about Gavin's care or the arrangements for our return trip to Kildrummond—since his final remark the night before, when I informed him I didn't want him for a husband. "I think you've made the right decision," he'd said curtly. "We wouldn't suit."

Watching his tall form walking ahead of me, I couldn't dismiss an aching sense of loss. Had I jumped to an overly hasty conclusion? Was it possible that Ian was guilty of nothing more than a sincere disagreement with me about sheep farming at Kildrummond? No. After I'd promised to marry him, his first thought was of my grandfather's discomfiture when we informed the earl we were getting rid of Crawford. And when I'd accused him of wanting to marry me only as a means of acquiring Kildrummond, he hadn't bothered to deny it. On Ian's side, at least, I was satisfied that there was nothing between us except a ravenous physical desire. Which I had to learn to stifle, because I was never going to give into it again.

The slow monotony of that silent journey, the necessity to hold Gavin as motionless as possible to avoid jarring his leg, wore on my nerves. I felt a sense of relief as we approached the turnoff to the castle, and, immediately beyond it, the wooden bridge spanning the little river as it splashed into Loch Linnhe. Then, looking past the bridge to the road leading south to Loch Leven, I glimpsed a small, familiar figure and froze.

"Ian! There's Nanny."

He halted the horses and stood waiting for the old nurse

to come up to us. She was walking slowly with her head down, seemingly unaware of our presence. As she drew near us, I saw with disquiet that she was mumbling to herself, and her clothing, normally so neat, was disheveled and dusty. Her wispy white hair escaped untidily from her cap. "Nanny," I called.

She jerked her head up, staring at me out of hostile black eyes. For a moment I felt a sense of panic, remembering how those fragile old arms had slammed a heavy metal candlestick down on my head.

"Nanny, we've been worried about you. Where have you been?"

Ignoring me, she trotted across the bridge, edged past our horses, and bounded up the path beside the river. "I'd better go after her," Ian muttered. "She should at least be aware that Murdoch's been searching for her."

Lashing the two sets of reins carelessly around a nearby tree, he ran after Nanny. He caught up with her before she'd gone more than a few yards. When she felt his hand on her arm, she whirled about. Her face wore an expression of terror, which faded as he began to speak to her. Their conversation lasted for several minutes, and I could hear nothing of what they were saying. After the first few moments, Nanny appeared to be doing most of the talking, waving her arms wildly as she made her points. Finally he turned away and Nanny broke into a run up the path. When Ian rejoined me, he looked bemused, close to shock.

"Is Nanny going to her cottage?" I asked.

"What?" My question broke into his abstracted mood. "Yes, she's going to her cottage," he said slowly, "even though I advised her to return to her Gypsy friends for a while. The longer her absence, the better the chances will be that the earl and Murdoch will have second thoughts about remanding her to the sheriff. She refused to leave."

"But if Murdoch finds out she's there. . . . " I bit my lip.

"You promised me you'd intervene with Murdoch for Nanny."

Ian gave a short laugh. "That was when my authority still counted for something at Kildrummond. For the time being, I think Nanny should be safe enough in her cottage. Murdoch and the earl have more important matters on their minds now than taking revenge on an old lady. After that . . . " He shrugged.

Ian's slurring remark about Murdoch and my grandfather, his glancing reference to the sheep-raising scheme, annoyed me. "I'll speak to Murdoch about Nanny," I snapped.

"Do that. You have more influence with Murdoch these days than I do, certainly."

I winced inwardly at the indifference in his voice. "Shall we go on?" I said. "I don't want Gavin to wake up before we reach his home."

We didn't encounter anyone as we passed the house and rode around the circular driveway to the stables. There several grooms eyed us with excited curiosity as we crossed the stable yard and headed for the glen. I didn't doubt that everyone in the house would soon know we'd returned. Above the stables, at the old wooden bridge, I caught a fleeting glimpse of Nanny making the climb to her cottage.

We entered the valley and turned left into the miniature glen where Jock Cameron and his tenants lived. Shortly after that we took the fork that led to the crofters' huts. As we approached Gavin's home, I was surprised to see Meg Cameron standing outside the cottage talking to Hallie's mother.

"Is that Gavin? Is he all right?" Meg called, running toward us. "We didn't expect you here so soon."

Gavin stirred at the sound of her voice, opening his eyes and whimpering faintly. Reaching up, Ian gently took him from my arms. Meg stared apprehensivelya at Gavin's bandaged temple. "Hallie sent word to her mother last night by one of the stable boys that Gavin had been hurt," she said.

"Lady Allendale had told her Gavin had broken his leg. She didn't mention anything about a broken head."

"The head injury isn't serious, but the leg—it's a very bad break, Meg. The surgeon says he'll walk, but he may limp."

"He'll need special care then, while he's recovering." Meg drew a deep breath. "I've just offered to take Gavin into our house. I know something about broken bones. Heaven knows my brothers broke enough of them! Gavin's grandmother is reluctant to let me take him—she knows Hallie won't like it—but I've insisted."

I thought about the dark and cramped interior of the cottage. I studied the befuddled, prematurely aged face of Gavin's grandmother. If she'd taken better care of the child, I wouldn't have found him injured, miles from home on the road to Fort William. "Meg, you're doing the right thing," I assured her. Her strained features relaxed.

Half an hour later, beaming and brandishing an empty bowl, Meg joined Ian and me in her parlor. "He swallowed every bit of the gruel," she announced. "Oh, Mistress Kirstie, he says his leg is hurting. He's asking for some of that nasty-tasting brownish medicine."

"Laudanum." I handed her the little vial. "Use it very sparingly. Four or five drops several times a day as Gavin needs it for the pain. Don't give it to him at all if he begins to look glassy-eyed, with pinpointed pupils. That could be a sign of an overdose. Give the laudanum to Gavin in a little water mixed with wine to disguise the foul taste."

His craggy face drawn with concern, Jock rushed into the parlor. "Mistress Kirstie, Master Ian, I saw your horses in the courtyard. You have news of the little lad?"

"He's here, in our house," exclaimed Meg. "He's got a very bad break in his leg, and I didn't think his grandmother could care for him properly. You don't object?"

"Nay, lass, you do as you think best."

"That child isn't going to limp, not if I can help it," said Meg with a determined frown.

Jock patted her shoulder. "I'm sure he won't. You can be powerful stubborn when you put your mind to it."

"You'll excuse me, Mistress Kirstie, Master Ian?" said Meg. "I want to give the lad his medicine."

As she left the room, I rose, saying, "Now that I'm sure Gavin is comfortable and in good hands, it's time for me to go." I flicked a glance at Ian. "Don't feel obliged to escort me. I'm perfectly capable of getting back to the castle by myself."

"Can you hold for a moment, mistress? You, too, Master Ian. I have something to say to you." As Ian and I waited for Jock to continue, he suddenly appeared to be struck dumb. He fumbled with the cap in his hands, and he looked around the room with hunted eyes as if he were desperately wishing for help to come out of the walls.

At last Ian said, "What is it?"

Jock swallowed hard. "It's my lease, Maister Ian. Ye'll no like wha' I ha' tae say," he began, lapsing into Scots as he sometimes did in moments of excitement. "I've decided tae accept the laird's offer."

Ian stiffened, and the blood rushed out of his face. "My God, Jock," he choked, "I thought I could depend on your decency. You can't mean you're taking the earl's bribe. You know your lease is all that's preventing a wholesale eviction from the glen."

Jock, too, had turned pale. "Bribe me? After all these years, is that wha' ye think o' me?"

"What else am I to think? Your lease has three years to run. During that time, if you hold fast, the earl can't bring in Crawford and his damned sheep."

"And in three years? I'll ha' neither lease nor money then, and the laird will invite that Crawford back again, or, if not Crawford, some ither sheepman frae the south."

"Jock, listen to me. Anything could happen in three years. I might persuade the earl to change his mind. He might die—"

"But I'd still be alive, Ian, and I assure you I won't change my mind," I said coldly. He flinched as if he'd received a physical blow.

After tossing me a puzzled glance, Jock turned away and began again to speak to Ian. His voice gained confidence as he talked, and the Scots accent was much less marked. "In three years time, my lease will run out, and I'll not have a home, nor will any of my tenants. Now, some time ago, I heard about a tacksman in the Hebrides who went across the sea to Canada, where he bought some land and settled all his tenants that he'd brought with him. That's what I'm going to do. I'll take the laird's siller, and with it I'll buy a better life for me and all my tenants in the New World. Sorry I'll be to leave Kildrummond, Master Ian, and sorry, too, to interfere with your plans for the estate, but I must think of my tenants first."

The anger and the tension died out of Ian's face, and all the vitality, too. His shoulders slumped and he looked defeated. "I can't fault you," he said with a twisted smile. "I had no right to question your integrity. I wish you success in Canada." Without another word or a backward glance, he strode out of the parlor.

Staring after Ian's retreating back, Jock muttered, "He's taking it hard. I wish . . . Mistress Kirstie," he appealed to me, "what else could I do? I've argued and pleaded with my tenants all these years, trying to persuade them to improve their land and their stock. How could I abandon them now?"

"You couldn't." I forced back my feelings of sympathy for Ian. He was wrongheaded and shortsighted and, yes, unscrupulous in his romantic dealings with me, but probably he sincerely believed his plans for Kildrummond were for the best. "You did what was right, Jock. May I tell my grandfather you've accepted his offer?"

* * *

When I returned to the castle after my visit to Jock's house, I felt so worn out emotionally that I hoped to avoid meeting any member of the family until I'd had a chance to rest. I was disappointed. Murdoch intercepted me as I was walking down the corridor to my rooms. "One of the footmen told me you'd come back, Kirstie. My God, what prompted you to go chasing off with Ian to Fort William merely because his bastard broke a leg? You know what gossip this is going to cause, don't you? You spent the night alone with Ian in a public inn. Everyone in Inverness-shire will be wondering if the two of you are lovers."

For the first time since I'd known him, I was totally out of sympathy with Murdoch. I interrupted him, saying "I daresay everyone in Inverness-shire has more important things to think about than me and Ian. Murdoch, aren't you going to ask me about Gavin's condition? The child was badly hurt."

"Oh. Well, of course. How is the boy?"

"He'll recover. He may not walk normally. Look, can we talk later? I'm very tired. I slept only a few hours last night."

Murdoch was all contrition. "What a clod I am. Of course you must rest. May I tell Gwyneth to expect you for dinner? My uncle will be eager to hear about your visit to Jock Cameron. Unless you'd care to tell me now whether the tacksman accepted our offer?"

Suddenly I wanted to scream. I felt like a shuttlecock, being attacked furiously by opposing battledores. "No, I would not care to do so. I'm going to my rooms now. I'll see you in the drawing room before dinner."

Murdoch looked abashed. "I'm sorry. You look exhausted. Don't let me keep you."

About to leave him, I thought of my meeting with Nanny and turned back. "Murdoch, I saw Nanny today. I think she was planning to go to her cottage. Promise me you'll let her stay there in peace. She never meant to harm me. She was only confused."

Ian had been right. In the press of events, Murdoch had apparently forgotten all about the old nurse and her attack on me. "Nanny?" he said vaguely. "Oh, of course. Poor old thing, I daresay she's not really responsible for the mad things she does. Let me speak to my uncle about her."

Relieved, I went off down the corridor. At the turning into the west pavilion, I glanced toward my grandmother's apartment at the end of the hall, feeling guilty. It was several days since I'd visited Elspeth, several days since I'd even thought of her. Was I beginning to give up on my hopes of bringing her back to normalcy? No, not yet. I'd take at least a few minutes to visit her now.

My knock was answered immediately by the young maidservant who assisted Maura and occasionally relieved her from her constant vigil over my grandmother. The maidservant stepped back respectfully as I advanced into the room, saying, "Mistress Maura, she juist stepped out."

Seeing Elspeth, my heart sank. She was sunk deep in a comalike lethargy. There'd been no improvement since my last visit. She appeared to be in a near-vegetative state, closer to dying than to living. I sat down opposite her, speaking to her softly. "How are you, Grandmother? I'm sorry I haven't come to see you for a while. Shall I bring my cittern the next time I come?" No reply, no evidence that she even knew I was talking to her. Then, as the little maidservant, taking advantage of my presence, moved quietly about her duties, tidying the room, I noticed, out of the corner of my eye, a small bottle on the table next to my grandmother's chair.

I really don't know what prompted me to pick up the bottle, to uncap it, to sniff it. I drew a quick, surprised breath. Only hours before, I'd given Gavin a draught of laudanum. Cautiously, I dipped my finger in the bottle and then brought it to my lips. No, I couldn't mistake the disagreeably pungent smell and the bitter taste of laudanum. Some time, very recently, I guessed, Elspeth had been given a dose of the drug.

And I'd have been willing to wager a goodly sum it wasn't the first time.

Slipping the bottle into my reticule, I rose, nodding to the maidservant and taking leave of Elspeth. "Good-bye, Grandmother. I'll come back soon."

As I went down the corridor to my rooms, I couldn't control my chaotic thoughts. For how long, and how often, had Maura been drugging Elspeth? I was tempted to say, since I'd started my regular visits to my grandmother. For some reason, Maura didn't want me to establish any kind of relationship with Elspeth. When it appeared that I was beginning to get through to the countess, had Maura started drugging her?

My steps dragged as a more alarming suspicion began gnawing at me. Could Maura have been dosing Elspeth with laudanum for many years? Why would Maura do such a thing? I'd gathered that the countess had become a recluse soon after the death of Fiona, and Maura had then become almost her sole companion. Could it be that Maura, for the first time in her unhappy, abused life, had come to believe she was essential to another human being, and that she was reluctant to share her sense of importance with the other members of the family? Had she decided to keep Elspeth in a more or less permanent state of oblivion, so that the earl and Murdoch and Gwyneth would assume the countess was slipping ever further into madness and it was therefore unnecessary to visit her?

It was difficult for me to conceive that Maura would do such an inhuman thing. If I was sure of anything, it was that she was passionately devoted to her mistress. She might actually believe, of course, that she was acting in Elspeth's best interests. But didn't such behavior verge as much on the deranged as Elspeth's wild attack on me during my first days at Kildrummond? And, if so, what was I to do about it? The other members of the family had come to accept the situation as it was, and my suspicions were just that, only suspicions. Except for the laudanum. That was concrete enough.

In my bedchamber, Emily was waiting to pounce on me with the familiarity of an old and trusted family retainer. "Mistress, wha' were ye about, traipsing tae Fort William wi' Maister Ian? I' the sairvants' hall, they're saying—"

It was too much. "Emily," I said coldly, "I don't wish to hear what the servants are saying. I had a very bad night last night, and I'm tired. I'm going to bed. Wake me in time for dinner."

After she left, and before I got into bed, I went to the window, opened it, reached into my reticule and emptied the little bottle into the shrubbery far below. I felt as if I were getting rid of something evil.

It was difficult falling asleep, even though I was weary enough to drop. Everything that had happened in the past few days came whirling into my mind like a kaleidoscope. The earl's plan to lease Kildrummond to Crawford. Gavin's accident. My quarrel with Ian. Jock's surprising decision to give up his tack and go to Canada. The discovery that Maura was drugging my grandmother. At length I did drift off.

Later, only partially refreshed from my nap, I changed into one of the fashionable gowns Nanny had adapted for me from Gwyneth's voluminous wardrobe. Emily was arranging my hair as I sat in front of the dressing table when the door of the bedchamber opened and Maura burst into the room. "Where is it?" she screeched, her unattractive face distorted with rage.

"Noo, see here, ye canna speak tae Mistress Kirstie like that," Emily declared, squaring around belligerently.

"Leave us for a bit, Emily," I said hastily. "I'll speak to Maura alone."

"Weel . . . "

"Run along, Emily." After she left, I rose to confront Maura, assuming a calm I was far from feeling in the presence of this gaunt, wild-eyed creature who was clearly almost out of control. "What do you want to see me about?"

"Don't play the innocent with me." In her anger, Maura had abandoned even the pretense of civility she'd grudgingly shown to me previously. "You came to the countess's rooms earlier today, and you took away a bottle of her medicine. I want it."

"Medicine? That was laudanum. You've been dosing my grandmother with the stuff for years, haven't you? Why? Don't you want her to get better? Do you think she's happy living as a vegetable?"

Maura gasped. Clearly she hadn't expected a counterattack on my part. She was still furious with me, but as she spoke I detected a trace of apprehension in her voice. "The doctor prescribed that medicine for the countess. She needs it. She must be kept calm."

"Perhaps some doctor, at some time, prescribed laudanum for my grandmother to make it easier to bear her grief when my mother died. I don't think he wanted the countess to take it for the next twenty years."

"She hasn't been taking laudanum every day for twenty years," Maura snapped. "I give it to her only when she becomes overly excited."

That had the ring of truth. Perhaps my imagination had been overactive in suspecting that Maura had been systematically drugging Elspeth into a coma for years. I thought it a mistake that a doctor wasn't supervising Maura's care of my grandmother more closely, and I still believed she'd been dosing Elspeth with laudanum to prevent me from getting close to the countess. Nevertheless, I felt a certain sense of relief. I'd been thinking, that, if Maura were really as irresponsible as I feared she was, I might be obliged to go to my grandfather and try to get her discharged. Now that seemed unnecessary. Provided she didn't have the use of the laudanum, Maura could probably be trusted to take adequate care of Elspeth.

I said calmly, "I couldn't give you the laudanum even if I wished to do so, Maura. I've destroyed it. You've been giving my grandmother too much of it, and it's not good for her. And I'm definitely going to continue my visits to the countess. Before long, I'm convinced you'll see a great improvement in her condition."

Maura's face altered. The anger changed to a kind of malignant coldness. "You don't know what you're talking about. You had no right to take the laudanum. You had no right to interfere in what doesn't concern you. You think you're helping my lady, but you'll end by destroying her."

She stalked out of the room. With a sigh, I sat down at the dressing table and finished pinning up my hair. I had little relish for going down to dinner with the family. I longed to have a tray alone in my room. Naturally that was out of the question. They would all be waiting to hear about my visit to Jock Cameron.

And indeed, the entire family—plus Master Crawford—was already assembled in the family drawing room when I entered. Murdoch hastened to meet me. "Here you are at last." He smiled. "I hope you're feeling more the thing after your nap."

Raising an eyebrow, Gwyneth said, "Well, Kirstie, I'm sure I'm very glad you've returned safely. However, I do trust you've realized how unwise it was to—"

"Gwyneth," said Murdoch warningly. "I don't think Kirstie needs a lecture at this time."

"Quite right, Murdoch," the earl remarked. "The less said about such an ill-advised errand of mercy, the better." He motioned me to a chair beside him. "Come sit with me. You went to see this tacksman, Jock Cameron, yesterday?"

"Yes, and today also. Jock is prepared to accept your offer."

"Oh, capital," exclaimed Murdoch in delight. "You've done it, Kirstie." Gwyneth expelled her breath in a long sigh of satisfaction. My grandfather allowed a faintly gratified smile to curve his lips. Master Crawford beamed, rubbing his hands together as if in anticipation of the profits to come. "Ye'll no regret our bargain, my lord," he said to the earl. "Frae this day, ye'll see a richer Kildrummond."

"But not necessarily a happier one," said a harsh voice. Ian was standing in the doorway. His clothes were dusty and disheveled; his thick tawny hair was escaping from its usual neat queue. I guessed he'd spent the day in the saddle. A sudden vision of the bare hills surrounding the "little lake of the blood" flashed through my mind.

My grandfather lifted his quizzing glass to look at Ian. "If you are favoring us with your presence at dinner, my dear Ian, I suggest that you change into something more presentable."

"I'm not dining here, sir. Not tonight, or any night. I know about Jock Cameron's decision to accept your offer, and I realize the way is now open for raising Lintons at Kildrummond. I came to find out if you wanted to accept my offer to stay on as steward until the last of the expiring leases has been terminated and arrangements have been made to clear the glen."

"That would be helpful, I believe. You're familiar with all the estate records. Thank you."

"No need to thank me. I have no wish to be helpful to you personally. I'm staying on to do what I can for our tenants as they prepare to leave the glen and move to the model villages"—Ian shot Murdoch a look of savage irony—"the model villages that are being prepared for them. Meanwhile, to avoid embarrassment for all of us, I'll no longer be staying at the castle except to work out of my estate office. I've arranged for a room at Davey Henderson's tack."

"As you will." The earl gave an indifferent nod.

"You're certainly a shining example of gratitude and family feeling, Ian," said Murdoch with a sneer.

"A direct reflection of the way I've always been received

at Kildrummond, no doubt." Ian bowed to the earl. "Good day, sir."

His face and his voice hadn't betrayed any emotion, but I couldn't believe that Ian, deep inside of him, didn't feel a sense of desolation at the thought of cutting his ties with this place that he loved better than any other on earth. Impelled by a sudden quick sympathy, I rushed after him, catching up to him in the great central hall.

"Ian . . . "

He paused, turning around to face me. The gray eyes were dead and cold.

I'd followed him on pure impulse. My mind floundered, searching for something to say to him. "Ian, I—I wanted to thank you for staying on. The tenants will appreciate it."

His feelings broke free from the iron reins that had restrained them. "My God, woman, why bother with this charade? You've no love for your tenants, no love for Kildrummond, no love for anyone except yourself. I should have listened to my instincts. From the day I met you I suspected you'd mean sorrow and distress for the people of this glen. Now you've destroyed us all."

The viciousness, the unfairness, of Ian's attack flayed my heart. My eyes flooding with tears, I stumbled across the foyer and down the corridor to the haven of the music room, where the candles had been lit in readiness for our usual nightly concert. Sinking into a chair, I covered my face with my hands and gave way to a wild sobbing.

"Kirstie, darling! What is it? It's Ian again, isn't it? What did he say to you this time?"

I shook my head, leaning gratefully against Murdoch's comforting shoulder as he knelt beside my chair with his arms around me.

"All right. You don't have to talk," Murdoch said softly. He handed me his handkerchief, a silky square edged with lace that typified Murdoch's sybaritic tastes. Mopping my streaming eyes, I began to laugh.

261

"What?" he asked, puzzled.

I sat up straight. "Murdoch, you'd rather be dead than unfashionable, wouldn't you?"

After a startled moment, he laughed, too. "I'll never be able to keep secrets from you, will I?" His face sobered. "We're so well suited, my dear. We could have such a happy life together. I love you so much. Won't you marry me?"

The affection and concern in his handsome face contrasted brutally with the look of black hatred I'd last seen in Ian's eyes. There could never be anything between me and Ian now. I was very fond of Murdoch. We shared many of the same tastes. If I married him, he'd help me ease our tenants into a new way of life. I smiled at him. "Yes, I'll marry you, Murdoch."

"I don't want to say good night," Murdoch said as we paused in front of the door of my bedchamber. His eyes fixed on mine, he hesitated for a fraction of a moment. Then he slipped his arms around me, bending his head to kiss me. His lips felt firm but gentle, not demanding any more than I wanted to give. So different from . . . I averted my face, pushing lightly against Murdoch's chest. He released me instantly.

"Was I rushing you? I'm sorry."

"Oh, no, it's just—I'm very tired. All those toasts to our future happiness. The discussions, going on and on, about how prosperous the family is going to be. Master Crawford, herding us through every step he'll take when he sends his Black-faced Lintons to Kildrummond."

Murdoch laughed. "There was a deal of talk, wasn't there? I'm not surprised you're fatigued. I'll leave you to your rest." He raised my hand to his lips. "Sleep well. Try to dream of me. You've made me very happy."

Stepping wearily into the bedchamber, I stopped short, groaning inwardly, when I saw Hallie talking to Emily. The day had been too long, too full. I didn't think I could bear a confrontation with Hallie about accompanying Gavin to Fort William yesterday. However, judging by the steaming pitcher of hot water on the washstand, she at least had a legitimate reason for coming to my room at this hour.

"Mistress Kirstie, Hallie's juist been gie'ing me the great news," Emily exclaimed, bursting with excitement. "Sae ye're gaeing tae wed wi' Maister Murdoch! The laird, he maun be verra pleased."

So, I thought, every servant in the castle knows about my betrothal already. Tomorrow the news will be all over the estate. "Yes, I think the earl is pleased," I replied.

Hallie dropped a sketchy curtsy. She murmured, "I wish ye happy, mistress." The triumphant expression in the bright blue eyes belied her show of respect. Without words, she was telling me it was her turn now with Ian.

As she turned to go, I said, "Gavin looked very well when I left him this morning. Mistress Cameron will take great care of him, you can be sure of that."

The blue eyes flamed with resentment. "Aye, no doot she will. Was that yer idea? Ye've been sae kind tae my son. Will there be something else? Then I'll bid ye good night." With another slight curtsy, she flounced out of the bedchamber.

"Weel, noo," Emily said in a disapproving tone, "that Hallie, she's no' respectful at a'. Mayhap I should ha' a word wi' the hoosekeeper."

"No, don't bother. I can manage Hallie." I yawned. "Hurry and get me out of this gown, Emily. I'm so tired I'll be asleep the moment I lay my head on the pillow."

As it happened, I didn't fall asleep immediately. Snuggling under the coverlets after Emily left, I lifted my hand to snuff out my bedside candle, pausing when I felt a small stiff object against my hip. I sat up, retrieving the object from beneath my body. My heart was pounding as I stared down at the tarot card. It showed a medieval knight on horseback, his visor drawn back to display the grinning head of a skeleton.

I remembered the day I'd come upon Nanny telling Emily's fortune with the tarot cards. I recalled the sight of Emily's terrified face as she gazed at the grisly portrait of the skeleton rider, and I heard the echo of her quavering voice saying, "Nanny! Isna that the death card?"

"Aye, 'tis the death card," Nanny had replied, "but it doesna ha' tae mean death. Forbye, it can mean many things: change, birth, transformation. . . . "

What message was the card intended to convey to me tonight?

Chapter XIV

When I woke up the next morning, my first thought, naturally, was of the tarot card I'd found in my bed the previous evening. I really hadn't lost any sleep over it. After my initial moments of panic, I'd reasoned that the "death card" merely represented a resumption of the spiteful petty persecution that had dogged me in my early days at the castle. No actual harm had come of it. It was Hallie again, I'd assumed, angry at me for accompanying Ian to Fort William when Gavin was injured. I didn't see what I could do about it.

When I went down for breakfast, I paused in surprise at the door of the dining room. My grandfather was sitting at the head of the table. It was the first occasion since my arrival at Kildrummond that the earl had breakfasted with the family.

"My dear Kirstie, you're going riding very early, surely," he said, raising his quizzing glass to gaze at my riding habit.

When I'd first arrived at the castle I'd been unnerved and intimidated by his practice of staring at me through his quizzing glass. Now I was used to it. "I'm going to visit Gavin immediately after breakfast," I explained.

Murdoch rose to pull out my chair for me. "I'll go with you," he announced.

"Murdoch, you're forgetting," the earl reprimanded him.

"Master Crawford is leaving us this morning. We have matters to settle before he goes."

"Aye, and that we do, my lord," said Crawford, speaking enthusiastically but indistinctly through an enormous mouthful of cold roast beef. He reached for a tankard of ale and drained it, wiping his mouth with his napkin and dabbing at several drops of spilled ale on his waistcoat. My fastidious grandfather barely restrained a shudder. "As I told ye," said the sheep farmer, "I ha' the preliminary papers all drawn up—"

"Subject to the changes we discussed last night," said Murdoch quickly.

"Aye." Crawford nodded. A faint shadow crossed his face. Evidently it still rankled that last night Murdoch and the earl had forced him to agree to a higher yearly rent.

"I'm sorry I can't go riding with you this morning, Kirstie," Murdoch said as he returned from the sideboard with a plate of rolls and a cup of coffee for me. "Business before pleasure, eh, sir?"

The earl smiled his wintry smile. "It's just as well you're not accompanying Kirstie," he observed. "As I understand it, this bastard of Ian's is staying with Jock Cameron's wife. You'd be out of your element, dear boy." He turned to me. "You're quite sure it's necessary to visit the child? Wouldn't it serve the purpose as well to send a servant to inquire about the boy's welfare?"

The arrogance in my grandfather's voice was quite unconscious, I was sure. Unconscious or not, his indifference to the plight of a helpless child disturbed me. "I'd rather go myself, sir, if you don't mind."

He shrugged, abandoning the subject. Shortly afterward he rose from the table, and, trailed by Murdoch and Crawford, left the dining room to go to his estate office.

"Kirstie, I'd like a word with you," said Gwyneth. While the rest of us had been speaking, she'd sat quietly in her place at the end of the table, sipping her tea and crumbling a roll into minuscule fragments on the tablecloth in front of her. There were dark circles under her eyes. Suddenly I had a fancy she'd aged several years overnight. She rose, putting down her napkin. "Shall we go to the drawing room? We won't be overheard there."

Puzzled but obedient, I followed her to the drawing room, where I sat down opposite her, my hands folded in my lap.

"I have a favor to ask of you," she began. "I'd like you to speak to the earl for me. I have a fancy to set up my own house in Edinburgh, and my income isn't sufficient for that. Please ask the earl if he'll consider doubling my jointure."

My face must have mirrored my confusion. "I'd be happy to bring this up with my grandfather, although I fail to see why you think I have more influence with him than you do. But, Gwyneth, why don't you speak to him yourself? And why do you want a house of your own? I thought, now that our money problems appear to be solved, that we'd all be living together in the family house in Edinburgh for a part of every year."

"That was before you and Murdoch were betrothed. Once you and he are married, you'll hardly want a widowed aunt living in the same house with you. When you first arrived here, I believe I told you that a house couldn't have two mistresses. Remember?"

I did remember. I also understood the misery Gwyneth was trying so hard to conceal beneath her stoic calm. Last night I'd been too full of my own thoughts and emotions to pay much attention to her. Now I recalled the mask that had slipped over her features when Murdoch and I returned to the drawing room and he exuberantly announced our plans to marry. Her impeccable manners had carried her through the evening—she'd wished us happy, she raised her glass in every toast—but after dinner she'd pleaded a headache and gone up to her rooms.

I'd never been fond of Gwyneth. Nor, I was sure, did she have any affection for me. However, I'd have been inhuman not to feel sorry for her now. Apparently she'd cared more deeply for Murdoch than I'd realized. She must have cherished a dream that some day he'd return her devotion. Now she had nothing to look forward to except a half life as a hanger-on relative by marriage in someone else's home.

"I hope you know I've no desire to turn you out of Kildrummond or the Edinburgh house, even if it were in my power to do so," I said gently.

She rose, raking me with cool, unfriendly eyes. "At this point I see no need for pretence. We've never liked each other, you and I. Often I've wished with all my heart that you'd never come here. I'm asking you for a favor that I think you should grant out of your own self-interest. You see, the earl won't want me to leave his household. He's grown to depend on me for many of his creature comforts over the years. Talk to him, persuade him to give me the income to live independently, and I promise you I'll go quietly. You needn't fear I'll ever interfere in your management of Kildrummond."

It had rained again during the night, and it was still dark and overcast as I cantered out of the stable yard a little later on my way to the glen. The gray, leaden sky exactly matched my somber mood. As a newly betrothed woman, I knew I should have been in higher spirits. After a night's reflection, I was convinced I'd made the right decision in marrying Murdoch. Still, I could see stretching ahead of me only a proper, dutiful, uneventful future. My heart rebelled at the reminder that never again would I experience those wild, bittersweet moments of physical ecstasy I'd known in Ian's arms.

My thoughts wandered back to the tarot card. Was I so sure Hallie was responsible for putting it in my bed? What if it were someone else? What if it were Nanny? The old nurse was back at Kildrummond, and her inexplicable hostility toward me was apparently unabated. She also owned a pack of tarot cards, and she knew, better than anyone, the significance of that grinning skeleton on horseback.

And what about Gwyneth, I thought suddenly, as I approached the wooden bridge over the river. This morning she'd revealed how thoroughly she disliked me. She'd told me bluntly that she wished I'd never come to Kildrummond. Was it possible I'd mistaken the face of my persecutor? All these weeks, could it have been Gwyneth, and not Hallie, who'd been relieving her resentment with those spiteful little acts of vandalism?

Ian's rangy black stallion was tethered to a tree on the other side of the bridge. Glancing beyond the bridge, I saw his tall form, halfway along the precipitous path leading to Nanny's cottage. He was talking to the old nurse. Both of them raised their heads at the sound of my mare's hooves on the planks of the bridge. They looked away from me immediately. For Ian and Nanny, apparently, I didn't exist anymore. I didn't know why it hurt so much, but it did. I urged my mare into the path leading to the glen.

My bruised spirits revived when I arrived at the Cameron's house. Meg greeted me with a joyful smile. "Gavin's feeling so much better today, Mistress Kirstie. He was hoping you might visit."

Gavin did look better, even though the area around his bandaged temple was still swollen and was turning purple, and the coverlets were mounded carefully over his splinted leg. "Is your leg very painful?" I asked, taking a chair beside his bed.

"A wee bit," he admitted with a slanting glance at Meg, standing beside me. "Mistress Cameron says she canna gie me tae much o' the brown medicine."

"An overdose of laudanum would be very bad for you," I assured him. I slipped my hand into the pocket of my riding habit and brought out the carved wooden box of dominoes. "I thought your mother wouldn't mind if you played with these while you were sick. Afterward—well, perhaps Mistress Cameron would keep the box for you."

A look of perfect understanding dawned in Gavin's eyes. Now he could accept my gift without offending Hallie. I spent a happy hour with him, teaching him how to play the game. It brought back memories of Calum MacDonell and my life in Normandy. How Calum had loved to defeat me at dominoes during those long winter evenings at Bassincourt! And how much I still missed him.

Later, sitting companionably with Meg in her parlor, sipping tea and munching a biscuit, I inquired about Gavin's immediate future. "He's doing so well with you, Meg. Do you think his mother and grandmother will allow him to stay with you until he's fully recovered?"

A cloud settled over Meg's brow. "I don't think Gavin's grandmother ever wanted to look after him. She's a sloven, and lazy, and Jock suspects she's a secret tippler. Hallie . . ." Meg shook her head. "Hallie loves the boy in her own way, but I've often thought she'd be relieved to hand his care over to someone else, if it weren't for—" She broke off.

"If it weren't for Ian," I finished. "She's always hoped Ian would turn to her one day. Perhaps he will, now."

"Never," Meg declared, with a decisiveness that was unusual for her. "A slut like that? She threw herself at him, you know, when he came home on leave and everybody at the castle ignored him. Each time, after he returned to duty, she'd sleep with any man who'd have her, including—" Her lips clamped firmly together, cutting off, I presumed, the syllables of Murdoch's name. After a moment, she said, "Is it true, what we hear? You're going to marry the laird's nephew?"

"Yes. Murdoch and I are betrothed."

"I see. Jock and I, we'd hoped . . ." Quickly she changed the subject, talking about her knitting, Gavin's care, any subject except Ian. He was the son she and Jock had never had, and now he was estranged from them, and the hopes they'd

270

once had of seeing me and Ian presiding together over Kildrummond had evaporated. "It will all be very different now," she said at last.

Yes, very different, I thought a few minutes later, as I rode slowly away from the Cameron house. The past few days had changed my life completely.

I reached the turning out of the miniature glen into the valley. A crofter was walking along the path toward me, and I greeted him with a nod and a smile. I was utterly unprepared for his move when he lunged at me, grabbing my bridle and causing my horse to rear. Barely keeping to the saddle, I struck out at him with my whip. "Get away from me! What do you want?"

The man released my bridle and jumped back far enough to be out of range of my whip. He looked frightened now, rather than frightening, as if he'd just realized the enormity of what he'd done in attacking the laird's granddaughter. "I want ye oot o' the glen," he blustered. "Ye'll soon be rid o' us. Maun ye come here tae gloat? Canna ye leave us in peace afore we're evicted?"

I recognized the man now as one of the crofters to whom Ian had introduced me. "It's Ben—Ben Strachan—isn't it?"

The man nodded sullenly.

"Ben, listen. I didn't come here to gloat over you. Truly, I want what's best for you. You're not going to be evicted with no place to go. The family has plans for new villages, where you'll be able to learn new trades—"

"Villages!" The man spat on the grass. "We know aboot them, we do. We'll all rot in hell afore we see ane o' they villages. Dinna think tae fool us." Turning his back on me, the crofter lurched off in the direction of his hut.

I continued on to the mouth of the glen, feeling increasingly troubled. That the news of the coming clearances was common knowledge already in the valley wasn't surprising. But this immense distrust of the artisan village concept on the part of the crofters must have originated with Ian. He'd

271

offered to stay on during the transitional period in order to be of use to the tenants. Was his real purpose to foment discontent and make it as difficult as possible for the earl to carry out his plans?

Still worried, I urged the mare into a canter over the wooden bridge. As I reached the far side, the horse stumbled and fell. I was thrown clear, but I hit the ground so heavily that I had to lie prone for several moments before I could gather my groggy thoughts. After I'd decided I wasn't badly hurt, I rose rather shakily, noting with relief that the mare had struggled to her feet and was grazing placidly. As I was walking over to her, my foot caught on what appeared to be a length of black cord. It was attached at one end to an upright of the bridge, and the rest of it trailed across the path into an adjoining thicket. I picked it up, my blood running cold. Held taut, it would have been about on the level of my horse's knees. It was obvious what had happened. Someone standing in the thicket had pulled the cord tight at the exact moment I crossed the bridge. Whether or not murder had been intended, I could easily have been killed.

Too unnerved to attempt to mount the mare, I led her slowly down the path toward the stables. Who had been standing in wait for me in the thicket? It would have taken some strength, I supposed, to pull the cord strongly enough to make my horse stumble. Was it another of the crofters, inflamed with rage over what Ian had told him about the clearances? And if so, did Ian realize how much violence he might be unleashing with his irresponsible talk?

I left the mare with the stable boys to be checked for injury, fending off their questions about my fall, and went into the house. At the head of the staircase on the second floor, I remembered my promise to Gwyneth and walked down the corridor to my grandfather's apartment. Best to get it over with. I hoped it wouldn't be too embarrassing for either of us.

As was usual with him at this hour of the day, the earl

was still in his elegant befrogged banyan. He was sitting in an armchair, a pot of chocolate beside him on a table. And once again, as he'd done on my last visit, he was fondling the jeweled dagger that had once belonged to a sultan.

"You've had a fall, I perceive," he said, looking with a mild interest at my mud-stained riding habit. "I trust you're not hurt. You really shouldn't ride alone, you know."

"Yes, sir." For once, I could agree wholeheartedly with my grandfather. I made a mental note to ask Murdoch to escort me the next time I went riding. And perhaps I should avoid the glen entirely for the time being, although that would mean I couldn't visit Gavin. "Gwyneth has asked me to speak to you," I said.

He raised an eyebrow, listening politely and without comment until I finished telling him about Gwyneth's request. Then he rather surprised me by saying, "I approve of Gwyneth's wish to set up a separate establishment. Tell her we'll work out the details of a new financial settlement for her when I've signed the final papers with Crawford. The sheep farmer is gone, by the way. I couldn't have borne his insufferable company for another day."

Ignoring his reference to Crawford, I gazed at him uncertainly, saying, "I hope you don't think I said or did anything to make Gwyneth feel unwelcome."

"Certainly not. Why would I think that? Gwyneth is an intelligent woman. She knows quite well that her day as mistress of Kildrummond is past. You and Murdoch will want to regulate your own household."

I left the earl's apartment to go to my own rooms with my mind in a welter of confusion. I'd always believed my grandfather was strongly attached to Gwyneth, depending on his daughter-in-law for companionship and for attending closely to his wants and foibles. Clearly Gwyneth believed this, too. Suspecting he'd refuse her request out of hand because of his reluctance to lose her, she'd called on me to buttress her arguments. Apparently we'd both misjudged his feelings. So far as I could tell, Gwyneth's departure didn't matter to him. He'd even said, with a careless indifference, "She knows quite well that her day as mistress of Kildrummond is past."

What a strange, cold creature my grandfather was. I knew Ian was convinced the earl cared for nobody except himself. Could that be true? I'd always assumed he was fond of Murdoch. Gwyneth had talked often about how close the two men were. But then, I'd also thought the earl was fond of Gwyneth.

When I reached my bedchamber, Emily wasn't there. As I was changing out of my riding habit, I discovered that my right shoulder was quite sore from the impact of my fall at the bridge. I used the discomfort as an excuse to keep to my rooms until dinnertime. In truth, my mind was so full of bewildering, fearful impressions from the events of the past few days that I felt physically weary. I played my cittern. I wrote a letter to Madame de Bassincourt, and another to Marie Christine. I opened a book. I tried very hard not to think at all, but it was almost impossible to keep my mind a blank.

Emily fussed over me when she came in to help me prepare for dinner. "Ye're looking verra peaky fer a newly betrothed lass. Ye should be shining wi' happiness. Ye've no' changed yer mind?"

"I'm feeling fine, and no, I haven't changed my mind about marrying Master Murdoch. I'll wear the blue silk tonight."

While Emily was arranging my hair, she said casually, "Ha' ye visited the countess recently?"

"I saw her yesterday, very briefly. Why?"

"Weel, ye ken the wee sairvant girl—Dilly's her name— who helps that Maura Fraser wi' the countess? Dilly's saying around the sairvants' hall that the auld lady is verra upsetlike taeday. Weeping and wailing and trying tae leave her rooms. Didna ye tell me yer grandmither's been verra quiet lately?"

I tried not to let Emily see how disturbed I was by her comment. Had I done a dreadful thing in taking away Elspeth's laudanum? Perhaps Maura had been telling the simple truth, that it was essential to give my grandmother the drug when she was in one of her agitated moods.

When I left my bedchamber to go to dinner, my guilt feelings were so great that my feet took me automatically past the turning out of the pavilion and down the corridor to my grandmother's rooms. As I approached, her door opened and Ian came out, followed by Maura, who clutched at his arm, exclaiming, "Now perhaps you'll believe what I've been telling you. She's evil, she must be stopped. And the laudanum. You must get it for me as soon as possible. Tonight, if you can. Please."

"I can't go to Fort William tonight, it's too important that I—" Ian stopped short when he observed me out of the corner of his eye. His face turned to stone.

From inside Elspeth's room came the sound of a crash and a wailing cry of "Fiona," followed by the low murmur of a voice I took to be that of the servant girl, Dilly.

Maura glared at me. Her face was almost unrecognizable from grief and fury. "Did you hear that? Are you satisfied with the mischief you've done?"

"Maura. This is doing no good. Please go back to the countess."

Ian's quiet voice seemed to have a calming effect on Maura. She put her hand on the door, then turned to plead, "You'll help me, Master Ian?"

"I'll do what I can."

She opened the door and went into the bedchamber. Ian swung around to confront me. "Is it true you destroyed the laudanum?"

"Yes." I looked back at him defiantly. "Maura was giving my grandmother too much of the stuff. It was turning the countess into a vegetable."

"That's your opinion. Maura's been taking care of the countess for years; you might have given her credit for knowing what was best for Elspeth. In any case, before you interfered, the countess was at least alive. She may not be, for

275

much longer, thanks to your meddling. Did you ever think it might be dangerous to deprive a person too suddenly of a drug she's grown to depend upon? But you wouldn't care about that."

The contempt in his voice cut like a knife. "Oh, I care," I said between stiff lips. "I care enough to try to help, anyway. Which is more than you do. You're stirring up the people of the glen merely to make yourself feel important, to get back at my grandfather for refusing to allow you to dictate how he should run his own estate. You don't care if someone gets hurt!"

A startled expression crossed his face. "What—?" He stopped short, his mouth hardening. "Think what you like." He wheeled and strode off down the corridor.

"Kirstie, stop!"

I looked up in surprise from the keys of the harpsichord. Murdoch was standing beside the instrument, looking down at me with an expression of mild exasperation.

"You omitted the refrain," he explained. "There you were, playing the second verse, and there I was, singing away at the refrain. It sounded very odd."

I hadn't noticed the discordance. It was the morning after my latest clash with Ian, outside my grandmother's door, and my mind wasn't on my music. "I'm sorry. I'm afraid I wasn't concentrating."

"Indeed you weren't," he retorted. "You were thinking of a thousand other things, perhaps, but not about our duet. Kirstie, what's the matter?"

"Nothing. Don't be silly." I picked away with one finger at the melody of "Gather Ye Rosebuds."

He seized my hands and pulled me away from the harpsichord. His face looked unwontedly grave as he asked, "You don't regret our betrothal?"

"Of course not."

"Well, then . . . " He hesitated. "Is it Gwyneth? She didn't come down for dinner last night, nor to breakfast this morning. Have you two had words?"

"No. Why should we?" I didn't like Gwyneth, but I certainly wasn't going to discuss her with Murdoch. If he didn't realize—and I found that hard to believe—that she was in love with him, I wasn't going to be the one to tell him. And I couldn't talk to him, either, about tarot cards, or Elspeth's dependence on laudanum, or Ian's betrayal of my love, or that black cord stretched across the bridge, without explaining why, since my arrival at Kildrummond, I'd kept these and all the other things to myself.

"I didn't sleep very well last night," I told Murdoch.

"Oh, is that all?" He laughed. "I was afraid you didn't love me. Look, if you're tired, let me help you to relax. Sit in that chair over there, and I'll play for you."

Murdoch was an excellent musician. I sat dreamily in my chair, listening as he slipped from Bach to Scarlatti to Handel. "Oh, I meant to tell you," he called over his shoulder. "Nanny seems to have disappeared again. I did speak to my uncle about her, and he's agreed not to notify the sheriff about her attack on you. So, to reassure her, I've sent servants with messages to her cottage several times during the past two days. She was never there. And no one seems to have seen her."

"She's probably gone back to the Gypsies. Ian told me she has friends and relations among them."

"Oh. Very likely." He was playing an air by Monteverdi now. "Speaking of Ian, one of the stable lads told me something odd this morning. It seems that Ian had his horse saddled at dawn today and went off to Fort William. Or that's where he said he was going. I wonder why?"

I thought I knew why. Last night Maura had pleaded with Ian to help her. He'd gone to Fort William to see his surgeon friend, the military doctor who had treated Gavin's injuries. Soon, possibly, Maura would have a fresh supply of laudanum. Unless . . . Doctor Smithson had appeared to be a very responsible physician. Friend or no, would he be willing to hand over to Ian a powerful drug intended for a patient he'd never seen? And what should I do about it? If Maura was right, and the countess really did require at least a minimal regular does of laudanum . . . Once again my thoughts were revolving in a wretched squirrels' cage of indecision.

"Well, I refuse to concern myself with what Ian may or may not be doing in Fort William," said Murdoch with a grin as he rose from the bench of the harpsichord. "He won't be around much longer, thanks be to the Almighty, and we won't have to see much of him, now that he's living with one of the tacksmen." A knock sounded at the door. "Yes, come in," he called.

Emily's face seemed vaguely troubled as she entered the music room. "A message for ye, Mistress Kirstie. I found this bit o' paper tucked under the door o' yer bedchamber."

One look at Emily, and I knew she'd unfolded the message and read it. I turned the piece of paper over in my hands. It was faintly yellowed and appeared to be a blank page torn out of the front or the back of a small book. On one side of the page were a few lines of writing in a nearly illegible scrawl: "Mistris Kirsty, I maun tell ye—come to my cotij Janet Cumming."

"What is it, Kirstie?"

I handed Murdoch the note. After he read it, he said in a tone of great surprise, "This is from Nanny? I had no idea she knew how to write." He studied the note, frowning. "She seems to be asking you to come to her cottage to hear something of importance. Strange."

I took another perplexed look at the piece of paper. "I hope she's not ill. . . . No, she can't be ill, if she was able to come all the way to the house to slip her message under my door. But in that case, why didn't she simply wait to talk to me?"

Murdoch shrugged. "Who's to say? Benighted old creature, she might have wanted to talk to you without fear of being overheard. Or she may have sent the bit of paper by one of the servants, or a crofter's child, or even one of her Gypsy friends, I suppose. It seems very odd, though. Will you go?"

"Oh, I think I must. Poor old thing, she's acted so strangely lately. Perhaps I can help her straighten out her thoughts."

"Then I'll come with you. Don't forget, your last encounter with her was nearly fatal."

"Murdoch, I thought we'd agreed Nanny didn't really mean to harm me. Besides, she crept up on me from behind when she hit me over the head. Old and feeble as she is, she'd be no match for me face-to-face. So thank you for offering to come with me, but I'd rather go alone. Whatever Nanny wants to say to me, she'd never open her mouth about it in front of you."

"It's all very well to say the old lady's harmless, but she *did* attack you," said Murdoch uneasily. "Oh, very well," he added when I shook my head at him. "I won't insist. What a nuisance old Nanny is turning out to be." He lifted my hand to his lips. "Don't be too long. I'd like a game of chess before dinner."

I sent Emily to my rooms for a shawl and a bonnet. I'd decided to walk, rather than ride, the short distance to Nanny's cottage. Taking the route with which I was so familiar from my daily walks about the estate, I crossed the formal gardens to the rear of the house, passed through the gate in the far wall and climbed the steep trail as far as the fork leading to the area above the stables. There I paused. Something impelled me to glance up the path ahead of me at the hulking walls of the ancient castle ruins, barely visible through the thick screen of trees. I'd avoided that upper path since my earliest days at Kildrummond. I'd avoided thinking about the terrifying sensation of evil and danger that had assailed me on the two occasions I'd stepped inside the great bailey.

So why, then, had those old memories surfaced in my mind now?

Shivering, I turned right into the fork, walking briskly as I skirted the stables and trudged up the hill to the wooden bridge. My pace slowed when I began the climb to Nanny's cottage. I wanted to help her if I could, and I hoped her summons meant that she no longer harbored the baffling animosity she'd displayed toward me since she'd fallen into that mysterious trance on the night of the Kildrummond ball. However, despite my assurances to Murdoch that I had no fear of the old nurse, I felt uneasy. What if she were still violent? Why did she want to see me?

That uneasiness persisted when I emerged from the path into the clearing in front of the cottage. There was no curl of smoke escaping from the chimney, as there would have been if Nanny had put the kettle on to prepare tea for my coming. I had a curious conviction that the cottage was empty. In my fancy, I imagined that the small front window of the house was staring at me with a hostile and unwelcoming air. At the same time, I couldn't rid myself of the eerie feeling that somewhere, close to me, an alien presence lurked and threatened.

Nonsense, I told myself crossly. How Père Chenvert in Bassincourt would scold me if he knew I was giving in to vague fears of the unknown. Slowly I walked across the clearing to the cottage and rapped on the door. I could hear the sound echoing through the interior of the house. I knew there was no one there. Pushing open the door, I stepped across the threshold, only to stop short when I stumbled against an overturned chair.

I automatically upended the chair with one hand and then stood still, glancing about the room. It looked perfectly normal, although without Nanny's sprightly presence it seemed rather lifeless. How odd, that she'd gone out without righting the chair. She must have been in a hurry, knowing I'd be arriving soon.

As I moved away from the door into the center of the room, my foot brushed against an object and sent it skittering across the floor with a metallic sound. I bent to pick it up, my eyes widening in surprise. The heavy gold seal was so familiar. The design etched into it—sheaves of arrows bound together with a band—was taken from the crest badge of Clan Cameron. From the day Ian and I had landed at the port of Edinburgh, when he'd changed from his Black Watch uniform into civilian clothes, he'd worn the seal constantly, suspended from his watch pocket. I'd always considered it a supremely romantic gesture. After the battle of Culloden and the defeat of Bonnie Prince Charlie, the wearing of the kilt had been proscribed, so Ian had flaunted the seal as a proud and defiant symbol to the world that he belonged to a fighting Highland clan.

I took a closer look at the seal. Adhering to the clasp at one end of its chain were several wisps of thread or fabric, as if the seal had torn away from the material to which it was attached. Yesterday I'd seen Ian with Nanny on the path leading to her cottage. Perhaps she'd invited him into her house, and he hadn't noticed when he left that his seal had parted company with the worn lining of his watch pocket. I tucked the seal into my pocket, making a mental note to send a servant with it to Ian's new quarters in the glen. Regardless of the state of our relations, I wouldn't deprive him of a possession he prized so highly.

From behind me I heard a series of scuffling noises on the other side of the door. "Is that you, Nanny?" I called. She didn't answer. I pulled at the door handle. The door wouldn't open. Growing increasingly exasperated, I kept tugging at the door handle with no result. After a minute or two of fruitless effort, I heard rustling noises coming from the ceiling above me. I looked up to observe with horror the flickering glint of flames. Almost immediately smoke began seeping downward. The thatched roof of the cottage was on fire; the rustling noises meant that the rats were abandoning their refuge. Slowly, agonizingly slowly, the horrifying truth penetrated to my brain. Someone had barred the door from the outside and had then set fire to the roof. Frantically I dashed from one to the other of the two tiny windows of the house. Neither of them was designed to be opened. I was trapped.

I screamed, knowing it was futile. The presence on the other side of the door had either gone away, or was lingering outside in the clearing to enjoy my torment. The smoke was becoming heavier. It was increasingly difficult to breathe. As I began tugging desperately again at the door handle, I was conscious of a growing sensation of heat. In no time, I knew, I'd be engulfed in a blazing inferno.

With a crash, the door burst inward. On the threshold, a tall form was beating out the flames around the door. Murdoch's voice called through the smoke, "Kirstie! Are you in there?" Forcing my trembling legs to obey me, I stumbled through the door and past the barricade of burning brush that had been piled against it. Murdoch caught me up and carried me to the edge of the clearing, where I lay back against his shoulder, breathing in long thankful gulps of pure air. With a sudden crackling roar the roof of the cottage erupted into a final burst of destruction.

"My God, Kirstie," Murdoch was saying, "I was afraid Nanny might still be violent, but I never thought of something like this."

I struggled to stand upright, staring at the burning cottage. In a matter of minutes, I knew, the structure would consist only of blackened stone walls. I felt sick and faint. I'd been very close to death in there. After a few moments I asked, "What made you come after me?"

"Well, I wasn't easy in my mind about your visit. I talked to Gwyneth, and she said that, to the best of her knowledge, Nanny couldn't read or write. So then my suspicions started to boil over, and I rode to the bridge to wait for you. Then, after you didn't appear, I walked up to the cottage. I wasn't sure you were inside, of course, but when I saw the blazing thatch . . . I rushed to the door. Someone had wedged a plank through the handle, and then had piled brush against the door and set it afire." He hugged me close to him. "God, Kirstie, I came so close to losing you."

I went into a paroxysm of coughing. He immediately said remorsefully, "What am I thinking of? You need to be put to bed immediately. Can you walk by yourself? You can? Then lean on me. I left my horse at the bridge."

After we arrived at the stables, Murdoch insisted, against my protests, on carrying me into the house and up the stairs to my bedchamber, past a bevy of curious servants who were staring at his singed and smoke-blackened clothing. He barked to one of them, "Inform his lordship that Mistress Kirstie has had an accident."

Though uninjured, I was badly shaken. For once I didn't object to being fussed over and scolded by Emily, who had me out of my clothes and into my bed before my grandfather, accompanied by Murdoch and Gwyneth, came to see me.

The earl's reaction was entirely predictable. After a perfunctory expression of gratitude for my safety, he exclaimed wrathfully, "Now, perhaps, you'll heed my opinion in the future. It does no good to deal mercifully with evildoers. If you and Murdoch hadn't persuaded me to overlook Nanny's criminal behavior, this wouldn't have happened."

I was glad when all of them left, glad to have an excuse for not going down to dinner. Physically I'd suffered no ill effects from the fire. My emotional state was another story. My mind couldn't reconcile the fact of attempted murder with my memories of the eccentric old nurse who'd welcomed me to Kildrummond so lovingly, so joyfully, as the daughter of the girl she'd adored from childhood.

Several hours later I had to face something infinitely worse. The maidservant who carried up my dinner tray also brought the news of Nanny's death. Some crofter children, prowling around the smoldering remains of Nanny's little house, had stumbled on her body in a ravine near the cottage.

"Auld Nanny, she'd been deid fer many hours," related the maidservant with a ghoulish relish. "She was stiff as a board. Cook says her heid was bashed in—"

I cut her off. "Take that tray and leave. You, too, Emily."

"Noo, Mistress Kirstie, ye need yer nourishment—"

"Get out, both of you," I said in a strangled voice I didn't recognize as my own. Emily's eyes widened. She turned abruptly, pushing the maidservant ahead of her, and went out the door.

I sank to the floor, covering my face with my hands, while I fought the waves of nausea pouring over me. Nanny hadn't tried to lure me to my death this afternoon. She was already dead. I knew who'd killed her. When I entered her cottage, I'd seen, without recognizing their significance, the mute signs pointing to the struggle that ended her life and to the identity of her murderer. The overturned chair. Ian's gold seal with the telltale shreds of fabric clinging to its chain, ripped from his watch pocket during the struggle and falling unnoticed to the floor.

Why had Ian killed Nanny? I didn't know. It seemed senseless. But I did know why he'd shut me up in her cottage today and set fire to it.

Over the years, Ian had grown from an embittered little boy into an embittered man, obsessed by his dream of one day becoming Laird of Kildrummond. When I displaced him as heir, he hadn't been able to hide his dislike and resentment at first. Then, gradually, it had dawned on him that by marrying me he could still achieve his dream. He'd almost succeeded. It was only when I unmasked him at Gavin's sickbed in Fort William that he'd finally had to face the truth that he could never take possession of the estate while I was alive.

He'd already tried once to kill me. His hand may not have jerked tight that black cord at the bridge, causing my mare to lose her footing and throw me—perhaps he enticed one of his crofter friends to do that for him—but the intent was his. Murder was the only alternative he had left.

Chapter XV

The day of Nanny's death seemed endless, dragging on through the rest of the afternoon and into the evening. Barricaded behind the closed door of my bedchamber, I was nearly oblivious to the passing of time.

"Mistress Kirstie, I've brought ye some chocolate," came Emily's voice from outside in the corridor.

I stopped in the middle of the room and faced the door. For hours now, I'd been pacing back and forth across my bedchamber, until it was a mercy I hadn't worn a hole in the carpet. "I don't want any chocolate," I called.

"But ye havna eaten yer dinner, nor yet yer supper—"

"I'm not hungry." I glanced at the clock. "Go to bed, Emily. It's very late."

There was a long moment of silence. In my mind's eye, I could see Emily's bony, anxious face. Then I heard the slow, reluctant footsteps receding down the corridor. Tomorrow I'd hear in no uncertain terms what Emily thought of my barricading myself in my rooms from midafternoon to past midnight.

Tomorrow. Oh, my God. Did I have a tomorrow, or, if I did, could I face it? Ian had tried to kill me. I knew him. He'd keep on trying until he succeeded. Even if I immured myself in the house, never venturing forth without a companion, he'd find a way to get at me, and I had no defenses against him.

Oh, I could report my suspicions to my grandfather and Murdoch, and they'd contact the sheriff at Fort William. Nothing would come of it, because I had no proof against Ian except for the gold seal I'd found on the floor of Nanny's cottage, and that pointed only to her murder, not to mine. Of course, the earl and Murdoch would be inclined to accept that proof. They'd always been only too willing to believe anything in Ian's disfavor. But the sheriff . . . The sheriff would say, "Why did Ian kill Nanny?" And I'd have no answer. The sheriff would say, "Ian could have a perfectly innocent explanation for losing his seal in Nanny's cottage." And that was true also.

Without proof, how could I accuse Ian of attempting to kill me in order to prevent his beloved Kildrummond from being turned into a vast sheep farm? He wasn't a nobody who could be jailed or transported or hanged on the flimsiest of accusations. He might be landless, he might be the son of a traitor, but he bore the title of Cameron of Inverloch, and that still meant something in Inverness-shire.

So what was I to do? These past hours of tormented searching for an answer had produced only one solution. The only way to save my life was to put myself beyond Ian's reach. I must leave Kildrummond. Perhaps I could persuade my grandfather to move his household immediately to the Edinburgh house. Failing that, he might allow me to make a visit to Bassincourt before my marriage to Murdoch. I'd speak to the earl tomorrow.

Suddenly I felt a hot rush of blood to my face. During these solitary hours, I'd confronted more than my agonizing fears for my life. Over and over again I'd found myself remembering the pressure of Ian's body against mine, the clinging touch of his lips, the knowing caresses of those long slender fingers brushing my skin. Filled with self-loathing, I'd been forced to admit that even now, knowing what I knew about him, I still wanted him physically. He was still a fever in my blood.

I drew a deep breath and walked to the window in an effort to distract my thoughts. I leaned my head against the panes to cool my hot cheeks. The full moon was high overhead, bathing the gardens below with a soft, translucent light that illuminated the neat paths and carefully pruned shrubs with almost a daytime clarity. Idly my eyes focused on the far end of the garden where I'd caught a flutter of movement near the rear wall. I blinked incredulously. That couldn't be my grandmother disappearing through the gate in the wall. She was never allowed to be alone. Maura, or the servant girl, Dilly, was always with her. In any case, where was she going in the middle of the night?

Slowly, reluctantly, I went to the door of the bedchamber, opened it, and began walking down the corridor, in semi-darkness save for the muted light of a single wall lamp. I must be wrong. The countess couldn't be prowling the grounds of the castle, unattended, in the middle of the night. Not unless . . . At the end of the corridor, I could see a faint glow of light spilling out into the hall. The countess's door must be open.

My heart beginning to pound, I raced toward that opened door and into the countess's bedchamber, where I paused, looking around me blankly. The darkened room, illuminated only by the faint glow from the banked coals in the fireplace and the moonlight streaming through the window, seemed to be empty. Then I heard a low groan. Something was stirring near the window. I hurried over there, dropping to my knees beside the prostrate form lying on the floor next to the massive armchair where the countess usually sat. "Grandmother?" I breathed.

It wasn't my grandmother. It was Dilly. She struggled to sit up, holding one hand to her head, her eyes dazed. Helping her to her feet, I said urgently, "Dilly, what's happened? Where is the countess? Where is Maura?"

287

The maidservant's face twisted with pain. She continued to clutch her head, muttering, "It hurts. . . . "

I guided Dilly into my grandmother's chair, pushing her hand aside so I could examine her head. I couldn't see any blood, but there was definitely a large bump forming behind the right ear. She must have hit her head against an arm of the chair when she fell. I didn't think the injury was serious. I put my hand on her shoulder, shaking her gently. "Dilly, please talk to me. Where is the countess?"

Her eyes were beginning to clear. A frightened, confused expression crossed her face. "I dinna ken. The countess, she's been sae restless taeday, wouldna eat, wouldna stay in her bed. Mistress Maura, she told me tae stay wi' the countess while she went down tae the kitchens tae fix some'ut tae make the auld lady sleep. But that was half an hour and more gone, and Mistress Maura didna come back, and the countess, she leaped oot o' her bed again and started fer the door, and when I tried tae stop her, she pushed me awa'. . . . Whaur be ye gae'ing, mistress?"

But I was already out the door, making for the staircase to the lower floors. I had to get to my grandmother as soon as possible, before she fell and injured herself on the winding paths above the garden. I was so frightened for her safety that I wasn't thinking very clearly. The vague thought did cross my mind that I should get help, but I dismissed it. There was no time to fetch Maura from the kitchens, or to rouse Murdoch as he lay sleeping in the far wing of the castle. In any case, their help wasn't essential. I was sure I'd be able to persuade the frail, confused old lady to return to her rooms with me.

I flew down the stairs, thankful for the household practice of leaving dim lamps burning to light the corridors and landings of the living quarters at night. Pushing back the bolt on the massive rear door, I ran into the gardens and dashed for the gate. When I emerged onto the path beyond the garden wall, I couldn't see the countess ahead of me in the moonlight

288

filtering through the trees. She must be moving faster than I'd have thought possible in her weakened state.

I started up the path, hoping to see the countess at every bend, but she was nowhere in sight. At the fork leading to the stables I halted. Which way had she gone? I made a barely conscious decision. I turned at the fork, running along the path to the point where I could see the stable walls and the trail winding up to the bridge across the river.

I didn't go on. I knew, with a sudden, sickening certainty, that my grandmother hadn't taken the path to the bridge. Wheeling, I raced back to the fork and swung into the steep path climbing toward the ruins of the original Castle Kildrummond.

I caught up with her as she neared the gatehouse. When I touched her arm gently, she looked up at me without surprise, but without recognition, either. She'd lost her cap somewhere, and her white hair was straggling down her back. Although she was wearing only a light robe, she wasn't shivering or displaying any other signs of discomfort from the chill of the night air. She appeared to be in a trancelike state.

I placed my arm around her shoulders, saying softly, "Grandmother, it's cold out here. Let's go back to your nice warm rooms." I tried to make her turn around. She resisted me with an unexpected strength, throwing off my arm and lunging forward toward the gatehouse a few yards away. Hurrying after her, I reached out for her as she neared the portal of the gatehouse, and then stopped dead in my tracks. The sound of voices and the glimmer of lanterns came from inside the bailey.

The horror I'd felt twice before in the ruined courtyard invaded my soul. Some malign force, repelling me even as it exerted an irresistible fascination, drew me into the portal of the gatehouse to stand beside Elspeth. The two people inside the bailey were too preoccupied to notice our presence.

I stared, transfixed, at the scene before me. In the flickering light of the lanterns, piles of dirt and stone were visible at several points beneath the walls, but what drew my eyes was the old well in the corner of the courtyard, which I remembered as being capped by a massive wooden cover. The cover had been removed, and Ian had lowered himself into the well, which to my bemused gaze appeared to be only a few feet deep. As I watched, he bent over repeatedly to pick up stones of varying sizes, which he tossed onto the ground beside the well. Maura stood near him, holding a lantern high.

"Stand back, Maura," Ian said suddenly. "I've come to a large slab of rock." In a few moments he'd maneuvered the slab to the coping of the well, and, with one final heave, sent it crashing against the rocks already scattered on the ground.

Maura leaned forward, peering into the well. "Ian, look," she said in a quavering voice. "That was Fiona's!"

Ian brought up an object that glittered in the swaying light of the lanterns. "So you were right all along," he exulted. "If this bracelet belonged to Fiona, it was buried here with her. She died at Kildrummond, not in France."

Beside me, Elspeth uttered a piercing scream. She bounded forward into the bailey, and instinctively I followed her. Ian and Maura had turned their heads at my grandmother's scream, their faces registering a kind of frozen shock. Elspeth snatched the bracelet from Ian, gazing at it, mesmerized, for several heart-stopping seconds. Then she dropped it, as if it was burning her hands, and, lifting her arms to the sky, she shrieked, "My baby! My baby is dead, and I'll make them pay for it!" She turned on her heel, screaming horribly and continuously as she rushed to the gatehouse and disappeared through the portal.

Maura recovered first from her paralysis of surprise. She wailed, "My God, Ian, I've got to stop her before . . . " She raced out of the bailey.

Scrambling out of the well, Ian checked his move to follow Maura. He stared at me with an expression oddly torn between triumph and regret. I felt an agonizing surge of fear.

He and I were alone here in this deserted place. If he wanted to kill me, this was his chance. Almost before the thought had crossed my mind, he bolted past me to plunge through the portal of the gatehouse.

I paid no attention to his going. My ears were ringing with the sound of the countess's eldritch screaming, receding but still clearly audible. I put my hands to my ears. How long would she keep it up? How long *could* she keep it up?

I moved stiffly toward the old well, stopping on the way to pick up the delicate filigree bracelet. It had the look of Fiona Cameron. I didn't doubt it had belonged to her. Ian's words had pierced my heart with the clamor of truth. I knew, even before I knelt on the coping of the well and forced myself to look down into its depths, what I would find: the remains of two bodies, their bones interspersed with the rotting fragments of the clothing Fiona and Marcel had worn on that night over twenty years ago when their lives had ended.

I rose slowly, my mind numb. I realized later that I must have been in a state of profound shock. I'd learned terrible things tonight, but I hadn't yet put all my impressions together to arrive at the ghastly and inevitable conclusion. I glanced around the deserted bailey, noting with a dull surprise that I no longer felt threatened by an other-worldly presence. Of course. If Fiona's spirit had been trying to reach me, to inform me about her murder and to implore me for justice, she could be at rest now.

Like an automaton, I walked out of the bailey. As I trudged along the descending path, I wasn't thinking of Elspeth or Ian or what I'd find when I reached the house. I tried not to let my mind come to grips with anything except the necessity to put one foot before the other. Time enough to know all the truth. Time enough to be hurt.

Still in a sort of half daze, I slipped through the rear door of the house and began climbing the stairs. At the landing on the second floor I heard a hubbub of screams and shouts, and suddenly I was jolted back to reality. My heart pounding,

I picked up my skirts and ran toward the east wing. From behind me came the sound of running feet. I glanced around hastily. A group of excited, half-dressed servants was pelting after me.

As I neared the open door of my grandfather's apartment, Murdoch burst out of his adjacent rooms, pushing his arms through the sleeves of his dressing gown. "My God, Kirstie," he gasped at the sight of me, "what's going on here? I heard somebody screaming to wake the dead—"

"Elspeth," I panted, pointing into the earl's sitting room. His eyes widened. He dove into the room and I followed hard on his heels. The bright moonlight shone full on my grandfather's tall form and the tiny figure whose fingers were locked tenaciously at his throat while the old voice, hoarse now from so much screaming, repeated over and over again her grief-stricken accusation, "You killed my Fiona and you killed Marcel, and now it's your turn to die!" Maura stood by, her hands covering her mouth, while Ian struggled to pull Elspeth away from her husband.

With a curse, Murdoch grabbed Ian from behind, wrestling him aside, then tore Elspeth's hands from the earl's throat and shoved her viciously across the room, where she fell heavily against a cupboard. My grandfather staggered backward, clutching at his neck.

"What is it? Have you all gone mad?"

We turned out heads to see Gwyneth in the open doorway, gathering her robe against her body with one hand while she held a lamp in the other. In the sudden brightness of the room we all remained motionless for a fraction of a moment, like actors in a tableau. Then Maura screamed, "My lady, my lady," and rushed to Elspeth's side, cradling the older woman against her breast, murmuring endearments. The seconds ticked by and the countess opened her eyes, looking around her blankly. Dropping to his knee beside her, Ian grasped her wrist, feeling for a pulse.

"Is she all right, Ian?" Maura asked tensely. "You know her heart isn't strong."

Ian shook his head. "I don't know. I hope so, but she's too old and fragile for such rough handling. Her pulse is very irregular."

Maura laid Elspeth down gently and leaped to her feet, hurling herself on Murdoch, who had helped my grandfather to a chair and was bending over him, chafing his wrists. The earl was pale and shaken but appeared to be breathing normally. "You devil, Murdoch!" Maura cried. "Devils, both of you! You killed Fiona, and you won't rest until you've killed her mother, too!"

Murdoch seized Maura's wrists, holding her off to prevent her from gouging at his face and eyes with her fingernails. "You're as mad as the old woman over there," he exclaimed furiously. "Kill Fiona? My uncle and I were here at the castle when Fiona died in France. And why would we do such a thing? Well, this is the end of you at Kildrummond, Maura Fraser. We're packing you off to the hovel you came from, or better yet, to a lunatic asylum. And we'll find someone to care for the countess who'll keep her safely shut up, with no opportunity to go roaming about, attacking her own husband." He pushed her away, so that she stumbled and almost fell, saying contemptuously, "Get out."

A burst of demonic fury seemed to seize Maura. Glancing wildly about her, she picked up a bronze paperweight from my grandfather's desk and raised it threateningly at Murdoch, who laughed in her face. Her eye fell on the glass case containing my grandfather's prized collection of knives and daggers. She lunged at the case, smashing it with the paperweight, and reached in to grasp the jeweled dagger that had once belonged to a sultan. She rushed at Murdoch, slashing at him with the weapon. He tried to grab her wrist to twist the dagger from her hand, but she seemed to have acquired a superhuman strength and evaded his hold. Suddenly Maura cried out and slipped to the floor, pressing her hand to her shoulder. Blood immediately began oozing from between her fingers.

As Murdoch stood looking down at her, the angry light faded from his face. The dagger fell unnoticed from his limp hand. Ian elbowed him aside and stooped to pick up Maura, carrying her to the connecting room, the earl's bedchamber. A moment later he came back, his hands stained with blood. "It's a serious wound," he said curtly. "I'll stay with her to try to stop the bleeding. Kirstie, can you and Gwyneth care for the countess?"

"Take her to my rooms across the corridor," Gwyneth offered.

"No, I think she'd do better in her own apartment, among her own familiar things." I raised my voice to the crowd of servants in the hallway. "One of you come in here. The countess must be carried to her rooms." To Gwyneth I said, "I can manage. You stay here. The earl may need you, or Ian."

I went over to my grandmother, who was sitting up and attempting to get to her feet. As I put my arm around her to help her, she said plaintively, "Where am I? This isn't my room." She looked straight at the earl, and then away from him to Murdoch, without registering any emotion at all. The great burst of angry energy had passed, and she seemed to be slipping into her familiar state of apathy.

One of the larger footmen came in, gathered Elspeth into his arms and carried her from the sitting room. As I followed him into the corridor, I spotted Emily among the crowd of silent, waiting servants. She came over to me immediately, her long, bony face scored with worry. "Mistress Kirstie, wha's been happening?" she muttered. "Terrible things the sairvants are saying. Her ladyship tried tae strangle the laird, Mistress Maura deid or dying. . . . "

I shook my head. "Maura's hurt, that's all I can tell you." I made a sudden decision. Elspeth was calm now, and very tired. I thought Emily could manage her. "Emily, I want you to go with the countess and care for her until I come. Dilly is waiting in the apartment. She'll help you."

As Emily went off toward the west wing, following the footman with his fragile burden, Murdoch came out in the corridor. "You're not going with the countess to her rooms?"

"I want to see how Maura is doing."

Murdoch put out his hand. "I hope you didn't believe anything Maura said. I think she must be as mad as my aunt—"

Cutting him off, I said, "I don't know what to think. Please, I don't walk to talk now."

"But Kirstie—" He bowed, standing aside to allow me to enter the sitting room. Gwyneth was measuring out a spoonful of a dark-colored liquid, which she stirred into a glass of water and handed to the earl. A medication for his heart, I presumed.

Gwyneth said in a shaken tone, "Murdoch, I don't know what's going on here, but it's been too much for the earl. He must rest. He can take the bed in your room—"

"No," said the earl. He was still very pale. "I'll stay here." He sat, not moving a muscle, his eyes fixed on the door leading into his bedchamber, from which we could now hear the murmur of voices.

Maura must be recovering, I thought. I sat down, willing myself to concentrate on Maura and her injury. I wouldn't let myself think about the questions that were thronging my mind, because, deep in my soul, I knew the answers to those questions could destroy me.

The minutes passed, and the four of us—the earl, Murdoch, Gwyneth and I—continued to sit in watchful silence. Gradually the voices in the next room became intermittent and then ceased. Ian appeared in the doorway, his face gray with strain. "She's gone," he said. "The blade must have nicked one of her lungs. I couldn't stop the bleeding. You meant to kill her, Murdoch, and you succeeded."

Murdoch sprang to his feet. "Damn you, Ian, you know

it was an accident. I was trying to take the dagger away from her, not kill her!"

Ian's voice was cold and controlled. "You killed her to prevent her from revealing that you and your uncle murdered Fiona and her husband."

Murdoch said venomously, "You'd do anything to blacken my name or the earl's, wouldn't you? You know the woman was raving. You know Marcel and Fiona weren't murdered. They died in France, Marcel in a fire, Fiona in childbirth."

"That's the story you've always told. Tonight I found their bodies in the disused well in the castle ruins."

Murdoch fell back a step, as if he'd suddenly received a blow to his chest. He gasped, "You couldn't have—if you found bodies, they weren't Fiona's and Marcel's."

"I also found a filigree bracelet set with seed pearls that belonged to Fiona. But I didn't need that proof of identity. I already knew Fiona and Marcel were buried in the ruins. Someone was watching you on that night twenty-odd years ago, when Fiona and Marcel tried to elope from Kildrummond. The countess saw her husband strangle their only daughter—"

"That's a damnable lie!" exploded Murdoch. "The countess never accused my uncle of such a crime. The earl and I found her in a swoon in the second floor hallway that night, clutching the note Fiona had left behind notifying us about her elopement. When my aunt recovered her wits the following morning, she said not a word about imaginary murders."

"Of course she didn't, then or thereafter. The shock of seeing her daughter die caused her to lose the memory of what happened that night. But she began reliving in her nightmares what she couldn't face in reality, and Maura Fraser was listening. Maura's known the truth almost from the beginning."

"Maura!" Murdoch snarled. "If you're calling on that lunatic for proof of your filthy accusations—"

The earl stood up, grabbing Murdoch's arm. His normal

air of brittle arrogance had vanished. "Tell them it was an accident," he implored in a trembling voice. "I never meant to hurt Fiona. I loved her. I only wanted to stop her from throwing herself away on that base-born French tutor—"

Murdoch turned on him, white-lipped with fear. "Sir, for God's sake, don't say any more!"

But it was too late. Sinking back into his chair, his hands partially covering his face, the earl went on talking as if the floodgates had suddenly burst on the impounded memories of twenty years. He poured out all the details of what had happened on that fatal night. . . .

Carrying a portmanteaus in either hand, Fiona had crept down the staircase after the family was safely in bed. Or so she'd thought. She didn't know that her father and Murdoch were sitting in the estate office, enjoying a late-night drinking session. Apparently the portmanteaus had been too heavy for her slight frame, and she'd tripped and fallen down the last flight of stairs, severely twisting her ankle. Leaving the port- manteaus in the foyer, where the earl and Murdoch found them when they strolled into the hall a few moments later, Fiona had hobbled to the rear entrance of the house to throw the heavy bolts and admit Marcel from the garden where he'd been waiting. When she and Marcel arrived back in the foyer for the portmanteaus, the earl and Murdoch confronted them.

In a drunken frenzy, the earl seized Fiona by the throat, shaking her from side to side while he denounced her perfidy in eloping with her tutor. After a desperate struggle, Marcel managed to tear the earl's hands from Fiona's throat, but it was too late. Her windpipe was broken. Inflamed with grief and rage, Marcel then attacked the earl, and Murdoch, un- able to separate them, grabbed a heavy bronze figurine from a table in the foyer and slammed it down on Marcel's head.

Now there were two dead bodies to dispose of. Placing the portmanteaus temporarily in the estate office, to be taken later to the attics and the contents stuffed into a locked trunk, Murdoch and his uncle carried Fiona and Marcel to the ruins of the ancient castle on the hill and dumped the bodies into a disused well. . . .

When the earl's quavering voice trailed off, I was released from the frozen horror that had engulfed me and held me petrified and silent in my chair. I blurted the first thing that came into my mind. "But if Fiona died that night at Kildrummond, she couldn't have had a child."

"That's right, Kirstie," said Ian quietly. "You're not Fiona's daughter. You're not the lost heiress of Kildrummond."

Suddenly Murdoch, too, appeared to emerge from the trance in which he'd been transfixed by the earl's terrible monologue. "Don't believe Ian, Kirstie," he snapped. "You know he'd say anything to injure my uncle. There's not a word of truth to anything you've heard tonight. You *are* Fiona's daughter, the heiress to Kildrummond!"

I stared at him, openmouthed. "But my grandf—the earl . . .

"My uncle is old and ill and in great distress. He doesn't realize what he's saying. I don't know who those bodies are that Ian claims he's found. They could be anybody. My aunt is a raving lunatic, has been for years, and nobody would believe her accusations against my uncle, if she ever made them. All Ian has for proof is Maura Fraser's word, and she's dead and can't repeat her lies."

Evidently believing he'd fully justified his denials, Murdoch tossed me a triumphant smile. It faded when he turned to face Ian and noted his expression of cold self-assurance.

"Proof? Oh, I have proof, Murdoch," Ian said. "How do you suppose I knew where to dig for Fiona's body? The countess couldn't tell me, she had no knowledge of the burial place. You've forgotten about Nanny."

"Nanny?" Murdoch seemed stupefied. "What's Nanny got to do with any of this?"

Settling back against the door frame, Ian crossed his arms over his chest and spoke, calmly and confidently. "On my way home yesterday from Fort William," he began, "I met Nanny, returning from her stay with her Gypsy friends. She talked wildly about some kind of trance or dream she'd had, in which she'd seen the dead bodies of Fiona and Marcel."

I made a sudden movement, remembering Nanny's collapse on the night of the Kildrummond ball, after she'd handled the brooch I'd inherited from Fiona. Ian paused, giving me a curious glance, but made no comment.

"I didn't pay any real attention to what Nanny was saying," he went on after a moment. "I thought she'd lost her wits temporarily. But later that day, I mentioned the incident to Maura. I don't quite know why, except that she'd been hinting, ever since Kirstie arrived at Kildrummond, that Kirstie couldn't be Fiona's daughter. Now she broke down and told me about the countess's nightmares. So this morning I went to Nanny's cottage to question her."

I caught my breath at this, and again Ian paused to look at me. On my way to visit Gavin at Jock Cameron's house this morning—no, it was past midnight now, so that happened yesterday morning—I'd seen Ian talking to Nanny on the path leading to her cottage. Later, when her body was found, I assumed he'd killed the old lady shortly after I'd seen them together. A cold fist seemed to be squeezing at my heart.

With a shrug, Ian continued. "Nanny was a little more lucid than she'd been the day before. Apparently when Kirstie showed her a piece of jewelry that had belonged to Fiona, Nanny had a sudden vision of seeing Fiona lying dead in a place she took to be the ruins of the old castle, and somebody, unidentified, was throwing rocks on the body. The vision wasn't straightforward, it was more a series of fleeting, shifting impressions, but they were enough to convince me I should dig for Fiona's remains in the ruins."

Murdoch said sourly, "Well? What's this trifle to say to anything? Nanny may have told you where to find some buried bones. What does that prove?"

"Nanny also told me she'd once told you about her vision. You'd encountered her running away from the house with Kirstie's brooch in her hand, remember? That was the day she'd been up in the attics and discovered that Fiona's belongings had never left the castle. Distraught, she told you then about her vision of seeing Fiona's body and Marcel's in the castle ruins. You laughed at her, telling her she was going mad. If she hadn't wandered away, probably that very evening, to seek comfort from her Gypsy friends and relatives, she'd have been dead long since. But you seized your opportunity today, didn't you?"

"A typical performance, Ian," Murdoch sneered. "Slandering me with the lying words of a dead woman. As I said, you've no proof against me."

A great change came over Ian. Suddenly he seemed much taller, and his voice rang out with a chilling inexorability. "Perhaps you and the earl aren't actually guilty of murder. Perhaps the killing of Fiona and Marcel was the accident you claim it to be. In any case, even if the countess were able to testify against you, no court would accept her testimony. However, I *can* prove you killed Nanny, Murdoch. Once again someone was a witness to murder. You know I'm staying with Davey Henderson, one of our tacksmen? A few hours ago, Davey's eight-year-old son broke down and admitted to his father and me that he'd seen the 'tall, white-haired man from the castle'—that was you in your elegant powdered wig—in the act of throwing Nanny's body into the ravine below her cottage."

A great shudder shook Murdoch's body. For a moment he stood immobile, as if the shock of Ian's words had paralyzed his limbs. Then he bent, snatching up the sultan's jeweled dagger, stained with Maura's blood, which had dropped from his hand minutes before. He lunged at Ian, the dagger raised high.

They wrestled back and forth in hard-breathing silence, equally matched in height and weight, as Ian managed to get a grip on Murdoch's wrist and struggled to maintain it. With one final desperate effort Ian wrenched the wrist sideways. With a shriek of pain, Murdoch released the dagger, which fell to the floor, its jewels winking in the lamplight. Slipping behind him, Ian dexterously twisted Murdoch's arms together behind his back.

"You'll pay for Nanny's death, Murdoch. And best of all, Kildrummond will be rid of you once and for all!"

Chapter XVI

It was such a lovely morning that it was hard to believe in the horrors of the preceding night.

The sun was shining directly into Elspeth's eyes. I moved her chair to a different angle. "There, is that better?"

"Much, much better, Fiona, dear," the countess murmured with a sweet, vague smile. Then her gaze sharpened. "But you're not Fiona, are you?" A moment later, the alertness faded from her eyes. She looked away from me, her face assuming the blank expression that had become so familiar to me in the preceding weeks.

Dr. Smithson was standing beside me, observing Elspeth. It was nine o'clock in the morning, some six hours since Ian had locked Murdoch into his rooms with a servant guarding the door. Ian immediately had sent to Fort William for Dr. Smithson and the sheriff, who had both arrived an hour previously.

The military surgeon and I moved away from Elspeth's chair. "What do you think of her condition?" I asked in a low voice. "Will she ever be normal?"

He shook his head. "I honestly can't tell you. I'm no expert in diseases of the mind. You say she lost her only daughter many years ago. In her grief, her behavior altered, and her family gradually became convinced she was mad. Also, you believe her attendant has been administering large amounts of laudanum to her, perhaps over a long period of time. It may be that these experiences—being shut away for so long from most human contact, brooding constantly about her daughter's death, being kept under the influence of a powerful drug—have themselves pushed the countess over the edge of madness, even if she wasn't insane in the beginning."

Was it possible, I wondered, that the discovery of Fiona's body had allowed Elspeth to achieve a kind of catharsis, by releasing, if only temporarily, some of her terrible buried memories? Aloud, I said, "She's much brighter than she was when I first saw her. A moment ago, as you observed, she seemed completely lucid. She realized she'd confused me with Fiona and corrected herself."

Dr. Smithson shrugged. "Time will tell, Mistress Cameron."

"How is my grandf—how is the earl?"

The surgeon appeared not to notice my slip. "Well, his heart isn't strong, as you doubtless know. He seemed weak and shaken this morning. Not surprising, really, in view of what's been happening here. Two deaths within hours of each other, the old nurse and the countess's companion—"

The doctor broke off, giving me a frankly curious look, which I ignored. A vestigial loyalty kept me from discussing the events that had shattered Kildrummond.

"I don't anticipate any immediate crisis in the earl's condition," the doctor continued after a pause. "However, I suspect he'll gradually become more and more of an invalid."

An end almost worse than death, I thought, remembering with what gusto the earl and Murdoch had looked forward to resuming their lives among the fleshpots in Edinburgh and London.

Emily, energetically tidying the apartment with the help of Dilly, answered a soft knock at the door and admitted Ian. "How is she?" he asked, glancing at the countess in her chair by the window.

"Quiet and peaceful," I said.

304

"Good. Perhaps Dilly could stay with her for a while. The sheriff would like to speak to you and to Emily."

I caught Emily's eye as an expression of something very like terror crossed her stolid face. Of course. Since the early hours of this morning, we'd both known she'd have to speak.

"I'd be delighted to sit with the countess for a spell," the doctor offered.

Ian and I walked down the corridor together, with Emily trailing behind. "I've just returned from the castle ruins with Sheriff MacLean," he said after a moment. "He completely accepts that the bodies were those of Fiona and Marcel."

I glanced at him as we began descending the staircase. His sharply angled faced was pale and drawn from weariness, and he still wore the dirt-streaked clothing he'd worn to excavate the old well, but he had an air of self-assured authority about him. Once more, he was the heir of Kildrummond, and no one could doubt he was completely in charge.

I stole another look at him. Only hours before, I'd been convinced he was trying to murder me. I didn't believe that anymore, of course. I was beginning to suspect I'd never really believed it, except perhaps during those first agonized moments after I learned of Nanny's death. He hadn't killed Nanny, which didn't prove he hadn't tried to kill me, I supposed, but I was acting on instinct now. This man may have been my enemy, struggling to wrest from me the control of Kildrummond, but I knew he wasn't my murderer.

In the family drawing room, Gwyneth was pouring tea for Sheriff MacLean, a large man with shrewd eyes and a calm presence. Gwyneth's hands were trembling so much that the cup she handed to the sheriff rattled in its saucer. Her face looked ravaged and old, and she'd neglected her normally meticulous toilet.

Silently and automatically, Emily served tea to me and Ian and then stood, waiting, behind my chair.

"Well, now, we have a very confused situation here," the sheriff began, glancing at each of us in turn. "I'm investigating four deaths, two recent, two that occurred many years ago. As I've told Major Ian Cameron, I've no doubt that the bodies in the ruins are those of Fiona Cameron and her husband Marcel. I've talked to his lordship, and I've no doubt, either, that the crime was manslaughter, not murder, and that there's no possibility of prosecution. The earl didn't make a formal confession, and no court would accept the testimony of his wife because of her mental condition. So that case is closed. Maura Fraser, now, and the old nurse, Janet Cumming, are a different matter. It seems clear they were both killed by Murdoch Graham—"

"Murdoch never meant to kill Maura," Gwyneth interrupted the sheriff. She was very pale. "It was an accident. As for Nanny, you'll never get anyone to believe he killed her, not on the testimony of a crofter's child."

"We'll see, Lady Allendale," the sheriff was saying, when a strange man burst into the drawing room. "Sir, the prisoner ha' escaped," the man reported.

The sheriff scowled. "And how, pray, did that happen? Major Cameron tells me he posted a servant to guard the door."

"I dinna ken, sir. I went up tae Maister Graham's rooms tae take charge o' him, as ye ordered, and I found the prisoner gone and the sairvant lying on the floor and his heid streaming wi' bluid. It looked verra bad, sir. I wouldna be surprised if the sairvant died."

I said quickly, "Emily, ask one of the other servants to tell Doctor Smithson there's a wounded man in Master Murdoch's rooms."

"Yes, do that, Emily, and then I want you back here," said the sheriff. To his deputy, he said, "Ride back to Fort William immediately and order the search parties out." The sheriff looked at Ian. "We may not catch Master Graham, you know. He has many friends in the area, and if he can reach Edinburgh he'll easily find a ship for the Continent."

"I can't understand how Murdoch managed to escape,"

said Ian, frowning. "I gave specific orders that his door wasn't to be opened until you arrived, Sheriff."

Instinctively I glanced at Gwyneth. She stared back at me defiantly. Her pallor was ghastly. No words were necessary. Probably I'd never know exactly what had happened, unless the unfortunate servant recovered to tell his story, but that Gwyneth had somehow contrived to free Murdoch, I had no doubt. Perhaps she'd brought food to him, and distracted the attention of the servant long enough to enable Murdoch to overpower the man. My eyes met Ian's. He'd guessed, too. Would he accuse Gwyneth?

He drew a deep breath. "Perhaps it's all for the best," he muttered. "I didn't relish the thought of seeing Murdoch, or the earl, for that matter, in the dock, laundering the family's dirty linen in public. Both of them are Camerons, after all."

The sheriff nodded. "There's something to that," he said sympathetically. "Now, then, Major, I must make a report on these four deaths. However, I'll confess to you that I'm not clear on many of the details. You've told me that Maura Fraser had known about the murders of Fiona Cameron and her husband for years. Why had she kept silent? And why did she choose this particular time to denounce the earl and Murdoch Graham? Nor do I quite understand about the old nurse's vision, and why it led to her death."

Looking unutterably weary, Ian sat silently for a few moments, as if to collect his thoughts. At last he said, "I can only speak from hearsay. I'd assumed all my life that Fiona and her husband had both died in a fire in France. That was the story the earl had always told. Then he sent me to Bassincourt to check on the letter Calum MacDonell had written to him. Calum claimed that Fiona had survived the fire and then had died after giving birth to Kirstie. At that time I began to doubt, not that Fiona and Marcel hadn't died in the fire, but that Fiona had lived long enough to bear a child."

Ian looked directly at me. "It all seemed too pat. You see,

a few months before, the earl and Murdoch had tried to persuade me to agree to Crawford's plans to turn Kildrummond into a sheep farm, and I'd refused. Now, miraculously, the earl had discovered a new heir. I would no longer stand in his way. I suspected you were an imposter, Kirstie, but I wasn't sure if you were a party to the scheme. Calum Mac-Donell may have been working on his own."

So that was it, I thought. That was why Ian was so cold and distant toward me from the moment we met. He thought I was knowingly and deliberately trying to deprive him of his inheritance.

He fell silent for a moment. Then he added, speaking to me in a low voice, as if I was the only person in the room, "I wasn't really sure you were an innocent bystander, until the Kildrummond ball. You were so hurt by my crude behavior that night. It seemed inconceivable you could have a guilty conscience. And I remembered how kind you'd been to the countess. Would you have done that if you didn't believe her to be your grandmother?"

I turned my head to look at my old servant, still standing behind my chair. "It's time to tell me the truth, Emily. You've known me all my life. You know whose child I am."

Guilt and sorrow and a great wistfulness mingled in Emily's expression. "Dinna blame yer faither, Mistress Kirstie. Maister Calum, he loved ye verra much, and he was sae afraid tae die and leave ye destitute i' a strange land. When he first became ill wi' his heart, he wrote to his auld friend, Maister Murdoch Graham, asking him tae find ye employment in Scotland, mayhap as a governess. Maister Murdoch wrote back, proposing a great deception tae foist off Kirstie as the heiress tae Kildrummond, and yer faither agreed. He had tae tell me about the scheme, do ye see, because of course I knew full weel that Sheila MacDonell was yer real mither, Mistress Kirstie. And I thought it was a guid thing, too, that ye shouldna end yer days as a pauper. Sae then Maister Murdoch sent some papers and letters and jewelry that ha' belonged tae Fiona, and when Major Cameron came tae examine them, he could only say they were genuine."

Emily looked so guilt-ridden that I reached for her hand, murmuring, "I know you must have thought you were acting for the best." Only the details of what she'd told us had come as a shock. Since the moment Fiona's body was found in the ruins, I'd realized, at least vaguely, that Calum and Emily must both have cooperated in furthering the claim that I was the long-lost heiress to Kildrummond.

And Père Chenvert, I thought suddenly, sitting up straight in my chair. Now I understood why my old parish priest had acted so strangely at the time of my father's death. During the administration of the Last Rites, Calum must have confessed to Père Chenvert the details of the scheme to foist me off as the earl's granddaughter. Bound by the seal of the confessional, the priest couldn't reveal to me that my father had lied about my parentage. All Père Chenvert could do was to try to dissuade me from going to Kildrummond by using any other argument that came to hand.

A trace of sympathy in his voice, Ian said, "Thank you, Emily. That's how I thought Murdoch must have managed the deception, but of course I was only guessing." Shifting his attention back to the sheriff, Ian went on. "When I returned to Kildrummond, Maura began hinting that Kirstie might not be Fiona's daughter, but she wouldn't explain why. However, she did produce a page from Kirstie's family Bible, giving the date of her birth as March of 1751. Fiona was last seen the previous January, at which time she didn't appear pregnant. She could hardly have given birth to a full-term child two months later."

Maura tore the page out of my Bible? The inconceivable, contradictory suspicions were beginning to race through my brain, but I couldn't stop to think about them now. I had to listen to Ian.

The sheriff spoke up with a puzzled frown. "I still don't

understand, Major Cameron, why Maura kept silent about the murders for so long."

"Because she was afraid for her mistress. After Maura learned from the countess's nightmares about Fiona's fate, she was afraid to accuse the earl and Murdoch of murder, for fear they would kill Elspeth to keep her silent, or at the very least send Maura away and put the countess in the care of strangers who would regard her as a madwoman."

"But isn't she mad?" asked the sheriff.

Ian shrugged. "Perhaps she wasn't in the very beginning, right after Fiona's death, but she was in shock. Her behavior was resentful and suspicious and rude, because she couldn't release the memories that were thronging her dreams. The family began to think of her as strange, or even mad, and Maura encouraged it, thinking the countess might be safer that way. Maura even started giving Elspeth doses of laudanum, which of course put her into a dull, nonresponsive state."

"When did Maura Fraser tell you this, Major? And how long have *you* known that Fiona died at Kildrummond, not in France?" the sheriff asked suddenly.

Looking startled for a moment, Ian replied, "Until two days ago I really didn't know anything. Then I told Maura about Nanny's vision of seeing Fiona's body in the ruins, and Maura broke down to tell me what the countess's nightmares had revealed to her, that Fiona and Marcel had been murdered and their bodies buried in the old castle. So that night I started digging in the ruins. Last night I found the bodies."

The sheriff cut in, saying briskly, "And the countess followed you to the ruins, and—wait, now. Why did she do that?"

Ian shrugged. "Maura and I discussed our plans to search the ruins in the countess's room while she was present. She seemed to be in a comalike state. We didn't dream she could hear or understand us, but she must have done. That's the only reason she would have followed Maura."

"I see," said the sheriff. "Well, then, the countess followed Maura to the ruins and apparently regained her memory briefly and returned here to attack her husband. Maura Fraser leaped to her defense and Murdoch killed Maura to keep her from talking. Yes, I think it's all clear now."

"There's something else that's clear now," said Ian. "Remember, I was alone with Maura before she died, and she opened her heart to me. She didn't want to die with Kirstie's attempted murder on her conscience. In God's name, Kirstie, why didn't you tell somebody you were living in fear for your life?"

There was a collective gasp. Even Gwyneth, sunk in her own private hell, raised her head to stare at Ian.

I said feebly, "I thought at first someone who didn't like me was playing malicious tricks. Hallie, maybe, because she was—" I shook my head. "Or Nanny. She turned so hostile after she had that vision. Or—" I glanced at Ian, then dropped my eyes, my face flaming.

"You suspected *me* of trying to harm you?" he asked, his voice incredulous. "How could you think that? You knew I . . ."

You knew I loved you? Could that be what Ian had meant to say? I swallowed hard. "I'm sorry, Ian. We'd disagreed about the sheep farming, and my grandf—the earl had insinuated you were scheming to marry me to get your hands on Kildrummond."

His face had turned bleak and cold. "I see. Well, it was always Maura. When you came to Kildrummond, she was positive you were an impostor, but she couldn't say so without revealing the countess's terrible secret. So, frustrated and angry, Maura started persecuting you. An anonymous note. A damaged length of dress material. Pages torn out of your Bible. A heavy dose of laudanum in your milk to make you sick."

But I didn't drink the milk. Poor Daffy drank it, and it

311

killed him. I felt sick, as I had that night when I'd seen Daffy's little body writhe in agony.

Ian must have sensed my sudden quick stab of revulsion. His expression softened slightly. In a moment, though, he continued, as if he had a dogged compulsion to tell his story completely.

"Maura stepped up her campaign out of desperation, Kirstie, when you started visiting the countess and it appeared you might be coaxing Elspeth back to normalcy. Maura couldn't run the risk that Elspeth might recover her memory completely and accuse the earl and Murdoch of Fiona's murder. So Maura began giving the countess heavier and heavier doses of laudanum to keep her comatose. And then everything came to a head two nights ago, when you agreed to marry Murdoch. For years Maura had looked forward to the time when I'd be the Laird of Kildrummond; she and Elspeth could be at peace then. She couldn't face the thought of having Murdoch in control of Kildrummond for the rest of his life, and so she decided to kill you. If you were dead, I'd be the heir to the estate, and she and Elspeth would be safe."

I shuddered, remembering that lethal black cord stretched across my path at the bridge, the horror I'd felt when I was trapped in Nanny's burning cottage. "I was sure it was Nanny who'd lured me to the cottage," I murmured, thinking back to that terrifying time. "She'd already shown she was capable of violence. She'd hit me on the head when I was examining those trunks in the attic. Of course, when her body was discovered, I realized she couldn't have set the fire—"

"Nanny didn't attack you in the attics," Ian exclaimed in surprise. "That was Murdoch. Oh, I can't prove it, but think about it: Nanny met Murdoch right after she came down from the attics. He accosted her because she was talking wildly, and because he noticed she was carrying Fiona's brooch. She told him she'd found Fiona's and Marcel's clothes in a trunk in the attics, together with other belongings they'd surely have taken with them when they eloped, and she'd also found a packet of Marcel's love letters to Fiona. She wouldn't have left them behind, either. All of which proved to Nanny she'd never left Kildrummond."

"I didn't find any letters in the trunk," I expostulated. I don't know why I seized on this point. To any reasonable person, it must have seemed unimportant, in view of all the terrifying and tragic and disillusioning facts that had engulfed me during the past two days.

"Of course you didn't," Ian retorted. "That's why Murdoch hit you over the head. He didn't want you to find the letters. He didn't want you, or anyone else, to have any reason to start thinking about why Fiona and Marcel had eloped from Kildrummond without taking their most essential possessions. You blamed Nanny for the attack, which suited Murdoch's purposes exactly. Now he could kill her with impunity. Who would suspect him? Anyone could have killed her."

"This is pure conjecture, Major Cameron, as I'm sure you know," said the sheriff disapprovingly. "If we succeed in capturing Murdoch Graham, the proof against him will consist of the crofter child's testimony that he killed the old nurse, and the servant's testimony, if he recovers, that Master Graham attacked him." The sheriff rose. "You'll excuse me, Major Cameron. I must be getting back to Fort William."

I watched, silently, as Ian accompanied the sheriff to the door and afterward went with him to accompany him to the stables.

Gwyneth aroused from her lethargy after they left. "At least I won't have to suffer thinking of you as mistress of Kildrummond, Kirstie MacDonell, when I'm in exile in Edinburgh," she said bitterly. "Where will you go? Back to your provincial friends in Normandy? No doubt they'll be kind enough to allow you to go on being governess to their children and their children's children for the rest of your life, and I wish you joy of it."

I couldn't feel any anger toward Gwyneth. She was suffering enough without any added ill feeling from me. Whether Murdoch was captured or not, Gwyneth must have given up forever any notion of happiness with him.

"Come with me to my rooms, Emily," I said to the old servant. "We have work to do."

In my bedchamber, I instructed Emily briefly to begin packing up all my belongings. She didn't argue. She saw as plainly as I did that I was finished at Kildrummond. She also assumed, without question, as I did, that I'd be welcome to resume my duties as tutor to Marie Christine at the Château de Bassincourt.

It didn't take long to pack. Excluding the gowns that Nanny had refurbished for me from Gwyneth's inexhaustible wardrobe, I'd be leaving with precisely the same amount of meager belongings I'd brought to Kildrummond.

"Find Master Ian and ask his permission to use one of the estate carriages to journey to the port of Leith," I told Emily. "I think he'll be generous."

I stood at the window overlooking the gardens, waiting for Emily to return. Gazing at the remains of the ancient castle, its walls rising above the screen of trees, I thought how ironic it was that on my first night as on my last at Kildrummond, those forbidding ruins should have delivered their warning that I had no future in this alien place.

I found it hard to believe I was leaving Kildrummond forever. Despite all the tragic and unhappy things that had happened to me here, I'd begun to feel as though I belonged. I'd miss some of the people here. Not the earl; I'd never felt any affection for him, try as hard as I might. Or Gwyneth; between us there'd never been anything except a guarded truce. But my grandmother . . . It was odd, I still thought of Elspeth as my grandmother, and I was very fond of her. How wonderful it would have been if I could have continued my visits to her, helping her with my music and my very presence to return to a somewhat normal life. And Gavin. Would I ever know if Hallie decided that Gavin's real happiness lay with Jock and Meg?

Then there was Ian. My heart was already bleeding at the thought that I'd never see him again. He'd become so much a part of me in these few short weeks. How could I face the future with this cold and aching void in the very center of my being?

"Where do you think you're going?"

I turned from the window to face Ian. Tired and disheveled and out of sorts, he still looked so beautiful to me. I steadied my voice, saying, "Back to Normandy, of course. Where else would I go?"

"You could stay here at Kildrummond. You could be the next Countess of Carrickmore."

I was having trouble breathing. "After everything that's happened, you still want to marry me? You don't mind that I had so little faith in you that I suspected you of trying to kill me? And what about the sheep? You know I don't agree with you about Master Crawford and the sheep—"

"Good God, woman, are you going to argue with me about sheep at a time like this?" With a rush, Ian crossed the room and crushed me in his arms. The pressure of his body against mine revived the familiar rush of desire, the aching longing to be physically united to him. "Oh, Kirstie," he muttered as his lips covered mine, warm and devouring. "I don't want to live without you, here or anywhere. I need you, I want you, I love you. Stay with me at Kildrummond."

I don't remember saying anything. I didn't need to. My clinging arms, my body strained against him so closely that I felt the rising urgency of his arousal, gave Ian his answer.

ROMANTIC SUSPENSE WITH ZEBRA'S GOTHICS

THE SWIRLING MISTS OF CORNWALL   (2924, $3.95)
by Patricia Werner

Rhionna Fowley ignored her dying father's plea that she never return to his ancestral homeland of Cornwall. Yet as her ship faltered off the rugged Cornish coast, she wondered if her journey would indeed be cursed.

Shipwrecked and delirious, Rhionna found herself in a castle high above the roiling sea—and in thrall to the handsome and mysterious Lord Geoffrey Rhyweth. But fear and suspicion were all around: Geoffrey's midnight prowling, the hushed whispers of the townspeople, women disappearing from the village. She knew she had to flee, for soon it would be too late.

THE STOLEN BRIDE OF GLENGARRA CASTLE   (3125, $3.95)
by Anne Knoll

Returning home after being in care of her aunt, Elly Kincaid found herself a stranger in her own home. Her father was a ghost of himself after the death of Elly's mother, her brother was bitter and violent, her childhood sweetheart suddenly hostile.

Elly agreed to meet the man her brother Hugh wanted her to marry. While drawn to the brooding, intense Gavan Mitchell, Elly was determined to ignore his whispered threats of ghosts and banshees. But she could *not* ignore the wailing sounds from the tower. Someone was trying to terrify her, to sap her strength, to draw her into the strange nightmare.

THE LOST DUCHESS OF GREYDEN CASTLE   (3046, $3.95)
by Nina Coombs Pykare

Vanessa never thought she'd be a duchess; only in her dreams could she be the wife of Richard, Duke of Greyden, the man who married her headstrong sister, Caroline. But one year after Caroline's violent and mysterious death, Richard proposed and took her to his castle in Cornwall.

Her dreams had come true, but they quickly turned to *nightmares*. Why had Richard never told her he had a twin brother who hated him? Why did Richard's sister shun her? Why was she not allowed to go to the North Tower? Soon the truth became clear: everyone there had reason to kill Caroline, and now someone was after *her*. But which one?

Available wherever paperbacks are sold, or order direct from the Publisher. Send cover price plus 50¢ per copy for mailing and handling to Zebra Books, Dept. 3516, 475 Park Avenue South, New York, N.Y. 10016. Residents of New York, New Jersey and Pennsylvania must include sales tax. DO NOT SEND CASH.

ELEGANCE AND CHARM WITH ZEBRA'S REGENCY ROMANCES

A LOGICAL LADY   (3277, $3.95)
by Janice Bennett

When Mr. Frederick Ashfield arrived at Halliford Castle after two years on the continent, Elizabeth could not keep her heart from fluttering uncontrollably. But things were in a dreadful state. Frederick had come straight from the Grange, his ancestral home, where he argued with his cousin, Viscount St. Vincent. After his sudden departure, the Viscount had been found murdered.

After an attempt on his life Frederick knew what must be done: he must risk his very life, and Lizzie's dearest hopes, to trap a deadly killer!

AN UNQUESTIONABLE LADY   (3151, $3.95)
by Rosina Pyatt

Too proud to apply for financial assistance, Miss Claudia Tallon was desperate enough to answer the advertisement. But why would any man of wealth and position need to advertise for a wife? Then she saw his name and understood why. *Giles Veryland.* No decent lady would dream of associating with such a rake.

This was to be a marriage of convenience—Giles convenience. Claudia was hardly in a position to expect a love match, and Giles could not be bothered. The two were thus eminently suited to one another, if only they could stop arguing long enough to find out!

FOREVER IN TIME   (3129, $3.95)
by Janice Bennett

Erika Von Hamel had been living on a tiny British island for two years when the stranger Gilbert Randall was up on her shore after a boating accident. Erika had little patience for his game of pretending that the year was 1812 and he was somehow lost in time. But she found him examining in detail her models of the Napoleonic battles, and she wanted to believe that he really was from Regency England—a romantic hero that she thought only existed in romance books . . .

Gilbert Randall was quite sure the outcome of the war depended on information he was carrying—but he was no longer there to deliver it. He must get back to his own time to insure that history would not be irrevocably altered. And that meant he must take Erika with him, although he shuddered to think of the havoc she would cause in Regency England—and in his own heart!

Available wherever paperbacks are sold, or order direct from the Publisher. Send cover price plus 50¢ per copy for mailing and handling to Zebra Books, Dept. 3516, 475 Park Avenue South, New York, N.Y. 10016. Residents of New York, New Jersey and Pennsylvania must include sales tax. DO NOT SEND CASH.

REGENCY ROMANCES
Lords and Ladies in Love

A TOUCH OF VENUS   (3153, $3.95)
by Patricia Laye

Raines Scott knew she had to hide her youth and beauty to get the job cataloguing rare coins. The handsome Lord Kemp doubted the intellectual skills of *any* woman, and had less than scholarly pursuits on his mind when he realized his new employee's charms.

REGENCY MORNING   (3152, $2.95)
by Elizabeth Law

When their father died, leaving them alone and penniless, the St. John girls were at the mercy of their aloof and handsome cousin Tarquin. Laurie had planned the future for all of them, including her sister's marriage to Tarquin. Plans rarely work out as imagined, however, as Laurie realized when she lost her heart to her arrogant cousin.

DELIGHTFUL DECEPTION   (3053, $2.95)
by Nancy Lawrence

Outspoken Charmain Crewes fled from home to avoid the arranged match with the rakish Earl of Wexford. When her coachman fell ill, she hired the handsome stranger who was watching her in the woods. The Earl of Wexford was in no hurry to tell her he was exactly the man from whom she had run away, until her charms captured his heart!

THE DUCHESS AND THE DEVIL   (3279, $2.95)
by Sydney Ann Clark

Byrony Balmaine had promised her wealthy uncle to marry the man of his choosing. She never imagined Uncle Charles would choose the rakehell Deveril St. John, known as the Devil Duke by those who knew of his libertine ways. She vowed to keep her promise to her uncle, but she made another promise to herself: the handsome duke may claim her in matrimony, but he would never claim her heart. If only he weren't so dangerously handsome and charming . . .

Available wherever paperbacks are sold, or order direct from the Publisher. Send cover price plus 50¢ per copy for mailing and handling to Zebra Books, Dept. 3516, 475 Park Avenue South, New York, N.Y. 10016. Residents of New York, New Jersey and Pennsylvania must include sales tax. DO NOT SEND CASH.

DISCOVER THE MAGIC OF REGENCY ROMANCES

ROMANTIC MASQUERADE (3221, $3.95)
by Lois Stewart

Sabrina Latimer had come to London incognito on a fortune hunt. Disguised as a Hungarian countess, the young widow had to secure the ten thousand pounds her brother needed to pay a gambling debt. His debtor was the notorious ladies' man, Lord Jareth Tremayne. Her scheme would work if she did not fall prey to the charms of the devilish aristocrat. For Jareth was an expert at gambling and always played to win everything—and *everyone*—he could.

RETURN TO CHEYNE SPA (3247, $2.95)
by Daisy Vivian

Very poor but ever-virtuous Elinor Hardy had to become a dealer in a London gambling house to be able to pay her rent. Her future looked dismal until Lady Augusta invited her to be her guest at the exclusive resort, Cheyne Spa. The one condition: Elinor must woo the unsuitable rogue who was in pursuit of the Duchess's pampered niece.

The unsuitable young man was enraptured with Elinor, but *she* had been struck by the devilishly handsome Tyger Dobyn. Elinor knew that Tyger was hardly the respectable, marrying kind, but unfortunately her heart did not agree!

A CRUEL DECEPTION (3246, $3.95)
by Cathryn Huntington Chadwick

Lady Margaret Willoughby had resisted marriage for years, knowing that no man could replace her departed childhood love. But the time had come to produce an heir to the vast Willoughby holdings. First she would get her business affairs in order with the help of the new steward, the disturbingly attractive and infuriatingly capable Mr. Frank Watson; *then* she would begin the search for a man she could tolerate. If only she could find a mate with a *fraction* of the scandalously handsome Mr. Watson's appeal. . . .

Available wherever paperbacks are sold, or order direct from the Publisher. Send cover price plus 50¢ per copy for mailing and handling to Zebra Books, Dept. 3516, 475 Park Avenue South, New York, N.Y. 10016. Residents of New York, New Jersey and Pennsylvania must include sales tax. DO NOT SEND CASH.

THE BEST OF REGENCY ROMANCES

AN IMPROPER COMPANION (2691, $3.95)
by Karla Hocker

At the closing of Miss Venable's Seminary for Young Ladies school, mistress Kate Elliott welcomed the invitation to be Liza Ashcroft's chaperone for the Season at Bath. Little did she know that Miss Ashcroft's father, the handsome widower Damien Ashcroft would also enter her life. And not as a passive bystander or dutiful dad.

WAGER ON LOVE (2693, $2.95)
by Prudence Martin

Only a rogue like Nicholas Ruxart would choose a bride on the basis of a careless wager. And only a rakehell like Nicholas would then fall in love with his betrothed's grey-eyed sister! The cynical viscount had always thought one blushing miss would suit as well as another, but the unattainable Jane Sommers soon proved him wrong.

LOVE AND FOLLY (2715, $3.95)
by Sheila Simonson

To the dismay of her more sensible twin Margaret, Lady Jean proceeded to fall hopelessly in love with the silver-tongued, seditious poet, Owen Davies—and catapult her entire family into social ruin . . . Margaret was used to gentlemen falling in love with vivacious Jean rather than with her—even the handsome Johnny Dyott whom she secretly adored. And when Jean's foolishness led her into the arms of the notorious Owen Davies, Margaret knew she could count on Dyott to avert scandal. What she didn't know, however was that her sweet sensibility was exerting a charm all its own.

Available wherever paperbacks are sold, or order direct from the Publisher. Send cover price plus 50¢ per copy for mailing and handling to Zebra Books, Dept. 3516, 475 Park Avenue South, New York, N.Y. 10016. Residents of New York, New Jersey and Pennsylvania must include sales tax. DO NOT SEND CASH.